The PROMISE

CRAIG TIMOTHY MICHAELS

Library of Congress Control Number: 2024915017

ISBN
978-1-964982-05-2 (Paperback)
978-1-964982-06-9 (eBook)

The PROMISE

ST. PETERSBURG, RUSSIA

ALTHOUGH THE RUSSIAN city's northern latitude readily afforded long, late-season, frigid nights, massive ice blocks from Lake Ladoga coursing through the main waterways would lower the temperature quickly, setting into motion late-season snows. Today's storm, a weather system blowing in from the Gulf of Finland, proved such an example with a bone-chilling 24° Fahrenheit. The biting bitter wind whipped sleet and snow seemingly every direction as Samantha trudged along Bolshaya Morskaya to the Hotel Angleterre, her residence of choice.

She had fled to St. Petersburg as a drastic means of escaping the unrelenting pain and grief inflicted by her megalomaniac, now ex-husband, Robert Barrett IV, and a powerful overbearing father, Ed Marissen. Although she held a genuine love for Rose, her mother, a complete separation proved imperative. Abundant financial resources provided the ability to remain indefinitely in this cold, distant city. The decision was hers and hers alone; Samantha Marissen chose to stay.

St. Petersburg! A much grander name than Leningrad, a name that burdened the city prior to the fall of the Soviet Union and communism. Peter the Great built this 'Window to the West' into a modern European city. Modeled by Italian architects, the baroque and neoclassical architecture with its network of canals, projected a European appearance. Even city residents consider themselves as European and just a bit more sophisticated than their countrymen to the east.

Determined to escape her past, Samantha discovered an historic and cultural treasure, the famous 'Venice of the North'. The city rests on 45 islands with more than 500 bridges, some narrow pedestrian bridges, others medieval or modern, and yet others giant drawbridges. Impressive historical monuments and exquisite palaces dot downtown St. Petersburg.

The Angleterre, renovated to its original splendor and situated next to St. Isaac's Cathedral, was within walking distance to the Admiralty, now a beautiful example of the Russian style, initially the construction site of the first ships of Russia's Baltic fleet. Also close by is the Bronze Horseman, the statue depicting Peter the Great as a fearless Roman hero, and the Hermitage Museum, home of one of the largest and most impressive art collections in the world.

Samantha's favorite locale, however, soon became the Nevskiy Prospect, the lively main avenue of St. Petersburg that houses the center of business and commercial activities, such as the cultural life; entertainment; Gostiny Dvor, the city's largest department store; and much more. Nevskiy cuts straight through the heart of St. Petersburg, from the Alexander Nevskiy Monastery to the baroque masterpieces of the Winter Palace and the Hermitage. Occasionally she felt that not enough time was available to absorb everything, although time no longer posed a problem.

Weary of her struggle against the elements, Samantha, smothered in sweaters, a scarf, a woolen cap pulled over her ears and forehead, thick gloves, fur-lined boots, and an insulated hooded coat, leaving only her eyes exposed to the harsh weather, finally reached the majestic over-sized doors of the hotel. An odd combination of the bleak and beautiful brought her peace and tranquility halfway around the world, far from her past with no thought of the future.

The entrance, manned by employees dressed as Russian Empire Guards, offered a welcome invitation to the warm, impressive, richly appointed lobby, although 'lobby' would do it no justice. She crossed the expanse to the elevator in her bulky, definitely unattractive outer garb, which concealed a forty-eight-year-old elegant woman with beautiful features: soft blue eyes, dark brown shoulder length hair, and the occasional smile, a smile once described as 'the smile of sincere love', a description recalled from her distant past.

Samantha dropped her coat, sweaters, scarf, cap, and gloves onto the floor next to the door, her boots near the fireplace. She spared no expense on accommodations; the fourth-floor Classic Room featured a view of St. Isaac's Cathedral, a king-sized bed, sitting area, satellite TV, internet access, an exquisite shower/tub, and a safe. More importantly to her, the room exuded a cozy warmth. She could request a fire but that meant interacting with another person. At the moment, she would rather be alone.

After preparing a cup of tea, Samantha stepped to the window and gazed upon Isaac Square, a daily ritual. Situated in the center of the square, the magnificent St. Isaac's Cathedral, considered one of the finest architectural monuments of the 19th century. Majestically designed with monolithic columns, sculptures, mosaics, paintings, marble and semi-precious stones, it was the main cathedral of the Russian Orthodox Church until 1917. Lazily watching the wind-blown sleet and snow cover the idyllic setting, she succumbed to exhaustion from her blinding, treacherous walk. Setting her tea on a small ornate table, she kicked off her slippers and lay across the bed; sleep, however, not an option.

Thoughts of what brought her to St. Petersburg continued to haunt her. If only those thoughts would fade, she could begin to live her life anew. Until then, she would continue to pray and place her faith in Jesus to bless her, protect her, and bring about recovery.

Samantha Marissen had been the wife of Robert Barrett IV, a most successful corporate vice-president. After the divorce, she found herself alone. The wives of his business contacts had been her only acquaintances, not friends, simply acquaintances. She had no children, no siblings, her life barren of relatives or friends. Robert Barrett IV would never tolerate children; they would cramp his fast-paced business life and, as he so boldly stated, "negatively affect his wife's body proportions."

Rob IV was a husband missing-in-action. Business was his life, his existence. Samantha fit as merely window dressing, a trophy wife. "Just shut up and be happy" was his rule, a rule he enforced physically as well as emotionally. The dark secret Samantha kept buried within was the denigrating abuse suffered at the hands of Rob IV. She experienced great relief when he left on business, a time of silence and peace, a time of prayer, but also a time of pain, pain knowing that to be her life.

Samantha, depressingly aware of the reality, found it to be a disgusting truth. Raised in a most wealthy environment, she married a man from an extremely wealthy family who would not be her choice today if presented the situation again, or so she hoped. In all honesty, she had feared living without wealth, having been raised to believe she could not live without every possible comfort. In retrospect, she learned the love of wealth, not wealth itself, is the root of all evil. As with many things, a need becomes a weapon if controlled by the wrong hands. Samantha's father and later her husband used wealth, her need, as a tool to coerce her into their demands. Sadly, she obliged.

Her nightmare began the afternoon her father met a longtime business acquaintance, Robert Barrett III, for lunch at *Fontaine's*, a high-class restaurant in Clayton Heights. The two reminisced with drinks until Ed informed Bob he must leave for an appointment and insisted on covering the tab. As they left, Bob mentioned his son, Rob, would be returning from business in Los Angeles Friday and joining the family for dinner. Would Ed, Rose, and Samantha like to spend the evening at the Barrett's home? Rob would enjoy a relaxing night with family and friends.

Ed, already attempting to develop a plan to maneuver Samantha and Rob together in order to drive a final wedge between his daughter and a strongly disliked Air Force pilot, immediately expressed delight at the invitation and joyfully accepted. Samantha, not the least bit interested, angrily fought her father's insistence, still suffering the guilt and anguish of so deeply hurting the man she thought she loved. No, she did love him; she had abandoned him to her fear. After a great deal of arguing and tears, she gave in, agreeing to attend. No one bested Ed Marissen, not even his daughter.

As the saying goes, the rest is history. Samantha and Rob IV grew into an unlikely item. Ed, like a champion chess player, planned six or seven moves ahead. He knew full-well this move could be great for business once he convinced Rob IV to accept a position at Marissen AeroSpace. Bob III's investments plus Rob IV plus Ed Marissen equaled greater success. After a bit of internal shuffling, a vice-president position opened and Rob IV jumped onboard.

Over time, under Ed's coercion, Samantha accepted Rob IV's third marriage proposal, succumbing to the knowledge this was to be the course of her life. Fear of losing her father's money doomed her to a life of quiet despair. The only means of maintaining her lifestyle was to marry the man of her father's choice. What shred of dignity remained?

Samantha often wondered what her life would be had she stood strong and run away with her Air Force captain, but now, far too late for such a dream. Certainly, she was a distant memory to him. If only she had…if only she had…her life replete with 'if only she had'.

For more than twenty years, Samantha lived the lie. Rob IV refused any treatment or counseling, denying his abusive behavior, believing a man's man is never the problem. She begged him time and again that they both make an effort at counseling, make a new beginning, try to make the marriage work. He would have none of that. Counseling exposes a chink in the armor, a weakness and an admission of failure. Never! Samantha ceased pleading as he grew more abusive, both verbally and physically.

Not only did her pleas set him off, he ridiculed and despised her Christian beliefs. She found, unfortunately far too late, he had lied about his faith. He had none. Rational people do not need a God, he would vehemently proclaim! His great success was due to his own work, not some god somewhere. Rob IV was the one who made things happen, no one but him! Anger so controlled him regarding Samantha's beliefs that during his last tirade he called her the worst any man could say about a woman, then pushed her violently into their bedroom wall, causing a concussion. He threatened more violence if she did not follow his lead at the hospital emergency room. As a result, the emergency room report stated she stumbled down the stairway, striking her head on the wall at the bottom of the steps. Both the attending emergency room doctor and nurse could only be suspicious of the injury/accident having found no other marks or bruising. She had successfully protected her husband, but solely out of fear.

Eventually, Samantha confided in her mother and father of the violent abuse. Her father advised her to do nothing; he would handle the matter. Terrified and on the verge of a breakdown, she begged her father not to speak to Rob IV; he would certainly take his anger out on her. She wanted to get away from him, as far as possible.

Did Ed Marissen love his daughter before business, or business followed by his daughter? Samantha read his reluctance to protect her as a decision of 'business first'. Glaring at her father and avoiding eye contact with her mother, she gathered her coat and purse and stormed from the mansion with no contact from that dreadful day.

The next two years proved a living hell as the divorce proceeded. Rob IV used every form of harassment known to destroy her will to fight. When forced to file a restraining order against him, he fought back attacking her character, stating how drunk and violent she was, the affairs she had, and the men hired to follow him; none of which was true. He feared for *his* safety and required a restraining order to protect him from her. Samantha, completely broken by the horrid mess, requested through her lawyers that if Rob IV ceased, she would walk away with nothing. Anything to end the torture. She did as promised, but what is nothing when one is the Marissen daughter?

Ed maintained silence during the proceedings, at least publicly. Samantha was never aware of her father's feelings or her mother's hatred and mistrust of Rob IV. Rose despised his ploys and maneuvers to eliminate those he considered expendable in order to reach the top of the organizational chart. Ed's admiration of Rob IV was based solely on the continued growth of the corporation, which surely had to prove Ed's leadership decisions were the cause of such continued success. Ed had certainly veered from the path, lost his way.

Ed Marissen came from simple means, learning survival during difficult times. He held his father, Roger, in low self-esteem since his father's struggles and many moves of that period placed great stress on his mother, Alice, who stretched everything as far as possible to keep the family fed and clothed. Ed worked any odd job he could find as a young boy, earning extra money to help his mother. He promised himself this would never happen to his future family.

And so, began the saga of Ed Marissen from the survival of his childhood to his rise as CEO, President, and owner of the business he built from a small machine shop he had purchased and built to the aerospace giant of today. Immediately following his high school years, Ed had taken on the job of 'gopher' at the small machine shop in Memphis, Tennessee after leaving his hometown of Chattanooga. The shop, Memphis Machine, made a multitude of parts for a few small plane manufacturers and also for one aircraft required by the military.

His position of 'gopher' referred to *"go for* this" or *"go for* that."* Through hard work, he revised the meaning of 'gopher' to *"go far"* and eventually advanced to shop manager reporting directly to the owner, Larry Owens. Five years later, Larry, who had three daughters, decided to sell the business and retire. His decision to manufacture plane components for the private sector while keeping his hand in the military pool paid off quite handsomely with a nice nest egg for his retirement.

Larry held a great appreciation for Ed and offered to sell the business to him. The idea of owning the business intrigued Ed but, unfortunately, he didn't have the courage to accept the deal and relunctantly turned down the offer. Disappointed to hear Ed's rejection, Larry called him into his office the following morning. Ed took the seat across the desk from his boss. Larry leaned forward, looked Ed in the eye, and told him he would not accept his rejection of the offer. To make it big, you have to take some risks, he told Ed. He then gave him a lower price for the company and offered to finance the deal himself. He explained to Ed that he would like to see the company carry on under similar management and he knew Ed was the man to do it. You don't need time to think it over, he stated. Just do it! You need to do it. Flabbergasted, Ed merely shook his head in the affirmative. A handshake finalized the transaction.

Ed found he had a natural ability for running a business and making profit. He assembled a small, efficient sales staff, divided the existing customer base among them and allowed them the freedom to seek out new business. He took the young, inexperienced staff and taught them what he knew about the manufacturing business before setting them completely free. All Ed expected in return was good, hard, honest work, which would be rewarded with additional compensation. If not, one warning, followed by the layoff when necessary. His honest approach and fair actions resulted in very few employee dismissals. He always made a point of calling everyone by name and making himself aware of his employees' families.

Wisely, Ed also hired knowledgeable individuals to oversee the areas of the business he felt the need for solid advice with decisions. Soon, the business became too much for the confines of the building. Ed expanded the square footage twice to accommodate the booming business. Occasionally, Larry would visit, only to be further astounded by and proud of Ed's accomplishments since acquiring Memphis Machine. He could rest assured he chose the right man to keep the business alive.

Ed, grateful for Larry's gift, knew without doubt he would never be in his current position without Larry's generosity. His respect for Larry Owens ran deep, so deep that he would not consider a change of the business name until both Larry and his wife passed on. At that point, the name Memphis Machine certainly did not convey the image of the larger, more complex business the company had become. Ed had major plans for the business, including a name change and possible move to St. Louis, Missouri. The St. Louis move would place the company in close proximity of Vandover Civilian and Military Air or Vandover CMA, which covered a growing segment of flight, the civilian passenger jet and the military fighter jet. Ed had an eye for the future and understood the need to develop continually new technology for the constant improvement and advancement of modern aircraft, military or commercial.

In his usual wise way, Ed left the responsibility of seeking land for a new structure or locating an appropriate existing structure in St. Louis to a St. Louis firm that would work diligently to bring a new business to town. Even the St. Louis banks were jumping through hoops to finance his project. Ed's only responsibility for the move would be to sit back, wait, and make the final decisions.

More important at the time was his wish to marry the young lady of his dreams, Rose Bennett. Rose came from one of the well-to-do families of Memphis and had met Ed at a major charity fundraiser. She thought him quite brash since there appeared to be no reason for his presence at the event; he didn't rank with the high society…yet. He was known locally as a successful businessman, although not in a 'respectable enterprise', whatever that meant. Ed took it to mean his business was a *commoner's* profession. He had not been born into wealth, so he was not 'old money'. However, if he continued to appear with the wealthy, they may eventually view him as an equal. He believed such thinking was the height of conceit but understood image was important to many of their type. The stereotypes ran both directions. He must play the game if their investment could someday be beneficial to his business. Again, his instincts paid off with his acceptance into that realm of society.

Rose agreed to see Ed not due to his growing wealth but for the same brashness she first criticized. What man would have the nerve to scale the castle walls of the wealthy and slay their egos with his? Their love grew quickly, too quickly for her parents. But over time, seeing that Rose loved him deeply and realizing his potential, the Bennetts gave their approval when asked for her hand in marriage.

The Marissen wedding soon became the talk of Memphis. Exquisite, elegant, and perfect, exactly the way Rose pictured her life with Ed. The possible move to St. Louis excited her since the distance between there and Memphis was not that great.

The move to St. Louis came quickly; everything fell into place under excellent coordination. Ed's main concern continued to be his employees; he would not desert any one of them. He presented an offer of relocation to each: those near retirement received a lucrative retirement buyout; those who could not move, a generous monetary package and assistance in acquiring new employment; and those who chose to relocate did so at company expense with Ed insuring no personal loss on the sales of Memphis homes in relation to the purchase of St. Louis housing.

The newlyweds settled into a very nice area of town and received well by their neighbors, as most people found Ed and Rose's southern air engaging. Ed, the gentleman and Rose, the exquisitely graceful southern belle, an image Rose was more than happy to promote. Life was wonderful.

Business thrived under the new name, Marissen Air, with government contracts to supply parts for Vandover CMA, the largest manufacturer of jet fighters in the country. But the world had changed. Space had entered the scene with a vengeance;

military rockets had become a vast necessity and space travel of all sorts, including civilian, became more prominent. Vandover CMA changed to Vandover Air and Space and sub-contracted the majority of components to Marissen Air. Ed, with his uncanny knack for speculation, had, two years earlier, built a large, technologically advanced plant in preparation for the inevitable responsibility.

In order to keep up with Vandover A&S needs, Marissen Air required three shifts, seven days a week. Once more, Ed figured the necessity of another name-change: Marissen AeroSpace. The name fit the times and the image. Imagine progressing from Memphis Machine to Marissen AeroSpace in such a relatively short period. Ed resided at the top of his game.

Although all was well in the business sector of their life together, he and Rose suffered one major disappointment: the Marissens were unable to have children. As a result, Rose fell into a deep depression. She desired a large family with Ed but her dream slipped into darkness.

After dinner, on a cool October evening, the phone rang; Ed answered. The Tennessee State Police informed him his sister Anne, her husband Tommy, and two of their children, eight-year-old Victoria and five-year-old Donnie, died instantly in a horrific car accident not far from their home in Chattanooga. Miraculously, their twelve-year-old daughter, Samantha, had survived with only a broken arm.

The State Police explained they could find no next-of-kin in the area and Ed verified he was her only living relative. Samantha had no one; she was alone but for Ed and Rose, the only family the little girl had. Ed requested no one tell her of the death of her parents and brother and sister; she needed family. He and Rose would tell her of the tragedy.

Ed explained the horrible incident to Rose, who,

momentarily, could not fathom such a disaster and was grief-stricken by the thought of little Samantha in the hospital with no one at her side. An hour later, they boarded the company plane for Chattanooga, reaching the hospital late that night and were immediately escorted to Samantha's room. Although the police report noted she "survived with only a broken arm", the many deep gashes, abrasions, bruises, and swelling transformed the pretty, young girl beyond recognition.

Rose comforted Samantha as best she could while Ed explained in a choking, faltering voice what took place that night. They wept. Samantha's inconsolable agonizing grief pierced Ed's heart as he sat helpless on the edge of the bed. Rose's quiet strength and courage took over as she cared for and loved the frightened lost child that night and throughout her hospitalization. Ed spoke with his lawyer soon after, instructing him to ensure Samantha's return home with the Marissens. He also provided instructions for the burial of Samantha's family in St. Louis, where she would now reside. "Take care of it," he had said and hung up the phone. Any other details could wait until later.

Time passed painfully as Samantha endured surgery upon surgery at a prominent St. Louis hospital to repair completely the compound fracture of her arm and rid her body of the scars; but the psychological scars of the loss of her family would require much more to heal. As soon as possible, Rose and Ed adopted Samantha, and through an utter tragedy, they became a family. Ed vowed to his sister, Anne, he would protect Samantha in every possible manner; she would never suffer again.

Samantha blossomed into a beautiful young woman but all the while Rose suffered great distress over her daughter's quiet demeanor, a quiet far beyond shy. She understood the reclusive quiet resulting from the loss of her family, but Samantha's inability to enjoy any facet of life deeply saddened her. Rose simply assured her daughter of her love and support.

Once recovered physically, Samantha completed her schooling, including college but was not yet prepared to take on the field of teaching to which she devoted her study. True to his word, Ed protected her but, unfortunately, more than necessary. Unable to leave the safety and security of home and the perpetual financial ease, she could not imagine a life of her own. The comfort of wealth combined with her father's smothering protection prevented Samantha from growing in maturity and responsibility. By now, both Samantha and Rose fell under Ed's control; every decision his because of his overwhelming need to "protect" those he loved.

Even so, Ed grew more distant, devoting his life to his business. The space program forged Marissen AeroSpace into an empire. Perhaps, Ed thought, the business should develop a far-advanced aircraft. Present it to government officials at some future date, possibly leading to one or more lucrative contracts, quite the opposite of normal procedure.

Nevertheless, he still found time to over-protect Rose and Samantha, such as that time he successfully destroyed her relationship with the young Air Force captain six years her senior. Ed performed the despicable act of hiring a private investigator to search the young man's past, which proved less than stellar. His findings revealed nothing illegal; the young man was simply a good bad boy. However, that was nothing more than an excuse; the reality, he did not want Samantha to marry a military man. Not only would he not make a decent living to support his daughter, he could be reassigned anywhere in the country, perhaps the world. He may be involved in a war. His daughter would not live her life under those conditions.

Rose, on the other hand, liked the young man and admired

his efforts, the time and hard work spent investing in his future. She was aware of his typical middle-class background, which made absolutely no difference to her. As far as his past, his past was exactly that…past. He had grown, matured, and now, proved himself to be a sincere, loving, caring, giving, and yet strong Christian man. Samantha loved him and, finally, experienced happiness. His presence, from the moment they met, uprooted her twelve-year depression. If only Ed had recognized that. Unfortunately, his blindness shattered Samantha's hopes and dreams.

As noted prior, Rose never cared for Rob IV. Arrogant and self-centered, he wanted only what best served him. He ridiculed Rose and Samantha's Christian beliefs, seeing no benefit in Christianity, laughing it off as something upon which weak people relied. Rose thought many times of Paul's Second Letter to the Corinthians that warns, "Do not be unequally yoked together with unbelievers. For what fellowship has righteousness with lawlessness?" It is not possible to do things to God's glory under such an arrangement.

Fourteen years earlier, Samantha, as a ten-year-old, had come to her mother and father on a muggy Tennessee evening and excitedly told them she wanted to give her life to Jesus. Her parents knelt with her that very moment as she spoke from her heart that "she was a sinner, Jesus died on the cross for her sins and was raised for her justification. Jesus Christ was her Lord and Savior; by his death and resurrection He had given her everlasting life."

Rose remained saddened by Ed's refusal to see and understand his daughter's precarious position; from whom should he truly protect her, a man who loved the Lord but not wealthy, or a wealthy man who disdained the Lord? This dilemma mattered not to Ed. Although Samantha's life should have been storybook perfect, her inability to stand up to her father's madness led to a huge mistake, a miserable mistake.

A single tear trickled down Samantha's cheek as she lay on the hotel bed. She swung around, sat up, wiped away the tear, and picked up her Bible. She moved to a chair near the window and opened to Psalm 139. She reached her favorite verse:

> Search me, O God, and know my heart;
> Test me and know my anxious thoughts.
> See if there is any offensive way in me,
> And lead me in the way everlasting.

The words brought Samantha peace. As a child of God, He knows her heart, her thoughts, any harmful or evil way in her. He will guide her through all obstacles. She left the Bible open in her lap, exhaled a deep sigh of relief, and closed her eyes once again, allowing her mind to drift to a better time; at least, the beginning of a better time.

* * *

A more beautiful Saturday morning would be difficult to imagine: sunny, cool, the grass sparkling with heavy dew. Samantha reclined on her favorite lounge chair near the pool of her parents' exclusive home anticipating the marriage of her friend, Gina. The two had been the best of friends since Gina introduced herself to the new girl at school in St. Louis, one year after the loss of her family and physical recovery. Their friendship grew into a bond so strong, they appeared more like sisters than simply companions.

Knowing the wedding would be dignified and luxurious,

she purchased two dresses, one for the morning nuptials and the second for the evening reception. Following her mother's advice not to over-shadow the bride, she kept her choices simple, yet elegant. Little known to Samantha, a major turning point would strike that morning for which she was unprepared.

As a twenty-four-year-old woman with a degree in Education from a major St. Louis university, she had desired to get out, apply for a position, and find her own place as a young adult should, but for her insecurities and overprotective father. After all, her mother hadn't worked, she consoled herself. She worried her attitude might simply be an excuse to justify her mistrust of life, to not experience true joy over something, anything.

As she dressed for the ceremony, she mused what the morning might be like on her wedding day. No matter, she thought, there's no one in my life and probably won't be any time in the near future. Relationships were difficult for Samantha, if not impossible; self-preservation ruled her socially. Her lack of simple, basic trust led to an immediate disinterest in anyone she met. Her customary pattern—a slight interest today, none by tomorrow. Possibly someday she would meet her knight in shining armor who would sweep her off her feet, who would heal her heart. Wow! Talk about dreaming.

She hastily dismissed her self-pity, wanting nothing more than to celebrate Gina's marriage; Gina, her one true anchor of friendship. Aware her mother had explained the loss of her family to Gina, Samantha never revealed her knowledge of the matter to either. Early in their friendship, Gina had questioned Rose of Samantha's past because she recognized a sadness in her eyes that couldn't be explained. Since that time, Samantha thought of Gina as more of a sister as a result of her concern. Gina understood when Samantha declined to be in her wedding; the ordeal would have been too much, although saddened her best friend would not be her maid-of-honor as hoped.

Samantha chose to drive her new metallic blue convertible Mustang to the church in Kirkwood. Keep the top up today; the hair must remain presentable for the affair. Pulling into the parking lot, she spied a rare empty space near the church entrance. Someone must have left early for some reason. As she neared the empty space, another car approached from the opposite direction. The driver stopped and motioned for her to take the spot. Samantha smiled and mouthed 'thank you' to the rather good-looking driver. After pulling into the space, she focused on the rear-view mirror as he drove to the back of the lot.

Inside the church, she took a moment to admire the large, beautifully colored stained glass window stretching across the entire front wall before asking a young usher if she should sit in a particular area as a friend of the bride. He directed her to a section reserved for immediate friends on the bride's side. The instant Samantha stepped forward she bumped into the parking lot guy, the driver who had kindly granted her the last close space. Once again, he stopped and motioned for her to proceed before him. She attempted to say 'thank you' but her voice failed.

Knowing full well he was behind, she made her way to the pew wondering whether the parking lot guy was a friend of Rich or of Gina's family. Why are you so nervous, she asked herself? Three young ladies scooted over, providing Samantha a seat on the aisle. She fidgeted a few moments with her beaded pocketbook before turning slowly to steal a quick peek for the parking lot guy. There he was, three rows behind on the groom's side of the aisle. He looked up, smiled, and gave a slight wave of recognition. Embarrassed, Samantha returned the smile and quickly faced forward.

Caught looking! Oh, well, she thought, he waved first…

and he smiled. She wanted to look again but didn't, that would be much too obvious. Who was he? She had attended a few functions where Gina or Rich, the groom, had been. She hadn't seen him before. Was he close to Rich? Samantha realized she smiled when she thought of him. Again, she had the urge to look back, but didn't want to make her attraction to him so transparent. Oh, great, did she just think 'attraction'?

The ceremony proceeded beautifully; the bride and groom gave their hearts and lives to one another through sincere, love-filled vows. The ceremony, with the exceptional music; Gina's mother crying; her father smiling; and the huge wedding party of four brothers and four sisters flanking the bride and groom, presented a wonderful scene. The moment arrived for the minister to inform Richard he may kiss the bride and introduce the happy couple as Richard and Gina Reynolds.

Applause spread throughout the church while the happy couple ambled down the aisle. As Gina passed her best friend she winked, just moments before Samantha noticed Rich and the parking lot guy share a quick left-handshake. Who is this mystery man, she wondered, and why do I care? The guests soon followed the newlyweds and wedding party to a receiving area adjacent to a reception room where coffee, tea, and light pastries would be served.

Samantha searched anxiously for the parking lot guy as she moved down the aisle alone toward the receiving line. Once again, she smiled as she thought of him as the parking lot guy. She knew nothing of this man but out of character, decided she would. Noticing him no more than ten feet ahead talking with his friends, Samantha squeezed through the crowd until almost next to him, purposely bumping into his right side while placing her hand against his back. Thinking someone had tripped, he turned quickly and held his arm in front of her, hopefully, to keep her from falling.

"Well, thank you again," she said in her best southern accent.

The parking lot guy smiled. "You're welcome. We seem to be bumping into each other quite often this morning."

"I believe I started on the wrong foot today. I do apologize for my clumsiness."

"That's all right. It's not every day I find myself this close to an attractive woman. Believe me when I say I don't mind."

Samantha, unprepared for the oddly spontaneous compliment, didn't know how to respond.

The reception line narrowed to single-file a short distance ahead. The twosome stood side-by-side in casual conversation until reaching the single file formation where the parking lot guy placed his hand on the small of her back and gently guided her before him, catching her off-guard. Samantha found she appreciated his polite courtesies. Although captivated by this man, she had yet to know his name. He did nothing out of the ordinary, still his actions and manners were kind and gentle, yet strong.

When Samantha reached the groom, she took his hand and with glistening eyes whispered, "Rich, take good care of Gina, she is a wonderful friend. I know you both will be happy forever."

"I will, you have nothing to worry about." Rich kissed her cheek. "Thank you for being such a good friend to Gina. She loves you like a sister. In fact, I think of you two as sisters."

He hesitated a moment, then vowed, "Samantha, I promise nothing will change. Gina will always love you, I love you."

"Oh, Rich, you surely know what to say. And you know I love you too. Thank you for everything."

Samantha side-stepped to Gina and held her hands as they did their little squeal thing.

"I'm so happy for you, Gina…and I'm so envious. You and

Rich have a wonderful love I can only hope for someday. You are a totally happy and beautiful bride. Congratulations to both of you!"

"Oh, thank you so much, Samantha! I'm so happy you're here. As soon as everything gets back to normal, we'll get together. We haven't spent enough time together. Wedding plans, I'm so sorry."

"Don't be sorry! This is the most beautiful moment of your life!"

"Thank you. Then Rich and I will see you at the reception tonight! You can tell me about you and Jim."

"Who?" Samantha asked, confused.

Nodding toward the parking lot guy, Gina replied, "Jim, the guy next to you. I thought you might be together."

"No…we're not."

Jim overheard and remarked, "We've been bumping into each other pretty much."

Gina leaned toward Samantha and whispered, "How are you this morning?"

Samantha's eyes welled up as she softly replied, "I'm doing well; I'm having a very good time."

"Good, good. I'm glad. We'll see you tonight. I love you, Samantha!"

"Love you too! Till this evening!"

Samantha watched from several steps away as Jim congratulated Rich and Gina with handshakes and hugs. He was truly happy for them.

"So, he does have a name," she laughed. "I like it…Jim, or James. I like James."

After a final moment with Gina, Jim joined Samantha, she clutching her small beaded pocketbook at the waist, he with one hand in his pocket. She searched for any reason to remain together. The awkward moment arrived.

Disappointed, she heard Jim express, now very disheartened, "Samantha, it was really nice to meet you this morning. Thank you for your company."

"Yes, it was very nice. Thank you too."

He extended his hand, she hers, for a parting handshake. Not exactly what she had hoped. James maneuvered through the guests to his friends as she watched. He didn't even look back! Samantha dejectedly selected a cup of tea from the hot refreshment table, joined a few acquaintances from college, and stood quietly, saddened, she thought that she had sabotaged what may have been a wonderful opportunity.

Amber, the nearest acquaintance asked, "So, what's his name? Did you guys connect? Are you going to get together?"

"Nooo," Samantha answered, "seemed like we were getting along pretty well. But I suppose what you hope for and what really happens rarely match. I do know his name is Jim…James, and I think he's from out of town, he mentioned that. He was… very sweet. I could have talked with him all morning; he was so nice, so much a gentleman. But, I guess that's not to be."

A sudden look of surprise swept over Amber as she glanced beyond Samantha.

Samantha almost expressed "What?" when she felt a light touch on her shoulder. It was Jim.

He bowed slightly at the waist and proceeded, "Miss Samantha, I must apologize for the manner our earlier pleasant conversation ended. I wonder if you might be at the ball tonight. If so, may I request the honor of a dance with you?"

She giggled at his very courteous and purposely exaggerated theatric query delivered in a perfectly horrid cartoon character impression of a southern drawl.

"James, sir, it seems my dance card is rather full." Again,

she exaggerated her southern roots following his theatric lead, trying desperately not to laugh.

"Well, lovely lady, I thought that may be the case, you being such an attractive, delightful woman." He raised her left hand with his right, "I'm sorry to have interrupted you. Thank you for your time, you are very gracious."

Again, bending at the waist, he placed his left hand on hers, the hand already held, "Lovely lady, I bid you fair afternoon."

Releasing her hand, he turned to depart, and acknowledged the observing friends, "Ladies."

Before Jim, or James, had taken a second step, Samantha called, "Sir, I see I do have one cancellation on my card. You may fill that space if you so desire."

"Why Miss Samantha, it would be an honor and a privilege. Till tonight then." With that, Jim, or James, smiled slightly, gave a parting wink, and left the reception.

Amber excitedly declared, "That was certainly different! I mean silly...but funny. He came back just when you thought he wouldn't! Isn't he..."

Samantha laughed an 'I can't believe what just happened' laugh. For the first time, she displayed humor and a boldness so unlike her. Perhaps because he was so very nice, unlike anyone she ever met. Not only that, he purposely sacrificed all dignity with his amusing return and simply awful southern whatever that was.

After returning home, she told her mother of her experience with James; how they met and the humor shared to know one another better. Rose laughed but advised her later, when Samantha asked for the fifth time how she looked, to relax and enjoy the reception. If the evening didn't go as hoped, she still had her friends.

Besides, Rose thought, how could he not be drawn to such

an attractive, sweet young lady? She had no recollection ever seeing her so excited, so happy. She prayed Samantha not be hurt treading in this unknown territory.

*   *   *

Gina's parents reserved the elegant, elaborate ballroom on the forty-fourth floor of the Metropolitan Tower in downtown St. Louis to accommodate the large number of guests invited to the reception. The décor of the immense room included plush subdued carpet, ornate wall and pillar design, and fine furniture, illuminated by exquisite crystal chandeliers and many forms of indirect lighting. Fifty-two round-tables were arranged symmetrically about the expanse, covered by white linen tablecloths with glistening silverware and Waterford crystal. A small candle in glass displayed the etched name of the guest assigned to that particular seat of ten chairs at each table with a colorful centerpiece of low-cut flowers, so as not to hinder the view of the guest seated opposite.

Samantha ventured so far as to beg a ride to the reception with Amber and her date, Brad, in the hope James would seek her out for the promised dance. Maybe, just maybe, he would spend a portion of the evening with her, perhaps, she hoped, the entire evening. She still could not understand what about this man fascinated her so. More than likely nothing would happen. Samantha knew something more substantial than silly humor would be necessary; the evening could not stand on that alone. An actual connection would require intelligent conversation. What if he wasn't really interested? But, he is interested, at least, he seemed to be this morning. Suddenly, Samantha realized the disappointment she would experience if his earlier flirtation amounted to nothing. Oh, my gosh! Don't over-think this, she reprimanded herself.

The entire scenario ran through her mind as she rode the elevator from the parking garage to the building lobby, then, up to the forty-fourth floor of the structure. The elevator opened to the plush foyer of the ballroom tastefully decorated with palm plants and flowers, comfortable chairs, and soft lighting. Samantha decided to keep her light wrap in case the room was cool. Entering the ballroom or reception area nearly took her breath away with the panoramic view afforded by the floor-to-ceiling glass that made up three sides of the room. Glancing across the expanse, she visually took in a large portion of the city, the Arch in all its sunset beauty, and the ole' Mississippi flowing by. She immediately realized how intimidated she felt near the windows of the forty-fourth floor. She endured heights, but this…a bit much.

As Samantha stood at the entrance to the reception, she scanned the area for any sign of James but the room much too large for any success. A pang of sadness struck as the familiar sense of loneliness attempted to invade the moment; how, so many years later, she needed her family, her mother and father, her sister and brother, how much she still missed them. OK, Lord, please let me enjoy tonight. This is Gina's party; please let me be happy for her and with her. Please, Lord.

She noticed Amber and Brad had located their table and motioned for her to join them. Samantha weaved through the tables until reaching them and found her seat with the candleholder marked Samantha Marissen. Next to her seat was another candle marked Unknown. How appropriate, she chuckled. She had been to other wedding receptions but never advertised as Alone. She checked the room quickly but still did not see James. If he was here, he may see her anxiously searching for him. She should appear more nonchalant.

The room began to fill quickly and with the arrival of the

wedding party nearing, Samantha recalled that James had never said he would spend the evening with her; he asked only for a dance, nothing more. As sad as that fact was, she felt better remembering he said nothing to lead her to think otherwise.

Samantha listened politely to the table chatter between her acquaintances, not really taking part. Without warning, she felt a light touch on her shoulder. Turning quickly, a most pleasant surprise greeted her.

"Miss Samantha, how are you this evening?"

"James, you're here!"

"I am. Did you miss me?"

"Why would I? I hardly know you!'"

The light banter of that morning returned as their icebreaker of choice.

He leaned down and whispered, "May I ask a favor of you?"

"I suppose."

He reached for her hand as she gracefully rose from her chair. At 5' 10" he stood several inches taller than she.

"I guess this really isn't a big deal but there is an extra chair at my table with some candle thing that says Unknown. As usual, I seem to be the odd man." He smiled slightly, glanced to the windows, then back to her eyes. "I'm with my married friends, and obviously, I'm not married. So, I hope you will join me for dinner. I promise you interesting conversation and my complete attention."

Samantha continued their eye-to-eye connection, "First, I agree you are an odd man. Second, there is also an empty seat at my table, so I suppose that makes me odd too. And third...I would love to join you for dinner. I promise *you* interesting conversation and my complete attention."

Jim grinned at the good news, "Mind if we take your candle with us. I wouldn't want to introduce you as "Miss Unknown.""

"Not at all! I would appreciate that very much."

After explaining the plan to her friends, Jim smiled and reached for her candle before departing for his table. Samantha had never been so bold, or brave, as to accept an invitation from a man she hardly knew to join a table of people she never met. Again, he placed his hand on her lower back as they wound through the meandering guests to his table. She experienced the same secure feeling she had that morning in the reception line.

Upon reaching their destination, all table conversation ceased.

"What? Are you so surprised there might be someone I hope to spend the evening with, that all your talk just stops?"

Simultaneously, everyone nodded 'yes'.

As the small group doled out trouble to Jim, Samantha shone with an inner glow, knowing he had said "someone I hope to spend the evening with." He did want to be with her. She couldn't believe it! Suddenly, the introductions begin.

"Everyone, I would like you to meet Samantha, the woman kind enough to accept my invitation. Thanks to her, I will not be sitting alone tonight.

"So…to start," he pointed out each couple, "Bill and Nancy, Neil and Sue, Bob and Liz, and last, but definitely not least, Ted and Carol."

They welcomed her warmly, to which Samantha smiled nervously and responded, "It's so nice to meet y'all. Do keep in mind that if James hadn't invited me over, I would be sitting alone too."

Bill looked at Samantha, then Jim, "OK, how do you do it? How do you rate such a nice attractive woman and with the southern style yet? And what's this James thing?"

Jim exchanged places with Samantha, placing her on his left. Sliding out her chair, he stated, "I'd rather you sit next to Carol. She's a very nice person. It's probably a little too soon to expose you to Bill."

An exaggerated "oooooh" rose from the table.

Samantha remarked, "Humor is so enjoyable; it lightens the mood and is an excellent icebreaker. Don't you think so, James?"

Before he could respond, Bill cut in, sweeping his hand around the table, "Whoa! Thank you! I'll have you know, these people have never appreciated my humor. But I have to ask, what's this 'James' thing? No one ever calls him James."

Samantha leaned toward Bill, closing the gap between her and Jim, "Well, I heard Gina call him Jim this morning and my first thought was 'I like James; to me, he looks like a James.'"

"All right, but I'll never get used to it."

"Maybe I'll know y'all long enough for you to grow accustomed to it." She did it again, verbalizing her wishful thinking. Samantha, immediately aware these were good people with no pretenses, felt very comfortable sitting with them.

Neil raised a couple of questions for the newcomer, "So, where did you find this old man?" as if he didn't know, "And more importantly, why have you consented to sit with him?"

Everyone, including Samantha, laughed. She could see they appreciated harassing one another. "Oh, we met just this morning and seemed to get along quite well."

Jim leaned forward with a hint of seriousness, "Well… you…I…uh…you know how sometimes you can just feel something. I hope maybe…you know."

His stumbling bumbling statement caught everyone off-guard; he actually implied he had an interest in a golly-gee sort of way. Samantha blushed; she felt the warmth in her cheeks.

"Why, Samantha, has Jim embarrassed you?" Sue kiddingly asked. "That's the Jim…I mean the James we all know and love! Wow, seriously," she laughed, "I'll never be able to call him James."

"Well, what if y'all call him Jim, like usual, and I'll call him James. Then, it'll be kind of special. And yes, he's been saying some very sweet things to me today." She laid one hand on his shoulder and gently held his arm with the other, "Haven't you, dear?"

Dear? She couldn't believe what she just said, even if in jest...or was it? Again, the party of ten laughed, chuckled, and groaned, his friends taking Jim and Samantha's banter with a grain of salt.

The arrival of the bride and groom with their entourage interrupted the conversation, followed by the loud melody of "Here Comes the Bride," initiating a prolonged session of cheering, whistling, and applause. Dinner was served, first to the wedding party, then the guests. No buffet line at this affair!

Samantha blended easily with Jim's friends, enthusiastically participating in the conversation revolving around the table. For no particular reason or perhaps every reason, she felt very much at ease taking part in the chatter with Jim, or James. At one point, with others involved in low-key table talk while eating, Carol leaned toward Samantha and quietly noted, "You've made quite an impression here. This is a good group, a close group; we're all just average working people. We've known each other for so long, kind of like a family. I hope we see more of you. You fit right in, and," she chuckled, "you seem to think we're OK too. I mean, we can be a little off-the-wall at times...maybe most of the time."

"Thank you, Carol. I am enjoying tonight very much. Y'all are so kind to include me like this."

Carol lowered her voice a bit more, while leaning still closer, "Jim seems very happy tonight. He's been so busy with the Air Force; I mean all the flight training and OTS, whatever that is, all that officer stuff."

A priceless expression spread over Samantha's face, which immediately caught Carol's attention. Slightly embarrassed, she asked, "Oh…so you didn't know? Jim hasn't told you? I'm sorry."

"No, what do you mean? I haven't a clue. Who is he?"

"Well, officially he is Captain James Paul Gordon, an Air Force pilot and, I think…what is that? Oh, yeah! An aeronautical engineer. Not too shabby for a south St. Louis boy."

Having no idea of his accomplishments, 'shocked' understated Samantha's reaction to the revelation.

Carol went on, "He's so quiet about it. Doesn't say much, doesn't brag, he's just a regular guy. You know, he flew in this morning from a base in Mississippi. He flies out Monday, something like 5:00 in the morning."

Samantha thought he might be from out of town but not an Air Force base in Mississippi. Why didn't he tell her? Well, there just hasn't been time she considered; then realized this was the first time she heard his last name, 'Gordon'…well, of course, she could have looked at the candleholder! How crazy is this?

Waiters scurried about the room pouring champagne for the upcoming toast. Soon after, a tinkling of glass signaled everyone to please turn their attention to the best man, Rich's older brother, Kevin, managed to touch on every emotion: memories of brotherly pranks, moments of love, anger, and humor, and ended tearfully with, "our entire family loves you, Gina, and we are ecstatic to welcome you as our new sister. We all wish you and Rich many wonderful, blessed years."

The hearty sounds of well-wishers burst across the room at the conclusion of the sincere toast. Samantha was so very happy for Gina. Not only was she a wonderful friend, but an entirely new family loved her for the very same reasons. She sighed, hoping for a similar experience someday.

Once settled in their seats, she turned to Jim and asked, "Do you think we could visit my table for a bit. I wouldn't want them to think I'm some kind of snob or something."

Folding his napkin, he responded, "You know, I'm here with you and my friends having a great time. I never gave that a thought. Sure, we can."

Barriers, buried deep in her heart, seemed to crumble with every word he spoke. Jim rose and explained to the table where they were going, but they would be back.

As Samantha stood, she stated sincerely, "Thank y'all for making me feel so comfortable. I truly cannot remember a better time. We will be back. I enjoy you guys too much!"

Before leaving, Jim snatched his Unknown guest candle sitting next to the candle he brought from Samantha's table. Their hands came together as they walked toward her acquaintances' table.

* * *

Ted leaned forward, as if sharing a secret. "Wow! She is really nice; I like her!"

"No kidding!" Bill added, "And she can dish it back, can't she?"

Carol chimed in, "She is very sweet. Do you know Jim hasn't even mentioned the Air Force to her? I know he never does, but I think she is different. I don't think that would sway her one way or the other."

"I just hope he feels the same about her as we do," stressed Bob. "We know Jim doesn't put much faith into relationships. I'd hate to see her hurt. I hope he knows what he has there."

"Bob, the eternal pessimist!" Neil stated mildly. "Even he would have to know she's a keeper."

Sue added, "She's so nice, he'd be a fool not to know that."

"Well, we are talking about Jim, aren't we?"

* * *

As they stepped up to her table, Samantha slipped her right arm under his left and introduced Jim, something she failed to do earlier in the excitement of the moment.

"Everyone, this is the parking lot guy I met this morning, James Gordon. James, this is Amber and Brad, my transportation this evening, Sarah and Tom, Emma and Bill, and Savannah and Ron."

The usual formalities followed: the handshakes, the smiles, and the routine actions everyone performs when an introduction suddenly takes place. A rather dull, one-sided conversation among Samantha's acquaintances made for an awkward situation. Their boorish behavior irritated her so, that after a short time she whispered, "Let's go back to your friends' table. They are much more fun…and adult."

"You're calling my friends adult? Careful, you may offend any real adults here tonight."

"You know what I mean," she squeezed his hand for emphasis.

"Yeah, I do. You do know my friends are now your friends."

"And I hope I can be their friend,"

"I think you already are. I can tell they like you."

Again, Samantha's heart surged with emotion, as she began to understand her world growing ever larger this evening.

She devised a lame excuse to leave, which appeared to have no effect, so they made their goodbye. While rising to return to the 'fun and adult' crowd, Jim left the second Unknown candle with its partner. As Samantha and Jim drew near to the 'fun' table, they observed the four couples preparing to roast them for attempting to rejoin the group. But, as soon as Bill began, another tinkling of glass interrupted him.

Rich stood with raised glass, "This toast is for my closest friends. Would you guys please stand?" He motioned toward their table.

Bob, Neil, Bill, Ted, and Jim rose slowly, cautiously.

Rich continued, "Thank you for being such good friends…always, including all the ridicule you laid on me for remaining single for so long. Well, thankfully, you can't do that anymore. I was just waiting for the right woman to come along…and she did. But I do want to thank you for the examples of your marriages. You showed me what a happy and blessed marriage can be. Gentlemen, I raise my glass in a toast of appreciation for your friendship."

Having never received applause from so many people…the five friends found the attention just a bit embarrassing, although Jim wondered why Rich included him as one of his married buddies, probably just a wedding day slipup.

Rich spoke again, "I'm sorry, Jim, but I would like you to remain standing."

He went on, "Now, I did make a slight mistake. Jim is not married…not yet. But, Jim, I've known you the longest, about twenty years and I've cherished every year of our friendship. You were always there for me when I was down and needed support, or when I was up and celebrating! I hope I've done the same for you. But anyway, Jim, things have changed and for the better. I hope my friend that it may not be long before you join the ranks. Everything has to begin somewhere. You're a good friend, a good man, Jim. To my very best friend!"

Jim blushed with embarrassment but Rich's words truly affected Samantha. She raised her eyes to Jim only to see him looking at her. She thought, everything does have to begin somewhere, doesn't it? Once the applause stopped, he sat and tenderly, softly kissed her forehead. Looking at him with glistening blue eyes, she smiled; it seemed she might cry. She did enjoy being with him and thought as Jim shared earlier, "a feeling, a real feeling."

An older couple walking past their table stopped momentarily to ask, "So, are you the young lady who is going to get this guy to join the ranks?"

Both Jim and Samantha laughed as she responded, "I don't know. We met just this morning!"

"Well, good luck to both of you. You make a cute couple!" The husband patted Jim on the back and gave a thumbs-up before continuing across the room.

*   *   *

Opening her eyes, Samantha found herself in the same room, alone, still depressed. The afternoon had slipped into early evening. Thinking of her past with James was sad, yet memories of a happier time.

She slid off the bed and closed the drapes. She couldn't help but think of her loneliness. There was no one to turn to…not now. She had thought of finding James; was he married, did he have children, was he happy? She quickly put the idea out of her mind; she hurt him deeply because of her cowardice. He must hate her; no, not now, but then. She was certain he no longer remembered her. She must put this behind her, including the memories of James and that awful, horrible, evening when her weakness and lack of character caused him such pain. Yet, the kindness, gentleness, and love of James slipped into her mind once again.

"I've got to stop thinking of him…this is just ridiculous. He is not going to fly in here and take me back with him."

She flopped back onto the bed and squeezed her eyes shut.

* * *

Samantha would never forget their first intimate contact… the innocent kiss of her forehead, how it almost made her cry. She knew that very night James respected her; he was a man, not a boy like her previous very infrequent dates. She thought Jim to be older but how much older? Not a lot, but more than she previously thought. College, Officers Training, flight training…all that had to take time…a lot of time. She decided she would not worry about that tonight. She was enjoying their time together and nothing would interfere.

Ted kicked back in his chair, "I'm going to grab something to drink. Carol? Anyone?"

Carol replied, "Yeah, I'll take another one of these, if you don't mind."

"We're good," Bill added as he looked to Nancy and held up his glass.

Bob and Liz waved off Ted's offer. Neil and Sue were on the dancefloor.

Placing his hand on hers, Jim asked Samantha if she wanted something, a soda maybe.

"I'd really like a sweet tea, but I know they won't have it. Y'all live too far north to appreciate true sweet tea. I can find it but I have to look real hard."

She removed her hand and casually took his. "I'll have a tea with lots of sugar. Not the same but it will do."

"Alright, Ted and I will be right back."

Samantha's eyes followed him as he and Ted left for the refreshments.

"Carol noticed and laughed a bit, "You like him, don't you?"

"Yes. Yes, I do, but I don't understand. Honestly, I have never felt this before. He makes me feel so at ease, as if he really cares. I feel this trust, this secure trust with him. I know this is so silly. I…I just hope he feels the same."

"I can…well, we all can tell he certainly enjoys being with you. He looks at you with those blue eyes and he's constantly smiling. Tonight is very different for him." Carol went so far, as to say, "I think he feels the same."

Samantha experienced an easy comfort talking with Carol, just another benefit of her excursion into the venue of relationships. She inquired shyly, "Do you mind if I ask you something?"

"Sure, what's that?"

"I think I'm a lot younger than James. Do you think that will bother him at some point?"

Carol smiled but answered seriously, "While you were at the other table, we," she chuckled, "we were talking about you two, and we know Rich and Jim are the same age and we thought you and Gina are too. So, if Jim can't figure that one out, well…pilots are supposed to be smart, aren't they? Besides, what difference does it really make?" She then added, "Sorry we were talking about you when you weren't here."

Carol's response relieved Samantha of her mild concern, and she was pleased to learn they spoke of James and her in their absence. She smiled and nodded in agreement.

"Where in the world did Ted and Jim go? You can get refreshments right over there!" Carol knew these guys well. "I tell you, you can't take your eye off them for a second."

Motioning toward the front of the room, Liz pointed out, "I think they're way up there. I'll bet Ted has a hundred questions about you, Samantha. Fortunately for us, you two are fair game tonight!"

"Looks like they're finally heading back." Nancy added to the gentle ribbing, "Ted either heard what he wanted, or he gave up!"

Samantha enjoyed being the subject of the mild barbs, and joined in the laughter as she watched James and Ted zigzag through the maze until reaching their table.

Ted set Carol's glass before her and dropped into his chair, "Whew, that was a long walk!"

Jim handed the glass of tea to Samantha, then took his seat scooting his chair slightly closer to hers. He waited. She stirred her tea and took a sip.

Surprised, she exclaimed, "Oh, my! Real sweet tea! I thought they wouldn't have any!"

Ted reached past Carol and tapped Samantha's shoulder. Carol moved out of his way with an exaggerated "Excuse me!"

Ted apologized, "I'm sorry, but I have to tell her this."

Jim interrupted, "Ted, c'mon."

"Don't be so humble, Jim, if that's who you really are. Anyway, we went all the way up front because Jim figured the head guy was probably there. Turns out he was. Jim asked him for a sweet tea and a Coke. The guy says 'we don't have sweet tea.' Jim asked if he was sure and the guy says 'pretty sure.' Jim places a big bill on the bar..."

Ted smacked the table in demonstration, jiggling the ice in their glasses. "Well, maybe not quite like that. But, Jim motioned the guy closer and says, 'If you can find me some sweet tea, this is yours.' Five minutes later the guy is back with a pitcher of the stuff, pours a glass full, and looks at the bill on the bar. Jim says, 'Take it, you earned it.'

"I tell you, I don't know this guy. He's under the influence of something...or someone."

With that, Ted purposely stared at Samantha until she and her new friends laughed at his obvious insinuation.

Embarrassed and shaking his head, Jim mildly retorted, "Ted, you never cease to amaze me; you can make every story sound like an adventure."

Again, laughter filled the air.

Samantha set the glass down, ran her finger slowly around the rim, turned to Jim and lightly kissed his cheek, "Thank you."

Surprised by her reaction, all he managed was a simple, "You're welcome."

The band, more of a small orchestral group, returned from break to begin their next set. Jim stepped up to the leader while his friends watched, motioned toward Samantha as he spoke, then waited until the opening bars of a romantic piece began. He turned to her and extended his hand.

"Seriously, Ted, who is this guy?" Bob quipped. Ted shrugged an 'I don't know' response.

Samantha smiled at Bob and Ted's exchange while noting Jim's invitation. She dramatically touched her fingertips to her chest as if to ask, "Who, me?"

She rose, removed her wrap, laid it across the back of her chair, and joined James on the dance floor. This was the first anyone had seen her elegant yet subdued azure dress, revealing one shoulder. The others soon followed the couple to the dancefloor.

As Jim took her right hand in his left and placed the other on her back, he reminded her, "You promised me a dance this evening. May I take advantage of that promise, Miss Samantha?"

"Why, yes you may, Mr. Parking Lot Guy, yes, you may."

Samantha appreciated that James made no attempt to draw her close. He seemed to do everything for her. Neither spoke during the dance, only swaying in unison to the music. He enjoyed simply holding her, sharing the music with her. And, she felt a secure comfort in his arms. Occasionally, their eyes met, bringing a smile to both.

Humorously, their friends, while supposedly dancing, all angled for the best view of the couple.

As the romantic melody blended into the next arrangement, Samantha and James wandered, arm-in-arm, toward the full-length windows viewing the St. Louis Arch, while the curious friends returned to their table.

Once near the windows, Samantha slowed to a stop. She took a step back.

"I'm sorry, I feel very uncomfortable this high up. I know nothing can happen; I'm just uncomfortable."

Jim held her hand and reassured her, "Well, let's take a couple of steps back then. I don't want you to be uncomfortable at this moment."

"Why this moment?"

Jim turned her face to his and slowly, softly kissed her. Samantha, lost in the moment, returned the kiss. After only a second he pulled back, looked into her eyes, and very quietly said, "Thank you."

Squeezing his hand, she smiled and nodded yes.

With a touch of uncertainty, she requested, "May I ask you something?"

"You may ask me anything."

Turning to the windows, she inquired, "How come you haven't mentioned anything about the Air Force?"

Jim chuckled, "So Carol said something to you, didn't she? I knew she would. I think she has this need to watch over me."

"She means well. I'm glad she told me."

He studied Samantha, then opened up, "I learned some time ago that to share my background with someone was the 'kiss of death' for any possible relationship. Suddenly, I became a trophy, someone to show off. I felt the only reason someone would be with me was to brag, "Look everyone, I'm dating a pilot!" I never really knew who liked me for me. Please understand…this is not an ego thing. If it was, I would take advantage of it…not hide it."

Sadly, Samantha felt the need to ask, "Do you think I might be like that?"

"Oh my gosh, no…no. From the very beginning, I felt… no, I knew you were different. I just didn't know where or how to begin. So, I'm glad you asked."

Relieved, Jim briefly outlined his decision to join the Air Force, his schooling, his officer and flight training, and his current status. She listened intently, wanting to drink in every bit of information about him.

"And so, I flew…well, I didn't fly the plane, I hitched a ride early this morning, got to my uncle's, shaved, showered, and barely made it to the wedding on time. If I had been one minute later, we probably wouldn't be having this conversation."

"And if I hadn't stopped to admire the stain glass windows at the church, I wouldn't have bumped into you in the aisle. I believe God has certain events laid out for us. If it is His will for us to meet today, we would meet. And I do believe this is what He wants. What we do with this meeting is what matters."

Samantha feared she may have surrendered too much information too soon and attempted to come up with something different to say. Her fear was soon put to rest.

"Do you really believe that? I mean the way everything has happened today; I would almost have to agree." Jim appeared sincere with his statement.

"Yes, I do believe that."

"If this were to grow into a…a…relationship, and I hope it does," Jim inquired, "can we talk about this more? I'm curious about your conviction. That is something I'm seriously missing and it is becoming more and more evident lately."

Oh, my, she thought, he said we may have…a relationship someday. I hope so too. "Yes, we can talk about it any time you want. I won't forget." She felt a certain giddiness over Jim's desire to see her and to actually plan to talk about her faith. Nothing could be more important to their future.

For now, she simply wanted to know more about him, "So, do you find your career exciting?"

He shuffled his feet and put his hands in his pockets. "Well, the actual career is exciting." Stepping to the windows, he faced her, "But…many times, it can be lonely. If you don't have that special someone…you know…to share with, or write to, or go home to, it can be very lonely."

Aware of her own pain and loneliness, Samantha cautiously followed him to the glass, "Well, I think you have someone now."

Her willing admission to share revealed an inner fear that needed to be addressed. She took his hand, "James, I must ask you," reluctantly, she continued, "Do you know who I am?"

"Let me see…aren't you Samantha, that extremely sweet, smart, beautiful woman who has grabbed my attention and dazzled me with her charm?"

Smiling broadly, she giggled, "Oh, James, how many times have you embarrassed me today? I've lost count." She paused to gather her courage, "But seriously, do you really know who I am, my full name?"

He thought for a moment, "Oh, my gosh, I can't believe it but I don't know your last name. I could have looked at your candleholder; it's right there! How can I not know your name by now! I'm so sorry."

She took a long breath, then exhaled, "I am…Samantha Marissen."

"Marissen…Marissen…Marissen?" Small wonder she was so apprehensive about telling him. "Are you speaking of Marissen like in Marissen AeroSpace? Are you related to the Marissen family?"

Raising her palms, she shrugged, "The daughter."

Jim's expression definitely gave away his surprise, "No! Really! No, I mean…really!"

"Really. Does that make a difference?"

His mind a jumble of thoughts, "I don't think so. Uh, no, I guess not. But what about you? I'm pretty much a nobody in the big picture!"

Never taking her eyes from him, Samantha declared, "You're somebody to me James Paul Gordon. I…I…like you. You have been so nice, so sweet to me today. You respect me. You are warm, caring; you are funny and you're fun. You have made today so very good." She smiled and added, "I do know this, back in the day you probably would be known as a Southern Gentleman."

Jim grinned, glanced to the side, and sighed, "Wow, Samantha, give me a minute here. I just need to get a handle on this. And…you're OK with me? Yes, you are. You said you are. I really don't want any of this to change. I…uh…I like you too."

With hands on her hips and head tilted, she plainly stated, "Well, Captain Gordon, let's not change anything then!"

"All right…I agree. Let's not change anything."

As they stood near the glass facing each other, still holding hands, Samantha felt a tremendous weight lifted from her shoulders; the longer she waited, the more difficult it would have been to tell of her St. Louis family name. Now, she decided to tell James the rest of her story, the whole story.

"There is another part of my life I want to tell you."

Still dazed by her initial revelation, he warily asked, "What's that?"

She hesitated a moment, then began, "I…umm…I am the Marissens' daughter, but not their biological daughter. I was born in Chattanooga, Tennessee and lived with my parents, my sister, and my brother until I was twelve. We were in a horrible, horrible accident and I lost them all that night; they all died—my momma and my daddy, my sister and my brother. My sister, Victoria, was eight, and my brother, Donnie, five. I was the only one to survive. Oh, my Lord, I miss my family so much."

Although the words grew increasingly difficult to express, she continued, "Ed and Rose Marissen were my only remaining relatives. Ed Marissen is my mother's brother, my uncle. They cared for me and helped me through the whole ordeal. They adopted me as soon as they could and raised me as their daughter. I call them 'mother' and 'father' out of a deep respect for all they have done for me. But...I will always love and remember my Momma and Daddy, and Vicky and Donnie. I will see them again, someday.

"I...I just wanted you to know everything about me."

As a tear trickled down her cheek, she rested her forehead on his shoulder. "I have never shared this with anyone...ever. I think I trust you, James. I don't know, I felt a need to tell you."

For twelve long years, her grief remained locked deep in her soul; tonight, the sorrow broke free.

"Oh, Samantha, I'm so sorry...so sorry."

Jim struggled emotionally to find the most sensitive and caring way to handle this unexpected turn of events. In the beginning, he held her shoulders but, slowly, his arms enveloped her as she softly wept; that being all she wanted, comfort... safety in his arms where she could allow her long-held feelings to escape. He held her close to shield her from nearby guests and allow her the freedom to cry as long as needed.

Eventually, he heard her quivering breaths just before she raised her head and made a weak attempt to smile. She lowered her head again, still attempting to calm herself, to recover from her long cry. She barely uttered, "I'm sorry. I'm sure I'm quite a sight."

"You are the most beautiful woman I have ever known."

"Oh, James, surely you're just trying to make me feel better."

"No, Samantha, I've never had someone open up to me like you just did. Thank you for trusting me enough to do this." In unfamiliar territory, he desired to do something. "Umm…would you like someone to help you with…well, you know?"

"Would I like someone to go with me to a Ladies Room to freshen up?" She laughed weakly. "Is that what you're trying to ask?"

"Yes, it is." He smiled at her mild attempt to lighten the mood.

"Yes, I would. Is Carol around?" Already, Carol had become her first choice.

"Yeah, she's looking this way." Jim handed her a fresh handkerchief from his pocket. She turned briefly to wipe away her tears but, instead, began to cry softly again.

"I'm sorry, James, I can't seem to stop."

"Please, take as long as you need. Carol's on her way. Would you rather wait?"

"No, no, I need to pull myself together. Thank you."

"I'm here for whatever you need. I'll always be here." He knew he meant what he promised.

As Carol approached, Jim asked, "Would you go with Samantha to a Ladies Room? I know she would appreciate your help."

Reaching for Samantha while staring at Jim, Carol sternly demanded, "What did you do?"

"What? No…nothing. Please, just help her. I'll explain later."

With an air of disdain, Carol made clear, "Yes, you will explain later."

She quickly grabbed both their handbags and assisted Samantha down a lengthy hallway to a little visited Ladies Room.

"Samantha, I'm so sorry. I really thought tonight would be different. What stupid thing did he say? Sometimes he makes me so mad. He can be so thoughtless…even heartless. I just don't understand. What dumb thing did he say? I'm sorry, I'm really angry. You're so nice…too nice for him. This is just so like him."

The walk down the hall focused on Carol's denunciation of Jim. Samantha desperately attempted to explain but failed to break through not only her own tears and sobs but also Carol's protests and attacks.

Once in the Ladies Room, the two women faced each other on the couch, "Oh, Samantha, I am so sorry…and then he has the nerve to have me try to patch things up. Well, better for you to find out—

"Carol, no…no!" She gathered herself enough to stammer, "You have…you have it all…wrong. James didn't…he didn't do anything…to hurt me. He was just…just the opposite."

"What?" Carol looked in disbelief.

"Really…" A calmness began to settle over her as she dabbed her eyes with Jim's handkerchief…then blew her nose. "We were sharing…our pasts when I told him of a…a terrible loss in my life."

She related the full tragic account to Carol, who first listened teary-eyed but by the end, wept with her.

"James was…comforting me as best he could. He is so good…so good to me. Oh, Carol, this is so confusing. I…I don't understand. I've just met him and I've told him everything. Honestly, I have never said anything to anyone about the loss of my family. My best friend, Gina, knows only because my mother…Rose explained everything to her without telling me. Rose has prayed for years that some kind of treatment or something would make a breakthrough. Now, I just blurted the whole story out to him; I've even told you. I just don't know what's happening to me."

Wiping away her own tears, Carol confided, "You know, Samantha, you and Jim just might have that very beginning of a relationship where you find you are just what the other person needs. It may be for a moment or a lifetime. I hope for you two it is a lifetime. Enjoy it. You look like you've been seeing each other for months. I just can't believe Jim…but, I suppose I should. You are such a sweet person; how can he not—

"Oh, no!" Carol exclaimed. "What have I done? I accused him of hurting you. I treated him horribly. We have to get out there!"

As they hurriedly readied themselves, Samantha spoke from her heart, "Carol…thank you. I can't tell you how much you've helped me tonight. I feel you're someone I can talk with freely. I hope…I hope I know you for a long, long time."

Carol looked at her in the mirror and smiled, "I think we're going to be very good friends."

At least twenty long, uncomfortable minutes passed before Samantha and Carol returned to the group. Jim stood as the ladies approached. Samantha stepped directly to him and hugged him tenderly as the rest watched, bewildered.

Carol was the only one to speak. Touching his shoulder, she expressed her remorse, "Jim, I am so sorry. I am. I misjudged you. Forgive me…please."

"There's nothing to forgive, Carol. I've had a little quiet time to think. My history doesn't lend much credibility, does it?"

Samantha, interrupted to explain to the others, "Please, James did nothing wrong. He was comforting me after I shared some things with him about my past. A flood of memories made me very sad…and I…I just broke down." She smiled meekly. "I'm really embarrassed y'all saw that happen, especially this being the first time we've met."

"Oh, Samantha, please don't be embarrassed," consoled Liz.

"We're embarrassed because we jumped to the wrong conclusion about Jim. We didn't know. We assumed Jim said something to hurt you. We should have waited until we knew what happened. We are all very sorry for what we did…aren't we?"

Together, the group agreed. Not yet known to them, the root cause of their snap judgment lay in the fact Samantha had won their hearts and the 'family' jumped to her defense.

Jim quietly asked if she had one more available slot on her dance card to which she smiled and nodded yes. They excused themselves and moved to the dance floor.

*　*　*

Samantha recalled Carol later sharing the brief conversation which took place during their last dance of the evening, wanting her to know the 'family' was aware of her loss and how deeply they regretted questioning Jim's motives. She hoped she hadn't crossed a line of confidentiality.

So very sad, Samantha thought, she had sacrificed such friendship for a future of pain and loneliness.

She remembered Carol telling her how she and Ted, Bill and Nancy, Neil and Sue, and Bob and Liz sat silently, unable to make eye contact with one another at their table, with Bob admitting, "Man, were we wrong. I feel like a fool."

Neil concurred, "Yeah, we all do. I mean, he did not deserve that."

Ted asked Carol the question everyone wanted to ask, "Before they get back, did Samantha tell you what she told Jim?"

"Yes, she did, and it was just awful."

She went into as detailed an explanation as time allowed which, by the end, the young women choked back tears and the guys had to swallow hard when Carol stated, "She told me she trusted him; she had never told anyone about that day…until

Jim. We should not have assumed he would hurt her. Never."

Of course, Carol hadn't crossed a line. She was a friend, a wonderful friend. They all were.

* * *

Samantha and Jim returned to the table hand in hand, like they had been together for months. Bob gripped Jim's shoulder, "Look, Flash, no…no jokes. I'm serious. We can't begin to tell you how sorry we are for what we thought. We're friends but we didn't act like it."

Jim addressed the table, "Look, believe me when I say I understand."

Turning his attention to Samantha, he took her hand as they sat face-to-face, "You told me of your past, I want to tell you mine."

His friends could not believe what they heard. Was he going to risk her knowing about his past in front of them?

"Do you want us to leave? We can go somewhere else, if you need," Ted respectfully requested.

"No, I want you all to stay. This is something you should hear.

"Samantha…I have not lived a good life…not at all. But I'm pretty sure you have. I want you to know that…something has been happening in me the last few months, something trying to tell me how wrong I have been. I've been looking for answers. I think, and I hope I'm not wrong, I think you are part of the answer. I think Rich and Gina are part of the answer. I see what has happened with Rich, how he has changed…and he has. I want that. I think you furthered this with our conversation earlier about how we met, and how it wasn't chance. I want to continue that conversation…I do."

Samantha's eyes never parted from his as he bared his past to her. He was confessing his life before her, before his friends. At that moment, their table seemed to be the only table, with just Samantha, Jim, and his friends present. The surrounding commotion faded far into the background as he explained all his life had been. He desperately desired to be honest with her.

Eventually, Jim finished with, "I can't change my past, I can't deny any of it, but no more, not today, not now, not ever again."

"I know," she responded softly, "I know."

Jim managed a meek smile. Samantha truly felt something happening in him. He faced the conviction of his life and resigned himself to his past. How interesting the oddity of the pair, one a hurting believer, the other a hurting non-believer. Perhaps this was God's plan; allow two broken people to heal one-another.

As they rose, Jim asked, "Are you OK with me, or did I make a mess of everything?"

"I don't think you, or I, made a mess of anything. I believe you are so close to making a very important decision."

"What's that?"

"Remember the conversation you want to continue? Well, I believe that will explain it all for you."

"I'd like that."

Shifting back to his friends, he admitted, "You know, when you chose to protect Samantha, that proved to me you like her, and that's good!"

Samantha glanced to her table and realized Amber and Brad had left.

Jim also noticed her ride had departed, probably assuming he would take her home.

"I see your friends abandoned you," he jokingly remarked. "Would you like a ride home?"

"I'd like that very much. Thank you, Captain."

Regardless of the humor, Samantha experienced mixed emotions about James taking her home; happy she would have more time with him, yet sad that he would see the Marissen estate. It's one thing to be told someone is wealthy, another to be confronted by it. Thankfully, Rich and Gina interrupted her moment of inner turmoil, finally visiting in their quest to spend time with as many guests as possible.

Bob began the verbal sparring, "Yeah, 'bout time you showed up. I missed a good movie on TV waiting for you."

Rich shot back, "We were wrong, Gina. We thought we saved the best for last. Looks like we saved the last...for the least...best, oh, never mind!"

"Whaaat?" everyone asked.

"Never mind, I'm just tired. I think I'm losing it."

"Hate to tell you this, pal, but you lost it long ago," came a parting shot.

The group gladly welcomed them, pulling over a couple of empty chairs from the next table. Gina sat on one side with the girls surrounding her, Rich on the opposite with the guys in their own small circle.

After accepting congratulations on the marriage and praise for the beauty of the day's events, Gina asked Samantha to sit next to her. She did, although warily.

"What, Gina, something wrong?"

"I don't know where to start, Samantha," she sighed, trying to keep her voice low. "From what I hear, you seem to be having a very good time this evening...with Jim...I worry about you...and Jim."

"I understand."

"He has a pretty shady reputation."

"I understand."

"He's probably not be the kind of guy you want to date."

"I understand."

Exasperated, Gina demanded, "Why do you keep saying 'I understand'?"

"Because James told me everything. He told everyone everything."

"What? Wait…what?" Incredulous, best described Gina's reaction, as she attempted to lower her level of shock and surprise.

"James has been wonderful. Honestly, I have not felt a joy like this for a long, long time. Not just a happy feeling but real joy. I can't explain this, just believe me…please."

Samantha scooted her chair closer to the new bride, "Gina, I feel so safe with this man, I actually shared everything about my family, my life, my thoughts. He was so caring, especially when I cried, I mean I really cried telling him about my family and how much I missed them."

"Tonight? Really?"

"Yes, right over there," she nodded toward the area near the windows.

"Wait, what happened?"

Carol, Liz, Sue, and Nancy angled away from Samantha and Gina to afford them the privacy needed. Samantha softly and emotionally shared the events with the bride, who slowly absorbed the impact the evening had on her best friend. To see such happiness in a woman who had experienced so little, gave Gina pause to reflect: is it possible this is really true or has Jim just found a new way to accomplish his goal? Why would Jim tell her about himself, while trying to succeed at a quick pick-up? Why would he do this in front of everybody, people he knew well, people who knew him? She had to admit, even she felt a surge of joy for Samantha! What a conundrum, happy for a dear friend, untrusting of the cause of her happiness.

Truthfully, Gina understood there was only one thing to

do. She would back off, allow this to play out. She should not interfere. Samantha would have to face the consequences of her decision, even if the end result proved painful. She prayed not. But, she would share this with Rich; he could keep an eye on his friend. What a shame to feel this way. If only, in some strange way, this could be true.

Samantha sighed, lowered her head, and revealed, "I also believe he wants something more out of life; I'm going to share the gospel with him tonight."

"What?"

Her eyes glistened, as she reported, "James wants to talk about it. He wants to hear more."

"Jim? Our Jim?"

"Yes, your Jim, my James…at least for tonight. Carol said something very sobering this evening. She said perhaps we are just what the other person needs, maybe for only a moment or, possibly a lifetime. I know this may be only for a moment, Gina, but I'm willing to take the time to talk with him. He's so sweet, I would love to develop a relationship with him, but only God's way. Yes, I am very happy tonight and I thank God for that. But, if James does not want to take that step, I cannot allow myself to pursue anything with him…but…he seems so ready."

"This is all so unbelievable…Jim?" Gina sat in silent wonder before taking Samantha's hand, "I suppose, but please, please, please know I'm always here for you, for anything, anytime."

"Oh, I know, I do know. Thank you so much for understanding, for being my friend."

Eventually, the party of ladies reunited and happy conversation resumed. Samantha stole a glance at James; he and Rich were involved in their own conversation, probably regarding the next time James would be home. Briefly, she prayed their time together to be more than just a moment.

The 'family' came together for one last bit of ribbing,

laughing, crying, and planning for the next get-together, maybe the 4th of July. The time came to call it a night. By this time, Samantha knew she had not experienced this depth of happiness since before the loss of her mother and father, and brother and sister. In one evening, she felt closer to this group, or family as they liked to describe themselves, then to anyone in a long, long time.

The entire family surrounded the couple for one last moment of fun which quickly turned into a time of thanks.

Samantha started by affirming, "I truly appreciate this evening, all of your laughter, your conversation, and, most of all, your support. Y'all are such a wonderful group…oops, sorry… such a wonderful family. I haven't enjoyed myself this much in quite some time. Y'all treated me like one of your own…" she choked back her emotions, "and I thank you more than I can ever repay."

The first to hug Samantha was Carol. "You have been a real joy tonight. We needed someone new here to help keep these guys in line." Softly, she added, "I pray all goes well for you and Jim. I would love to see you both again!"

"Thank you, Carol, thank you for everything."

Everyone followed with hugs and kind words for the newcomer. Jim laughed that he was yesterday's news. What could he do to get back into the limelight? Bob mentioned, and everyone agreed, that if Samantha agreed to come to their get-togethers, he could come with her. She truly enjoyed her inclusion in the family and thought, perhaps, God had blessed her with the beginning of a new life.

* * *

Samantha rolled over on the hotel bed, the room light still on. She filled a glass with bottled water, turned off the lights but one, and relaxed in the over-stuffed chair. Remembering moments from twenty-something-years past was therapeutic and, more than likely, romantically exaggerated. Sitting in the dimly lit room, she returned to her memories.

* * *

Jim held the car door open as she gracefully slid into the seat. She hoped he was anticipating their eventual discussion; she prayed he meant what he said. Hoping to keep the moment light until then, she spoke of the beauty of the wedding ceremony that morning. Nothing delighted her more than when he asked if she would continue the conversation begun at the reception.

She responded that, yes, she would; she wanted to make certain he truly wanted to hear because this was a serious matter.

Reaching for her hand, he simply stated, "I am serious. Tell me everything. When you're finished, I'll ask any questions I have. I'm military; listen first, ask questions afterwards."

"Yes, sir, Captain," she laughed as she saluted.

"Remind me to show you how to salute properly when we're finished."

"Yes, sir!" she saluted again…and, again, incorrectly.

Jim insisted, "I'll have you saluting properly before the night's over."

"OK, how about I just go back to being a plain civilian."

He smiled, "There is nothing plain about you."

"Nor you," she replied.

"James, I want you to know, I'm ashamed to say I've never done this before. We should all be looking to share the gospel… Jesus commanded us to do just that, 'Go out and preach the gospel to all nations.' But then, I've never met anyone who should hear it more. You seem to be so open and ready to hear."

"Bring it on, Hon."

Surprised by his response, she began, "Your friends invited me to be a part of *the family* tonight. So does God. He invites us to be a part of His family. We don't deserve this invitation. We've sinned and rebelled against God, and only those without sin can be a part of His family."

"But how—

"You said you would hold your questions until I was finished, Mister."

He saluted, "Yes, Ma'am!"

"OK…We've sinned and rebelled against God, and only those without sin can be a part of His family. Yet, God's son, Jesus Christ, made it possible for us to accept this invitation. He died on the cross, taking our sin, all sin, past, present, and future, upon Himself so that we could be forgiven. Jesus then rose from the dead, making a new, eternal life possible for us.

"So, the Bible says, 'God proves His own love for us in that while we were still sinners, Christ died for us' and 'If you confess with your mouth, Jesus is Lord, and believe in your heart that God raised Him from the dead, you will be saved.' This is found in the Book of Romans."

"How do you—

"Shhh. I truly feel you are at this point. God is waiting for you to respond to His invitation. If you want to have a new life in Christ, you must repent of your sins, which you began tonight when you told me and your friends about your past. Tell that to God, admit to God that you are a sinner and ask Him to forgive you and repent of your sins, or turn from the sins that have kept you from God, and accept Jesus' gift of forgiveness. Confess your faith in Jesus Christ as your Savior and Lord. Express your repentance and your faith by praying a prayer that I can lead you in…if you like."

James, now very quiet, just nodded. Samantha thought she

noticed him wipe his eyes as he drove. Giving him time, she said no more until he asked for final directions to her home. Once there, she directed him where to turn into the property, never before realizing how intimidating the tree-lined drive could be, especially when exposed for the first time to such an exorbitant exhibit of wealth. She motioned to the far side of the circle, opposite the arched doorway, where to park.

Oh, my Lord, she prayed, what is he thinking? Please do not let this be the end of what could be beautiful. Be with him, Lord, and me. Bring him to you, please.

Jim took a moment to compose himself as he walked around the rear of the car. He fumbled opening her door, staring in amazement at the majesty of her home. He had never seen an authentic mansion up close.

Looking over her home, Samantha felt a sudden sadness. "I'm sorry," she said softly, "I've never seen this through someone else's eyes."

"Don't feel that way, please. Your family can't be faulted for hard work and success."

He straightened her wrap across her shoulders, enabling her to draw it together for warmth. The early spring night had grown quite cool; their breath slightly visible. He had yet to respond to her invitation to pray.

Dejected, Samantha spoke so very softly, "Well, James, thank you for—

"Wait," James almost pleaded, "Aren't you going to pray with me? I can't have the evening end without that. I want to do this…now. This is what I need, and I want you to be the one."

Tears filled her eyes as Samantha hugged the man she truly desired to know. His arms, strong yet loving, held her as he had at the reception. She thought he might be embarrassed; he would not release her until bringing his emotions under control.

"Let's sit on the bench under the tree. We can pray there."

Beneath a crescent moon, she took his hands and asked him to pray with her…

"Dear God, I know I am a sinner. I believe Jesus died on the cross to forgive me of my sins. I believe Jesus rose on the third day to give me eternal life. I'm sorry for all the wrong I've done and ask you to forgive me. I now repent of my sins and accept your gift of eternal life. Thank You for Your love, forgiveness, and a new life in Jesus Christ. From this day forward, I choose to follow you. In Jesus' name, Amen."

Both sat silent in the cool night air, eyes closed, his hands in hers, heads bowed. Samantha understood that whether anything developed between them or not, this night could never be taken away. This memory would be a bond of Christian fellowship forever. No one comes to Christ without remembering who led them and who prayed with them. Regardless of any circumstances, they would remember one another as long as they lived. She thanked God again that He had given her the understanding that if nothing came of their relationship, He had granted her the blessing of being the one to pray with him.

Jim raised his head to see Samantha smiling, her eyes brimming with tears. She took his face in her hands and kissed him lightly.

"Welcome to God's family, James. You have blest me tonight in so many ways. Thank you."

"I'm certain I should thank you."

Reflecting a moment, he asked, "Is there something I should do now?"

"There's nothing you must do, but there are things you should want to do." She thought a moment, "Is there a chaplain at your base, someone you can tell what you've done? I'm sure he will be more than happy to guide you in the right direction."

"Probably, and I will, but what about now? I don't want to let this moment go!"

"Well," she didn't want to put him on the spot, "You could come to church with me in the morning. I go with my mother every Sunday…it's kind of a thing since my father doesn't go with her anymore. But I could go alone…if you want."

Nudging a little closer, Jim surprised her with his response, "Actually, I would like to meet your mother. Just go like you always do, and I'll meet you there. I really want to do this."

"Are you sure?"

"I'm very sure; I've never been more certain of anything in my life." He looked to her left, then to her and added, "I hope we can continue to see each other."

"I believe that can be arranged, Mr. Parking Lot Guy."

Jim had no idea of the joy Samantha experienced, a first after many, many years. He had accepted Jesus; he wanted to attend church with her and her mother; and he wanted to continue what had begun today. She hoped he felt a similar joy.

"I wish we could spend more time together. You have made such a wonderful decision tonight. I could talk with you for hours." Tapping her lower lip with her finger, she excitedly declared, "Wait a minute," she quickly rose from the bench. "You asked what you could do? Don't move, I'll be right back."

Samantha nearly ran across the circle and disappeared into the shadows of the entrance. Several minutes later, she emerged with the same energy.

She returned to the bench, panting from her sprint, her wrap still across her shoulders. "I want you to have this, please."

"What is it?" Jim couldn't make it out in the darkness.

"You should begin to read the Bible. This is my Bible…I want you to have it. Read the Gospel of John. John's gospel says it all," her breathing began to settle. "If you want, we can go through this together."

"Samantha, I can't take your Bible."

"Please, do. Then, you will have one right away. I want to give it to you. This is a very special night; nothing would make me happier than if you would accept it."

How does one turn down such a heartfelt offer? "Thank you…I do accept. I can't tell you what…what this means…to me. I don't…I don't know what…to say." Words became very difficult. Never before had someone cared enough to share her most precious possession.

Jim hesitantly placed his arm around her and asked, "Samantha, please tell me…do you really want to walk down this path with me, to see where it may lead?"

"More than anything in the world."

* * *

After giving directions to the church and sitting with him for what did not seem long enough, Samantha kissed Jim a last time for the evening, prayed with him, and sent him on his way. No matter what, the memory of the evening; the release from her sorrow; the leading of a new Christian; and the discovery of potential love could never be taken away. As she entered her room and hung up her wrap, she had to ask herself, "Did today really happen?"

Kneeling at the foot of her bed, she prayed more earnestly than ever:

"My dear precious Lord, I cannot thank you enough for this evening. You have given me everything I ever needed…all in one day. You gave me the opportunity to lead a lost person to you; then, you gave me the possibility to grow to love that man, the very man you sent to release me from my past. Watch over us, bless us and protect us. Help me to help him wherever I can and that he continues to help me heal. And, Lord, I ask that this be true and lasting…and, if at all possible, please let my family know…I think I'm going to be all right. I pray this in Your holy name my Lord, Jesus. Amen."

Twenty minutes later, Samantha lay in bed, reliving the evening in her mind, the very faint scent of his cologne still present. What an evening, she sighed, knowing she would have a wonderful report for her mother in the morning. She closed her eyes. The phone rang.

"Who in the world would call at this time?" she sleepily mumbled as she rolled over to answer.

"Hello?"

"Samantha! This is Gina! Sorry to call so late, but we had to know!"

"Had to know what?" she intentionally taunted her friend. "Where are you calling from?"

"From the hotel, and you do know what I mean. Tell us! We're dying to know. I told Rich what you were going to discuss with Jim tonight. What happened?"

"Oh, that," she paused for effect.

"Samantha!"

"OK, I'm sorry. I'm just so happy about this!"

She proceeded to relay the full account of the events following the reception. Gina and Rich listened together on the other end, occasionally interjecting a "Really?" or a "He did!" and, eventually, a "Praise the Lord!"

"This is great news!" Rich rejoiced. "I don't know what to say, Samantha, but you should be very happy. You accomplished in one evening what I've been hoping for a year!" Deep within, he truly felt great happiness for his best friend and Samantha.

Samantha placed the credit where she felt it belonged, "You laid the groundwork, Richard; God let me bring him home."

"And you did it so well. Thank you, Samantha, you are a great friend! I'll leave you with Gina now; I'm sure she wants to know about the other stuff." And, he was right.

"So, what else happened?"

"What else what?" Samantha teased.

"Please, just tell me."

"James wants us to see where tonight may lead. He's going to meet me at church in the morning!"

"No!"

"Yes!"

Gina relayed the news, "Rich, Jim is going to church with Samantha in the morning!"

Samantha heard in the distance, "No…really?"

"Tell Rich…really!"

The remaining conversation consisted of every detail regarding Samantha and James' potential relationship, and closed with a tearful, yet joyful, promise to get together following the honeymoon and Jim returning to St. Louis. Samantha hung up knowing that since the loss of her family, she had never felt more content with her life than tonight.

Sunday morning, she woke early and joined her mother for a cup of coffee in the breakfast room. Normally, morning conversation seemed out of the question but not today, she had much to share and all good. Rose never said, but she had mixed emotions about the young man who 'gave' his life to Jesus. Maybe so, but many a young man has said what needed to be said in order to fulfill his quest, she judged. But Samantha seems so certain; her exuberance convinced Rose, grudgingly, to see for herself. If he doesn't show, she deduced, then, everything was just a ploy, a sad ploy that would inflict much pain to her trusting daughter. She regretted not having an earlier opportunity to meet the young man who stole her heart. A mother would have surmised his motives.

Rose appreciated Samantha attending church with her since Ed no longer did. She didn't know for certain but strongly suspected her husband never believed. Perhaps that was the reason she had such difficulty accepting Samantha's story of the previous night. Just wait and see, and pray he is truly the new Christian she thinks he is.

Samantha and Rose reached church thirty minutes early, just in case. As many of Rose's friends began to arrive, Samantha excitedly shared her story with them. Rose wished she hadn't, again just in case, fearful her daughter not only would be hurt, but also embarrassed. Every passing minute convinced Rose he was not coming. She wanted to cry for her daughter. How could he do this to her?

"I suppose we should go in, the music is beginning."

"No…wait. I think that might be him." As a car drove past the entrance toward the back of the lot, Samantha hurriedly stepped to the doors, "It is him!"

"Samantha, wait," Rose called, but too late. She swept out the door, making her way to the rear of the church parking lot. Rose sighed, "At least he's here."

Several minutes later, the couple entered hand-in-hand. Samantha immediately introduced the obviously nervous young man to Rose.

"Mother, I would like you to meet James Gordon, the gentleman of last evening. James, this is my mother, Rose, a very loving and gracious lady."

Jim took her hand, "Good morning, Mrs. Marissen. I'm very happy to meet you. I am sorry, I definitely wanted to arrive early but I was held up by two trains just down the street. As soon as the first crossed one way, a second passed the other. I couldn't believe it. I wanted to make a good impression this morning; I really did. Forgive me, I'm sorry we didn't have time to talk before the service."

Rose placed her hand on his, "Don't even worry about it. This is Kirkwood; it happens to everyone at one time or another. So nice to meet you, Mr. Gordon."

"Jim, please."

"All right, Jim. But you must call me Rose."

"I will…Rose."

Relieved to find him polite and a gentleman, Rose relinquished her earlier rash judgment, and decided to allow time to determine any thoughts about Jim Gordon.

As the three progressed down the center aisle, Jim had to smile; two days in a row he found himself attending church. Reaching an available pew, Rose entered first. He placed his hand on Samantha's back to guide her behind her mother. She immediately remembered the feeling of the day before. Not only that, she noticed a few people smiling as she and Jim moved next to Rose.

Once settled, she whispered to him, "I'm so glad you're here…and you have your Bible with you. Thank you!"

Taking her hand, he whispered back, "I'm glad too. I had to

see if everything that happened last night was real…and…I'm happy to see it was, and still is." He proudly added, "I read part of 'John' last night, but I'll need your help understanding it all."

She smiled, "I'll always be here to help."

He gently squeezed her hand, "And I'm here for you."

After the opening hymn, Rose quietly expressed to Samantha, "You never said he was handsome," followed by the slightest smile.

She grinned and replied, "I'm pretty sure I did."

After the pastor pointed out a few of the church events scheduled during the week, he asked everyone to stand for the reading of the Bible verses that would be the subject of his sermon. After the reading, Samantha sat just a bit closer, resting her shoulder against his arm; she simply wanted to be near him. As the pastor made references to particular Bible verses during the sermon, she helped Jim find the verses in 'his' Bible, truly enjoying her role as teacher.

She couldn't help but smile as she observed Jim, listening, hearing the Word for the first time. The Gospel of Matthew, chapter 13 came to mind: "But blessed are your eyes, for they see, and your ears, for they hear."

Following the service, a smattering of church members gathered around Rose, Samantha, and Jim to greet the young man Samantha had enthusiastically spoken of earlier. Jim found himself shaking hands while responding to questions and generally enjoying his inclusion into this church family. Any initial nervousness soon evaporated with each new introduction. Samantha made an intentional effort not to mention his Air Force background. She would leave that to him.

Laughter and friendly conversation floated among Rose's fellow church members, who seemingly enjoyed speaking with the young man. Please, Lord, Rose prayed, I ask that he be real.

Lastly, Samantha introduced Jim to their pastor, Mark Rodgers, and excitedly informed him of James' decision, "James gave his life to Jesus last night, it was beautiful. The whole night was beautiful," to which Pastor Rodgers congratulated Jim, welcomed him to the church, and offered his help in any way.

As the conversation of the previous evening grew, mostly between Pastor Mark and Jim, Rose listened intently and began to realize Jim's testimony may well be true. His sincerity in relating how the past months had weighed heavily on him, and how he felt the need for something beyond himself initiated a positive change in Rose's view. She sensed in him a great deal of thanksgiving for Samantha's intuitive command of what he required.

Samantha, meanwhile, stood quietly at James' side as he declared so honestly to Mark, his story and to give such credit to her. When he spoke of their day together, a wave of embarrassment nearly swept her over. But, at that moment, nothing mattered except James; she truly believed there may be an excellent chance something could develop. One fact of which she was certain; trust had overshadowed her pain. With James, she experienced safety, strength, and joy.

A wave of relief flowed over Rose as Jim spoke of the marriage of his friend and how Samantha had made the day the best of his life in so many ways. The final convincing point occurred unexpectedly while Rose and Jim listened to Samantha giddily describing the candleholder situation at the reception to the pastor. Jim turned to her mother and privately assured her he would never say or do anything to hurt or take advantage of Samantha. Rose's heart melted, knowing for certain her daughter had every right to be as happy as exhibited that morning.

The conversation drew to a close; Pastor Mark congratulated

Jim again, letting him know he was welcome any time. If he wanted to meet the next time he was in town, that could be easily arranged.

Jim, Samantha, and Rose enjoyed a casual lunch that afternoon; Jim told of his Air Force career and his assigned base in Mississippi. Rose laughed, mentioning he should have no problem with Samantha's southern manner of speech. Their time at the restaurant proved delightful. Impressed with his determination and success, his newfound Christian life, and his respect and care for her daughter, Rose found she truly liked and admired the Air Force Captain for the right reasons and hoped to see him again.

After the three returned to Rose's car at the church parking lot, Jim gently caressed Samantha's face and kissed her softly. "I'll call you tomorrow evening."

"I hope so," she whispered, knowing today would be the last time she would see him for a while.

He brushed her cheek with his finger, "I will, I promise."

*   *   *

Samantha had just nodded off in the dimly lit hotel room, when a knock at the door startled her. She shuffled to the door to investigate. Looking through the peephole she noticed two men in the hallway. Before opening the door, she asked who they were and what they wanted. They responded that another guest complained their heating system was not working. They were to check out the problem. Their heavy Russian accents made the explanation difficult to understand. Samantha asked them to repeat the reason; they did, while displaying their IDs.

"One minute," she said, "I want to check with the front desk."

"We understand," one of the men answered loudly.

The phone rang several times before an answer, "Front desk,

how may I help you?" Thankfully, the responder's accent wasn't as thick.

"Yes, this is room 442. There are two maintenance men at my door to check the heating system in my room, but I'm not having a problem."

"We are sorry for inconvenience. There is complaint on your floor. All rooms need check for safety. Is good to call before opening door to person you do not know."

"All right, I understand. Thank you."

Samantha hung up the phone, unlocked the door, and pulled the chain free. Slowly, she opened the door and the two men apologetically entered her room. One, with a toolbox, stepped to the thermostat, popped the cover off, and inspected the inner components. The other appeared to take temperature readings around the suite, or so it seemed.

The man at the thermostat called Samantha over to explain the problem. While watching but not understanding the explanation, an arm suddenly slipped around her neck. She felt the prick of a needle. Attempting to scream, time stopped; her world faded to black.

UNITED STATES

APRIL 2, THE day the United States broke the back of the largest Russian spy network in this country since the 1950s. Twelve Russian agents in seven major cities had been hacking military, political, and weapons manufacturing databases for several months, feeding the information to secondary agents in obscure third world countries before re-routing the stolen data to Moscow. Unashamedly, twenty-three American citizens assisted the Russians by supplying access or security codes to accomplish their sinister plot. In depth background checks of the Americans showed none suffered financial troubles, personal problems, or any sort of disaster. Their only focus, simply money, the all too well known Achilles heel, American style.

Fortunately, the NSA, CIA, and FBI had uncovered the operation months earlier, redirecting computer connections to vast banks of misinformation. The era of the shifty-eyed, trench-coated spy vanished with the appearance of the computer 'geek', the lifeless slob rotting in his apartment night after night attempting to crack the codes of giant corporations. Recruitment of these characters proved quite simple when presented with the challenge of government agency and defense contractor systems. Throw in a few bucks for their efforts and you can build a sophisticated operation led by a relatively small assembly of foreign agents.

Nevertheless, the entire foreign agent web collapsed when the

National Security Agency intercepted several communication and transmission tests sent by the weak-link incompetent apartment dwellers. Instead of allowing their fingers to do the walking, the hackers let their fingers do the talking, keyboard talking, and pride brought about bragging, albeit very little, of the upcoming security breach. Greed can bring about results, but pride will eventually destroy the project and those involved.

The political outrage broadcast over media airwaves boisterous, continuous, and quickly annoying. Annoying because, in the typical political atmosphere of the day, consisted of nothing but mindless chatter without substance. The general principal of the day: take a grave misfortune and parlay it for political gain, any type of political gain. Whine…a soundbite, complain…yet another. The current administration found itself in quite a quandary: How should the affair be handled without angering the Russians who will obviously plead innocence? Or, more importantly, how should the proof be exposed without appearing as buffoons for the near disaster occurring in the first place? Although the attempt failed, the party residing on the opposite side of the congressional aisle will attempt to further their cause by creating an artificial fear among the people. How do we know for certain that the country's security wasn't compromised?

Three factions quickly formed: the politician who hid under any rock to avoid voicing a position; the politician who proclaimed, "I didn't believe this could happen"; and the last with the usual, "I told you so!" Unfortunately, the media, with their love affair of fools, ignored those true representatives of the people wanting to defend the United States against external as well as the new world internal attacks. The problem, too many congressional representatives and senators unable to make decisions with the chains of party and lobbyists wrapped tightly around their ankles. The Administration's decision: the twelve Russian agents would be tried as spies and the twenty-three American citizens as traitors; something the U.S. government hadn't the courage to do in decades.

OUTSIDE ST. PETERSBURG, RUSSIA

SAMANTHA MARISSEN REGAINED consciousness slowly, painfully, definitely confused. What happened? She struggled to recollect the events that led to her kidnapping. No, it wasn't kidnapping, she thought, or was it? Finally, she raised herself on one elbow and opened her eyes enough to squint about her confines, utterly disgusting conditions compared to her hotel. Her head throbbed with such intensity, she collapsed back onto the mattress. Only then, did she realize she lay on an old single bed. Next to the bed, a lamp atop a well-worn nightstand emitted barely enough light to allow visibility across the room. Dim light sufficed; a brighter light would intensify her nausea.

Head pounding, Samantha groggily recalled the memory of the previous night. Was it last night? She had no idea how long she had been out. Who were the men in her hotel room? Who assured her they were legitimate? What was this about?

With no warning, an uncontrollable urge to throw up surged through her body. Frantically, she searched for a place to do so. Despite her pain, she stumbled toward a door in the corner and found a small, dingy, dark bathroom. Sanitary conditions meant nothing at the moment; she dropped to her knees and threw up violently into the filthy toilet. Her body convulsed with gut-wrenching heaves until nothing remained to be expelled. Supporting her head above the bowl, she broke down and cried uncontrollably.

"Miz Marissen!" bellowed a large balding man in a thick Russian accent.

Samantha, still hunched over on her knees, turned toward the frightening voice, looking miserable with tangled hair, vomit on her mouth and chin, beads of sweat covering her face, and tears of terror streaking her cheeks.

"Get up! Get in to room!"

Sobbing, she stood slowly and tried the sink faucet which spit out cold water. She wiped her face with her hands as best she could but found no towel and no mirror. She staggered to a chair the large, balding Russian pointed to, and carefully lowered her aching body.

"Why am I—

"Stop!"

Shaking from fear, sickness, and the cold, she numbly nodded.

"You are held for passing Federation classified information to foreign agents! We hold until evidence complete! Do not resist! Understand?"

Samantha nodded again. The large, growling Russian stormed out, slamming the door behind him. She heard the clicking of the lock.

"Oh, my Lord, what's happening? I've done nothing. Help me, Lord, help me, please." She looked upward through tear-blurred eyes, then buried her face in her hands and wept.

MARISSEN ESTATE– ST. LOUIS, MISSOURI

ERIC, THE MARISSENS' head butler, rang the bedroom of Rose and Ed. At 5:30 in the morning, he did not expect a civil answer. Much to his surprise, Ed answered in a sleepy but calm voice.

"What is it, Eric?"

"Sir," he hesitated, "There are two men from the CIA in the downstairs study. They must speak with you now."

"What! Tell them I'll be right there."

"CIA?" Ed mumbled to himself as he slipped on his robe. "What could they want this early?"

Rose rolled over, half asleep, "What's happening?"

"Wait here, I'll check it out." he answered, stepping out of the bedroom.

Eric stood at the entrance to the study as Ed marched in. Two agents rose and displayed their IDs, allowing Ed to quickly scan them before asking, "What is so important that you show up at 5:30 in the morning? Couldn't it wait?"

"Mr. Marissen, please. You may want to have a seat. We have disturbing news."

The agents divulged as much information as available regarding the arrest of his daughter, Samantha Marissen, in St. Petersburg, Russia five days earlier by the Russian Federation on the charge of international espionage. Five days had passed before the Russians alerted our State Department of the arrest, they informed him. Regretfully, her exact whereabouts were unknown, and now, little time remained before the news media learned of the event and began the butchering of meager facts.

Rose overheard the report while waiting on the stairway outside the study. She hastened into the room, "What's happened to my daughter? Where is Samantha?"

Ed put his arm around her and responded, "Rose, Samantha has been arrested on some trumped up charge in Russia. This is absolutely ridiculous!"

Glaring at the two men, he continued, "There is no way possible anyone can believe this. Outrageous! What's being done to bring her home? I'll do whatever is needed. Just tell me!"

"Mr. Marissen, we don't know yet. We were sent to inform you of the situation before you heard it elsewhere. We are deeply concerned for your daughter's welfare. You will receive information as we do."

The overwhelmed couple collapsed onto the leather couch, holding one another for strength, Rose crying, Ed pondering what to do next.

"We're sorry to invade your privacy like this, Mr. and Mrs. Marissen, but our orders are to remain with you at this time. Is there somewhere we can position ourselves without being in the way? We will be in constant contact with our superiors. Please try to remain calm while we do our job."

"Yes, yes," Ed mumbled. "Eric, show these gentlemen to the breakfast room. Get them some coffee."

Rose rocked as she cried, "My baby, my poor little baby."

Ed held her close, trying to be strong for his wife and Samantha, now helpless to protect either.

MARISSEN ESTATE– ST. LOUIS, MISSOURI

EARLY MORNING NATIONAL TV broke the big story. Talking heads busily performed pointless interviews with clueless politicians, while broadcasting mind-numbing speculation. Somewhere in the circus might be a shred of thoughtful truth.

Ed and Rose watched in disbelief. The reports of the Marissen arrest took on a sense of urgency with a possible explosion of political ramifications. Relations with the Russian Federation already strained to the breaking point over the seizure and arrest of the Russian spy ring, and now, retaliation with the arrest of not just an American citizen, but the daughter of the wealthiest man in America.

Two distinct viewpoints floated about for consideration. The first and most accepted explanation: Samantha Marissen—the victim of an outrageous plot to deflect guilt from the Russian spy ring fiasco onto the United States involvement in their own tangled espionage web. The second, promoted by a crude, rotund, hack of a filmmaker: A wealthy divorced woman— Samantha Marissen, involved in such a scheme simply for the excitement, the thrill of the games for the rich and famous. As he would so eloquently denigrate one who could not respond, Samantha Marissen merely wanted to hurt her wealthy father as an act of revenge or retaliation. Although he drew his usual flock of followers, most believed the raggedy, waddling, filmmaker simply desired another axe-grinding, desperate attempt at serious acceptance.

One of the CIA agents quietly entered the room, pardoned himself, and handed a cell phone to Ed. "Mr. Marissen, the President would like to speak with you."

Surprised by his announcement, Ed took the phone, "Mr. President?"

"Yes, Mr. Marissen…Ed, this is Donald Burton. I want you to know how very sorry I am to learn of your daughter's illegal arrest. Rest assured, I know this is nothing more than a smokescreen to lessen the attention given to the broken Russian spy ring. We will do everything in our power for the quick and safe release of Samantha. This has my complete attention until it is resolved."

Ed's only question, "No one knows where Samantha is being held?"

"Sorry to say, at this time, we do not. I do expect that to change very soon."

"Please…find her. Bring her home."

"We will, Ed. We will."

The conversation concluded, he returned the phone to the agent, leaned back on the couch, and held Rose close. Strange, he thought, he'd spoken with presidents before but that was business; this is his daughter.

WASHINGTON, MISSOURI

NOT ONE TO sleep late, Jim Gordon completed his daily three-mile run by 6:30 a.m. Three miles doesn't seem like much, unless living outside Washington, Missouri. The distance over his normal route became a real workout, taking him over hills, through a valley, and up a steep grade to his cabin.

Four years earlier, Jim retired from the Air Force after thirty years. Unbelievable…thirty years. Where had the time gone? Over the course of his career, Jim qualified to pilot high-performance jets, such as the F-15 Eagle and the F-16 Fighting Falcon, as well as his involvement in the development of the F-22 Raptor. His Air Force adventure started with the typical medical examination and interview prior to admission, followed by his degree in Aeronautical Engineering.

Adhering to the requirements of a fighter pilot, Jim excelled in mathematics and physics and completed the professional officer's course, flight training, field training, and weapons practice. Along with his physical and visual excellence, he possessed the ability to remain alert throughout any length mission. The average citizen is unaware how much more than steering a plane is required of a fighter pilot. Flying alone, the pilot must make rapid decisions, use the most advanced technology available in navigation and communication systems, and operate the armament and fire control systems carried on his aircraft. Hours upon hours of training and air practice demand physical and mental acuity.

Under normal conditions, a fighter pilot works an eight to ten-hour day training and learning new flight exercises regulated by the number of hours they must spend on the ground (a 12-hour rest) in between flights. During wartime, such as Jim's Mideast tour, following the same flight regulations, a pilot performs the same daily routine: fly a mission, return, eat, sleep, get up and fly another mission. Missions can involve flying above ground troops protecting them from danger with air strikes; delivering bombs on target; or defending the pilot's airspace incorporating flying tactics.

'Colonel James Paul Gordon, Retired', the title didn't sound right and probably never would. Upon retiring, Jim took a year off, traveled some, and built his cabin or had it built depending on how and when he told the story. For a short period, he attempted painting…on canvas, not walls. A 'total lack of talent' could not begin to describe his ineptitude. Soon, Jim realized he had to work again, to fly again. Having free time is great as long as you have someone to share your experiences.

He never married; had a few relationships but nothing serious ever developed. Not that Jim was incapable of love, no one had been able to capture his heart. In the off-chance he did meet someone, the relationship predictably ended quickly since all signs showed there could be no future…but that was OK. He once loved a woman more than he could ever love again and would never settle for less. He opened up to no one; his pain remained deep within and he left it at that.

Jim interviewed with an airline that catered to small business, flying executives to and from various destinations. No one understood why a retired Air Force colonel would want to fly a smaller, slower private jet, but Jim knew. He had to fly. Bargaining from the start that he be allowed to choose his flights, unless something of an emergency arose, Small Business Air, SBA, offered him an immediate position with substantial compensation. His experience as a pilot, a flight instructor, and a man with no ties made him a solid investment. He accepted the offer several days later; SBA was happy and the job kept Jim in the air.

His friends: Rich and Gina, Ted and Carol, Bill and Nancy, Bob and Liz, and Neil and Sue, all married with grown children, remained in contact with Jim. Never a party, birthday, barbeque, or holiday passed that Jim wasn't invited to one or another's home.

One year after their wedding, Rich and Gina had a beautiful daughter, but sadly, could have no more. Jim loved the little girl, viewing her as the daughter he and his Samantha might one day have. As promised, the Reynolds named the baby Samantha, after Gina's best friend. Over time, young Samantha thought of Jim like an uncle, a title he cherished after his loss. Now a beautiful young lady, she blest Jim with her humor, her outgoing personality, and her love.

Years earlier, Gina explained to young Samantha the history behind her 'uncle' and his Samantha. She detailed the life-altering split and how her best friend simply dropped out of everyone's life immediately after. From that moment, young Samantha wanted her 'uncle' to always know of her concern and love for him, especially during his Mideast tour. She wrote daily and prayed for him every night, not realizing the impact she had on Jim, the special meaning she gave his life.

Reaching the top of the steep grade, Jim stood in the crisp early morning air and surveyed his kingdom; a four-room cabin consisting of a kitchen, bedroom, living room, and an extra room used as an office, sort of, and a bathroom. Settling down with a good book, most times the Bible, filled his non-flying time while relaxing on the rustic front porch. A good rain only added to the ambiance; listening to the rhythm of the drops bouncing off the tin roof. From his porch, Jim enjoyed the beautiful vista of tree-covered rolling hills. Tall pines surrounded the remaining perimeter of the property, providing the privacy he desired.

Every morning before his run, Jim set the coffee maker timer to ensure the aroma of fresh coffee filled the room by his return. This morning was no different. He poured a mug of brew, grabbed the remote and clicked on the TV, immediately noting something major must have happened.

"What's today's big story?" he muttered.

After a sip of coffee, he eased back in the recliner and closed his eyes. He was tired enough this morning to doze off, and almost did until he heard the name "Marissen," or so he thought. He sat up and leaned forward.

The morning news people were discussing an international event that occurred earlier in St. Petersburg, Russia. Jim listened for the name again, just to make sure. After several minutes, the anchorwoman repeated,

"Our breaking story this morning is the arrest of Samantha Barrett, or since her highly publicized divorce, Samantha Marissen, daughter of billionaire Ed Marissen, in St. Petersburg, Russia. It appears she has been charged with espionage, passing on highly sensitive material to an unknown third party. For more on the story, we take you to Tom Spencer in Moscow."

"Good morning, Tina. The atmosphere in Moscow is tense, as the head of the Russian Secret Police, Victor Federov, has been less than candid in his remarks. According to Federov, 'the main threat is foreign intelligence services have planned all along to steal sensitive materials of the Russian government in the areas of military weapons research and development, which raises serious concerns regarding the security of the Russian Federation.' No one is certain what the ambiguous statement means.

"Federov reportedly stated that the FSB is currently dealing with more spies than ever and has curtailed the spying and other sabotage activities of nine agents recruited by foreign security services.

"The question that should be asked, according to an anonymous American Embassy official is, 'Has the Samantha Marissen case been fabricated by the FSB as a clear provocation against an American citizen in retaliation for the recent arrest of the Russian spy ring in the United States?'

The official explained his statement saying, 'The Russian secret police are traditionally excellent in the fabrication of false spy cases. There can be no doubt that the FSB along with Russia's many special services are a powerful tool for the inexperienced Kremlin leaders in their push to bring back a totalitarian regime in a country where democracy never truly existed in the first place.'

"These are strong words," Spencer continued, "released by the United States Embassy in the hope of exhibiting Russia in the worst light possible in order to gain international support. It is still very early in the crisis to understand all that is happening. We are told a press conference will take place sometime today, but as of yet, no word.

"Reporting from Moscow, this is Tom Spencer. Back to you, Tina."

"Thank you, Tom. Obviously, we will stay with this story throughout the day to keep you informed. We will return after this short break."

*   *   *

Jim stared at the screen in disbelief of what he had just heard. The report stirred feelings he buried long ago of Samantha, now a woman in harm's way in a hostile country. He knew she was incapable of anything so ridiculous. This must be a fabrication. What was she doing in Russia anyway? His concern soon turned to regret, a deep regret that he had not fought for her. He should never have allowed her father to stand in their way. Over the years, he worked hard to ignore that guilt and pain, sometimes successfully, many times not.

Jim turned off the TV, poured another cup of coffee, and numbly stepped out onto the porch. Lowering himself to the edge of the top step, he scanned the rolling hills that normally brought him a sense of peace, but not this morning. Not now. Sweet, innocent Samantha. Watch over her, Lord. Bless her... protect her, please.

* * *

Thoughts of their time together raced through his mind, as if only yesterday. As a thirty-year-old Air Force captain, Jim hitched a ride on a transport from Columbus Air Force Base in eastern Mississippi to Scott Air Force Base, Illinois, not far from St. Louis, for the wedding of his best friend, Rich Reynolds. He and Rich had been the longest lasting bachelors in their tight group of friends. Along came this sweet young thing who swept Rich away. She was sweet, he recalled, and quite attractive too. Jim and his friends razzed Rich about their age difference, but that's all it was...razzing. Gina came from a well-to-do family but one would never know. She soon became one of the 'family.' Rich had many wonderful reasons to fall in love with 'the one'.

Prior to crossing paths with Gina, Rich had been invited to attend a Promise Keepers weekend in St. Louis, where he gave himself to Jesus Christ at the time of invitation. Rich was always considered a 'good guy', but the change in him affected Jim profoundly. From that day, Jim questioned his own life, his purpose. Rich spoke with Jim many times about his new-found faith; he never rejected the thought but never accepted it either.

Jim's Uncle Dave picked him up at Scott AFB and made it back to his home with barely enough time for a shave and a shower. Dave lived alone after his wife passed earlier in the marriage and never remarried. Jim roomed with his uncle after his father, Will, suffered a fatal heart attack; his mother, Bonnie, died four years earlier from cancer when he was eighteen. At the time of his father's death, Jim had already enlisted in the Air Force. Dave offered him a place to bunk anytime he had leave. With a room of his own and all the freedom of a typical roommate, the arrangement worked well.

His uncle's home turned out to be a place of security, something Jim had not experienced as a child and adolescent. Although his mother died of cancer, she also suffered as an alcoholic, while his father spent most of his time in his own self-involved world. If the day didn't revolve around Will Gordon, there had better be one heck of a good reason. Lessons on how to treat a woman with respect, or the proper role of a father or of a man for that matter, were non-existent. Jim eventually wondered if his mother turned to alcohol because of her emotionally abusive husband. He also questioned if the lack of siblings resulted from his father's self-centered, self-absorbed life.

Jim flew into the house and up the stairs with his bag while Dave returned to his easy chair and Saturday morning paper, chuckling as he sat back and listened to the frantic preparation taking place. Twenty minutes later, Jim bounced down the stairs in his suit, hair still wet, and tie draped around his neck.

"Sorry about the rush, Dave, but I'm already behind schedule. Thank goodness my suit was here, and it fits. I'll be back after the wedding; we'll talk then. And thanks for the use of your car. You're a lifesaver!"

"Good! Just get there on time, but be careful. Enjoy yourself!"

Jim hurried out the door but had to turn back for the keys. He jumped into the car and sped from the house. "Slow down," he warned himself. "A ticket is the last thing you need this morning." Thankfully, the early Saturday morning traffic wasn't too bad. He should get to the Kirkwood church on time, barely. Surprisingly, he managed to tie a perfect knot at one of the stoplights. Already a good day, he thought.

During the drive, Jim couldn't help but think he was now the sole bachelor, thirty-years-old and attending his best friend's wedding alone. Never a long-term relationship kind of guy, he had little confidence in his social abilities, which, more than likely, accounted for his casual party life; live like there's no tomorrow. He knew the last thing any good father would accept was his daughter associating with him. On occasion, he would cautiously pursue a young lady but once she learned of his Air Force background, she inevitably transformed him into a sideshow, something to be displayed. Eventually, he determined not to speak of his career unless absolutely necessary.

The fact that he was not Rich's best man did not disturb Jim; Rich had a brood of brothers and the oldest deserved the honor. However, missing the rehearsal dinner did disappoint him but, he knew Rich would be his best friend to the end. Rich had put up with a lot; he owed Rich much, more than he could ever repay.

In his rush, and his thoughts, Jim almost drove past the entrance of the church parking lot. He abruptly whipped the car into the driveway, spied an empty parking space near the front of the church, and made a dash for the spot. Another car, approaching from the opposite direction, aimed for the same space. Jim immediately noticed the driver and her smile, stopped, and waved her into the empty slot. She mouthed 'thank you' and, of course, smiled again. He quickly drove to the rear of the lot to the next available parking space.

Hustling through the rows of cars to the church doors, he spied the 'smiling driver' several yards ahead and thought she certainly appeared to be attending the wedding alone. She is pretty but it was her smile that attracted him. No! Not today, no more! I'm tired of being alone, he yelled at himself. I want more than that! But I'm not going to hurt another person, not her, not anyone! I'm tired.

Jim stopped in his tracks; a cloud of disappointment and depression enveloped him. He truly was tired. He did want more. But what? Maybe…maybe he wanted what Rich found, but where do you find that? Rich had made many attempts to talk with him but he ignored his words, not purposely but lazily. The mysterious thoughts overwhelmed him. Jim looked around the lot, then decided not today. He was going to enjoy Rich's wedding, support his friend, and talk to him later, when things settled down. Perhaps he would share the dream with him, an unsettling dream, one he could not forget. Shaking off his malaise, Jim proceeded to the church doors.

Once inside, his eyes bounced straight to the 'smiling driver' asking a young usher for direction. He turned to his right searching for his friends and, sighting them on the groom's side, stepped into the middle aisle the same moment as the unknown young lady; she bumped Jim forward into the side of the last pew, sending a resounding echo throughout the church causing several guests to turn toward the source of the noise. Jim straightened himself and motioned for her to go ahead of him. Again, she smiled and silently mouthed 'thank you.'

Jim followed as she seemed to glide down the aisle, a

sophisticated and attractive woman in blue, a light blue, a sky blue—definitely her color, he thought. At one point, the sunlight shining through stained glass, colorfully illuminating her shoulder length hair, bouncing in step with her pace. He quickly looked away, he would not be enticed. And besides, she was probably far too nice for him anyway.

He stepped into his pew, three rows back of the 'smiling driver' but on the groom's side. His friends, Bob and Liz, Ted and Carol, Neil and Sue, and Bill and Nancy, welcomed Jim warmly with handshakes and greetings. As usual, they were a pleasure to see. He felt home.

Stretching back, he took that first deep cleansing breath of relaxation after his hectic morning and glanced toward the 'smiling driver' as she turned in her aisle seat making eye contact with him. He smiled and gave a slight wave to say "hi." She returned the smile and quickly faced forward. Several times, he thought she almost turned back again.

Bob tapped his shoulder and whispered, "Settle down Junior, she looks way too nice for you!"

Knowingly, Jim quietly stated from the side of his mouth, "Ya think?"

Remaining focused on the ceremony grew increasingly difficult as his eyes constantly wandered to the 'smiling driver,' but during a moment of personal reflection, Jim recalled, right in the church, a disturbing dream he experienced some weeks before, an intense dream he could not forget. The memory of the dream returned with remarkable clarity—

He stood alone in the center of a magnificent hall, the arched ceiling and floor exquisitely constructed of seamless cream-colored, highly polished marble. The peak of the ceiling rose, at least, eighty feet high with no visible means of support but for the flawless glass windows wrapped around the massive structure offering a striking panoramic view of the wondrously lush green fields beautifully landscaped with stately majestic trees; light breezes flowed gently through their thick canopies. Never before had he experienced such serenity.

Behind him stretched a low wide marble wall encasing a glistening, soothing pool of placid, pure, crystal-clear water fed by a spring visible on the distant side. Utter awe of the absolute beauty of the structure and spring-fed pool overwhelmed his mind when, without warning, he found himself outside facing the facade. Making his way through the grass toward a nearby path, away from the hall, he sensed he was not alone; another walked with him, yet several steps behind out of his sight. Jim did not attempt to see his companion but initiated a one-sided conversation regarding the fascinating hall and the calming, peaceful fields of green.

As he approached a small grove of trees, the path split in two. He stumbled to the left and down into an expanding dark wood. Struggling to return to the upper path, his slide continued deeper into an ever-darkening forest. Regardless of how he grasped and clutched at the undergrowth of thorny, musty brush, his twisting and turning descent into the menacing darkness persisted until he slammed face-down into the very lowest point of the slimy, filthy, stench-ridden path. The one behind did not follow. He was alone and blind in the blackest darkness.

Straining to bring his surroundings into focus, he panicked; fear burst forth in his mind and heart. He slipped and fell several times into the muck and mire attempting to rise but when, finally upright, observed with great difficulty that he stood alone on a cold, dark, dank, dangerous street with no comprehension of his whereabouts and no direction. A stark realization came to light, the realization there was absolutely nothing he could do to save himself. Crushed by a chilling childlike fright, he spun frantically to his left, then right, and seeing nothing familiar with no means of escape, cried out in despair. There must be a way out! Never before had he experienced such terror.

Rubbing his eyes with his fingertips, Jim felt great relief it had been only a dream, yet disturbed by its clarity, as if he had just dreamt it again.

Applause filled the church, snapping Jim to the present, as Rich and Gina began their march down the aisle into the rest of their lives together. Jim noticed Gina wink at the 'smiling driver' just before he thrust out his hand to shake Rich's as he passed. Once the remainder of the wedding party exited the sanctuary, the guests surged to the receiving area. His friends chatted, enjoying one another's company as Jim wondered where the 'smiling driver' might be. Please, just forget about her! What's the big deal? Why did he even care? He pushed thoughts of her from his mind and forced himself to join his friends in conversation.

As the crowd inched forward, a hand suddenly pressed against his back while a soft voice expressed, "Oh, I'm so sorry."

Jim turned quickly, expecting someone had tripped. What a shock! He was face to face with the 'smiling driver.' His mind buzzed with the realization of her presence and barely heard when she remarked in her soft southern voice, "Please forgive me."

He managed to say something about bumping into each other again, which he thought lame but she laughed and agreed. During this introductory period, they followed his friends in the reception line that led to a beautiful, glassed-in receiving are where coffee, tea, and light pastries were available. While he and his still unnamed 'smiling driver' moved forward, Jim self-consciously attempted to begin some typical small talk. He noticed, however, that she seemed attentive…and smiled. When she spoke, he hung on her every word, sincerely interested in what she said. He enjoyed her soothing, southern accent, finding her very demeanor comforting, even relaxing.

Nearing the wedding party, he placed his hand on her back and guided her before him. She seemed to want to say something, but didn't. He was a mix of emotions. Should he continue down this road or not? He was well-aware if he didn't make some sort of impression before reaching the end of the line, it would be the end of the line…for him. She was so nice, so sweet, and she actually talked with him, almost as if interested but, more than likely, just his imagination working overtime.

Jim soon realized that while he was trying to figure out what to do next, the 'smiling driver' had already reached Rich and appeared to know him quite well. Rich had been holding out on him, probably for the best, he laughed to himself.

He caught the tail-end of Rich's response, "Samantha, Gina loves you like a sister…

Soooo…her name is Samantha, very fitting, very classy, most appropriate.

Samantha moved on to Gina; he watched as the two performed the mandatory 'squeal of happiness' only young women can do. Jim smiled, sharing in her happiness for Gina.

Rich broke in, ending his daydream, "Jim, are you here to congratulate me or just to stare at another attractive woman?"

"Yeah…No! Sorry, just lost in my thoughts. Congratulations, Rich!" He wrapped his long-time friend in a bear hug. "I wish you and Gina the very best and I want to see plenty of kids! Between you both, they'll be beautiful girls and handsome boys!"

Jim overheard Gina exclaim, "Samantha, I thought you and Jim were together…you're not?"

"No…we're not," she responded. Disappointed her answer wasn't more positive, he popped in his stupid line about bumping into each other. Still, she laughed.

Leaning toward Jim, Rich asked, "You're not interested in her, are you? You haven't made any moves?"

"No…no, I haven't…and I don't intend to. She's really nice, I won't do that. I'm done with all that." He stopped, looked at the floor, then continued, "You've been a great friend, Rich. I was going to save this for later but…I need to talk to you…but I want to listen this time."

"Seriously? You're serious! Sure, even tonight if you want!"

"We'll see. I don't want to interfere with your day. But I do want to talk."

"You betcha! I won't let you put it off!"

Pointing at Rich, Jim just smiled. "Thank you."

The best friends shook hands again followed by another bear hug before Jim stepped to Gina. Samantha stood to the side as her best friend and Jim exchanged a hug and a kiss on the cheek.

"Gina, you are an absolutely beautiful bride. I know I have nothing to say about this, but there is no one I would rather see Rich spend the rest of his life with than you. You are wonderful!"

Embarrassed, and surprised by his compliment, Gina kissed him again on the cheek. As she did, she whispered, "You're not going to hit on my friend, Samantha, are you? She's a very sweet, shy friend and I don't want to see her hurt."

"No, I won't. I promise. You are right, though, she is very sweet. But how come I've never seen her?"

"Oh, I don't know. I guess she's one of the lucky ones! You would only break her heart." Gina nodded toward Samantha, "I think she's waiting for you, so…please don't."

"I won't, Gina, I promise."

Taking a deep breath, she glanced again to her best friend, then Jim, "I'm sorry, Jim, she's had enough pain in her life."

"Yeah, then she certainly doesn't need any more, does she? I'll…I'll see you and Rich tonight." Before he stepped away, he barely whispered, "I love you both."

Realizing a sadness in him as he left, Gina almost called him back. He had never mentioned anything about loving her and Rich. The guests kept coming; sadly, she had to let Jim go.

He stepped toward Samantha, knowing what he had to do. Gina was right; his past proved the best thing to do was to walk away. But he wondered, what pain had she suffered? Facing one another, he looked into her eyes. Neither said anything.

Dejected, Jim reached out, "Samantha, it was a pleasure talking with you this morning."

She took his hand and responded, "Yes, thank you, James, it was very nice."

Their parting handshake a major disappointment, he turned to his friends on the far side of the room and walked off without looking back.

Naturally, they wanted to know what happened but Jim had no response, only a question, "Have you guys ever seen her before? You know, the young lady I was talking to in line."

"Lady?" Bob repeated.

"Yeah, lady. She is really nice, really sweet. I enjoyed talking with her."

Bob apologized, "Sorry, Jim. I, uh, I don't know what I thought. You threw me off there."

"No, I understand. Why would you think I'm serious?" Jim began to see how the image of his past affected everything. Another pulse of regret throbbed through his mind.

Neil attempted to drive the conversation through the heavy somber mood, "I think I would remember someone like her…

but I don't."

"And it's a good thing you don't." Sue laughed as she poked him in the ribs.

Bob, attempting some humor, spoke out, only to regret his statement immediately, "Didn't I warn you she was probably too nice for you?"

"Yeah, you did…you did. Oh, well, I should get back to Dave's, get some rest, spend some time with him." He stared at the marble floor a moment, then looked up, "But…you know…I have to say something to her. I don't know why, but I just can't just walk away like this. There is something about her." Jim cleared his throat, "I'm sure this is a suicide mission, but here goes. I'll see you guys tonight."

He walked away from his friends, hands in his pockets, without even a simple good-bye.

"Is it me, or does Jim seem really down this morning?" Ted voiced with sincere concern.

"Yeah, he does. Maybe he's just tired from his hectic morning." Bill attempted to give reason for Jim's change. "Who knows what time he had to get up to get here."

As he drew nearer to Samantha, Carol muttered under her breath, "I hope he knows what he's doing; she seemed very nice. I just hope he doesn't consider her some kind of a challenge."

From a safe distance, they observed as he approached her from behind and touched her shoulder. She turned with a look of surprise.

"What's he doing?" Neil asked.

"I don't know," Bob chuckled, "He's bending over or something. Whatever it is, she's not running away."

They noticed Samantha laugh politely, otherwise, only pointless body motion. She'd say something to Jim; he'd answer. They got a kick when he took her hand in his and bent over again; Neil almost choked on his coffee when Jim released her hand, motioned to her friends, and began to walk away.

"Wow! I don't believe it," Bill declared, somewhat shocked, "I guess she shot him down. When was the last time that hap—

"Not so fast…not yet!" Carol exclaimed.

Samantha must have called to Jim, he stopped and turned. She smiled while speaking, he responded, and then departed. But, they did notice her smile. What the heck just happened?

"I guess we won't know till tonight," Bob ventured.

* * *

Jim's friends located their table in the enormous ballroom, large enough to accommodate the several hundred guests invited for the social event of the season. 'Old money' is the term one would use to describe Gina's family, a family that called St. Louis home since the mid 1800's. The fortune made in the beginning grew over time simply because of so much. Properly invested, no family member would ever have to work, as was the case. Philanthropy ran deep in her family, so did politics; several members ran and won State offices over the years, while many others represented charitable causes over the years, eventually including Gina.

Although young, she matured into a level-headed, well-balanced young woman who had already created several worthy social programs, many for young pregnant single mothers, and children, alone and abused. Gina generally put in more than forty hours a week finding daycare or mentors for children, employment for single mothers, and healthcare and support for pregnant girls. She had asked Rich if he wished to join her mission explaining God watched over those doing his will. Rich would consider the opportunity but, initially, wanted to continue in his field. Gina knew his heart and waited patiently.

The group made themselves comfortable as large numbers of guests began to arrive in their finest attire. The 'family' laughed as they figured to be the only middle class people in the building, other than employees. "I hope somebody doesn't expect me to bring them a drink, or something," Bob laughed.

As soft music played in the background, Jim rushed to the table, "Sorry I'm late; I needed to spend some time with Dave. We don't see each other that often; we had a lot to talk about."

He tugged at the cuffs of his shirt to extend slightly beyond the suitcoat sleeves and then made another adjustment to his tie.

"Is that a new suit, you bum?" questioned Bob in his most serious voice. "Did you go out and buy a new suit? Is that why your late? Is there someone you're trying to impress? We know it's not us. I'll bet it's that 'Lady' you were asking about, isn't it? That's even a new tie, right?" he pressed further.

"OK, you got me. I don't have a lot working for me, and my only suit was really old, so I thought, it can't hurt. I don't know what, but there is something really different going on tonight. All I ask is, don't ridicule me too much in front of her…if she does spend some time with me. When we're alone, you can tear me apart all you want."

The four guys came to Jim, "Don't worry, we won't. We joke around a lot, but this seems important to you. So…we won't say anything. Just be on your best behavior…or all bets are off!"

The joking around and laughter with the guys put Jim a little more at ease, but he had to ask, "Have you seen her? I need to find her before everything starts."

"Whoa, jet jockey, slow down!" Bob pressed. "Can't you acknowledge us before you go traipsing off to find your 'Lady'?"

"Wait a minute! You said you wouldn't give me any trouble tonight. Are you backing off on your promise already?"

"Oooh, Jim, that promise was only not to have fun at

your expense in front of her," Ted informed the unsuspecting bachelor. "I look around and I don't see her anywhere near you at the moment…although…I do see someone who looks like her about seventy-five feet away." Ted motioned toward the center of the room.

"Ted, really? Yes! That's her. Thank you, really, thank you."

"You are welcome. So, go see if she remembers you." Ted smacked Jim on the back to send him on his way.

"OK, Roger Ramjet, go do what you need to do." Bob added.

Jim straightened his tie one last time. Bill and Neil kiddingly gave him thumbs up.

"All right, I hope to be back soon…and not alone, like that candleholder implies."

He set off for her table, not really understanding why, but well-aware he was violating the very rule Gina enforced with him. As he approached, he swore he would do nothing to hurt her; she was so different. If nothing more, he would see that she had a nice evening. Besides, she may not want to spend the entire evening with him.

He nearly lost his nerve as he drew closer. "Wow, she is really attractive. Bob is right; I'm way out of my league!" Her dark hair swayed over her shoulders as she played with one lock. She wore a blue dress, again blue, her shoulders covered by a matching wrap. Amazing how much one can notice in only seconds.

Attempting not to be too obvious, Bob supplied details of the event from his vantage point. He mentioned as a reminder, "If this doesn't go as he hopes, be supportive. I was thinking, tonight has to be a little depressing. He's alone. We're all married…and happy." He looked around the table, "Right?" Everyone laughed but knew he was right. They were all married, and yes, happily.

"Whoa, they're standing. Don't look, he's pointing to our table. She's motioning to hers. Excellent! She's coming. They're walking this way!" Looking away as they approached, Bob had to add, "We have ETA in six, five, four, three, two..."

Laughter encircled the group over Bob's play-by-play call, a perfect cover as the two reached their destination. Introductions, jokes, and general merriment quickly put the newcomer at ease. She made a solid first impression, and why not? Smart, witty, and attractive, mixed with her southern charm proved a most endearing combination. Lively conversation bounced around the table until dinner's end, Rich's brother presented the toast, an extremely warm and sentimental toast, followed by Rich honoring his married buddies with a sincere 'thank you'. Rich then toasted Jim, speaking of their lengthy friendship and their bachelor days in a humorous, brotherly manner. Rich closed with a mild insinuation that Jim's single days could be nearing an end.

The 'family' didn't understand but did take note of Jim's gentle kiss to Samantha's forehead; no wisecracks followed, as if the kiss was a solemn moment, and for Jim, it was. Something about this woman baffled him from the beginning; her thoughts, her interaction with his friends, and her attention magnified his interest in her tenfold. He felt to be a different man, a new man. He even enjoyed his new name, James.

Carol had the perfect view of Samantha after Jim kissed her forehead. She observed a woman searching the eyes of a man she obviously felt something for already. Yes, Carol understood at that moment, this young woman was falling for Jim in the truest sense. Oh, Lord, please watch over her. We hardly know anything about her, but she seems so nice. Protect her. And watch over Jim. Let him do nothing to hurt her. We may never see her again, but I ask that, for tonight, we enjoy one another's company.

Later, out of character, Jim requested a romantic piece from the band leader, his friends amused he even knew anything romantic. He and Samantha danced, not noticing the 'family' had surrounded them, watching every move. Carol did note how respectfully Jim held Samantha as they swayed to the music. The Jim of today exhibited a sincerity; no 'moves' tonight, only what appeared to be a mature, caring attitude toward a most endearing woman. As minor as it appeared, his extra effort to provide a sweet tea drink for Samantha opened Carol's eyes to a possibly new Jim. She thought of his life before; saddened that, though on the outside appeared glamorous, inside was nothing more than a dark void.

As the piece drew to a close, the newest couple drifted to the windows hand-in-hand while the group returned to their table. Ted and Carol took over as the designated commentators due only to a better vantage point. Their first assignment, a description of the kiss, which everyone agreed, was handled quite professionally…the reporting, that is. Unfortunately, the observations afterward consisted of nothing more than unheard conversing.

For Samantha and Jim, the window conversation would be the starting point of a greater understanding of each other beginning with Samantha shyly questioning why he had yet to mention his Air Force career. Realizing she must have spoken with Carol, he hesitated a moment, then explained his reluctance to share information regarding his Air Force background. As Jim shared more of his life, barriers of self-preservation crumbled, allowing him the freedom to open his life to another person, something he feared for years.

At one point, she mentioned her belief that God planned certain things for us; we can choose whether to follow, or not.

She believed God wanted them to meet that day and nothing would stop the opportunity from happening. After his past months of inner turmoil, Jim believed she may be right; at least, he hoped. Knowing someone, her God, was in control offered security, a knowledge he no longer had to 'go it alone'. How he wished that to be true.

Fearing he may have slipped up when he spoke of a continuing relationship, he shared his desire to talk about life, about God, and where he fit. His promise to speak with Rich jumped to the forefront of his memory, but as odd as it seemed, Jim decided he would rather share that discussion with Samantha. Emotions stirred within him when she excitedly admitted she wanted to talk further and that she would not forget. No matter how short a time, that meant at the very least, a moment of a future with her.

As Samantha and Jim continued sharing snippets of their lives and thoughts, he could not fathom that this woman, this kind, beautiful, caring woman, might actually like him. Samantha caught him off-guard when she hesitantly asked if he knew her name, her full name. He did not. After a long, slow breath, she stated, Samantha Marissen. Several seconds later, Jim grasped the connection between her and the family name 'Marissen'. The intent of her question became obvious. Would his feelings differ once he knew her as the daughter of the Marissens, a prominent St. Louis family name? Dazed by the implications of her honesty, he questioned his social stature in comparison to hers, that he was pretty much of a nobody. She nervously confessed she liked him and why; he admitted to his affection for her. The revelation of her family background would change nothing, they agreed. He didn't say, but every moment she spoke broke new ground. Although he cherished her candor, her next confession would put his fortitude to the test.

Cautiously, Samantha stepped closer as she opened her life to him, divulging the tragic account of the loss of her family twelve years earlier. What he heard disturbed him to the depths of his soul. His heart broke as she told in a faltering voice of the deaths of her mother, father, sister, and brother, how much she loved them and missed them. She explained the Marissen's selflessness during the course of her recovery. She raised her eyes to him as a single tear trickled down her cheek. As more tears followed, regardless of her attempts to resist, she rested her forehead against his chest. Jim had held Samantha by her shoulders, but in an effort to comfort her better, wrapped his arms around her, granting her the opportunity to cry freely, privately. He now understood: this was the pain Gina spoke of, a pain like no other, not to lose one family member…but all, in an instant. His desire at that moment was to do anything he could for her, although he knew there was nothing except to hold her…and he did, as long as needed.

Meanwhile, at the table, Ted nudged Carol as soon as he noticed the different sort of conversation and Samantha's reaction. Carol's reaction, "Oh, no! She's crying! What did he do?" The entire group watched, searching for any hint as to what happened.

"I don't believe it," Bob sighed. "What could he have done? He just doesn't take the time to think about someone's feelings. I don't get it! He seemed so different tonight. Usually, we don't know who he hurts, but we do tonight. I like her. I don't know about you but I'm telling him tonight it's about time he grew up, enough of his immaturity…I don't know…but I'm telling him something!"

"It's time," Carol agreed, "but we do it together, like an intervention. He needs to know when he's with us, we're not going to put up with his immature antics!"

"Carol, calm down," Ted pleaded, "we'll take care of it. It's a shame; she's so nice."

"I know, I really like her. She is so sweet." Carol sighed, "Maybe we can keep her and dump Jim, eh?"

*   *   *

Jim held Samantha gently yet lovingly until gathering herself enough to humorously request a little help from Carol, if possible. She accepted his offer of a handkerchief but softly began to cry once again. That she felt comfortable enough to cry in his arms about such a tragic event provided him a sense of worth and the assurance that he truly did care for her. Tonight proved to be much more than a simple dinner date.

*   *   *

"Oh, look! Now he wants help," Carol complained. "OK, nobody backs out! We tell him tonight…together! Where's her purse? I'm sure she wants to freshen up before she leaves. Who wants to take her home? Ted, we'll take her home. At least she will be with people who like her. Maybe we can stay in touch. I wouldn't be surprised if she didn't ever want to see us again!" She exhaled sharply, "I'll be back."

*   *   *

When Carol reached the couple, Jim asked that she accompany Samantha to the Ladies' Room. As the old saying goes, "If looks could kill…" The unfortunate scene left him stuttering "but… but…" as Carol huffed away with Samantha.

He comforted himself knowing Samantha trusted him. Carol would learn the truth when talking with her. Jim knew he could never, would never hurt Samantha; she deserved to be loved completely and unconditionally. What! Did he mean love in the general sense or the possibility that he could love her? Earlier, he hoped there could be something between them, but…love?

Returning to a table of silence, he slipped into a defensive mode, stubbornly blurting, "What?"

Someone mumbled a response, but he paid no attention. Their belief that he would hurt Samantha cut him deeply but he understood their thinking. Yet, he wished he had been given the benefit of the doubt…at least, until the misunderstanding could be resolved. Nevertheless, he learned a severe lesson; there are consequences for actions. Integrity is nearly impossible to regain once lost.

What seemed a lifetime passed before Samantha and Carol returned. Jim stood, Samantha hugged him tenderly, thoroughly confusing everyone. Carol apologized for her misjudgment but Jim explained his past left little credibility. Samantha broke in and made clear what James did for her and why.

After Jim and Samantha stepped to the floor for a last dance, Carol revealed Samantha's tragedy; the accident and the death of her family, her mother and father, and sister and brother. The realization their actions were not of friends brought about a deep regret over their treatment of Jim. The evening had revealed a changing Jim, particularly when he poured out his heart to Samantha and his friends, exposing his past, how he wasted his life…and how, recently, he had been plagued by guilt, how wrong he had been. He was searching for something, and Samantha, Gina, and Rich were part of the solution. He was fed up with his life; he wanted change. And, he credited Samantha with furthering his quest earlier, truly desiring to continue discussing God and life.

Drawing his confession to a close, he openly admitted,

"…no more, not today, not now, not ever again" to which she responded "I know".

'I know?' How could she say 'I know' with such trust? Her belief stunned him. She understood he honestly meant what he said and she trusted him. Jim felt as if he was being prepared for some sort of life change, but what? A final thought struck like a bolt of lightning; his friends chose to protect Samantha, a move that pleased him. The fact they were willing to guard her meant she had become a member of the 'family' that evening.

With everyone involved in one conversation or another, Gina and Rich visited their table to much ribbing. Rich attempted to joke they saved the best for last. Gina joined the girls and Rich, the guys. After some general guy talk, Rich sat next to Jim.

Jim laid his hand on his shoulder, "Rich, how are you enjoying married life, so far!"

"It's good, very good! But, hey, I need to ask you something."

"What's that?"

"Remember this morning when I asked if you were going to try something with Samantha and you said you wouldn't, you were past that."

"Yeah, I remember."

Spreading his hands, he asked, "So, what are you doing?"

"I'm sitting here, talking with you!"

"C'mon, you know what I mean."

"OK, promise me you won't interrupt; you'll wait until I'm finished?"

"You've got my word."

Jim lowered his voice, "All right…this morning, my intention was to walk away from her after I spoke with Gina in the reception line…just walk away. And I did…at first. But something called me back to her; not something selfish, something good, almost pure…if that makes any sense. She was so nice…just so nice. I haven't done anything I regret. I would never say or do anything to hurt her.

"We talked about many things: who she is, when she…when she lost her family; we talked about God and our lives. I told her about my life…everything! I told her I was finished with that; I didn't want any part of that ever again. You know what she said? She said, 'I know.' She has more faith in me than I do. Samantha is…a remarkable woman. If she agrees, I'm not going to stop seeing her, Rich. Not for you, or Gina."

Rich stared at Jim without a word, not angrily but a look of peace, and, finally, a smile. Placing his hand on Jim's shoulder, he calmly stated, "I'm glad. I believe you too."

Jim broke out in a wide grin, relieved to hear his friend also had faith in him. He needed Rich's support.

"I hope Gina will forgive me for not listening to her. Really, Rich, I love you guys. You're like a brother and sister to me. I feel like a huge weight is being lifted off me tonight."

"Which reminds me, Jim, do you still want to talk? We can tonight yet, if you want."

Sheepishly, Jim glanced to his left, then back to Rich, "Actually…I hope to talk with Samantha later. I'm ready. I hope you don't mind."

Rich laughed, 'So, you'd rather talk to some pretty woman than me? I guess I'm good with that! Mind if I tell Gina?"

"Would you hold off saying anything to her? I've let her down so many times, she may think whatever I say to Samantha is nothing more than a ploy for something else. And I don't blame her. She has had every right not to trust me."

"This reminds me so much of my story. Gina discipled me when she found I had recently accepted Jesus Christ as my Lord and Savior. And, I'm sure you know, Samantha is a strong Christian too. Let me ask you one question: Are you looking for that tonight?"

"Yes…I am," Jim sighed, in relief.

"Oh, my gosh, that's great! But I won't say a word to Gina, I won't have to; she'll find out."

Leaning back in his chair, Jim crossed his legs at the ankles, and laughed lightly, "This has been one full, exhausting day."

"Oh, yeah, tell me about it!" Rich agreed wholeheartedly.

"No…all seriousness aside, compared to your day this is a piece of cake…get it?" as Jim held a piece of wedding cake in front of his friend's face.

Rich chuckled, "Oh, man, your jokes are always sooooo lame."

"And yet, after all these years, you still laugh!"

* * *

The day played out as a wonderful experience for Jim, a new and exciting experience. He met a most beautiful woman who captivated him with her humor, her kindness, and her trust in him. Samantha also won the hearts of his friends who, by evening's end, lovingly adopted her into the family.

* * *

Samantha and James did continue their discussion during the drive home, with Samantha comparing God's invitation into His family to James' friends welcoming her into theirs. From there, she shared the Gospel with him, as straightforward, yet poignantly, as should be. By the time she finished, he knew he was at the end of himself; he had nowhere left to run. His life, as he had lived it, meant nothing; she must be sharing the way with him, she had to be. Why shouldn't he just turn to Jesus, let Him take over?

James heard Samantha's offer to pray with him. Was it possible that his emptiness could be replaced by Jesus; that he could begin his life anew, a complete fresh start? How could he not accept her offer to pray?

As he pulled the car around the circle, he had to blink several times to clear his vision; tears kept filling his eyes. Embarrassed, James walked around the rear of the car to wipe his eyes before opening her door. She must have thought he refused her offer as she sadly thanked him for the evening. He immediately expressed his need for her to lead him in the prayer. Tearfully, joyfully, lovingly, Samantha did just that, for which James would be forever grateful.

Not only would she be the person to lead him to Christ, she gave him her Bible to read, to study, to have as his own. He held her Bible close during the drive back to his uncle Dave's. As he reached the porch, he sat on the low brick wall, and stared deep into the night sky. He spoke to God, probably the second prayer of his life—

"Dear God, I want you to know how thankful I am for tonight. I am thankful to You…and to Samantha for what she has done for me. I ask you, God, help me to learn about you and how to pray. I want to know as much about you as Samantha does. She loves you and knows you well. Please protect us in everything. I know this prayer is so scattered…but I'll learn. And, thank you for introducing me to Samantha. She is a wonderful woman I could very easily love, which, I think has already begun. She gave me her Bible tonight; she wanted me to have a Bible from the start. She suggested I read the Gospel of John. I know everything that happened today is your plan and that I am now a part of that plan. She is yours and I will not do anything to hurt her, ever. You saved me through her; maybe I'll be able to do something for her someday. Oh, one last thing…I am sorry for the way I lived my life; what a waste of precious time. I do turn from that life to You. I love you, God, and thank you. Amen."

*   *   *

His mug empty, Jim stood slowly, stretched, and entered the cabin for a refill. He flipped the news on to a head shot of Samantha Marissen. Having not followed the public gossip of her divorce, the photo was the first he'd seen in many years. Forty-eight–years-old, they reported. Jim couldn't take his eyes from the screen, remembering the most wonderful woman he ever knew. Her deep blue eyes, her hair, and the smile that never failed to warm his heart; all of the visual reminders of the loving, caring, sensitive, God-fearing Christian woman she was, and he felt certain, still is.

He held no grudge, no anger against Samantha. Why should he? How could he? She did only what he had done… gave in to Ed Marissen's irrational, illogical, irresponsible, and overwhelming demand. The one person he would never forgive, James Paul Gordon, coward.

What if…? Samantha Marissen, the great 'what if' of his life. He prayed God grant her the strength and courage she needed, and that a quick release be negotiated. Sadly, Jim knew prayer to be the only action he could take.

OUTSIDE ST. PETERSBURG, RUSSIA

ALTHOUGH AWAKE, THE rattle of the handle and opening of the door startled Samantha, making sleep impossible. Every sound induced a paralyzing fear. A small, frail woman shuffled across the room, placed a tray of food on the nightstand, and crept out. The food, as usual, consisted of a skimpy sandwich and watered-down soup; nothing changed, if she ate, she ate for sustenance only.

With no view of the outside, Samantha lost her ability to determine day or night, morning or evening; she lost all concept of time, a form of mental torture, she explained to herself. Every day, or she thought every day, the large, balding, bellowing Russian, accompanied by an older woman, questioned Samantha incessantly of her role in the espionage operation. The older woman, never uttering a word, sat and took notes.

The Russian inquisitor shouted, cursed, and demeaned Samantha with horrid threats that her lack of cooperation could result in life imprisonment with no chance of release or ten years, maybe less, if she confessed. Terrified as she was, since there was nothing to confess, she would confess nothing; the United States would protect her.

Unknown to Samantha, however, the CIA struggled to discover her location. Negotiating with the Russian Federation ended in futility each session; the conditions for the release of Samantha Marissen revolved around the freeing of the agents arrested in the simultaneous nationwide raid of the extensive Russian spy network on April 2. Fourteen guilty agents swapped for one innocent American woman, unthinkable! Nevertheless…the freedom of our lone American remained of the utmost importance in the mind of every citizen. As long as Intelligence knew nothing of her whereabouts, serious negotiation would continue as hollow and weak.

Without fail, the large, balding Russian reported daily that no contact had taken place with the United States regarding a release deal. Different versions of the reports brought her to the brink of believing the lie. Lack of sleep and nutrition, combined with a constant, dreadful fear drove her toward serious depression. More than two weeks passed since her abduction; the majority of countries stood in unison with the U.S., a most uncommon position, in efforts to free Ms. Marissen. The inexperience and new-found leadership of the Federation had not planned the United States to be the favored nation in the crisis. Like a cornered animal, their long-term reaction remained dubious.

Only now did Samantha realize the repercussions of her decision to be alone in the world, a test of faith following her abusive, loveless marriage and her long-ago shameful denial of James. She coveted her freedom, her family, and a return to a life of hopes and dreams. Finding herself in a deeper test of faith so immense, she dropped to her knees in the presence of God, rededicating her life to her Lord and Savior, Jesus Christ.

* * *

Occasionally, after immersing herself in prayer, peaceful thoughts of the past bubbled to the surface, one time in particular to a decisive moment of change. Shortly after the exhilarating weekend of Rich and Gina's wedding, James called just, as he explained, to hear her voice and to let her know he would return to St. Louis in three weeks, a shorter time than he imagined. He hoped she would be there. Surprised at his comment, she reminded him of her promise; he would have someone to call, or write, or come home to. She would not make that serious a commitment without a heartfelt sincerity. He knew it to be far too early, but he truly desired to express his feelings for her. Jim held back but did apologize for his doubt.

Oddly enough, her eagerness to place someone other than herself first brought a realization, a self-awareness of her spoiled, little rich girl image, except the image displayed a reality. Samantha's time separated from Jim helped her to discover money and possessions do not bring pleasure or happiness; if so, short-lived. After twenty-four years, she decided the time had arrived for a change in her life.

Unfortunately, or fortunately, Samantha found little in common with her University acquaintances, who filled their lives with travel, which could be fun; expensive clubbing, which was definitely not; or simply spending family money foolishly. She desired more.

Arriving home after an uneventful boring morning, Samantha made a spur of the moment call.

"Hello."

"Hey, Gina, this is Samantha! How are you?"

"Samantha! I'm so glad you called Good timing! We just got home from our honeymoon. It was wonderful! What's up?"

"Would you like to meet for lunch tomorrow? My treat!"

"Oh, I'm sorry, tomorrow is a mess. You know, just got back in town. Can we make it Thursday?"

"Gina, I really need to talk with you. This is very important!"

"It's not Jim, is it? What did he do?"

"No, nothing. In fact, he is wonderful! But he does have a lot to do with why I want to talk with you."

"Can you tell me now?"

"This is something I'd rather talk to you in person about."

"All right, let me check here…yeah…yeah, I can do this. How about we meet at Lil's Desserts at six today, and I'm holding you to your treat. OK?"

"Lil's, today? In Webster, right? That's terrific! Oh, Gina, I really appreciate this. I'll see you at six. You're the best!"

"OK, six! See you there!"

Six o'clock took forever to arrive. Samantha, seated at a table on the outdoor patio shaded by enormous oaks, waited anxiously for Gina. Ten minutes later, Gina rushed into the outdoor setting to be immediately greeted with a hug from her exuberant best friend.

"Sorry," Gina apologized. "I thought I would be even later than this but I actually made most of the stoplights. How are you? You look great!"

"I'm good, very good!" Samantha answered. "How are you? You certainly look happy!"

"I am happy! Everything is wonderful. Our honeymoon was perfect! Romantic, fun, relaxing. It felt so good to kick back after all the wedding activity."

"So, how was Canada? As good as you thought?"

"Oh, listen, this was so great…"

Gina shared details of the places she and Rich visited while in Canada. Twenty minutes later, she finished the abbreviated version; the unabridged report saved for another day. Once again, Samantha dreamed of the same experience…maybe with James…maybe.

"So, tell me about you and Jim. Sounds like the reception

was quite a night for both of you. I apologize for jumping to conclusions about him. He can be a very sweet guy and I love him, but I love you too and I didn't want to see you hurt and… well…I'm so sorry. I just never expected what happened. The whole chain of events is wonderful. Rich is ecstatic. He asked me to tell you, he's happy you're the one Jim turned to for his moment of commitment to Jesus. Neither of us know anyone more deserving."

"Oh, thank you guys. I don't know if I'm deserving, but all I can say is I was so happy the night he accepted Jesus. He attended his first church service with me the next morning. I've never been blest like that. And then, to hear he truly wants to see me again. He is the nicest, sweetest, most caring man…and he respects me. We talk as often as we can and I can't wait to see him again. He wants me to teach him all I can about the Bible; he has a zillion questions. I love it! And obviously…I enjoy any opportunity to talk about him!"

"Samantha, I am so happy for you, really. How about when Jim comes into town, the four of us get together. I know Rich would want that."

"That sounds wonderful! I know James would like that too!"

Gina laughed, "I believe I'll never think of him as Jim ever again. I love the 'James' thing you do."

"Like I said, it's special if I'm the one to call him James."

"I like that. It's sweet."

The waiter interrupted to take their order, which didn't take long; both ordered the chocolate, chocolate crème pie topped with chocolate swirls and a chocolate ice cream scoop as a side.

"So, tell me what's on your mind?" Gina asked, returning to the conversation. "Sounds important."

Samantha related to Gina her need to do something with her life other than playing the rich girl. She needed to do something worthwhile; she had the time, she should put it to good use.

Gina thought for a moment, smiled, and asked, "Has Jim done this to you? Did he say something to you? I don't mean in a negative way. Has he had some influence in your decision?"

Samantha thoughtfully, earnestly expressed, "This is good, very good. James, without saying a word, has shown me what it is to do something with passion. Despite his background, you know…his parents gone, no immediate family; he has pretty much taken care of himself. I want to do that. I want to do that for him. I want him to be proud of me like I am of him."

"Oh, my gosh, Samantha. You really have fallen for this guy. I'm so happy for you! To see you come out of your shell like this…is wonderful! What does your mother think? Is Rose OK with Jim?"

"She loves James! She thinks the world of him, almost like he's the son she never had." Samantha hesitated, then continued in a softer voice, "She really does like him, and she met him only once…at church, the morning after your wedding. But, I tell her just about everything we talk about. She is so happy that James is the guy, as she says, "who caught my fancy." She's worried about me for so long, I'm happy she can finally relax. I tell you, I have never felt more alive. Sharing my loss with him means everything to me. I never understood I held it all inside. I do believe God led me to share it all with James. He knows everything about me and still wants to be with me."

"And you know everything about him."

"But, I know the 'new' him and the 'new' him is the man I'm falling in love with."

"Samantha! Do you realize what you just said?"

A moment of silence, then, "Yes…I do. I'm not going to be afraid to admit it. I am falling in love with that man; I'm falling in love with James Paul Gordon!"

"Do you know how good it is to hear you sound so happy…I mean, you are happy!"

Very softly, she verified Gina's declaration, "I am truly happy."

Gina leaned toward Samantha, "OK, so tell me, what do you want to do with your life? What do you think is worthwhile? You know I'll help in any way I can."

"You may change your mind after I tell you."

"I don't think so," Gina encouraged her.

Samantha nervously shifted to a more serious approach, "Gina, I'd like to work for you. No pay, nothing. Just let me be involved like you. Show me what needs to be done. I could tutor the girls…or something. I'll do whatever you need."

She studied Samantha and her sincerity, "Yeah, yes, you certainly can! You've opened a few avenues here that I've been considering. You would have to learn a lot in a short period of time and, I could really use the help. Besides, it might be fun to work with my 'sister'. When do you want to begin this venture?"

"Whenever you want!"

"Well, then, how about this coming Monday?"

*　*　*

Grateful…happy…frightened, three emotions Samantha experienced simultaneously as she began her venture into the world of responsibility. Monday morning, she was to meet Gina downtown at 9:00 AM but arrived by 8:30. Samantha spent that day and the next four, meeting everyone connected to the foundation and discussing where and how she could assist. That week and the weeks following, she spent familiarizing herself with Gina's dream and soon discovered, as others also found, the major downside. Whenever a shortfall of donations occurred, Gina covered the difference. Samantha, well-aware Gina could easily subsidize the programs, soon realized delays in necessities occasionally caused gaps in the overall care of the women and children. A charitable cause of this magnitude should not waver in support; the need should be made public with an organized, educational approach to attain and maintain a consistent flow of donations.

Nearing the final hours of a Friday afternoon, Samantha invited Gina to Lil's Desserts again for their now favorite treat to discuss an idea she had. Once the usual conversation about Rich and James concluded, Samantha began her pitch, "Gina, you have shown me every area of your foundation and I know your staff very well. I believe I can do something good for your dream." She paused for a breath, "I want to try to raise funds for your programs; not just accept random donations but purposely work for them. And not part-time, full-time…a full-time drive for funds. What do we have to lose? I believe I can do this!"

Sitting across from Samantha with a spoonful of chocolate cream, Gina momentarily said nothing while seemingly examining the dessert. Finally, shifting her gaze to her friend, she smiled and stated, "I like your idea. I know you could do it. Something like this would take an initial financial outlay. I think we should bring Rich into this discussion; he has the business acumen for this, but the project is yours, Samantha. This is why you're here!"

"This is so exciting! I was thinking, we'll need brochures and letters to start, develop a list of potential donors, and then…" She beamed, having possibly devised a way of becoming an integral part of Gina's mission. Wait until James hears about this! Her excitement spilled into the evening, so much so, she called James in Mississippi to tell him. She loved his enthusiasm and support; he was as excited as she. Her feelings for him grew even stronger that night.

Samantha and Jim's time apart worked in their favor; his

career taking off, so to speak, while she invested her heart and soul toward the success of Gina's dream. Her efforts brought no monetary compensation, only the satisfaction of her contribution for others. Over the next several months, she became quite proficient at fundraising. At the start, she spoke to groups at local churches, clubs, and small organizations. Her cause, and her name, opened doors to one-on-one discussions with financial executives regarding potential company or employee donations. Soon after, Samantha advanced to speaking directly with upper echelon players. Success with one business or organization meant others followed in support of such a worthy cause. Her abilities far exceeded what she thought possible.

All things do work for good. As a result of her relationship with Jim, Samantha had grown in giving of herself, reaping an abundant reward for Gina's dream, now known as HOPE, providing a home for young pregnant girls with nowhere to go, a temporary residence for abused women and their children, and a place for at-risk children and their mentors to meet for counseling, friendship, and activities. The Lord works in mysterious ways.

As good a Samantha had become at her work, one incident stood out when speaking at a Christian Woman's Breakfast of around 750 attendees, held as a major fundraiser. Although Gina rarely spoke at events, Samantha insisted, since HOPE had been her dream from the beginning, and the women deserved to see and hear the one who began it all. So, after the breakfast, Gina presented a brief history of HOPE, from its inception through today then, turned the floor over to Samantha.

She stepped to the podium, exuding the aura of the professional speaker, and placed her topic cards in front of her, although she rarely, if ever, referred to them, until this morning. A short time into her talk, she noticed someone enter the dining hall through the far doors to her right. He remained at the back wall until one of the ladies invited him to join them. As he walked to their table, Samantha realized the man was James… in uniform! She hesitated, mixing her excitement of seeing him with the subject matter and lost her train of thought. After several flustered seconds flipping through the topic cards, she continued detailing the programs, highlighting many of the success stories.

Jim smiled to himself over her quick recovery, watching with admiration while she spoke to almost 800 people, relaxed, as if talking to friends around the kitchen table. He still enjoyed her comforting southern demeanor and soon found himself listening to the information about HOPE with great interest. Her ability to dispense facts and figures so succinctly with occasional humor impressed him greatly. When she finished, a group of HOPE volunteers passed out modest gift bags for everyone, which included a pledge card. Most filled out the card at their tables including Jim.

Samantha hurriedly attempted to speak with the various women who approached her with words of thanks or questions regarding HOPE until she reminded herself James would not leave; he would be there at the end. She and Gina remained to answer as many questions as necessary. Finally, Gina suggested Samantha visit the tables in the back of the room; she would handle the front. Thanking those surrounding her as she made her way to the rear, she eventually reached James' table where she heard him remark, "…and she and I are seeing one another."

As she slipped her arm around his waist, Jim explained, "I had just mentioned that I knew you. They were all talking about how good a speaker you are and I had to brag a little."

"Kind of like a girl bragging on you when they find you're a pilot?" she teased.

Jim smiled a knowing smile and draped his arm around her shoulders, "Yeah, kinda like that."

Samantha's comment opened the gates to a flood of questions about the Air Force and flying. Patiently, he responded to each one, reminding himself he would get even someday. Meanwhile, she enjoyed having her arm around him, taking full advantage of the handsome image he presented in his Air Force blues.

Once the crowd thinned, she stated, "Please warn me the next time you plan to show up…I was so nervous."

"Nervous? Why? You've done this so many times before."

"Yes, but not in front if you."

Turning toward her, he assured her, "You were terrific this morning! I can't begin to describe how impressed I am. I couldn't do what you do. I am so proud of you, your work, your dedication, your passion. You're really something!"

His words meant so much to her. He couldn't do what she does? A man who flies fighter jets couldn't do what she does? What a wonderful compliment…he was proud of her, and her passion.

"By the way," she asked, "what are you doing in St. Louis? I thought we wouldn't see each other for another week or so."

"Well, Vandover needed to refit one of our F-16s with an upgraded radar system for testing. The original pilot is sick, so I volunteered last minute for the flight…and here I am."

"You flew an F-16 here? That's gotta be a thrill, flying into your hometown in an F-16!"

"It is," he admitted, "but usually no one knows."

"I've never known you to fly home in a fighter. If anything, isn't it like a T-37 or 38 or something?"

"Hey, you're getting pretty good at this stuff. Want to sign up?"

"I think I'll stay with what I do best…keeping my feet on

the ground. There's no way I could ever zoom across the sky like that!"

"I bet you could if you had to!"

"Yeah, well, don't hold your breath." Samantha abruptly stopped and asked, "When do you have to leave?"

"I have a briefing in about two hours, but after that, not until tomorrow afternoon around 1:00. I'll fly to the southern Missouri area, test the new system, and fly home…to Mississippi."

"Wow! You're moving up! Isn't this what you wanted?"

"I can always be reassigned but, for now, this is great!"

"I know getting reassigned is always a possibility," she sighed, as she looked down, "I hope it's not for a while." Pausing, she looked up, "Remember, I will be here for you when it happens."

Jim took her hands in his, "I hope you know what that means to me. You are a very special lady." He kissed her lightly. "So, how about dinner tonight?"

"Of course! It would be a pleasure, Captain Gordon, to dine with you tonight!" Samantha prayed for the day they would declare their love for one another, although now may be too soon according to what everyone would think. She felt truly loved by James; he will tell her when he's ready. She was more than willing to wait.

Glancing to the side, then to her, Jim hesitantly asked, "Listen, Samantha, would you…umm…would you like to watch me take off tomorrow? I saw what you did this morning; I would like to show you what I do. It's nothing big but you're the first I've ever asked."

Wide-eyed and grinning, she jumped at the opportunity, "I'd love to, that would be so exciting!"

That evening over dinner, James and Samantha covered a wide variety of topics from light-hearted to serious, enjoying every moment of their unexpected time together. Jim thought several times, as he listened, how he wanted to confess his love for her, but knew it had to be far too soon. He certainly didn't want to rush her into anything; he would wait a while longer.

With their time drawing to a close, he explained the best location in the terminal to see his takeoff. Taking her hand in his, he whispered, "Just wave when I go by. I'll be watching for you."

"Please, I'll bet you say that to all the girls!"

"Only one…ever."

* * *

By noon at the airport, Samantha, her mother, and Gina were in their seats at the mid-terminal location Jim suggested. Samantha asked them to come with her not only to share in the excitement, but also to show the pride she had for him. To most, his departure would be no big deal. To her, it meant everything.

The Vandover hangars were visible far across the runways and taxiways. Jim warned of a possible long delay before takeoff; commercial flights received precedence. To occupy time during the wait, she shared some of her aircraft knowledge.

"Did you know the F-16 is actually called the F-16 Fighting Falcon? Some pilots call it the Viper because it looks like the Battlestar Galactica starfighter. And, the Thunderbirds air team use the F-16 in their air shows."

Gina chucked and commented, "Perhaps you should be out there and Jim here with us. How do you remember all that stuff?"

"Oh, they're just silly little facts, but fun."

The three kept lookout on the Vandover hangars, watching for motion of any kind. Samantha's mother, Rose, was the first to point something out.

"No, I don't think so, Mrs. Marissen," Gina ventured. "That

has only one tail; I think Jim's would have two."

"Oh, Gina. What am I to do with you?" Samantha giggled. "The F-15 has the twin tail, the F-16 a single."

With that, Rose declared, "I am impressed; you really do know your facts!"

"Well, Mrs. Marissen, it's only because of that Air Force boyfriend of hers!" Gina jokingly threw out.

Although the word sounded rather juvenile, Samantha enjoyed the idea Gina thought of James as her 'boyfriend', never really having had a boyfriend.

The F-16 idled on the taxiway forty-five minutes as Jim awaited clearance from the tower. What an experience for Samantha: a fighter jet with James in the cockpit preparing for takeoff! She feared taking her eyes from the F-16 thinking she might miss something when, suddenly, the craft moved forward and swung around onto the runway. She quickly moved to the windows for a better view, followed by her mother and Gina.

As she observed in eager anticipation, Samantha remembered James' request for her to wave. Anxiously, she covered her mouth with her fingers. At that moment, she felt the need to pray,

* * *

Dear Lord God, please watch over James every time he must fly. Do not allow any harm to come to him in any way…ever. This is a selfish prayer because he is my love and I need to know I did all I could to keep him safe…and all I can do is pray. Bless him, Lord, protect him. He is yours now. I ask this in the name of Jesus Christ, my Lord and my Savior. Amen.

* * *

The intense whine of increasing thrust penetrated the terminal windows, sending a shiver down her spine. In a flash, the jet roared down the runway and lifted off directly across from the three. Waving her fingers, Samantha whispered, "Good bye, my love."

She watched with tears in her eyes as the jet climbed and arced to the south out of sight. It all happened much too fast.

May 15, Friday: Marissen
AeroSpace Corporate Offices

ST. LOUIS, MISSOURI

NOT ONLY HAD Rob Barrett IV lied about Samantha and her lifestyle, he physically and emotionally abused her, which enraged Ed Marissen. Like it or not, he knew he failed Samantha when he did not handle the situation immediately upon revelation of the ugly truth. The only resulting good, Rob IV feared venturing too far from his office during or after the divorce proceedings. He hoped for a rather lucrative buyout when the explosion of his dismissal took place.

That morning, Ed calmly walked into the reception area of Rob IV's office, told the assistant he would be in Barrett's office if needed, and proceeded unannounced. Rob IV looked as though he might pass out when Ed abruptly entered. Ed did not allow him time to speak.

Quietly, Ed declared, "I've wanted to tell you this for the longest time, you pompous fool. You're fired! Get out of my building…now!"

Rob IV leapt up, waving his finger at Marissen, "You can't just fire me! You owe me something for my time!"

Although extremely angered, Ed remained externally calm, "I owe you nothing." But then he continued loud enough for others to hear, "You abused my daughter…and now she is in danger! I was so wrong to bring you into my business, into my family…I have never regretted anything more." Returning to a lower volume, he stated, "I'm not waiting for you to pack up; we'll send your belongings to you."

With that, he signaled toward the door; two armed guards entered, grabbed the struggling Rob IV under his arms and bodily removed him from the building. By the time he drove off campus grounds, his security clearance had been revoked and all passwords wiped clean, as though he had never existed at Marissen AeroSpace.

Marissen stopped at Barrett's administrative assistant's desk and lowered himself into the adjoining guest chair. Her look displayed fear, a fear she was next to go. Instead, Ed rested his arm on her desk, leaned in and expressed, "Don't worry, Linda, you'll always have a position here. Why don't you take the day off? Besides, you have been promoted. That position you applied for…it's yours. I believe you are more than capable of handling the responsibilities. So, on Monday, report to Tom McKinley. He's on the fourth floor, west side. I'll check with you Monday. I'm sorry about this morning."

"Oh, my gosh, sir, no…that's OK. I don't know what to say, thank you!"

"You're welcome. Now, go. Relax. Enjoy the weekend. Don't forget…Tom McKinley, first thing Monday! Congratulations, you deserve this!

ST. LOUIS, MISSOURI

ED AND ROSE no longer watched TV coverage of Samantha's plight; the networks ran short of anything new and turned to clichés or trivial facts to fill the void. Every network felt it necessary to have a memorable name for the story, hoping the audience would remember theirs. Unbelievably, one network did a cheap knockoff of a well-known world event decades earlier, AMERICA HELD HOSTAGE. Sadly, the Samantha Marissen story bore the name, AMERICAN HELD HOSTAGE. Imagine the amount of money paid by the network for the letter N.

Rose Marissen fell into a deep depression requiring nearly daily medical attention. No government agency had been able to locate her daughter. Twelve years earlier, she made a covenant with God to keep her daughter from all harm out of a deep respect for Samantha's parents, Anne and Tommy. She felt she had failed.

Ed, expressing no emotion regarding the 'incident', refrained from outward anger, frustration, and remorse until the day the dam cracked, releasing every emotion toward the two CIA agents on duty, following another day with no news of his daughter.

The daily routine continued, "We are sorry, Mr. Marissen, we have nothing new to report on the location of your daughter. We hope to have something tomorrow."

"First of all," Ed shouted, "My daughter has a name… Samantha! From now on, you will refer to her by name! Maybe then you will see her…and us…as real people. And second, what in the world are you bumbling fools doing? Seems any other time we can get a satellite image of some nut in a public restroom, even which stall! What is so difficult about this?"

"Mr. Marissen, please. The issue is an inability to reach our contact, but we are certain a window of opportunity will be available soon. Our contact does not want to risk discovery. Where would we be then?"

Ed thought the agents had just attempted a mild form of intimidation, "You will not make me back down on this. Do you pull this on people who have no recourse? Do you know who you're messin' with this time? Your lack of information this far into the 'incident', as you like to call it, is reprehensible! I want a meeting with your superiors and I want it now…and I want those…those media clowns off my property and away from the gate…now!"

When Ed Marissen issued a demand, people usually responded. Although extremely influential, he normally did not abuse his ability to voice an opinion, but people did pay strict attention to him. In a final gesture of anger, he grabbed the first available object, a small statue, and hurled it into the mirror above the fireplace, sending shards of glass across the room.

A meeting would take place the following day.

Exhausted from his tirade, Ed lay on the sofa in his study, a multitude of thoughts racing through his mind. Only one thought jumped out, his stubbornness to stand by Samantha in her time of need. She walked out that day with no intention of returning…ever. How sad, he thought, a father refusing, even just hesitating, to place his family before business. In his mind, there would always be time to repair the chasm between

Samantha and him; after all, he was the problem solver. But not this time; he neared emotional collapse. The world seemed to be closing in on him.

And Rose, his precious Rose. The belief she would never see Samantha again would be the end of her. Oh, how he had confined her, fenced her in; never allowing her the freedom to experience the wonderful adventures the world has to offer.

Slowly lifting himself from the couch, he made his way to the bedroom where Rose finally slept with the aid of medication. Ed kicked off his shoes and slipped into the bed next to his wife. He held her hand and whispered, "Rose, I'm so sorry. I love you. I'm going to do all I can to bring Samantha home." With tears in his eyes, he kissed her cheek.

He remained with Rose until the following morning. After a couple of slices of toast and a cup of coffee, he readied himself for the meeting he had demanded. High-level directors from the State Department, CIA, and FBI would be in attendance. He was ready.

The contingent arrived at 10:00am sharp. Eric led them directly to Ed's plush, private meeting room, finished in Cherrywood paneling with a matching conference table surrounded by comfortable chairs, fashionable artwork, and complete with a selection of pastries and coffee.

"Sit, gentlemen, please, and help yourselves to whatever you want before we begin," Ed announced as he briskly entered the room. No one accepted his offer.

The CIA director began, "Mr. Marissen, we have—

"You have nothing," Ed calmly stated. "I'm certain your report says, 'We still have no information on the whereabouts of your daughter.'" he stopped for emphasis, "Her name is Samantha," he interjected. " 'We hope to know something by tomorrow.' However, one line should be added, 'We are completely inept and will resign ASAP.'"

"Now, Mr. Marissen—

Ed calmly cut him off again, "The next time anyone says anything at this table, it will be constructive and not whiney, weak excuses. Now, what is the plan to bring my daughter back safely?"

"We are attempting to negotiate that very deal. We cannot break protocol."

Through clenched teeth, Ed growled, "What protocol? You think the Russians are following any kind of protocol? They are playing us like fools!"

He fired the question he had wanted to ask all along, "Why can't we demand her release…or else. Are we so weak-kneed we can't flex our muscles when it comes to an American citizen in danger?"

The Director responded indignantly, "We can't just demand we get our way! Do you realize the repercussions of such an act?"

Ed turned to sarcasm in desperation, "Have you boys been under so many cowardly presidents, that you no longer have a backbone? What does the President have to say about this?" His southern demeanor grew stronger and more demanding.

"Mr. Marissen, I can only repeat we are doing everything we can to free your daughter—

"Her name is Samantha!"

"We are doing everything to free Samantha. Please be patient." The Director could say no more.

Ed terminated the meeting, "Gentlemen, your best isn't good enough. This meeting is over."

WASHINGTON, MISSOURI

JIM ANSWERED THE door, "Rich, Gina, Samantha! How are you? Come on in! Samantha, how's your dad been treating you? Still behaving badly?"

Rich shoved Jim's shoulder, "Really? Are you kidding? I've been second guessing myself for twenty years, letting her call you 'uncle'.

"Will you two ever stop?" scolded Gina. "You've been doing this forever. Don't you ever get tired of it?"

"Never!" they responded in unison.

"So," Jim wondered, "why the surprise visit? I certainly wasn't expecting to see you guys today."

Rich and Gina glanced to their daughter, Samantha, who answered for everyone, "We're here to see how you're doing. We haven't heard from you since the so-called 'incident' in Russia. I'm worried about you...we all are."

Gina took Jim's hand, "Is it OK if we stay a bit? You know, just to talk a while. And you better not tell us everything is fine."

"But I am fine," Jim stated unconvincingly. "Yeah, please stay, the company will be good," he finally confessed. "Have a seat."

"This is really awkward, Jim," Rich admitted, "that after all this time, to ask you about Samantha. I mean, you never brought her up in any conversation. You can't bury those feelings forever." Pointing to Jim's head, he added, "There must be some turmoil in there. Tell me."

Jim stared at Rich for a moment, then looked out the front window for several seconds. Pinching the bridge of his nose and exhaling a long breath, he confessed, "All right, I'll tell you. I worry about her constantly. She shouldn't be there. She's alone. I'm sure she's scared…who wouldn't be? I want to do something…but I can't. I can't just sit here…but, that's all I can do."

Turning back to his visitors, he added, "Rich," his voice wavered, "this is crazy…but…I still love her. I always have…I always will. I am just so…lost."

"I can't even begin to imagine," was all Rich could respond.

The following morning, Sunday, Jim woke earlier than usual, shaved, showered, dressed, and climbed into his old, reconditioned Jeep to head to church. He thought he would find peace and fellowship there, although none of the congregation knew of his relationship with Samantha.

Reaching the main road, he took a left toward the city instead of turning right to his church. Why? He didn't know. Jim simply drove until he reached the exit that would take him to the church he and Samantha first attended, the very church he met Rose Marissen.

Pulling into the parking lot, he immediately took note of the new, large lobby…probably for gathering before and after services. Easing himself from the jeep, he slowly approached the addition but stopped short and glanced up, reassured by the three crosses still mounted atop the roof.

Jim thought, well, Lord, here I am. What do I do? "Help her, Lord, she is alone, be with her, please." He entered the church with people he did not know, but once inside met fellow Christians not seen in years who welcomed him warmly. He soon understood God had led him to this church this morning because he needed these people, people who loved him, people who never forgot him, people who comforted him, people who prayed for Samantha and him. When he returned to his jeep after the service, he thanked God for bringing him home.

MARISSEN ESTATE, ST. LOUIS, MISSOURI

ED MARISSEN PACED the length of the conference room, totally frustrated with the CIA response, or lack of. They can't find her and if they did, they wouldn't rescue her. All they want is to continue talking! Most times, talk accomplishes nothing! At the very least, now is the time to talk tough, if you insist on talking. Ed fumed as he pondered his next move. How could he force the issue? He couldn't, at least until Samantha was found, but he could plan until that moment.

Snatching the phone, he punched the HQ button.

"Marissen AeroSpace, Mr. Marissen's office."

"Becca, this is Ed. Get me Sonora."

"Yes, Mr. Marissen, right away."

"Becca, hold on. I'm sorry, I didn't mean to snap at you; got a lot on my mind. Would you get me Sonora, please?"

"That's OK, sir, I understand. One moment."

The line rang once, "Sonora, Merrill Pierce. What can I do for you, Mr. Marissen?"

"Merrill, the project. What's the status?"

"Everything is progressing on schedule, sir. We are still anticipating an October completion."

"All right, Merrill, I want that moved up to September 1. You can do that, right?"

"Mmmm, possibly, Mr. Marissen, but that will require three full shifts, seven days a week…and that may not do it."

"Now, I'm talking all tests complete and ready for a go!"

"Yes, sir, that's what I assumed you meant."

"One more thing, Merrill. How's the second one coming along?"

"Should be complete by November…I think."

"I want#2 completed ASAP, and I want Blakely in the#1 simulator 24/7."

"Anything else, sir?"

"I also want Moore and Webster in the OV simulator with Stephenson and Malone in the IV simulator."

"Yes, sir. May I ask why the schedule is being bumped up so drastically?"

"No, not at this time."

"We'll get right on it."

"Thank you, Merrill."

"Yes, sir."

Now, that's how it's done…action taken!

OUTSIDE ST. PETERSBURG, RUSSIA

WAS IT ANOTHER day or night? She couldn't tell. Even when the hall door opened, all light was blocked. Samantha experienced confusion, hunger, and fear. The meals were both not enough and horrible; her weight loss now evident. The daily inquisitions continued, except the bald man now entered alone, which frightened Samantha. He had no problem resorting to physical harm, always appearing on the verge of something truly evil. Would he harm her today or worse?

The fat, balding Russian's harsh treatment consisted of intimidation, threats, fear, or physical harm to force her confession to a crime she did not commit. Of course, a confession could be forged, but how much more convincing if written in her own handwriting.

Sleep was sporadic, sometimes only two to three hours before the regimen began again. Sleep deprivation and grueling questioning many times brought on violent sickness and depression. If not for her prayer time, she would, more than likely, break under the strain and pressure. Only by the grace of God did she make it as far as she did.

Personal hygiene was of no concern. She was blindfolded and led to a cold shower possibly once a week and a clothing change about the same. One toothbrush, no toothpaste. Samantha turned desperate enough to brush her teeth with hand soap, being extremely careful not to swallow and to rinse at least ten minutes. The taste was disgusting but brushing gave some semblance of cleanliness.

Today, the fat, balding Russian, whom Samantha nicknamed Igor, burst through the door as she lay on the bed. A younger man in uniform followed.

"Get up!" bellowed Igor.

"No, I will not!" She froze with fear, knowing the outburst would cost her dearly. Why did she scream at him?"

Enraged, Igor pulled her from the bed by her arm, shouting she should respect him when he entered the room. After cursing Samantha, he slapped her just above her left ear, the location of the concussion suffered at the hand of her ex-husband. The force of the strike sent her sprawling across the floor. Pulling her up by the hair, he struck her left cheek, hard. She attempted to grab his arm to relieve the pain of his grip on her hair. Igor glared into her eyes as a madman, then yanked to the right, throwing her to the floor, where she collapsed and rolled backward, slamming the back of her head on the rough wooden floor.

Igor loomed over her, snarling, "You have guard now. You might kill yourself. But... worth more living."

Staring wide-eyed at the young man, Igor growled, "You! Keep her alive!" and stormed from the room.

Samantha curled up on the floor, shaking, sobbing in pain and fear. The young man knelt beside her and touched her shoulder. She lurched away in terror, covering her face with her arms.

"No...no harm. Be still. I help."

She lowered her arms just enough to see his face. He showed no anger. In fact, the young face was serene, even sad, his voice comforting. He reached out and waited until she warily allowed him to grip her hand. The young Russian slowly assisted Samantha to her feet and over to the bed. Again, she broke down and wept.

The Russian soldier could only watch in despair.

* * *

Samantha fell into a fitful sleep, drained from the pain of her beating and fear of the next. If the situation did not change, her body would fail physically. Emotionally, she already experienced total loss. Her world, what little she had, now gone.

Several hours later, the young soldier attempted to wake Samantha gently, so as not to frighten her. He failed. As her eyes fluttered open, she saw him near and screamed, throwing her arms over her face for protection.

He spoke softly, "No, not to worry. You safe. No pain."

Only then did she recall the face, the voice. Glancing nervously across the room, she noticed a cot in the opposite corner, presumably for the young soldier, her guard. As she lowered her arms, the young Russian could easily see the severe bruising on the left side of her face, and her lip, which bled during her restless sleep. He pulled a towel from his duffle bag, dampened it, and cleaned the dried blood from her lip and cheek as best he could.

In faltering English, he tried to reassure her, "I watch, nyet…uh, no…guard…not watch."

Trembling, she spoke in a raspy voice, "Thank you. Was that yesterday?"

"Yes…you…OK?" So far, his English rough but understandable, although not much had been spoken.

Samantha forced herself to sit on the edge of the bed, "My head hurts, my face hurts, my jaw hurts…other than that…no." She smiled weakly, attempting to be strong.

"Good," he responded in relief to see her sit up and answer. "I have food. You must eat. They come to take soon."

Samantha bent over, holding her head in her hands and moaned, "Ugh, I can't eat any more of that slop. I'd rather starve to death."

"No! Do not!" he begged.

"No, I won't. That's just an expression. I won't."

"You live. I see you live."

After removing the lamp, he slid the nightstand in front of her. Two trays were on the floor; one, a breakfast of toast, eggs, fried potatoes, and milk; the other, her customary bread and soup. The young man pushed the chair to the opposite side and placed both trays on the nightstand, his tray for her and hers for him.

She stared at the food, then him, "No, I can't."

Leaning over the nightstand, he pointed to the food, "Eat… or they take!"

After a moment of hesitation, Samantha ate as if the finest meal sat before her, devouring every morsel. When finished, she looked to the young Russian, "Thank you."

He handed her the glass of milk, which she quickly drained. After flushing the soup, he took the glass and stacked the trays outside the door. He moved the nightstand and lamp back into position and sat on the edge of his cot, fidgeting with his fingers.

With a quivering voice, Samantha spoke, "I don't know why you did what you did…thank you," her voice extremely weak.

The young Russian hoped to keep her talking, anything to put her more at ease, if possible. He signaled her to listen as he began to speak quietly, "Yest…yester…day, not to happen ever…no. No beating…no. I stop. Must not be. Sorry…I hope to talk good."

"Better," she corrected him.

He smiled, "I hope to talk better. OK?"

"OK." She returned a faint smile.

Minutes passed with nothing said. Finally, she whispered, "What is your name? I should know your name."

"Nikolai. Your name…I not know."

"Samantha, but Sam may be easier. Call me Sam." No one called her Sam; she didn't like it, but, obviously, this was different. "May I call you Nik?"

"Nik," he tried. "Nik is good."

"How long have you spoken English?"

"Not long. I speak OK."

"You speak well. At least we can talk. That's good. I don't know any Russian. I'm sorry. The more you speak, the better you'll get."

"You teach?"

"I can, if you want. You seem to know what I say. Do you have a hard time remembering the words?"

"Yes, but I…try."

"You do well,"

"Thank you…Sam."

"You're welcome, Nik."

Samantha's conversation with Nik temporarily relieved some of the stress. To have someone to talk with was a Godsend. She remembered he said he would not allow any more physical harm. She didn't want to pursue the subject; maybe she misunderstood.

But she had more questions, "Nik, what day is it?"

"You do not know? June fifteen…Monday."

"And the time…what time is it?" She tapped her wrist in demonstration.

Looking at his watch, he reported, "Twenty…umm… minutes after seven…in morning."

"Oh, my gosh, thank you! I didn't know the time or day or if it was morning or evening."

She lay back on the bed and closed her eyes. Nikolai watched over her, despising what happened. He would not allow any physical harm to come to her again.

Samantha prayed for God's protection and that the horrible ordeal would soon end. She thanked Him for sending Nik, hoping the soldier's kindness true. The chance he would turn against her loomed as a possibility; he may use false compassion to get what they want from her.

MARISSEN ESTATE, ST. LOUIS, MISSOURI

THE FRONT ENTRANCE bell chimed. Ed's first thought, "Another pointless report coming. Here we go." Eric led the agents into the study as Ed made his way to join them. He stepped into the room, closed the door, and position himself looking out the window.

"Well, gentlemen, go ahead and give me the usual. You still don't know where Samantha is, but you may possibly have something in several days. Am I right?"

"Actually, Mr. Marissen," the Director began, "she has been located. This information is not to be released to the public to maintain the highest level of secrecy."

Ed spun around, "What! You found her? Where is she? How is she? Is she all right?"

"She is, but we believe she will be moved soon. From here on, we will know the when and where. We have an informant imbedded in the immediate group holding her captive. He cannot get information to us daily, but what we have is good."

"Where is she? I just want to know where she is!"

"Again, this is not to be released; she is being held east of St. Petersburg. We believe they will move her to a more secluded area, one that would be difficult to find. They have no idea we will know their every move."

Although excited by the news, Ed returned to his reserved, business formality, "What is our next move? Where do we go from here?"

"Mr. Marissen, a plan is in the works. However, diplomacy remains the most sensible method to gain her release. Diplomacy and patience."

Agitated, Ed demanded, "And what if diplomacy fails? What then? We all know the United States will not release the Russian spies. What happens then?"

"Mr. Marissen, we will keep you apprised of every development." The Director pleaded, "Please work with us; that's all we ask."

Ed lowered his head and sighed, "I apologize. At least we know where Samantha is. I know you are doing as much as you can with what you have. Thank you."

The meeting ended on a civil note; his complimentary and agreeable attitude passed, an act, a very convincing act. If his own government would not rescue Samantha, he would.

"Rose, I must tell Rose!"

NEIL AND SUE'S– GLENDALE, MISSOURI

ST. LOUIS, INDEPENDENCE Day, hot and muggy; fairly typical of an eastern Missouri mid-summer day. The backyard party at Neil and Sue's home became more of a gathering of friends worried about another and one absent for twenty-three years. Jim spent much of his time flying for SBA to occupy his time and his mind. The 'family' still recalled the days of Samantha and James, although many years had gone by. Excluding Gina, Samantha had known the others a little more than two years before disappearing from their lives. During that period, she had become as close a friend as any.

A large canopy of trees covered Neil and Sue's yard and one-third of the pool, keeping the degree of "uncomfortability" (Neil's own word) relatively low. The conversation soon shifted to Samantha and her horrid ordeal.

"I can't believe they're still holding her; it's been almost three months, hasn't it? I mean, why?" Neil's question seemed unanswerable.

Rich tried, "So many demonstrations are going on in Moscow and St. Petersburg. There's a lot of unrest. The last I read, many Russian people think their government is wrong and are fed up. The Russian Federation can either crack down on their own people or prove Samantha is a spy."

"Good luck with that!" Ted interrupted.

Rich closed with, "If they forcefully silence the Russian people, the whole world will know they are struggling to hold on to their power base. They are on the brink of collapse…a trial with a resulting guilty verdict might quiet things down… at least for a while."

"Wow, you really thought this through!" Liz asserted. "But isn't that a pretty foolish thing to do for such a temporary solution?"

Bill laughed, "In my opinion, we're not talking about the brightest bulbs in the chandelier to start with."

Carol expressed a different concern, "I worry about her being held in a hostile country, Russia for goodness sakes. They haven't even allowed her to speak with any American official, no contact with anyone. We don't know how she's been treated; we don't know her physical condition. I feel so bad for her. Her life has not been a life that any one of us would want. She lost her family; she lost Jim; she went through a terrible marriage and divorce; and now, she's lost her freedom."

"I know," Gina agreed, "Samantha was…is my best friend. She is such a good, sweet, kind person. I miss her dearly. I think I understand how Jim has felt these past years…I think we all do."

"By the way, where is Jim?" Bob asked. "He is coming today, isn't he?"

"Oh, yeah, he's coming." Gina finished refilling her tea. "He got in late last night from Florida. He's probably just sleeping in."

"He's been doing a lot of flights lately," Rich added, "I worry about him."

Gina reassured everyone, "I'm sure he's OK. He's strong. Flying keeps him occupied."

"Well, he's taken this pretty hard. He feels helpless, like, after all this time, he let her down."

Nancy hushed everyone, "Quiet, I heard a car pull up. We need to talk about something else!"

With the group expecting Jim, Samantha Reynolds entered through the side gate instead. "Oh, really nice, you guys. I've heard more conversation at a funeral. Lucky I got here first to critique you terrible bunch of actors."

Gina greeted her with a big hug, "Baby, what are you doing here? I thought you had a barbeque to go to."

"I do, but I wanted to see Jim before I went. I wanna make sure he's OK." She gave her dad a peck on the cheek.

He leaned back in his lawn chair, "Samantha, I hope you realize how important you are to Jim. Even now, he lights up when you're around. You're the only one who can make him laugh. Most times, I can hardly get a smile out of him. You remind me a lot of his Samantha."

"Me too, Hon." Gina agreed.

A little embarrassed, she lamented, "I really wish I could have known her…oops, I think I hear that jeep of his. Make it party time!"

As if on cue, Jim stepped through the gate carrying a huge watermelon. "Hey! What's up? And my favorite 'niece', I'm glad you're here. Thanks for having me, sorry I'm late. I was wrapping up some plans." He set the watermelon in Rich's lap.

"Can a guy get something cool to drink around here?"

"Oh, sorry, Unc. Puh-leeze, allow me to get you something!"

Samantha trotted to one of the coolers, grabbed a cold soda, and handed it to Jim with a curtsy. "Pretty hot today, eh? Oh, yeah, how hot is it in your fabulous jeep?"

"Not bad at 70 miles an hour!" Jim laughed, "You just won't give me a break, will you?"

She caught her father's grin and quick wink and returned a smile.

Bob continued the harassment, "So, what are these plans that are so important you think you can walk in here as late as you want?"

"You know, Bob, I don't have a smart remark to fire back. I must be slowing down. Or, maybe you don't get on my last nerve, like you used to."

"Oh, no! Maybe you're the one losing it, Bob!" Ted exclaimed.

Nothing better than friendly hearty harassment to revive a party mood with this group.

Jim spoke softly after the introductory fun, "Seriously, I appreciate you guys always including me, for years…especially now. You're a great group of friends. So, I want to do something in return."

Bob couldn't hold back, "So, you brought a watermelon?"

"All right, you managed to do it, you got on my last nerve! I guess you haven't lost it."   Again, a good laugh followed. Jim felt blessed to have his 'family'. Without them, he would be lost. Looking around the group, he moved to the center, "I think you're all in a position to take some time off in a couple of weeks, beginning Saturday the 18th. You'll need the whole week. This includes you, Samantha, if your mom approves."

"Hey, what about me?" Rich begged.

"OK…if your mom…and dad…approve."

"That's better!"

"So, what's happening?" Samantha asked excitedly.

"I'd like for all of us to go to Naples…Florida, not Italy. What do you think?"

"What? How? That would be great, but how?" The questions flew.

"Look, everybody, sit down and let me explain." Jim took a

seat on one of the coolers and began, "I've flown this group of execs for a major hotel chain back and forth across the country for a while; they always ask for me now. I've been invited to a few of their after-business dinners and during one of the dinners, the owners made me an offer I finally couldn't refuse."

All eyes focused on Jim; Samantha asked, "What, what?"

"The owners of the hotels gave me a great deal to stay at their Naples resort…along with all of you! As far as getting there, they will pay SBA for us to fly down in my jet…well, the one I fly for SBA. But, everything else is on me, and I don't want to hear any objections!

"One thing, and it's not bad. We fly to Naples on Saturday morning; the next day, I fly the owners from Naples to St. Louis, stay here Sunday and Monday and fly them back to Naples on Tuesday. I'll be back with you by Tuesday evening at the latest…barely three days! You guys spend a week in a beautiful spot, relaxing and enjoying yourselves."

Samantha could hardly contain herself, "You know what is really great? After all these years, we get to fly with you!"

Jim stood slowly, put his arm around her shoulder, and admitted, "Yeah, it will be good, good for all of us."

With some rescheduling and a few changes here and there, the group would have their 'family' vacation. Jim had his opportunity to give back to those who had been so kind to him for so long.

RICH & GINA'S HOME– KIRKWOOD, MISSOURI

JIM RANG THE doorbell, surveying the neighborhood as he waited.

"Just a minute!" a voice shouted from a distant room. A minute later, the door opened.

"Jim!" Gina laughed. "You still have that knack of showing up when least expected! Come in. How are you?"

"I'm OK. I know it's only been a week, but I needed to get out, be with some friends. I hope you don't mind."

"Oh, you know we never mind. You're welcome anytime. I'll get Rich; he's out back."

Jim scanned the living room and the hall. He always liked Rich and Gina's home, the same home purchased shortly after the wedding. They raised their only child, Samantha, in this house; all their memories stored here, everything. Thoughts, such as these, were especially sad. His Air Force career had been exciting and satisfying, but now, only a memory.

"Jim, what's up? How ya doin?"

"Hey, Rich, just needed to get out for a while…see some friends. Couldn't think of any better than you two. Am I interrupting anything?"

"Just weeding the garden, but I'm always happy to put that aside…so, no."

Gina joined the boys with some cool drinks. "Please, make yourself comfortable." She paused to sip her tea. "I'm glad you're here. Last week was good for everybody, I know talking about Samantha doesn't solve anything, it's just that we're all together and…I guess, misery loves company. What else can I say?"

"It is good to be together." Rich leaned toward the coffee table, setting his tea on a coaster. "We remember her because we love her, just like you do, Gina, and you, Jim. No one has forgotten her. Maybe we can't do anything concrete, but we can certainly pray for her…which we all do, I'm sure."

"All the time,' Jim agreed.

The somber mood soon interrupted by a knock at the door. "I wonder who that could be?" Gina knowingly asked. "Why don't you answer, Jim? Give her a little surprise."

Opening the door just a crack, Jim spoke through the gap, "We don't want any! Need I release the hounds?"

"Need I have that fancy mode of transportation hauled away? It's blocking my parking spot!"

"Your spot? I thought you relinquished that when you moved out!"

"You know, Colonel Gordon, some benefits last in perpetuity!'

"OK, you win!" He opened the door wide, "I can't top that word. How are you, Hon?"

Samantha bounced in, hugged her uncle, and giggled, "Much better, now! I didn't know you were going to be here!"

"So, what are we…chopped liver?" Rich complained.

"Eeew! Really?" She kissed her mom and dad.

Gina filled Samantha in, "Jim dropped by just to be with friends."

"What? Nobody home at his first stop?"

Jim joined her in the fun, "Actually, the first two places

I stopped!"

"All seriousness aside, will you just stop?" Rich sat on the edge of his chair, shaking his head, "I don't know how much more of this I can take."

At last, a bright spot in the day as they enjoyed the pleasure of family, of friends.

Moving into the kitchen, the four sat around the table, almost a ritual when together. Jim stretched, extending a leg alongside the wall. "I need to bring this up. It's been bothering me the last few days…but, do you guys think it's wrong to go to Florida during this time? I feel guilty, like a lack of respect for Samantha. I don't know. What do you think?"

Rich, Gina, and Samantha shared glances among one another, not really knowing what to say. Gina offered first, "I do see what you're saying, but, I don't think it's any kind of disrespect to her. You…we all care about Samantha. We all love her. You have been, I think, under a lot of pressure. You've put a lot of blame on yourself; you want to do something for her…but you can't. None of us can. But, as we said before, we can pray for her. The decision is yours, Jim, and we will all respect that decision, regardless." Gina, Samantha, and Rich lovingly covered his hands with theirs, as a sign of caring concern and agreement.

"I definitely wanted to give all of you this trip." Jim stated softly, "I wanted everyone to know how much I appreciated my inclusion in everything: birthdays, anniversaries, births, even deaths. You have all been so good to me…so good." He sighed deeply, "I suppose we should go. I do know what I feel for her is true and nothing can make it less. Thanks…I just needed to talk this out."

Samantha spoke from her heart as she continued to hold his hands, "Uncle Jim, and I do consider you my uncle, you are the sweetest, kindest man I know next to my father, and I love you. Don't ever, ever change. I hope to meet someone like you two guys someday."

After a light lunch, Jim prepared to leave when Rich extended an interesting thought, "I wonder how the Marissens are handling this? Rose was always so nice; she even put up with me."

"I miss her." Jim chuckled, "She was like a mother to me. I always enjoyed when Samantha, her mother, and I would occasionally go out for dinner. I think Rose enjoyed it too."

"What about her father? What was he like?" Samantha nosily inquired.

"Samantha!" Gina chided.

"That's all right, Gina." Jim protectively responded. "Funny, isn't it? I never met him, ever. Guess he disliked me that much. But, no love lost on either side," he felt an old emotion swell in his chest.

"They gotta be hurting, to go through this now, so late in their lives. I mean, they're not old, but old enough. I guess late seventies, eighty by now. Last I heard, her father still runs Marissen AeroSpace; doesn't want to hang it up, I suppose. It always was his life." Jim found the more he spoke of Ed Marissen, the tighter his stomach became.

Samantha didn't hesitate to add bitterly, "All I know is, they fouled up everything between you and Samantha. I guess I should feel bad for them…but it makes me sad when I think of what they did to you."

"Mrs. Marissen really had nothing to do with what happened," Jim stated in her defense. "She couldn't stand up to Ed Marissen…not many people could, probably still can't.

"I can't blame anyone other than myself. If I had stood up to him; demanded a face-to-face talk. What an…he never confronted me to my face…and I let him get away with it! Perhaps, had I shown some courage, maybe Samantha would have stood with me! I have no one to blame but myself. This is not self-pity. It's just the truth!"

No one spoke a word. Sometimes, silence is best.

"I'm sorry," Jim muttered, embarrassed by his outburst. "A lot of years broke out in a short time."

"Why don't you sit down for a bit. Don't leave yet. There's something I have to do, actually, I need to do. I won't be long. Just don't go anywhere; I'll be back." Gina turned and ran up the stairs to the bedroom.

Twenty minutes passed before she returned, during which time, Rich, Samantha, and Jim discussed the upcoming trip. Jim felt the correct decision had been made; the time away would do everyone good.

"Well, there you are!" Samantha voiced accusingly. "Dad was about to send a search party upstairs. We heard you on the phone."

Smiling broadly, Gina sat next to Jim and explained, "I just got off the phone with Rose Marissen!"

"What, why?"

"Because you won't. She is really hurting, she sounded awful. Rich, I promised we would visit her soon. She needs the company. Mr. Marissen is in Arizona." Gina couldn't spill the information fast enough.

Jim quietly asked, "You didn't say anything about me, did you?"

Gina placed her hand on his shoulder, "I didn't have to. She asked about you, asked if we still kept in touch with you. You really should go see her…think about it, please?"

Jim stood, walked to the front window, turned to Gina and almost wondered aloud, "Where did you come up with her phone number? I know that has nothing to do with anything, but where?"

Giggling more out of accomplishment than anything else, she told of searching an old yearbook for Samantha's home phone number…and there it was, and it hadn't changed. She had to go through some guy, Eric or something, to get to her, but Rose remembered everybody."

Jim leaned back on the couch, rubbing his face with his hands.

"What do you say, Jim?" Samantha pushed. "You should visit her. How about now? You're just sitting here with us." She put the finishing touch to her argument, "Besides, as far as I remember, you usually do the right thing."

He straightened up, looked her straight in the eye, and calmly replied, "All right Samantha, I'll go…but…you'll come with me."

Suddenly, the tide had turned, "Why? She doesn't even know me. What purpose would that serve?"

"As far as I remember," he responded, "you usually do the right thing."

*　*　*

"My last trip down this road is not a pleasant memory."

"You'll be fine, Jim. Don't worry. At least you know Ed Marissen isn't there."

"Tell that to my stomach. I haven't felt this nervous since… well, since the first time I met my Samantha. I really wish you could have known her. She was quite the lady. Your mom and dad would agree how similar the two of you are…or were…or could be. You know what I mean."

She took note of Jim's reference to 'my Samantha' before agreeing, "Yeah, since this Russia bit has been going on, mom and dad have mentioned a few things like that."

As he pulled around the final curve, news people could be seen crowding the Marissen gate, waiting for anyone to make an appearance. The numbers were not as large as prior to Marissen's demand that they be dispersed.

Jim eased the jeep to the side of the road and looked over the scene. Getting in appeared relatively impossible.

Samantha questioned the situation, "So, what now?"

"The best approach is to come out of nowhere, strike fast. What's the worst that can happen? They tell us to leave."

The jeep lurched forward as he threw it into gear and drove to the gate. Jim made a quick attempt to get Samantha a little uptight, "Don't forget, these are the government's top security guys. Don't say anything to get them mad."

"What do you mean?"

"I mean, just be cool."

"Cool, what's that?"

"Ooh, you might have a problem."

Initially, the small annoying clog of media parted but eventually closed in. Microphones were jammed in their faces while others simply shouted questions in their direction. A special agent near the gate signaled Jim to turn around and leave the premises. Extending his arm out the jeep, Jim waved his ID toward the agent, knowing he would not be able to see from that distance. He hoped the agent would grow exasperated and come to the jeep to inspect the ID. Instead, the agent radioed another and soon two additional agents drove to the gate from the mansion. The three stepped into the crowd demanding they back up or face arrest for hindering an investigation.

Once cleared, the original agent motioned for Jim to pull forward. Jim glanced at Samantha and grinned noticing she had the look of a deer caught in the headlights. Two agents took their positions at either side of the jeep while the third stationed himself at the front of the vehicle.

The agent on Jim's side demanded his ID, which he handed over immediately.

"Colonel James P. Gordon. Am I supposed to know you?"

"More than likely not," Jim responded.

Irritated by the media and now this interruption, the agent snapped, "Let's try this again; tell me who you are and what you're doing here, or turn around and leave."

Pointing to his ID, Jim explained, "I'm Colonel James Gordon, Retired, an old friend of Rose Marissen. I stopped by to visit, my niece and me."

Samantha stared straight ahead, expressionless, not wanting to look anyone in the eye for fear an agent might ask her a question. She glanced sideways at Jim and noticed him looking back with the slightest smirk. The agents gathered for a conference near the gate, occasionally eyeing the jeep and passengers. Finally, one pulled a cell phone from his pocket and punched in some numbers. Jim and Samantha could tell he was reading information from the ID while pacing across the drive and back.

Suddenly, he slipped the phone back into his pocket, walked to the jeep, handed Jim his ID and said, "Follow the car to the circle and wait for an agent to escort you to the door. Sorry about the delay, Colonel."

Jim fired up the jeep as the agents turned their car around. Samantha sat silent until she sarcastically repeated, "Sorry about the delay, Colonel…Sorry about the delay, Colonel. What is that?"

As they made their way up the drive, she nervously laughed, "OK, I guess you got me!"

The short drive to the mansion was as intimidating as he

remembered; down a slight grade with a bend to the right, then back up to the large circle at the front entrance. Another agent stepped from the entryway, motioning for Jim to park on the opposite side of the circle.

As Samantha pushed herself out of the jeep, she stood in awe, inspecting the front of the mansion.

"Wow!"

"Yeah, that was my reaction the first time I saw the place…wow!"

"From what my mom told me, you were pretty impressive that night, the perfect gentleman."

"Don't let that get around."

"Please…you are a gentleman. But, don't worry, I'll never tell."

Her comment brought out a thin smile. He took a deep breath and exhaled, "Let's do this before I back out."

"Too late! We're past the point of no return."

Samantha and Jim followed the agent up the steps through the massive stone entrance to the mansion.

Eric the butler met them in the hall, "Mrs. Marissen will be with you shortly. Please make yourselves comfortable."

The duo moved cautiously into the elegantly decorated sitting room, where Jim, rocking heel to toe, hands behind his back, revealed, "My gosh, Samantha, I feel thirty again. Not much has changed…I'm still overwhelmed." Slowly, he turned 360°, taking in the view.

"This is amazing," she admitted, as she wandered about the room, scrutinizing everything.

All too soon, Jim heard footsteps approaching. His stomach tightened and his rocking came to a halt. Samantha scurried next to him from a far corner. Rose entered through a rear entrance to the room and hesitantly advanced toward the odd couple. She stopped abruptly, looking intently at Jim.

"Oh, my, Jim! It is you!" Her hands covered her mouth.

A moment later, she rushed to Jim, throwing her arms around him, sobbing into his chest. He stared at Samantha with a "What do I do?" look. She shrugged. Relaxing, he held Rose in his arms, allowing her to cry.

After some time, Rose stepped away, wiped her eyes with a tissue, stared first at Jim, then Samantha. "I'm so sorry. With all that has happened…and then, you're really here, I…I just didn't know what to think."

"It's all right, Rose. I am here…I'm here for whatever you need. It's so good to see you."

"Oh, my goodness, it is so good to see you! I can't begin to tell you how good it is."

They held each other again.

In only a moment, Samantha felt certain Jim made the right decision. Rose Marissen had missed Jim like a mother misses her son.

"This has been a very strange day." Rose attempted to explain, "First, Samantha's friend, Gina calls. Then, you come by. See what I mean…very strange."

"I can tell you what happened." Jim related the day's events to Rose, wrapping up with, "…and that's why I'm here. Hope you don't mind."

"Oh, no, never. I'm so glad!" She turned to Samantha, "I'm so sorry, I must have left my manners upstairs. Are you Jim's daughter?"

"No, Mrs. Marissen, you spoke with my mother, Gina, earlier. My parents are Gina and Rich Reynolds. Your daughter is who I'm named after!"

"You're Samantha? I haven't seen you since you were a baby! Let me have a look at you." Rose took Samantha's hands, "My goodness, you're all grown; it's been far too long."

Sweet memories of Rose came to Jim's mind: memories of her soft, comforting, southern manner, how she always made everyone feel at home. He remembered how he loved her as a son loves his own mother. Not surprisingly, he still did.

Motioning toward the couch, Rose insisted, "Please, make yourselves comfortable." She stressed, "Ed's not here. He's at one of his facilities, in Arizona, I believe."

Dismayed, Jim asserted, "You shouldn't be here alone."

"Really, it's all right. He needs something to keep his mind occupied. He's a wreck, worried about Samantha. I can't tell you how you have lifted my spirits this afternoon. Thank you for coming."

"You have helped me too," Jim asserted, "Seeing you and talking to you after so much time was necessary. I'm sorry for losing contact with you."

"We can always say what should have been. What we should do is correct whatever we can and move on. You are here, Samantha is here. We build from here." Rose, realizing her hope that Jim not drop from her life again, smiled at the reality of their reunion. Her long-lost son had returned home.

Out of curiosity, she hesitatingly asked, "Did you stay with the Air Force?" Another pause, then, "Did you…ever get…"

To ease her faltering attempt to inquire if he ever married, Jim responded straightforward, "No, the Air Force became my life after…afterward. I never married. I retired four years ago as Colonel."

"I'm so sorry, Jim. I wish things had been as they should have. If I could remove the last twenty-five years—

"Rose, it's all right. What's happened is past. I'm here so you know you're not alone We all are concerned. We all care. You are not alone in this."

Putting up a strong front, Rose declared, "Thank you, thank everybody for me."

Following another brief pause, she continued,   "I know you loved flying. I'll never forget that day we all watched you take off at the airport. Your mother was there, Samantha. It was so exciting; just made me shiver. Samantha was so proud of you, she…I'm sorry…I didn't mean to—

"That's OK, Rose. I remember that day, too. I was excited she was there, that you were all there. Gave me a chance to show off." He then recalled, "In fact, just the day before, I snuck into a breakfast meeting, or something, and listened to Samantha give one heck of a talk to something like seven or eight hundred people. Flew in real early, called Rich, and he filled me in on where, so, I just showed up. Found out, only women were there. Felt kinda funny, but she did a great job."

Rose thought a moment, "I remember! Samantha told me about what you did, how she lost her train of thought when you walked into the room." She paused, then added, "She also told me what you said to her afterwards."

"I meant every word."

For the next two hours, Samantha Reynolds sat back and enjoyed the conversation carried on between the long-separated friends. She learned more about Jim and Samantha during that short visit than ever could have been picked up in random bits and pieces. One happening she could hardly believe came from Rose. Jim responded in his "aw shucks" manner and let it pass. Not wanting to interfere, Samantha simply listened; she would definitely question Jim later.

Jim's Samantha once asked if he would like to perform a piano duet with her of "Glorious is Thy Name" as special music just before the sermon on Pastor Appreciation Sunday. The church pianist, Jeff Barnes, had put together for her a four-hands piano duet of the familiar hymn with a memorable melody. It had a familiar chorus that tends 'to stick in your head just by hearing it'. Since Jim wouldn't return to St. Louis until that weekend, they practiced the arrangement of the piece separately. They were finally able to practice together just before the service and, thankfully, all went well. Rose commented how Samantha had blossomed as a young woman during the time she and Jim were together, although she never pictured Samantha performing a piano duet arrangement at a Sunday morning service.

Rose laughed a moment, recalling the happier time, a moment that slipped into muffled sobs as her thoughts turned to worry for Samantha. Moving to her side, Jim held Rose once again to comfort a mother in deep despair.

"Rose, if you need anything, call me. I'm in and out of town these days. I'll give you my cell number; contact me anytime."

"Thank you, I will." Drying her eyes, she placed her hand on his, "She loved you, Jim, with all her heart. She…none of us could stand up to Ed. How foolish can we be?"

"I've asked myself that question a thousand times."

*   *   *

Before leaving, Jim spoke alone with Rose; Samantha returned to the jeep. As she thought of what just occurred, tears filled her eyes, a realization of all the people hurt by one man's selfish demand twenty-five-years earlier. The sudden bounce of the jeep as Jim climbed into his seat caused her to flinch. She quickly attempted to angle her face from his sight.

"Hey, what's the matter?" he whispered.

She shook her head to signal nothing.

"Your dad will be awfully upset when he finds out I made you cry."

Samantha turned to him, tears streaming down her cheeks, "You didn't make me cry." Meeting Jim's gaze, she confessed, "I always heard you and Samantha loved each other...I just never...never understood...how deeply—" She reached across the gap between the seats and, clutching his shirtsleeve, pulled her face into his shoulder and cried softly.

Jim held her as she cried, knowing she truly did consider him a member of the family; she cared that much about all that happened, then and now. He did have family, and he cared for his 'niece' just as strongly. Between his time with Rose and the realization that, aside from childhood scratches and scrapes, he had never seen Samantha cry, truly cry out of emotion, a deeper sense of empathy ignited, a level of concern he had not allowed for many, many years.

Slowly, Samantha straightened up, "Oh, my gosh. I'm so sorry, Jim."

He smiled, "No...don't be sorry. I need to thank you, for what you do for me."

* * *

Rose shuffled to her room, happy for the events of the day, yet, very sad she didn't share the news the CIA found her daughter. She couldn't afford to jeopardize Samantha's safety but felt Jim should know.

OUTSIDE ST. PETERSBURG, RUSSIA

RECLINING ON HIS cot, Nikolai thought Samantha finally asleep when Igor charged into the room.

"Up! Time to interrogate!"

Once awakened, she refused to move. She was tired, tired of fighting, tired of the fear, tired of every facet of her imprisonment.

Igor muttered something under his breath and violently grabbed her wrist shouting, "You get up!"

He jerked Samantha from the bed, dragging her to the floor. She began to kick and scream, "Nik! Help me! Please!"

For an instant, Nikolai froze. What to do? How!

Lifting his prisoner to her feet, Igor flung her against the wall, backhanding her across the face. He positioned himself to strike her full force once more.

At that moment, Nikolai's hand snared Igor's wrist while wrapping his arm around the thick neck. He forced the interrogator's hand up behind the back.

"Aargh! Stop!" commanded the fat man in excruciating pain.

Nikolai did not. He increased his grip while tightening his arm around Igor's neck. Igor bellowed in Russian as Nikolai maintained dominance, "You cannot do this! She is my prisoner! I am in charge!"

Incensed, Nikolai growled, also in Russian, "You pig! I am

here to protect her! From you, if necessary!"

"You cannot!" his speech becoming grunts. "You…cannot… remove…me…"

Nikolai quickly readjusted his hold on the stammering fat man, greatly intensifying the pain. In a last futile attempt to stop the young guard, Igor, with eyes bulging; a beet-red face contorted in unbearable pain and fear; short, erratic, sputtering breaths; and saliva drooling down his chin, dug his heels in and forcefully backed Nikolai into the wall. But, he had no more and dropped to his knees facing Samantha, now squeezed into the corner, knees tucked under her chin, arms wrapped protectively around her legs. She watched in horror as the scene unfolded, having no concept of the strength the young Nikolai possessed.

Heaving Igor to his feet with the fat man's neck tightly locked in the crook of his arm, Nikolai violently twisted his head to one side, causing him to drop to the floor. He laid motionless, eyes open before Samantha.

Throwing the door open, Nikolai ordered two men to dispose of Igor's body. Samantha understood nothing of what he said, but as Nikolai shouted stern orders he pointed toward her, a frightening motion; she no longer knew what to think or expect.

He slammed the door and leaned against the wall breathing deeply, relieved the incident over. He turned to Samantha still huddled in the corner, sobbing. He knelt and examined her injuries. Knowing she was in pain, he gently reached under her arm, assisted her to her feet and to the bed. As she sat on the edge, he held her shaking hand and whispered, "I…am…sorry. Not want you hurt…never! Do not…uh…fear. Do not…fear."

Tapping himself on the chest, he emphasized, "I am friend… friend. Tovarich. Friend. Tovarich."

Samantha looked to him, tapped his arm, and asked, "Tovarich?"

Nikolai smiled, "Da...yes! Tovarich...friend!"

Although he emitted kindness, she had just witnessed a cold anger of which she initially believed him incapable. Samantha had experienced abuse before, but never witnessed such a violent end to life, the death of an evil man. She felt no remorse, only relief. Thankfully, Nikolai's protection may have saved her life, yet she feared the result of Igor's death. How would those of higher authority respond? Would she be the one to pay the price?

Nikolai seemed to offer comfort and reassurance when he attempted to explain, "No anger. You see...no anger. Doctor is to come. You be...OK. OK?"

He wrapped a blanket around her shoulders; she shivered uncontrollably from the dark experience. He continued to hold her shaking hand as they waited. An hour later a light knock at the door startled her. No one knocked before, only unannounced entry. Nikolai opened the door to a medical person, who cautiously began to inspect and treat Samantha's injuries. Before leaving, the medic instructed Nikolai to keep a close eye on her; she may have suffered a concussion. She required rest but must remain alert for a period to ensure nothing wrong. Hours later, she slept as he diligently watched over her through the night.

Beginning the following day, Samantha ate proper meals; showered, not daily but regularly; and given personal hygiene supplies along with changes of clothing. She thanked God for the mercy he had shown her. Nikolai's promised protection appeared authentic.

CHESTERFIELD AIRPORT– CHESTERFIELD, MISSOURI

CHESTERFIELD AIRPORT SECURITY directed the five cars to an unused hangar converted into a garage for overnight travelers. While the field crew transferred the baggage to Jim's jet, his guests relaxed in the lounge sipping coffee prior to takeoff. Saturday morning, the airport a virtual ghost town at the early hour.

Jim entered the lounge in his SBA Captain's uniform, removed his cap, and announced their flight was prepared for departure.

Looking him over head to toe, Rich felt obligated to remark, "What's with the uniform? I'm impressed!"

Jim smiled, "Yeah, I thought you'd like it. Take advantage of it; you know I'm not capable of remaining so cordial."

"With your military background, you're probably more than capable. It's these guys that drag you down," Samantha jokingly chided the men of the group.

"Hold on!" Bob fired back. "What's she doing talking so early in the morning? Don't you have a rule about not speaking with anyone until at least 10:00am?"

"Now see what you've started!" Rich simply shook his head at Samantha's ability to spar with the guys. For whatever reason, she fit right in with everyone, maybe because of her special connection with Jim or her outgoing personality, or both. Hard to say, but she was well-liked by all.

Displaying her dry humor with Gina, Rich, and Jim, she confided, "You know, I feel a little out-of-place with you old folks. Try to keep your topics current so I can take part."

Chuckling at the early morning silliness, Jim nudged Samantha and reassured her, "I think you'll have a good time, regardless of your mom and dad."

The eleven travelers strolled across the already warm pavement to the awaiting jet. To the right of the door stood a young man, Jim's co-pilot for the flight, who introduced himself as he assisted the ladies up the several steps into the plane. The young pilot extended his hand to Samantha, the last to board. She hesitated but placed hers on his.

"Good morning! I'm Scott Larimore, Captain Gordon's co-pilot for this flight. Welcome aboard!" He smiled broadly as she began her ascent.

Stopping midway, she responded to his formal introduction, "Good morning, Scott. I'm Samantha Reynolds and I'm happy to be your passenger this morning." He released her hand as she entered the plane, glancing back briefly.

With Larimore staring into the plane, Jim stepped up and slapped him on the back, "Time to get this bird off the ground. Let's roll."

The young man turned to Jim and asked, "Who's the brunette?"

"Which one? A couple of them probably add the color."

"You know, the last one to… Wait a minute, you're kidding, right?"

"Are you?"

"What? No! You know who I mean. Don't you?"

Samantha paused inside the plane to view Jim and his co-pilot in conversation from one of the aisle windows. He seemed to be slightly taller than Jim, she thought. Dark hair, nice smile, mmm…no, a very nice smile, brown eyes. Oh, better get to my seat before somebody wonders what I'm doing.

"Oh, the last one? She's the daughter of my best friend and his wife who are with us this morning. Obviously, that makes her a close friend of mine." Jim strained to maintain a serious demeanor.

"Oh…sorry, sir. Didn't mean to…uh, you know—

"Yeah, I know." He smiled. "C'mon, let's go."

Jim climbed aboard first and stepped into the cabin to hear Liz exclaim, "Jim, this is fantastic! You get to enjoy this all the time?"

"I do. But don't forget, I sit up front, not back here!" A calm satisfaction filled his heart to see his friends talking and laughing while awaiting takeoff. Life seemed so different after his time with Rose and Samantha.

Walking the length of the passenger area, Jim warned his friends with mock authority, "Need I remind you, this is genuine leather upon which your posteriors rest?"

Reaching the aft of the cabin where Rich, Gina, and Samantha chose to spend the flight, he momentarily reclined across the aisle simply to harass Samantha. "So, what's the story? Fixing your hair and putting on makeup? I thought you girls did all that at home…you know…just in case."

"Just in case? You didn't tell me your co-pilot was cute. A little warning would be nice! And, I thought your co-pilot's name was Ben, not Scott."

"Oh, Ben. He decided to move on; I don't think he was cut out for this kind of schedule. Scott has been flying with me on a trial basis the last few weeks, so don't distract him. This could be a 'make or break' week. It's the final week of trials." Again, Jim had to stifle a smile trying to maintain an air of seriousness.

He added a slight zing, "By the way, Scott already found you attractive when your hair was in a ponytail and you wore no makeup. Tell you what, I'll send him down here before we take off. Be ready!"

"No you won't! Besides, he can't, he's trying to impress you for a job."

"Have fun, gotta get back up front. Don't want to leave Junior up there by himself too long." Jim smiled and laughed as he patted everyone on the back during his return to the cockpit. Samantha felt something different about him, nothing big, just…something.

Several moments later, Scott Larimore exited the cockpit area to double-check the door, or so he wanted the passengers to believe. From the rear of the plane, Samantha observed the young pilot once more: yep, later twenties or so; about six feet tall; brown hair roughly combed; as he came closer, she again noted his dark brown eyes…oh, no, he was walking down the aisle. Jim did what he said he would do!

Stopping at the Reynolds, he introduced himself again, "Hi, I'm Scott Larimore. I met you all separately when you boarded. I hope I'm not intruding, but I thought it would be good to meet you as a family. I apologize, but I mistakenly thought she," he glanced toward Samantha, "this young lady was flying alone. I'd like to welcome you aboard."

He extended his hand toward her but Rich took and shook it instead. "Scott, glad to meet you! I'm Rich and this is my wife, Gina. Samantha is our daughter. I hope we see more of you on our trip!"

Smiling nervously, he stuttered, "Heh, yeah, I mean yes, sir. Yeah, well, I better get up front. The boss doesn't like to be kept waiting. Nice to meet you…again."

As Scott stepped up the aisle, Samantha called, "It was nice to meet you, Scott. I hope to see you later!"

She kept her eyes on him until he closed the cockpit door, not failing to catch his final look and smile. What a smile! A broad smile, a sincere smile, she thought.

A minute later, amid the low whine of the twin engines, their pilot announced, "Ladies and gentlemen, thank you for flying SBA. I am your Captain, James Gordon. Please fasten your seatbelts. We are prepared for departure to Naples, Florida, a distance of 1010 miles at 485 miles per hour. Sit back, relax, and enjoy the flight."

As the jet taxied to the runway, Samantha again wondered about the subtle difference in Jim's demeanor. She couldn't put her finger on it, but something was different.

"Mom, Dad, have you noticed anything different about Jim this morning?"

Gina glanced to Rich, then back to her, responding, "No, not really. Should we?"

Oh, I don't know, it's probably nothing. There just seems to be something different in his actions…his voice. Never mind, I'm sure it's just me."

Turning slowly onto the runway, Jim brought the jet to a pause awaiting final clearance from the tower. A message crackled over the com, "OK, everybody, are you ready?"

The cabin broke into applause as the jet moved forward, gaining speed as it roared, wheels rumbling, down the airstrip until lifting free of the earth climbing toward the ceiling of blue. The city dropped away revealing the Missouri River to their right and moments later, the Mississippi River on the left.

Once Jim and his co-pilot settled into the flight, Larimore announced over the com, "Ladies and gentlemen, located in the galley directly behind the cockpit, you will find a couple of carafes of fresh coffee, regular and decaf…mmm, excuse me a moment… (muffled conversation) Did we make that yesterday or this morning? Oh, yeah…OK. (Return to normal level) Yes…fresh coffee, brewed just this morning for your enjoyment. Also…there is fruit juices, pastries and whatever. So, help yourselves. And if someone would, I could go for a cruller…I love the way that just rolls off your tongue…the word, not the cruller. OK, yeah…gotta go."

Many moans and groans emanated from the travelers, yet they showed no hesitation partaking of the early morning treats. For a short time, the eleven laughed and conversed as one large group, including comments on the 'Gordon' type humor of the co-pilot and the obvious spark Samantha and he experienced. She attempted to act offended but fooled no one.

As everyone returned to their seats, a few noticed Samantha remain at the pastry counter. Liz slipped back up the aisle and asked, "Need a hand with something?"

Looking as if she'd been caught with her hand in the cookie jar, Samantha sheepishly inquired, "Which one of these is a cruller?"

Grinning, Liz pointed and said, "Those two. Why don't you take one and give the other to the co-pilot? I think he'd like that."

"That's a good idea! Wait a minute, you're messin' with me, aren't you?"

"Maybe." Liz responded, giving Samantha a nudge and a wink.

Oh, well, she thought. I'm right here in front of everybody. There's no way to do this without being seen. She knocked softly on the cockpit door. After a brief, muffled conversation, the door opened with Scott in the entrance.

"Yes, ma'am. How may I help you?"

Suddenly, Samantha became aware of her nervousness, "I,

umm, I brought you a cruller since you seemed to want one. I hope that's OK."

"This is great! Thank you, Samantha. It is Samantha?"

"Yes…yes, it is. You're welcome."

Neither said a word for a moment. Finally, Samantha noted, "You're right, cruller does kind of roll off your tongue…the word…not the donut."

He smiled, took the napkin with the cruller, and mentioned, "Thanks, again. I owe you one."

"OK!" She smiled. "I'll see you in Naples!"

"I'd like that."

"OK, bye."

"Bye."

She returned to her seat; he closed the cockpit door.

As Samantha approached Rich and Gina, she rolled her eyes. "Uuugh! I was so ridiculous! I must have sounded like a twelve-year-old. He probably thinks I'm such a child." She flopped into the seat next to her mother.

"What? We didn't see anything." Gina made an attempt to minimize her daughter's self-imposed embarrassment.

"I was taking a nap," mumbled Rich.

Samantha reclined the seat, crossed her arms, and closed her eyes.

* * *

"Well, Junior, how did it go? She brought you the donut, eh?"

"Yeah, and then I sounded like a fool. I couldn't say anything intelligent. Brother!"

"It sounded like it went OK."

"I owe you one? That sounds OK?"

"What would you say if you could do it over?"

* * *

Samantha hadn't touched the cruller she brought back for herself. She had to laugh; I probably did sound like a twelve-year-old, but he did thank me. She chuckled out loud when she thought, why wouldn't he thank a twelve-year-old?

* * *

Suddenly, the hum of the com with the crackle of the microphone drew everyone's attention. "This is Scott, your co-pilot. I would like to thank the very nice lady who brought the cruller to me. I can honestly say I have never had a donut delivered by such a nice person. I would have added 'pretty' but your mom and dad are here. I don't want them to get the wrong impression of me. Oh, darn! That cruller just rolled off my tongue again! The cruller…not the word. Anyway, I'll see you in Naples! Over and out."

* * *

"Well, there you go, Hon! How about that?" Rich and Gina laughed at the short message for Samantha.

"Oh, brother, who is this guy? Is he going to be with us for the week?" Bill wondered.

Carol reminded everyone, "He and Jim have that weird schedule, remember? They'll be back Tuesday some time. At least, I hope he comes back with Jim. Seems like he could be a lot of fun, doesn't he, Samantha?"

– NAPLES, FLORIDA

TWO HOURS AND fifteen minutes later, all eyes gazed upon the shimmering Gulf waters as waves rolled toward the shore like thin ribbons of white from their present altitude and distance. The deep hum and thump of the wheels lowering hinted the time for fastening seatbelts had arrived.

Scott soon voiced over the com, "All right, all seriousness aside, fasten your seatbelts and return your seat to the upright position."

'All seriousness aside.' An instant awareness swept over Rich, "Do you know who always said that…and still does? Jim! The co-pilot, Scott, acts and sounds like Jim thirty years ago! Same off-the-wall humor! I hope he really is as nice a guy as he seems."

"He is," Samantha said as a matter of fact.

"And how would you know that?" Gina asked.

"One," Samantha began, "Jim wouldn't choose someone who's not, "And two," she concluded, "I just know he is."

"Well, OK! I guess that's good enough for me." Rich jokingly agreed but, as a father, hoped she was right.

Samantha turned toward her mom and dad and whispered, "I heard something the other day," she looked around, insuring no one was listening. "Are you aware Jim can play the piano?"

"You know," Rich remembered aloud, "Come to think of it, he did…wasn't bad at all. He hasn't played for quite a while. I think he and Samantha did something together years ago."

"Yeah, I found out about that Saturday when Jim and I visited Mrs. Marissen. They were having the greatest conversation and she brought that up. I almost fell off my chair. I never knew!"

"Didn't his mother insist he take lessons?" Now Gina attempted to draw out details from the past.

"I'm pretty sure that's how it was." Chuckling, Rich relayed more, "He said he hated taking lessons but he never intentionally missed one. Despite his family life, he always made the effort to please his mother; he did love her."

"Don't forget that, Samantha," advised her mother. "You can usually know how a man will treat you by the way he treats his mother."

"What was Jim, eighteen, when his mother passed?" Samantha felt her pain for Jim return as she thought of the disappointments throughout his life.

"I believe so," her dad responded. "Bonnie was her name. She was very nice."

*   *   *

"Sorry to be such a pain this morning," Scott mentioned after they received final approach instructions from the tower.

Jim had to laugh, "Trust me, I understand. In my younger days, I seemed to be an 'open mouth, insert foot' kind of guy."

Surprised, Scott questioned his statement, "You? You seem too quiet, too reserved, too formal to be like that."

"Believe me, I was."

"So, what changed?"

"I met someone."

"And she changed you?"

Jim thought before answering, "No…she didn't change me; she was the catalyst of my change."

"Must have been some woman."

"She was."

"Was? What happened, if you don't mind my asking?"

"It, umm…it didn't work out. She and I went our separate ways."

"Man, that's a shame."

Pausing again, Jim quietly affirmed, "Yeah, it was."

"Boss," Scott hesitated. "Could I ask you a question?"

"I'm sure you could."

"OK, sorry about the poor English. May I ask you something?"

"I don't see why not."

"Is it OK with you if I spoke with Samantha? I don't want to offend you or her mom and dad. This is a serious question. She seems to be really nice and I'd like…uh…you know, don't you?"

"She is nice…and I do know. It's fine with me. You seem to be a nice guy, but you'll have to pass Rich and Gina's inspection."

"Yeah, I think her dad is a little leery of me; I couldn't tell what he thought."

"I'll fill you in on a little something. If you want to survive this week, remember…," he hesitated while adjusting the angle of descent, "Just remember, don't worry about Rich. He's going to try to have some fun with you. He is a great guy. If he likes you, you're in."

"You're sure?"

"I've known him for more than forty years, I'm sure."

* * *

Back in the cabin, Ted laid his hand on Carol's, and promised, "I know you don't like the landing part, but this will be over in a minute."

With that said, the jet gently touched down and the reverse thrusters fired, dropping their rolling speed dramatically.

Jim's voice came over the com, "Ladies and gentlemen,

welcome to Naples where you will be basking in the sun, frolicking in the Gulf, and just making a general nuisance of yourselves for a period of one week. We thank you for your patience as we bring the plane to a stop. We will join you as soon as possible. "

Scott took control, and following the landing crews' directions brought the plane to its designated stopping point after which, he systematically performed a checklist shutdown. Only when all was in order did the two exit the cockpit to greet the eleven happy passengers.

Carol was the first to greet Jim, "The landing was great! Thank you."

He smiled, remembering Carol and Ted had experienced a harrowing landing during a sudden thunderstorm several years back, "Always easier when there's no wind shear or crazy crosswinds."

Scott prepared for the passengers to disembark, this time assisting the ladies down the steps. As the Reynolds family reached the front of the cabin, Rich placed his hand on Jim's shoulder and sighed, "After all these years, I finally got to experience your flying. I gotta tell you, you're good. If it wasn't for today, I would never have known how easy it must be to fly one of these things."

Jim just shook his head, "You still don't follow your mom's advice: If you can't say something nice, say nothing at all. Keep in mind, you're here, over 1000 miles from home; it's a long walk back!"

Gina put an end to the shenanigans, "Please, gentlemen, and I use the term loosely, let's get to the hotel before you start again. At least there I can pretend I don't know you."

"Wow, Mom! Nice work stifling these two." Switching gears, Samantha directed her next comments to Jim, "Really,

Unc, that was great; I've never flown in a business jet before. Is it anything like flying a fighter jet?"

He hadn't really thought about it, but now that she brought it up, he shared his first thought, "Imagine you drove a Formula I race car for the majority of your career, then had to switch to your dad's car. Probably something like that."

"Not unlike your jeep," Rich immediately tossed out. "By the way," he slyly questioned, "Do you call yourself 'Captain' when you drive that?"

With one eyebrow raised, Jim extended his arm toward the exit as an invitation to disembark, please.

Rich, Gina, and Samantha stepped from the plane to the already hot, sun-drenched tarmac followed closely by Jim. The timing could not have been better; a pair of limos pulled up, one white, the other black. Moving to the front of his speechless friends, Jim ordered, "All right, break into two groups and hop in. The luggage is already on its way to the hotel, right Junior?"

"Right, boss!"

Rich, Gina, and Samantha entered the black limo first, followed by the pilot and co-pilot. Once the juggling of seats settled, an obvious vacancy remained, the seat adjacent to Samantha's, which Scott took but only after a quick look to Jim for approval.

Lowering himself into the plush accommodation, he stated apologetically, "Hope you don't mind. I could sit over there."

Samantha quickly responded, "This is fine. No sense in your sitting away from us."

Gina turned to Jim, "Really, you shouldn't have! I've never experienced anything like this."

"Just kick back and relax," he reprimanded her. "This is your vacation."

Scott reached over and tapped Jim on the knee, "So, boss…

Jim, how did I rate this?"

Initially, Jim directed the explanation to the Reynolds, "I needed a good co-pilot, someone I could count on," and then to Scott, "You seemed to fit the bill. Not only do you have to be capable, in my book, we have to get along. There can be some pretty long days when we'll have to sit next to each other for a good deal of time."

Rich broke in, "I can tell you this…if he likes you, you're in; if not…well."

"I suppose I'll know after this week."

Jim displayed a hint of a smile as reassurance.

Up to now, the stunning view of the stretches of beach passed unnoticed until Samantha glanced to her right. "Oh, wow! Would you look at that? It's absolutely beautiful!"

The tropical view observed between the palms halted their conversation as the glistening waters of the Gulf breaking on pristine sand captured their attention.

Reaching toward Jim, Gina asked, "Is our hotel near the beach? Look at these places, right on the beach! Wouldn't that be—

At that instant, the driver turned into the palm lined brick entryway of the Grandeur Hotel and pulled up behind the white limo under a wide, curved, stone supported canopy where two attendants awaited the guests' arrival. The drivers scurried around the luxurious sedans to open the doors for their passengers. As an attendant approached, he formally addressed the group, "Ah, Mr. Gordon and guests! Welcome! Follow me, please."

Stepping from the limo, Samantha observed the surroundings complemented by the doting personnel and meekly stated, "I believe I'm a little underdressed for the occasion."

"I agree," Scott whispered from behind. "Wait, not that I

agree you're underdressed. I agreed we all are, all of us…not just you."

She slowed until next to him. "Scott, I see how you get all embarrassed at times. That tells me you're concerned about people. Don't lose that concern. Don't ever change." She smiled and caught up with Rich and Gina.

After regaining his composure, he reassured himself, "I suppose that went well, sort of."

The second attendant opened the stately brass and glass door motioning the guests toward the busy front desk to sign in and receive their keycards. Samantha entered and waited for Scott and Jim to follow. As Jim reached the open door, the white-haired formal attendant greeted him, "Good morning, Mr. Gordon. How are you this fine day!"

"I'm good, Max. What's up with you?"

"Ah! Not much is happening," Max chuckled. "But, it's always good to see you!"

"And good to see you!" Handing a couple of folded bills to Max, he confided, "Take good care of my friends this week. It would mean a lot to me."

"Thank you! I'll make sure they receive the best care. Good to have you here!"

"Great! Thanks, Max."

Once in the lobby, Samantha offered Jim a compliment, "I want you to know, you never fail to impress me. You're such an old-school gentleman. Like I've said before, I hope to meet someone really nice someday."

Jim smiled at the flattery. "You will, Samantha, I believe you will."

When Jim stepped up to the front desk, the manager informed him that the hotel owner, Mr. Morelli, would appreciate a moment.

As the group milled about the desk, Jim nudged Ted, "Would you get everyone over to the elevators marked '11 thru 16'? I'll meet you there in a few minutes."

Morelli stepped from his office as Jim crossed the area behind the front desk to greet the ever-smiling exec. The business friends shook hands firmly, exchanged pleasantries, and laughed for several minutes before concluding their brief encounter with a final handshake after which Jim strolled through the lobby to the elevators.

"Who was that?" Bill inquired.

"Just the CEO I told you about, the guy who owns this place." Jim attempted to minimize the moment, "No big deal, he's a nice guy."

Bill spoke for all, "No big deal! He made all this happen! We should thank that guy!"

Jim chuckled, "You'll get your opportunity."

The elevator doors opened; everyone entered, not knowing what to expect. Jim inserted his card into the slot and pressed **14**. The security system denied access to the 11th floor and above without a proper keycard. The elevator opened to the 14th floor, giving pause to the small group mesmerized by the exquisitely appointed décor.

"All right, I believe we have the six rooms at the end of the south side," Jim instructed. "Sorry, Junior and I get the corner room…just part of the deal."

"Heeey…wait a minute!" Scott inspected his room card, "I really don't have my own room, do I, boss…Jim? We're sharing a room, aren't we?"

Playing on Scott's humor, Jim smiled and explained, "Let me put it this way, Mr. Larimore; if it's late and you're in the room, all is good. And I suppose it works the opposite way too, although, I'm too old to get in trouble."

"Mmmm, OK, boss!" He turned to the group with upturned hands and a look of 'whaaat?', which drew a snicker from everyone, including Samantha.

"You're not alone, Scott! I'm rooming with my parents. What do you think of that?"

"That might be different," he ventured. "I'd be very protective of someone like you too."

Samantha's cheeks faded to red as she attempted to cover her embarrassment with nervous laughter, almost giggling.

Jim disrupted the minor moment, "All right, ladies and gentlemen, rest up if you want. There is no timetable, you're on your own. I only ask that we have our dinners together. Otherwise, just relax and enjoy yourselves. Mr. Larimore, you're with me…for the moment."

"Jim, wait!"

"Yeah, Carol?"

"We want to thank you for this wonderful trip, this beautiful place…everything! Thank you so much."

"You're welcome. I hope you know how much I appreciate all the years of your friendship. Now, go! Have fun!"

Jim followed Scott into the suite which consisted of a sitting area, a kitchenette, two king-size beds, and a full complement of furniture. Artwork adorned the room, with exotic plants completing the décor. Full-length arched windows overlooked the Gulf of Mexico, offering a serene vista of God's beautiful creation.

"Wow, Jim…boss, I didn't notice this before, but did you know that every suite has a balcony! I'm going to check this out!"

Jim, on the other hand, stretched out on the bed kicking off his shoes as he did. He continued with mixed emotions about the trip; treating his friends for their unwavering support over the years, spending time in such a beautiful locale while

Samantha was held somewhere in Russia as a political prisoner. He had spoken with Rose, to explain the business offer of the trip and his reasoning for presenting the gift to his friends. She advised him to accept the offer for his friends. Doing so did not mean he thought any less of Samantha. When looking at his predicament in that light, the guilt would subside…for a while.

Rolling to his side, Jim made a quick call seconds before Scott returned from the balcony.

"Wow, you would not believe the view…and the breeze. What a place! I can't believe I get to be a part of this. Thanks again, Jim. I appreciate the opportunity."

"That's alright. Don't forget, you're going to be working part of the week," he reminded him. Propping himself on his elbow, Jim asked the young man, "So, what are your plans for today?"

"I don't know, boss. Would you mind…Sorry, I have to ask you…does it bother you when I call you 'boss'? 'Cause, if it does, I'll stop."

Jim yawned, "Knock yourself out, I've been called worse."

"Jim?"

"I thought you wanted to call me boss."

"Yeah, but this is a more personal question."

"OK," Jim swung his feet over the edge of the bed and sat up. "What is it?"

"If you don't want me to do this, just tell me—

"Scott?"

"Sorry, boss…Jim. Would it be OK with you if I asked Samantha down to the beach?"

Jim flopped back on the bed, "This time, I hope you don't mind…I called her and asked if she would go to the beach with you so I could get some rest. She said she would be ready in ten minutes. You better get a move on, Junior."

"You're kidding! Really? You're not kidding! Great! Thanks, boss."

"No problem."

* * *

Soon after Scott dashed off, a light knock at the door interrupted him. He crawled over the bed, made his way to the door, and opened it a crack to see the hall filled with his guests.

"Jim, c'mon. Let's go to the beach. It's beautiful!"

Opening the door fully, he leaned against the frame, "Sorry, I want to get a little rest; have to fly out early in the morning. Give me a couple of hours and I'll be ready. OK?"

"Fair enough! See you in a couple!"

"Reserve a spot for me."

He returned to the bed, laying back on the pillow with hands behind his head. He found himself at peace; no longer his emphasis on self-pity but on true concern for Samantha.

"Lord," he prayed, "Watch over her every moment of every day. Bless her and protect her. She means so much to so many. You saved me through her. I thank you for that. I only wish there was something I could do for her. I can pray…for her… and for the opportunity to see her again."

After his time of prayer, he dropped off to sleep.

* * *

Strolling along the Gulf shore, Samantha and Scott stopped occasionally to investigate an odd-looking shell, allowing the warm water to wash over their feet.

"You know I fly for a living, so tell me about you. What do you do, Samantha Reynolds?"

"Well, actually, I work with my mom and dad at an

organization called HOPE that my mom began almost thirty years ago."

"HOPE?"

She picked up a striped shell, looked it over, and dropped it back on the beach. "The organization offers support for unmarried pregnant girls, homeless and abused women, and at-risk children. I never thought I would enjoy working with my mom, but I love it!"

Scott looked to the horizon, then to her, "That must give you a great deal of satisfaction, just knowing you're helping people who really need someone."

"I do, but everyone has a different calling." Samantha stopped and turned to him, "What we do today is important. Whatever we do now is preparation for what God has for us tomorrow. We are never finished."

Scott grinned with a look of relief and nervously inquired, "You are a believer, aren't you?"

"What do you mean?" With a look of surprise, she continued, "Yes…I am a Christian. But why are you asking?"

Laughing out loud, Scott confessed, "This is all coming together now; it's starting to make sense. I hope you don't mind."

"What makes sense? What are you talking about?"

"Sorry, let me tell you what I think." Slowly, they sat at the water's edge for his explanation. "Over the course of several flights, your uncle has led me into some interesting conversations centered on Christianity and my beliefs…my faith. Looking back, I think he was checking me out, testing the water as to how serious a Christian I am."

"And are you?"

"Yes…I am."

Stretching her foot into the water, she confided relief to his admission, "I'm glad. I'm really glad. I don't know what you think, but I'm happy we met this morning. I'm even happier to know you are a believer."

Scott raised from his elbows and gazed across the expanse of gulf water. "Do you know what I wonder?" Momentarily hesitating, he went on, "I wonder if Jim had this in mind all along? Not planning everything; just making sure we had the chance to meet. Nothing more than that. I don't know. That's pretty far-fetched."

Samantha chuckled, "You may be right! Why would he ask me on this trip? This was for his friends. And he did tell me he thought I would enjoy it. And…he did set up this time on the beach. Why…that sly uncle of mine!"

"So, is Jim related to your mom or your dad?" A reasonable question.

"Jim's not my real uncle, but to me…he is. Umm, what's the best way to explain this?"

Samantha decided to start at the beginning, "Before I was born, he was in a serious relationship that later, due to all kinds of unfortunate happenings, was…ruined, not by him but someone else. Anyway, during their time together, she brought Jim to Christ, in fact, the very day they met! I never knew her, but I always thought what she did for Jim was a true gift."

Her eyes grew misty as she continued, "I'm sorry, I found out just this week how much they loved each other." Wiping beneath her eyes with her index fingers, she went on, "Jim and my dad have been best friends since they were kids, so when his relationship fell apart, my dad…and my mom made sure Jim always had a way to stay involved with all his friends, the people you met today.

"So, as I grew up, Jim became a major part of my life. About as soon as I could talk, I called him Uncle Jim and I've never stopped. I love that man and I'm so happy he's a part of my life."

Scott placed his hand on hers as he asked, "Who was this woman? What's her name?"

"Samantha."

"Samantha? Your name?"

"Actually, I was named after her. She and Jim were still together when I was born. She was my mom's best friend and everyone figured Jim and Samantha were forever."

"I know Jim mentioned a very influential woman in his life. Maybe that was her."

"I'm sure. There's been no one since. You know he made a career of the Air Force. I guess that's what carried him through all these years."

"So, why doesn't he look her up?"

Samantha sighed in resignation, "This is becoming more involved than I intended. Can I trust you not to let Jim know that you know?"

"No…I won't. I like Jim…and I admire him. I wouldn't tell him. I would not jeopardize your trust." His words carried the sound of honest sincerity.

"So, why hasn't he looked her up?"

Staring straight ahead, Samantha continued the story, "Jim was devastated by their breakup and he designed his life around anything that kept him from thinking of her. My mom told me he knew she married a very wealthy man which, I'm sure, hurt him deeply. It's no wonder he forced her out of his mind. The amazing thing is he has never held any anger or hatred toward her. I am sure he has always loved her."

"OK, I get it; she's married. That's why he hasn't contacted her."

"Well, she's no longer married."

"All right then…back to my original question, why doesn't he contact her?"

"She's not available to be contacted right now."

"Wait. What? Anyone can be contacted anywhere today. I mean technology makes everyone contactable…contactable…I don't know if that's even a word, but you know what I mean."

Samantha leaned back, bracing herself with the palms of her hands on the sand. "She's out of the country in a remote area right now."

Very confused, Scott probed further, "How remote? Siberia or somewhere?"

"OK, I don't know if Jim would want you to know but I'm going to tell you. I've probably told you more than I should have but it probably wouldn't be right not to finish the story. You must never let him know I told you."

Looking her in the eye, he promised, "I want you to trust me; I won't ever tell him any of this."

A soft breeze blew several strands of hair across Samantha's face as she began. Unexpectedly, Scott gently brushed her hair aside, immediately embarrassed he had. She caught his hand and whispered, "Thank you, that was kinda nice, kind of sweet."

He grinned and nodded appreciation.

She began again, "Samantha is out of the country. She is in Russia…against her will."

A knowing look of realization overtook him, "Not that Samantha…Samantha? What's her name?"

"Marissen."

"Yeah, Samantha Marissen! She and Jim? Wow, who would have thought? I can't imagine what that's like, to know she's in danger, alone; and he still has feelings for her. That a lot to carry on your own."

Scott turned to Samantha, "I wish there was something I could do."

"There is," he heard her say, "since you're his co-pilot, you can be there when we can't. You know, just be there for him. I would appreciate that."

"I would, but I'm not officially his co-pilot; he hasn't decided yet."

"I think you will be. I know Jim's ability to judge character. I do think you will be."

* * *

Jim made good his promise and met his friends on the beach at one o' clock wearing baggy yellow trunks, an orange muscle shirt, his Air Force shades, and a fedora-shaped straw hat to everyone's delight. A delightful, relaxing afternoon passed talking, laughing, reminiscing, and re-enacting the glory days of Frisbee. Sitting beneath the palms, surrounded by friends, observing their smiles and accompanying banter, he knew the correct decision had been made.

Jim leaned forward, raised his sunglasses, and spotted Samantha and Scott approaching. Good! They would join the party in time to discuss dinner, after which everyone would be free to do whatever they wanted, although he felt certain the group would remain together. The young pair reached the circle of occupied beach chairs to a warm reception and an offering of a cool drink.

Jim stood and pointed to a couple of unused chairs, "Grab those and join us; we're going to make plans for dinner."

"Great idea, boss!"

"Hold on, I'll help." Samantha danced through the sand to drag one of the chairs to the palm-shaded patch.

Scott situated the chairs within the arc of partiers and, placing his hand on Samantha's back, guided her to the one nearest her mother. Gina immediately noticed the 'hand on the back' and had to smile; she knew well the same courtesy performed some years earlier by one Captain James Paul Gordon.

"Excellent work, Junior."

"Junior? You're calling me Junior in front of everybody?"

Jim looked over the sunglass frames and calmly stated, "You call me 'boss'; I thought I'd stick with Junior. What do ya think?"

"So, if I wanted to open it up for discussion, I'd lose, wouldn't I?"

"Yep."

"OK, boss, since we discussed the matter, Junior it is!"

Good-natured laughter rolled around the arc-of-friends until Bob asserted, "Jimbo, I think you should choose him for your co-pilot. I mean, he's already won the best comedy side-kick award."

"Possibly, but I do have one off-the-book question for him."

Scott moved to the edge of his chair and resting his elbows on his knees, faced Jim and asked, "What's that, boss?"

Jim leaned forward, "This has nothing to do with flying, but…were you able to survive your afternoon with Miss Samantha Reynolds?"

Surprised by the off-the-wall question, he responded, "I think…I suppose." Smiling, he turned and pleaded a response from Samantha, "Did I? My future may depend on your answer."

Emphatically, she answered, "Yes, you did." Moving her eyes from Scott to Jim, she repeated, "Yes, he did! He reminds me of someone, but I just can't put my finger on the name. It'll come to me eventually!"

Jim sipped his tea, set the glass down, leaned back and folded his hands, "Very good, Junior. You've proven you can handle yourself under stressful conditions, kept your wits about you. Congratulations!"

* * *

By early evening, everyone desired only a relaxing dinner after the long day's activity. The hotel restaurant, just off the main lobby and by no means the signature dining room, presented a fine meal for Jim and his guests. The final dinner, planned for the last evening of their stay, would be held at the exquisite 'Paradise View" located on the top floor of the Hotel Grandeur, hopefully accompanied by a magnificent sunset.

As the meal drew to a close, Jim rose, making known he had an important announcement. The table grew silent; all anticipating his next words. Taking an opportunity to extend the mystery, he walked slowly behind his seated guests until standing behind Scott and placed his hand on the young man's shoulder. Samantha, seated to Scott's right, glanced up to Jim and smiled; she thought she knew what was to come. Scott, with raised eyebrow and a nervous smile, eyed Jim's hand on his right shoulder. Several snickers were heard from the group who found him a welcome addition to the party. Within one day, he won the friendship of the close-knit family.

Jim cleared his throat and squeezed Scott's shoulder. "I want to let everyone know before we take off tomorrow morning, that I want nothing more than to offer the position of co-pilot to Mr. Scott Larimore with the hope of his acceptance."

For the first time that day, an air of seriousness overtook Scott. He stood and turned to Jim, "Jim…sir, I am grateful you would offer me an opportunity like this. I am honored." As he reached to shake Jim's hand, he happily declared, "I accept your offer. When do I start?"

Samantha, in joy for the young man, quickly stood and hugged him. "Congratulations, Scott!"

Not expecting such a reaction, he returned her hug. "Thank you, Samantha. Really, thank you."

Rich, Gina, Bob, Liz, Bill, Nancy, Neil, Sue, the entire group stood to applaud. Scott viewed the friendly, happy faces and understood the security Jim found with these people. Jim had been blessed with the kindness and care of a very special family.

As the group returned to their seats, Jim informed them, "I'm sorry to leave early, but we've got an early flight tomorrow, right Junior?"

"Right, boss." Scott stood to whisper, "I'd like to stay here awhile…spend some time with Samantha."

Jim smiled and leaned toward Scott. "You don't need my permission." Nodding to Samantha, he uttered, "Ask her."

"Oh, sorry. I'm not asking you; I just wanted to let you know."

Jim chuckled and patted Scott's upper arm, "Good, that's how it's done. See you in the morning."

Before Jim could step away, Scott reinforced his appreciation, "Thank you for your support. I won't let you down."

Jim replied with all sincerity, "I know. That's why."

Before leaving, Jim addressed his friends, "I'm happy we were able to spend this evening together. It meant a lot to me. I want you to know that. I do ask that we keep Samantha in our prayers. At one time, she was one of our family; in our prayers, she still is."

Shifting his attention to Scott, he warned, "Don't let her keep you out too late."

* * *

After an evening of pleasant conversation on the exotic deck overlooking the moonlit Gulf with the sound of distant waves washing ashore, Scott escorted Samantha to her room. He waited patiently as she searched for and finally found her keycard amid a myriad of items in her purse. She fidgeted nervously with the card until it slipped from her fingers and bounced off his shoe. He retrieved the card and placed it in the palm of her hand.

"Thank you." She hesitated for only a second, "Well, you certainly had an exciting evening."

"Yes, I did. I would never have guessed I'd spend the evening with you; I was already happy with our day together."

"You know I'm speaking of the co-pilot offer," she offered with a sly grin.

"Maybe, but I'm thinking of my time with you. I really enjoyed today. Thank you."

Flustered by his compliment, she replied, "I didn't know if anything would come from this morning, but I'm happy it did."

"Perhaps it went well because of our conversation on the beach. You shared some pretty personal information about Jim and Samantha. I'm surprised he spoke about her tonight."

Samantha nervously glanced around the hallway and whispered, "Remember, you promised not to say anything to Jim about—

Raising a finger to his lips, he shushed her, "I remember… and I won't. I don't want to lose your trust, ever."

Smiling, Samantha admitted, "I don't think you could."

Shuffling his feet, Scott said in a low voice, "I guess I better get going; have to leave by five in the morning. I promised your uncle I would never let him down, and I won't."

"You guys be safe. I want to see you both Tuesday evening. I…umm…I am happy you two are flying together. I know you'll make a good team."

"And now I can be there for Jim…just like you said." Chuckling, he asked, "Are you sure you didn't have something to do with his offer?"

She grinned, "No, sometimes, I believe I can see what he thinks of someone. I see he likes you, not just your abilities but your character."

Scott held her hand between his, "Sooooo…based on that,

may I assume you and I will get together Tuesday?"

"I've never known my uncle to be wrong."

*   *   *

Very early the following morning, Jim and Scott made their way across the empty hotel lobby to the waiting taxi for the commute to the airport. Nearing the door, Scott noticed a dark-haired woman asleep in one of the overstuffed chairs. Quietly, he detoured her direction and gently touched her knee. Her head popped up immediately.

"Samantha, what are you doing here?"

She sprang from the chair, "Umm, oh…I didn't mean to fall asleep. I…I wanted to say good-bye, and I wanted to tell you again how much I enjoyed yesterday. I hope you did too."

"I did, and I'm…I'm touched by you being here. Funny, I thought the same. I'm glad I got to see you this morning and tell you what a great time I had last night."

Suddenly, Jim appeared at the open door, "Junior, let's go! Samantha! What are you doing up so early?"

"Long story, Unc. Better get to the airport! See you Tuesday, Scott."

"Yes, I will see you Tuesday," he reassured her. "By the way, I like the ponytail."

SONORA COMPLEX, ARIZONA

PROMPT AS ALWAYS, Merrill Pierce awaited the arrival of the Marissen AeroSpace private Lear jet at the western end of the Sonora Complex runway. Once the aircraft touched down and came to a full stop, Ed Marissen descended the few steps and was met immediately by Merrill in a camouflaged Hummer. As he entered the vehicle, the jet already began its short tow to an also camouflaged hangar. The tightest security enveloped every aspect of the Sonora Complex.

The Complex, located within the northern expanse of the Sonora desert in Arizona, concealed the manufacture of a top-secret project financed privately by Ed Marissen. A number of employees signed on for the Sonora project: scientists, engineers, designers, machinists, computer analysts/programmers/technicians, plus all supporting personnel; accepted only after a grueling background investigation but, in the end, approved by Mr. Marissen. The finalists, those chosen for the project, were rewarded with a fine salary for the strenuous and sacrificial undertaking.

Out of necessity, many weeks at a time were required to maintain the project schedule. A full-time employee meant a repeated schedule of four weeks at Sonora followed by two weeks at home. Former Naval personnel employees compared life at

Sonora to time on an aircraft carrier, since all operations but the five-mile-long airstrip and the camouflaged assembly area/ hangar, operated below ground. The underground operations included laboratories, test chambers, simulators, manufacturing, mess halls, entertainment centers, and living quarters, which compared in size to a typical hotel suite. No one residential room was better than another, not even Ed Marissen's.

All above ground structures and access ways matched the surrounding land, making aerial sighting extremely difficult, if not impossible. Merrill Pierce followed markers along the roadway to the concealed entrance of the subterranean complex, and spiraled down, much like a garage ramp, into the massive concealed structure.

Pierce pulled the Hummer into the ventilated parking area; Ed transferred his belongings to an electric powered transporter, similar to but slightly larger than a typical golf cart. The two traversed the full length of the first underground floor to the section reserved for conference rooms. Ed notified Pierce the day before that he required a meeting with him of a highly sensitive nature, which made a good night's sleep for Merrill nearly impossible.

Inside the smaller conference room, Ed removed a thermos of hot coffee and two mugs from his bag. He poured a cup for himself and another for Merrill. After pacing across the room and back several times, Ed seated himself across from the project manager who had been nervously observing the maddening routine.

After a minute or so, Ed began, "Merrill, I wanted to meet with you this morning to explain why everyone has been busting their humps the last seven weeks. Now, this is only between you and me…The CIA has located Samantha."

"That is great news!' Pierce exclaimed. "Must be some relief for you and Rose."

"Some," Ed agreed, "but I cannot share this with everyone, not yet. The CIA and State Department want no one to know of their findings; the government wants to continue discussions with the Russians about her release and return. I try to understand their logic, but I believe if we are going to talk, at least talk tough! Otherwise, talk is only…talk! Nothing accomplished!"

Agitated, Marissen rose from the table and returned to pacing. "Therefore, it is my belief that if my daughter's safety is of no concern to them…then…then, we go in and get her out!"

A moment of heavy silence hung in the air before Merrill countered, "But Ed, can we do that? How? Isn't that like treason, or something?"

Ed swung his tall frame around and, leaning on the table, stared directly at Pierce, "I understand your reaction. It is not my intention to do this without government knowledge. I haven't figured all this out yet but, there isn't anything wrong with completing the project earlier than planned. Honestly, Merrill, I'll do nothing if you're not on board.

"Remember that Texas oil guy who rescued his crew from the Mideast after they were taken hostage for three months. That was a government approved operation. He hired his own men and with government cooperation, gained inside contacts to advise him on everything. His team was in and out with the hostages in a matter of one hour. Publicly, it was an individual operation unknown by the U.S. government. There never was any international uproar,"

"But this is Russia!"

"So what! The entire world believes they are guilty and we are the victim. Just this once, the world believes us. I say, use this to our advantage! It won't appear as aggression, just private self-defense.

"Merrill, I won't do anything without government approval. I have already floated the idea; the rest is up to them. Don't worry, I won't allow blind anger to color my decisions.

"There is absolutely nothing wrong with completing the project ahead of schedule, which is the most likely scenario. You are the project manager, Merrill. Are you OK with this?"

"As you have just defined this, Ed…yes…I am."

"Fine, Merrill, fine."

* * *

Pierce steered the battery-powered vehicle with Ed riding shotgun down the main aisle to the expansive assembly area. Marissen enjoyed the assembly of his 'babies' as he called them. Some years earlier, he promised that Marissen AeroSpace would develop and manufacture a revolutionary, futuristic product and accomplished just that with the evolution of a three-segment design.

The original project was to be a unique fighter, the XM or experimental model, advanced far beyond todays aircraft, consisting of new aerodynamics, new weaponry, and a new propulsion system.

The second phase became the development of the Orbital Vehicle, or OV, designed 50% larger than the NASA shuttle not only to increase the size of the work area, but to accommodate a crew of up to sixteen. Behind the flight deck of the OV and extending to the bay entrance were a series of crew quarters, two in each. The Orbital Vehicle, unlike any previous spacecraft, had the ability to maneuver under its own power after reentry rather than glide to a predetermined landing site.

The third phase, and most impressive, was the design of a radical new method of inserting the Orbital Vehicle into orbit. The Insertion Vehicle, or IV, could be best described as a magnificent aircraft capable of piggybacking the OV to the required altitude and speed prior to separation. Once separation occurred, the IV would return to the launch point while the OV would propel itself into orbit. The initial cost of the IV became irrelevant after the realization of the multiple insertions the craft made possible. One IV could place a minimum of three OVs in orbit within a twenty-four-hour timespan.

The uniqueness of the three craft was their sameness. Other than a difference in size and function, the three bore a striking resemblance in external design, sometimes compared to the underside of a typical clothing iron in basic shape. Not to be confused with the flying wedge of the past, the craft were of a narrower, sleeker shape, more similar to an arrowhead. Design included angled dual tailfins for added stability.

Ed frequently stopped to speak with those involved on each craft, shaking hands and swapping stories; extremely proud of those who designed and built them. However, times are different today. He still spoke with his employees but within a more subdued atmosphere and a sense of urgency. Merrill pierce had purposely leaked to the employees an explanation of the sudden timetable revision as only a small window of opportunity remained for demonstration of the three craft to government officials. If the deadline not reached, the demonstration would wait another year.

Acquiring the greatest minds and imaginations available to expand and intensify every aspect of the three craft brought about amazing discoveries:

- A powerful, innovative propulsion system by scientist Steven Hamilton
- A radical aeronautical design by scientist David Thurmond
- A far-advanced weapon system by scientist Charles Rice

- New and exciting uses of electromagnetism by scientist Mark Burchfield
- A futuristic camouflage/stealth breakthrough by marine biologist and scientist Lisa Kerrick
- Ultra-realistic XM, OV, and IV simulators by computer scientist Nathan Garcia

Ed's focus today remained the flight simulators working in unison to present a complete mission. Three crews trained to take part in an intricate, complicated flight simulation; the takeoff of the IV; the separation and entry into orbit of the piggybacked OV; and the flight of the XM-1, now locked in the belly of the OV. Ed and Merrill would view the simulations on a 24' x 12' screen. Both men nervously awaited the initiation of the test; Merrill as Project/Complex Manager, and Ed, who had set his dream of the massive project in motion years earlier.

Another independent, yet important, simulation of the total test mated the OV and IV, which under real-time conditions took place in the massive assembly/hangar area of the complex. All missions depended on the successful mating of the two craft. The large screen snapped to life when the simulated 'Super Crane', as the assembly crew named it, had just completed lowering the OV into the cradle, a large, recessed area in the upper body of the IV.

The mating crew performed all mandatory checks to ensure the OV mated in perfect alignment with the IV. Upon attaining the necessary flawless alignment, activation of an electromagnetic locking system secured the two craft as one; no possible separation could occur until deactivation of the system. A complete piggyback procedure necessitated four hours of turnaround time, a minimal amount compared to a conventional shuttle launch preparation.

Commander Mike Parker and Captain Tim Moore manned the controls of the IV simulator while Commander Kyle Webster and Captain Dan Malone operated the controls of the OV. Glen Blakely, a civilian test pilot, would fly the XM simulator.

Ed's split-screen monitor displayed views of the IV and OV flight decks simultaneously. The difference between the computer-generated views and reality were, for all practical purposes, non-existent. The countdown, no different from decades past, began with the familiar monotone drone. At the-6 second mark, Moore initiated the launch sequence for the IV causing a tremendous buildup of thrust as Parker focused on the percentage mixture of the three gases, which must be 38% - tank 1, 30% - tank 2, and 38% - tank 3. [Steve Hamilton demanded that at this point in time for security reasons, the gases remain unidentified.] The IV self-monitored the electromagnetic seal. As a mandatory failsafe, if the percentages of gas mixture measured incorrectly $^{+/-}$1%, or the electromagnetic seal failed to properly align the two craft, the mission would shut down on the launch runway.

Countdown for the simulation continued, 3...2...1... launch! The sight from the IV flight accurately displayed the vehicle exploding down the runway, while the OV monitor switched to an external, ground level side view. A computer-generated symbol signified the point necessary for a successful liftoff, and Malone hit the mark dead-on.

Marissen had determined the simulated test be handled manually; computer controlled launches, separations, and landings are great as long as the crews understand all aspects of manual override, if necessary. He grinned at the perfection of Captain Moore's liftoff, a precise 40° lift angle attained at the designated launch point at the necessary speed. So far, so good.

The split-screen gave way to an exterior side view of the

mated IV and OV as a second countdown began. The OV would not fire its thrusters until separation and clearance from the IV or severe damage could occur, both craft plummeting to earth. The sky grew darker and a curvature of the horizon became noticeable as the countdown reached zero. Commander Parker reversed polarization of the electromagnetic fields, forcing the OV from the back of the IV. Immediately, the IV nosed down, veering starboard of the OV. As designed, the separation procedure took place within a 1.8 second timeframe. Upon clearance, the OV fired its thrusters. A burst of tremendous acceleration pushed the OV to the 17,250 miles per hour required for orbital insertion. The IV, having completed its portion of the mission and began its return to Sonora Complex.

The remainder of the simulation involved the undocking of the XM-1 from the OV. Blakely initiated disengagement from the OV. A major design difference between the Marissen AeroSpace Orbital Vehicle and the NASA shuttle lay in the bay design and location. NASA designed the shuttle cargo bay located in the upper fuselage with the bay doors to open and remain open for the duration of a mission for cooling purposes. The Marissen designers positioned the bay in the underside of the OV with no need to open the bay access doors, since the camouflage/stealth skin prevented heat absorption.

From his simulator, Blakely successfully undocked, reentered the atmosphere and returned to Sonora followed by the reentry and landing of the OV. Although the flights of the three craft were a simulation, the actual test should be no different... except lives will be at stake and the loss of equipment possible. Everyone understood the risks involved when signing on for the project.

*   *   *

At the end of the grueling day, Ed flew to St. Louis to be with Rose, who remained unaware of the motive behind his trips to Sonora.

NAPLES, FLORIDA

SCOTT PACED THE floor with his pack slung over his shoulder. After an uneventful return flight, both men looked forward to the remaining three and a half days in Naples. Jim observed the young man marching back and forth across the colorful imported area rug.

"Better slow down, you may have to replace that carpet, you're going to wear it out. You got somewhere to go?"

"No, boss, I'm just anxious to get back to the beach and all."

"And all! Jim chuckled, "So, what percentage of 'and all' is she?"

"What? Who? No! I mean...OK...I don't know what I mean."

"But I know what you mean." Jim smiled at the memory, "Kinda frustrating, but still a good feeling."

Scott moved closer to Jim, shifting the pack from one shoulder to the other, "If we're on the same page, I agree. We are on the same page, aren't we?"

The elevators doors opened; a half a dozen vacationers spilled out into the lobby. Jim and Scott entered as the sole occupants for the ride up.

With a quick half-smile, Jim replied, "Junior, you are the shy one. I'm speaking of Samantha and you know it."

"Yeah, I know it. It's frustrating. I know what I think I feel, but I don't want to give in to it until I get a feeling for how she feels. I don't want to rush into anything." For the first time, Scott broke the male 'seal of disclosure', "I'm coming off a bad breakup. It's been awhile, but it made me overly cautious."

"Do you still love her?"

"What?"

The doors opened to their floor, they stepped out. Jim faced Scott, "Do you still love the woman involved in this breakup? I need to know."

"No, not at all! It's over, absolutely! I'm just a little gun shy. You know what I mean?"

Looking past Scott, then back, Jim responded, "Yeah, I'm pretty sure I do." They continued down the hall toward their room, "I'm sorry, I just don't want anyone hurt here."

Scott stopped short, "I won't hurt Samantha. I like her. She's really nice. I'm being ridiculous, I know. It feels so good having someone who seems interested."

For the first time, Jim felt as though he was offering fatherly advice, "I'm going to throw out this one reminder and that's it…and I want you to think about it. Do you know anyone who would get up at 4:30 in the morning and wait in a hotel lobby to thank you again for the evening before?" He raised an eyebrow as he finished.

Scott grinned, "You're right, and I feel good knowing you're OK with this. You are OK with this, aren't you? It's like I have three parents to impress here."

"Just two. I am protective of Samantha," Jim admitted, "but she doesn't need me to make decisions for her. And don't worry about Rich and Gina. They are regular parents of a regular daughter."

"Gotta tell you, boss. I should have talked to you earlier. I'm usually not too nervous or shy but she's different. You know, different."

"Yeah, I get it…different." Again, he understood, looking back to his own past.

Jim held the door of the suite open for Scott to enter and tossed his bag into the corner next to his bed and stretched out for a few moments rest. Scott set his pack on one chair and flopped into another.

Interesting, Scott thought. Jim says she doesn't need him to make decisions for her, yet she says she makes certain decisions based on knowing what he thinks. If only they knew what each was thinking…except, she should already know that. OK, time to stop thinking.

Jim tossed out a suggestion, "What do you say? Sit by the pool for a while? There's time before dinner."

Kicking off his shoes, Scott closed his eyes and exhaled deeply, "Sounds good, but I want to swing by Samantha's room first…to see if she's there."

"All right, ten minutes."

"Hold on, boss. I thought you said no time schedule."

"Hmm, so I did. OK, I'll be leaving in ten minutes."

Ten minutes later, Scott knocked on the Reynolds' door anticipating what he would say when she answered, except…no answer.

Jim pulled the door to their room closed and ambled toward Scott. "Not there, eh?"

Turning to join him, Scott muttered, "No, she's not."

"So, you had everything you were going to say all planned, and…bam, nothing, right?"

"OK, stop it," Scott laughed. "Sometimes you scare me, telling me what I'm thinking. It's eerie."

"At one time or another, we've all been there," Jim began, "when we have the perfect—

The soft 'ding' of the elevator interrupted Jim's words of

wisdom.

Gina, Carol, Sue, Liz, Nancy, and Samantha streamed from the elevator entangled in several conversations mixed with laughter. The instant Scott saw her, he called out, "Samantha!" and picked up his pace to greet her.

Meeting in the hall, neither was sure what to do or say until he asked, "What have you ladies been up to?"

Motioning to the others, she told of their day, "We spent half the day at the spa. It was wonderful! I had beauty treatments for everything; we all did!"

"Well, that was a waste of time!"

Everyone knew he didn't intend for his comment to come across as it did. Jim raised his eyes to the ceiling, shook his head, and half-smiled.

Once he realized how his statement must have sounded, he stammered, "No! Wait! What I…uh, what I meant…was… uh," he took a breath, "What I meant was, you are already beautiful. Anything else is unnecessary. You cannot improve on perfection."

Samantha beamed, "You smooth talking air jockey! Like I said, you're kinda cute when you do that!"

NAPLES, FLORIDA

FRIDAY EVENING, THE dinner reservation set for eight o' clock. Jim and Scott stepped from the elevator and led by the Paradise View maître de' through the restaurant and down two steps into an exclusive corner dining room offering a full southwest sunset vista. A large, round table for fourteen readied in the center of the room awaited its guests.

Scott scanned the area, taken by the vivid décor and beauty of the view from the sixteenth floor. Small wonder Jim requested everyone be prepared for a formal dinner.

"We have some time before everyone shows. I'm going to step out on the patio. Want to join me?"

"Sure, be there in a minute. I want to see if Samantha is at the elevator."

Tonight was class, no doubt; Jim had neglected nothing. Scott quietly brought one flaw to the attention of the maître de'.

"Fourteen place settings are at the table…there are thirteen of us. Jim, uh, Mr. Gordon, out on the patio, will be alone… well, not alone, he'll be with us, but…you understand?"

"Yes sir, I understand. I'll take care of it."

Scott stopped him, "Listen, I don't want to bring this to his attention, so would you wait until I distract him?"

"Yes sir, he will never know."

"Excellent, thank you." Scott slipped a bill into his hand.

Leaning against the half-wall of the patio, Jim peered over

the Gulf as he recalled the week, a well-needed respite, time to reflect and pull together his hopes, dreams, and prayers, a time for renewal. He had come to the decision: when Samantha returned home, he would contact her and ask her to forgive him for not standing up to her father so many years before. He would tell her how he still—

"Jim, sorry about that. She's not here yet." Scott's interruption snapped him back to reality.

"Oh…yeah. No problem."

"You OK?"

"I was just thinking; I'm happy this worked out so well. I think everyone enjoyed themselves."

"Don't even wonder. Your friends had a great time being together…and with you. I can tell they think a lot of you…and Samantha Marissen. Don't say anything, but…I know. Good or bad, we are very much the same."

"You're all right, Mr. Larimore. I like you. You're a good man. And I know my friends think highly of you. I don't know why, but they like you."

"One thing, I'll never have an ego problem working with you!"

"I know. That's one reason I chose you."

"As your co-pilot or…what?"

"Exactly. I know you are good at what you do…but, I also hoped you and Samantha would hit it off this week…and I think you have."

"Sooooo…you were doing little matchmaking as a sideline?"

"Yep. Hope you don't mind."

"Mind? Are you kidding? Samantha is…well, she's everything!"

Jim grinned, pleased that his plan appeared good, "Well, you can't get any more descriptive than that!" He paused before continuing, "I hope you don't mind me saying, and I'll say no more, I'm glad you told me of your previous relationship. I believe you made the right decision. Not because of Samantha, but…it was right.

"By the way, where is the 'everything' girl?"

"Funny, she wanted to meet me up here. I didn't ask why, I just said OK."

"Smart man, I believe you'll do well." Jim looked over the gulf waters, "Why don't you wait inside for her? My bet is she wants to surprise you."

"Jim, thanks for everything. And thanks for telling me I made the right decision. I thought I did; I needed to hear that from someone I trusted."

Facing Scott, he simply responded, "You're welcome. Now, go! Meet the 'everything' girl!"

As Scott entered the dining room, he noticed the maître de' had taken care of the extra place setting. Good man. He understood his admiration of Jim, his boss and his friend, wanting nothing to possibly cause him any sort of pain. He found it good to have a guy he could appreciate and emulate. Now, if only Samantha was here; he anxiously longed to be with her.

"Scott."

He turned from the table to see Samantha standing at the entrance of the room in a simple pale yellow, sleeveless dinner dress. Her dark hair swayed across her shoulders as she gracefully descended the steps and walked slowly to him.

"Samantha…you are beautiful."

Stepping to her, he gently placed his hands on her shoulders, and looking into her eyes, said, "Hi."

"Hi," she responded.

The beautiful young woman and handsome young man faced each other appearing as a couple of middle schoolers struggling for words at their first boy-girl party.

The almost romantic moment reverted to real-time with Rich's, "She looks great, doesn't she?"

Under different circumstances, that interruption could have been considered rude. At this moment, Scott considered it a thankful diversion.

"Yes, sir. Yes, she does!"

Gina hugged her daughter as she confided to Scott, "We went shopping this afternoon. Samantha wanted something nicer than what she brought with her; said she wanted to look pretty for you tonight."

"Mother!"

Scott took Samantha's hand and made their way to their table along with her mom and dad. Jim entered from the patio as his remaining guests arrived en masse. The formal finale had begun.

Multiple conversations, jokes, and laughter flowed throughout the room; sounds that filled Jim's heart with joy. His Air Force career had filled his life with adventure but stability and consistency rose in priority. After the many years of loving care and support, he finally had the opportunity to reciprocate. Bob and Liz, Ted and Carol, Neil and Sue, Bill and Nancy, Rich and Gina, and now, he hoped, Scott and Samantha blended into one family, in one place, at one time.

Glancing toward the door, Jim noticed the owners of the hotel who had made the week possible, and motioned for them to join him. The three met near the windows, clasped hands, and laughed over comments unheard by the others.

The distinguished man stepped to the table, cleared his throat, and announced, "Excuse me, may I have your attention. I ask that you all be seated. I have two or three things I would like to say before you begin your meal."

The couples took their seats as the gentleman continued, "Good evening. My name is Joseph Morelli and I want to thank you for being here tonight. The beautiful woman next to Mr. Gordon is my wife, Shari. It is my pleasure to welcome you to our restaurant this evening. I must tell you that Mr. Gordon… Jim, always speaks very highly of you and, now, I understand why. I hope you have enjoyed your week with us." He turned to Jim, "Everything has met your expectations?"

"You have exceeded them, Joe. Thank you!"

"You see, Shari and I travel between our hotels around the country and SBA respects our wishes that Mr. Gordon be our pilot of choice. Obviously, he is a good pilot but, more than that, he's just…a nice guy. Several months ago, we expressed our wish to do something for him but he turned down the offer, in a nice way, of course."

Morelli smiled as he added, "Shari usually gets her way, and so, here you are."

The group laughed at his line.

Joseph slowly circled the table until reaching Scott, "I do want to welcome Mr. Larimore, a fine addition. He has the opportunity to learn from one of the best."

Scott stood to shake his hand. "Thank you, sir."

Morelli continued, "Am I to assume this lovely young lady is Samantha?"

Surprised and flustered, she turned in her chair, "Yes…yes I am."

"Well, Mr. Larimore…Scott, requested a small surprise for you this evening as a 'thank you' for the enjoyable week he has spent with you."

With that, he motioned to a waiter near the entrance to the room who in turn signaled another. The young lady entered bearing a narrow crystal vase holding two roses, one open, one not, and placed it before Samantha. She hadn't a clue as to what to say.

"Let me explain the meaning of the full-bloom and the tight-bud rose. The full-bloom represents the week already spent together; the tight-bud symbolizes time yet to share."

"Mr. Larimore, it's been a pleasure." He shook his hand once more. "And, Miss Reynolds, I hope you enjoy Scott's gift."

She smiled broadly, 'Oh, my gosh, yes, I will…I do!"

"Good!" Morelli declared, "Then, let's continue the evening!"

As Scott sat down, Samantha leaned toward him and whispered, "I can't tell you what this means to me. I'm glad you're such a romantic; what a pleasant surprise." He placed his arm around her as they responded to a combination of compliments and friendly harassment from around the table.

Gina smiled, fully aware of Samantha's enjoyment of the moment and possible future relationship with Scott. During their week together, she and Rich had come to appreciate, no, like the young man; even joking if any man could be worthy of their daughter, it seemed he could. Again, she laughed to herself thinking of the similarities between Scott and her daughter and Jim and his Samantha.

Rich took Gina's hand, expressing, "You know, Hon, Jim is my best friend…and now I may have to put up with his clone. What have I done to deserve this?"

"I heard that! Should I take that as a compliment?" Jim paused to hug Gina as he made way to his seat between them and Samantha and Scott.

The Morelli's promised an elegant meal for his friends and followed through exquisitely. Soft background music, excellent cuisine, along with the most courteous service, rendered an almost fairy tale evening. Shari paused the dinner for a magnificent sunset viewing from the patio before continuing with the main course. Time well-spent in conversation, stories of the past and a few present, and just a general feeling of true friendship.

As the waiters served the desserts, Jim tapped his glass and stood looking over the table. "I would like to make a toast: To friends, the greatest friends a man could have. I pray we continue to be blessed with one another…" His voice faltered, "I…ahem…I…also pray for the safe return of Samantha…that she may find she was never forgotten."

Everyone agreed in a moment of silent remembrance and their own prayers for a lost friend.   As Jim sat, Bob rose and stood behind him, "I, also, would like to say something.

"Jim, speaking for all of us…and don't interrupt me. If you do, I'll take you down. No brag, just fact."

Bob grinned and continued, "I want to be the one to express this, since I've given you the most grief over the years, you know…Flash…jet jockey…air jockey…Roger Ramjet, and on and on."

Jim chuckled and muttered, "Oh, yeah, I know."

"We want to thank you for your generosity. You speak of us as good friends. Well, you are a good friend, always have been and we deeply appreciate your friendship. And…I want to add; some years ago, you made a statement to the effect of—once a man loses his integrity, it can never be restored. Not true! You are a good Christian man, a man of the highest integrity, and, whether you realize it or not, you've always been there for us; the many times one of us needed the hand of a friend…you were there. We are happy and proud to call you our friend."

"Well said, Bob! Yes, yes!" Agreement saturated the table of friends, of family.

Before Bob returned to his seat, he declared, "She will be back, Jim," and jokingly added, "Even if you have to go get her!"

Light conversation and laughter returned to the table, sometimes rapid-fire, other times a lob awaiting a smash, as the delightful evening of friendship, food, and fun carried on. Suddenly. Mrs. Morelli stepped quickly to Jim's side and whispered that Joe needed to speak with him, he was waiting near the elevator. Jim excused himself and followed her out of the room. All table talk ceased as the others wondered what happened. Did anyone overhear what was said?

No one had any idea. Better to simply wait and learn the details from Jim. With the lack of conversation, the sounds of the outer dining room took precedence—other conversations, silverware on china, the tinkling of ice cubes—all easily heard.

A somber Jim reentered the private room to his place and leaned forward on the back of his chair.

Gina asked quietly, "What is it, Jim?"

He straightened up, "Joe...Mr. Morelli is aware of my... our concern for Samantha and just informed me the networks are reporting two, maybe three explosions have occurred in Moscow, possibly in one of the business districts. It's early morning there. No report on the number of casualties yet. Russia's security service is trying to keep a tight lid on this. They're placing the blame on those who want to overthrow the current regime, which could put Samantha in harm's way."

OUTSIDE ST. PETERSBURG, RUSSIA

NIKOLAI KNOCKED AND waited several seconds before entering the room, Samantha's cell, and settled on the edge of his cot rubbing his face. Something troubled him and she wondered what…and why? She noticed, for the first time, he carried a sidearm. What had changed?

"Nik, what's wrong? You're carrying a gun; you're concerned about something. I can tell. Something is wrong. What?"

He looked up, exhaled deeply, and explained, "Sam, they want to move. Too much danger to keep here. Time to move…soon."

"Why? I am a prisoner in your country. What can I do? What can anyone do?" Samantha did not understand. "And why do you have a gun?'

Nikolai answered as best he could, "Under…ground bring down government to have freedom. In Kitai-Gorod, rebels use four bombs…three days past."

She stared wide-eyed, puzzled. "What is Kitai-Gorod?"

"Is business…center, by Red Square. Shops, banks, and all there."

"Was anyone hurt?"

"Seventy-two hurt…112 dead."

"Oh, Nik, I'm so sorry. That's horrible."

"They think rebels…use you…make disorder."

"Why? How would I figure into this mess?"

"I do not know. Make world see Russia in bad way. If you hurt…government blamed."

Moving to the center of the small room, she pleaded, "What do you mean? What could happen to me?"

Nikolai stepped to her to confide, "Nothing happen; I protect. Nothing to happen."

Samantha moved to the chair and quietly asked, "Where would they move me? When?"

"Plan is Moscow…in month for trial."

"Trial? For what? I have confessed to nothing, and I will not confess to something I did not do! I've done nothing against your country! Nikolai, you must believe me!"

For some reason, perhaps Nikolai's kindness and protection, caused her to think the ordeal near an end. This turn of events flooded her mind with overwhelming fear.

Although aware of reports concerning evidence and captured conspirators' confessions to be used against her, Nikolai chose to remain silent. Enough had been said.

Samantha fell on the bed facing the wall as she prayed, "Where are you, Lord? Why this? Please help me, I've never felt so alone. My life has been a living hell ever since I abandoned James so long ago. I'm so sorry I keep returning to him; he was the last good experience in my life…and, of course, you are with me, Lord. I turn all this over to you. Please…help me."

She devoted a lengthy period in deep, personal prayer, praying for strength, patience, and a peace she thought impossible. Only her Lord could supply that peace. "Fear not, for I am with you always," words she repeated as a source of consolation.

Near the end of her prayer, she thought of her family, her mom and dad, her sister and brother, and how much she still missed them. They were wonderful, she remembered. Barely middle-class, they were a happy, caring family who loved the Lord.

Searching for quiet memories, Samantha smiled to herself, recalling a time she became very upset with James, disappointed he had to reschedule his leave due to a sudden reassignment of a practice mission. She was certain he had something to do with someone else…and told him. He could not believe she would think he would do that to her and told her if that's what she thought, then there was nothing he could do or say. She did not hear from him for two weeks; he was so hurt. She found then how much she loved him and wanted to be with him. She knew she had to call him. She even thought of driving to Mississippi to apologize. Before she could, he called to tell her how sorry he was for what he said and that the last two weeks made him realize just how much he wanted to see her. Samantha could not allow him to take the blame; she told him the whole mess was her fault, her stupid insecurity!

"And it was my foolish insecurity that caused me to lose him forever. Forgive me, Lord, for hurting the man I loved. My prayer for him is…I hope he is happy, very happy with someone he truly loves, and I pray she loves him and knows how good a man he is."

Nikolai broke the silence; he could no longer bear to see her hurting, "Sam, I believe you not spy. Not to worry…I believe you."

Samantha rolled over and looked to him as tears filled her eyes. She turned and buried her face in her arms. He heard her sobs and waited. Shortly, she pulled herself together, sat up on the edge of the bed and wiped her tears with her hands. Relieved to hear Nikolai believed her, she knew this was from God; He heard and answered her prayer for strength, patience, and peace.

At least she could rest in the knowledge Nikolai knew the truth. She thanked God for His gracious response.

That evening, as they ate their usual meal, Nikolai took note of her quiet mood and inquired, "What is wrong, Sam?"

Without looking up, she responded, "You have been very kind and I appreciate your concern." Hesitating a moment, she continued, "Nik, I have been held here for three months and I've not been able to read my, my…Bible. I miss reading my Bible. Do you know what they've done with my Bible? It means a lot to me in so many ways. It brought me peace and helped me pray through difficult times."

Nikolai fidgeted slightly, as if nervous with what he was about to ask. "Are you…umm, a believer? Is that it? A believer?"

"Nik, you are getting much better with your English. I suppose talking every day has helped. Thanks for trying so hard.

"Am I a believer? Yes, I am. I believe in Jesus Christ and what He has done for me that I would never be able to do on my own. Are you?" She hoped for a positive response.

"No…no, I am not. I do not say 'no' only. I do not know."

Samantha pressed on, "What do you mean?"

"I know one who tells me of Jesus. I hear her. She is good. She asks me to take Jesus. She asks me to…to pray with her."

Almost pleading, she declared, "Oh, Nik, you must listen to her. You must believe. You must give your life to Him; make Jesus your Lord and Savior. His promise is eternal life for those who believe."

"You sound like her," he mused. "She is good teacher."

Picking up on something in his voice, she probed, "So, a she. Do you have someone special?"

Nikolai appeared to blush when he responded 'yes' to Samantha's pointed inquiry.

"Tell me about her. What's her name? When did you meet?

How long have you known her?" The questions rolled off her tongue rapid fire.

He grinned, then looked at the floor, embarrassed.

"Her name is Anechka."

"That is a beautiful name."

Nikolai wanted to tell more. "She is like you, only young."

Samantha looked straight at him with a grin.

He attempted to clarify his statement, "No, I mean you look like her, only old."

She laughed at his muddled attempt. She actually laughed. And so did he, warily.

He continued, "Her hair is brown…but brown eyes. She is little shorter than you. And, she is beautiful as you."

Now, Samantha blushed. Many, many years had passed since she last heard a compliment.

"How long have you known her? How did you meet?"

"Two years. Two years, now. We meet at wedding party. We…not know till after party."

"What did you not know?" The irony of his story tugged at her heart and immediately put aside her memories.

Appearing as a schoolboy, he shyly answered, "We like each other."

"And now?" she pressed. "How do you feel about her now?"

Embarrassed by the question, he hemmed and hawed, finally mumbling, "I do not know."

"What? You do not know?" Samantha asked straight out, "Do you love her?"

Nikolai hung his head and sighed deeply. Raising his eyes to her, he stated, "I do…much!"

Without hesitation, she asked, "Have you told her?"

"No, I do not know how."

"Nik, look at me." Now, she had his full attention. "You

simply tell her what's in your heart."

"I want that…but not to see her till later."

Suddenly, Samantha understood he meant after her trial. The revelation snapped her back to reality.

With a deep longing for the same, she advised him, "When you do see her, tell her how much you love her…and she will tell you of her love for you."

Nikolai asked, "How do you know?"

"Because you're a military man. She waits for you every time you're gone, right?"

"Da…yes!"

"Well, there you go! No woman will wait five minutes for a man she does not love." She paused several seconds before adding, "If you love each other, don't deny it, and then, don't ever let go. Don't allow anyone to interfere with your love and your lives. If you love Anechka, cherish her forever. Hold her, love her, care for her. You marry that young lady! Do you hear me?"

He smiled at her lecture, "Yes, I hear."

Nikolai wondered briefly, then questioned Samantha, "Do you love some…man?"

A completely unexpected question, yet she answered honestly, softly, "Yes…I do."

Concerned, Nik simply said, "He must worry now."

"No, I don't think so."

"But…he does not love you?"

Downcast, Samantha whispered, "He did, but I hurt him very much."

Nikolai grimaced, regretting his question.

July 29, Wednesday, Chesterfield Airport

CHESTERFIELD, MISSOURI

JIM AND SCOTT arrived early at Chesterfield Airport, a muggy morning with heavy fog rolling low across the river bottoms. Experience told Jim shortly after sunrise, the fog would burn off quickly, and visibility return to normal. Normal, he laughed. Nothing about his life these days could be described as normal.

Thankfully, his new co-pilot, Scott, bunked temporarily at Jim's cabin until he could complete his move from Boise, Idaho. The arrangement worked well: Jim kept up with the latest scoop on his niece, Samantha, and he could monitor the Larimore/Reynolds relationship. He also found it necessary, and a relief, to share the story of Samantha Marissen with Scott. Carrying his concern for her alone had placed a heavy load on his shoulders, especially now that violence raised its ugly face in the Moscow bombings. A willing Scott, now a friend, took a portion of the load by simply listening.

Carl Thompson, a flight controller and acquaintance of Jim's, routinely stopped in the pilot's lounge for coffee prior to his shift and today was no different. Oh, for a cup of coffee, Jim thought as he entered the lounge. Carl ambled to the coffee urn the same moment as Jim and Scott.

"Jim, who's the new guy?"

"Carl, this is Scott Larimore, my co-pilot. Scott, Carl Thompson."

"Nice to meet you, Carl."

"Yeah. Jim, I just heard that Samantha Marissen spy chick and you had a fling some years back. Did I hear right?"

Attempting to contain the shock of his question, Jim demanded, "Where did you hear that?"

"Are you kidding? It's been all over the news this morning! Where have you been? You're gonna be a celebrity!"

How do you explain that you were reading the Bible and in prayer before leaving home and talking business with your co-pilot on the ride to the airport. Jim wished he had heard this before coming in.

"C'mon, Carl, you know you can't put much stock in that."

"Whether you can or not, is it true?" Carl wasn't about to let it go.

Jim attempted a simple response, "Yeah, I knew her a long time ago, but not much more than that."

"Really? How was it, dating the daughter of one of the richest guys in the country."

"Look, Carl, it was no big deal, just a few dates, nothing more. There's nothing to it."

Carl would not halt his pursuit, "Jim, you know St. Louis. Everybody knows everybody's business. These news people will dig for anything to keep a story going, and now, they'll be looking for you…real soon."

Great, thought Jim, just what I need! What do I do now?

Carl continued to make a nuisance of himself, "So, did you ever think you would date a future international spy? That's gotta be good for the ego, man. At least, she was doing it for our side. Hey, was she doing it for you?"

That comment did it. Scott stepped between Carl and Jim, forcing Carl to stagger back, splashing hot coffee on his hand and pants. "Hey! What the—? Are you crazy, man?"

"Look, Carl," Scott stated slowly and succinctly, "I don't know you, but I think you probably crossed the line with that last statement, so I suggest you back off and shut up."

"What? Your boss can't take care of himself?"

"Oh, I know he can." Scott chuckled. "I just saved you a load of embarrassment. You're lucky that's only coffee on your pants."

Carl ached with anger, but thought better and hesitantly slinked back to his chair, glancing toward Scott several times as he did.

* * *

Jim stepped outside the lounge, took a sip of coffee, and slowly strolled around the northern wall, noting the fog had begun to lift. Their flight would be only a bit late departing.

Scott caught up with him, "Sorry, boss. I know I shouldn't have done that, but that little weasel just—

"That's OK, he is a weasel…and it was funny. Now, I just have to figure out what to do. This news media stuff could get sticky."

Reaching in his jacket pocket, Jim pulled out his cell phone and punched in a number. Although the hour was early, he felt the call necessary. The line rang only once before an answer.

"Good morning, Marissen residence. How may I help you?"

Jim guessed it was Aaron or Eric, or whoever. Geez, doesn't that guy ever sleep?

"Eric?" he guessed. "This is Jim Gordon. May I speak with Mrs. Marissen?"

"I believe she is unavailable at this time, sir."

"This is very important, Eric. I think Mrs. Marissen would be more upset if you didn't let her know I called."

"One moment, sir."

Scott attempted to remain nonchalant realizing Jim had just called Samantha Marissen's mother. *What other surprises does this guy have up his sleeve?*

Several minutes passed before Jim heard Rose's groggy response, "Jim, I got up as quick as I could. Is something wrong? Did something happen in Russia again?"

"No, no. Nothing has happened over there." He paused a moment, thinking, perhaps, he shouldn't have called. Suddenly, his concern seemed unimportant.

"I'm sorry to bother you with this, but it's possible the news media are ready to jump on a story about Samantha and me. You know I have no problem admitting it, but it would just turn into a feeding frenzy for the sharks…a completely unimportant story…and completely irrelevant at this time.

"The same thing happened with her ex-husband, except he used it to bury her reputation. More importantly, I'm afraid they'll come after you again."

"What can I do, Jim?" Now wide-awake, Rose readied herself for action.

"I'm flying to Florida this morning; I'll be back tomorrow night. If this does turn out to be another media circus…well, to stop it, maybe you could have your spokesperson put out a statement denying that I was ever anyone important to Samantha or your family. I think that might stop this mess before it begins…coming from you."

"I can, but you know that wouldn't be true. You are very important to me…to us. But, I'll do it right away. Thank you for the warning."

"No problem. By the way, how is Mr. Marissen doing?"

"He's back at Sonora…in Arizona, something about completing a major project. It's good for him, but I wish he was here."

"Tell you what. When I get back, you, Samantha, and I will get together again."

"Oh, Jim, that sounds so good. I'll send a car for you this time. You won't have to worry about the reporters and all."

"Excellent! Looking forward to seeing you again." The plans raised his spirits, and he hoped hers also.

"All right, Jim. You be careful." Rose wanted to say she loved him as her own son, but wanted to tell him face-to-face.

OUTSIDE ST. PETERSBURG

"NIK, WHAT'S GOING on out there?" The sudden commotion scared Samantha from the bed.

Slowly, Nikolai raised himself from his cot, unaware anything had happened. He froze, realizing Samantha had warned him; he should have warned her. If something had happened to her at that moment, he would have failed in his duty.

He leapt from the cot, pulled on his boots, and grabbed his gun. Samantha, always in a bright colored jumpsuit, stood fearfully in the center of the room.

"What's happening? Don't let them take me! Please! Don't!"

Nikolai wondered how she could know if this was the time for her move; he had not been informed of any change in plan. Maybe this was not the move. But, what then? Drawing the gun from its holster, he motioned for her to get behind him. Terrified, she followed his directions, awed by his composure. Unknown to Samantha, his calmness only a front. Inside, his gut churned and his mind raced for an answer to, "What would he do should the wrong person come through the door?"

The longer he and Samantha waited for the door to open, the greater the intensity of their fear. Carefully, he backed the two of them into the bathroom where he figured to have at least another second to make that decision.

A shout came in Russian, "Nikolai! We are making the

transfer tonight…now!"

He shouted back, "We are coming!"

Returning the weapon to its holster, he grabbed his canvas bag, then Samantha's hand to lead to lead her through the door. She resisted his pull. He saw the terror in her eyes. Quickly, he leaned toward her and whispered, "I let nothing happen."

Nikolai remained in front of Samantha as a shield between the soldiers and her, as they descended a steep stairway. His action not correct procedure, but he would protect her any way necessary.

For the first time in her three-month imprisonment, Samantha saw her 'cell' to be an upstairs room in what appeared to be an old two-family apartment building. Any sound heard must have been muffled Russian conversation; any food prepared elsewhere.

At the bottom of the steps stood a tall, thin, middle-aged, gray-haired man twirling a set of handcuffs for her transfer to the new location. After cuffing both wrists tightly, he slipped a blindfold over her eyes, but before he did, Nikolai recognized the fear in her eyes as she sobbed, "No, no. Please, no."

Another soldier forced her, stumbling and tripping, into the dark. Nikolai followed the small contingent to a van, questioning himself, "What can I do? What now?"

In desperation, with a voice of authority, Nikolai sternly ordered, "Stop! I will stay with the prisoner during the transfer. She is my responsibility and I will see this through. I want nothing to happen on my watch. All has been good; no need for mistakes now!"

He climbed into the back of the old van and continued, "Remove the cuff from her right wrist and cuff my left. Now, she cannot run and I still have access to my weapon!" Sarcastically, he added, "See how it should be done? This reprimand remains here. Do not forget what I taught you tonight!

"Now, give me the key! It is time to depart!"

Though terrified, Samantha still wondered just how much authority Nikolai did have. At least he would remain with her; at least she would not be alone. The rear doors slammed shut and the van lurched forward.

He and Samantha had the unpleasant opportunity to make the trip on a metal bench bolted to the sidewall of the van. The stiff shocks provided a rough ride; seemed most of the trip covered older roads at best. Nikolai tightened a strap across their laps as a seatbelt, hoping to hold them in place.

After a short time, he reached behind her head to loosen the blindfold; she had to reach back with him due to the handcuffs. The knot tight but he managed to untie the cloth and lay it to the side.

In the dimly lit interior, he could barely make out her face as she sat in silence staring at the opposite side, a single tear ran down her cheek.

Nikolai broke the silence, "Sam, I will not let harm be. You must trust."

Samantha turned to him, "Nikolai, who are you? Please answer me. You protect me. You make sure I have food, clothing, and, well, my basic needs. I am a prisoner, but you treat me like a…a friend. Why?"

"Do not forget, Sam. I believe you not…umm…guilty. You not prisoner. I am to guard."

"Nik…God has blessed me with your protection. I don't know where I'd be without your protection." Wiping away tears with her free hand, she continued, "You remind me of someone I knew, someone who made me see life for what it was…and what it should be."

Nikolai smiled the slightest. "Who?"

"Oh, he was…I'm sorry, it's not important…not anymore."

Several quiet, rough miles later, Samantha asked, "Where are they taking me?"

Nikolai stared ahead, not pleased with his answer, "I…I do not know."

CLANDESTINE

"NEITHER OF US will refer to the other by name…ever! Got that?"

"Yes, but why?"

"You have a serious gambling problem, am I right?"

"Uhh…yeah, I suppose."

"Your wife will leave you if you don't quit, right?"

"Yes, but—

"No buts! You would lose your kids in the process?"

"Probably…yeah, I would."

"You owe a lot of money, don't you?"

"Yes."

"Can you pay off your debts?"

"No."

"How would you like to have it all paid off?"

"Sure, but how? Why?"

"How about one favor for another?"

"Like what?"

"If you talk, I can and will ruin you. If you accept my offer, you will never have another financial problem, ever. You can turn this down, but you talk and your family will suffer."

"I'm listening."

"You're working on a project at Sonora, right?"

"Yes…I am. But how do you know?"

"I don't want that fighter to succeed, the XM project."

"What are you saying? You…you want me to sabotage the project?"

"Yes."

"But there is much more to it than just the fighter."

"If one-third fails, it all fails."

"So, you know the project?"

"Are you interested?"

"How much are we talking?"

"Enough to take care of your debts and your family for a good while. I'll take care of everything. You just spend it."

"I'm not sure—

"You in or out?"

"I have to decide right now?"

"Now!"

"I…I have no choice, do I? I'm going to lose everything, my wife, my kids, everything. Yeah, I'm in. I have to. When does this have to be done?"

"As soon as possible! Nothing until the job is complete, and remember, keep your mouth shut!"

SONORA COMPLEX, ARIZONA

MERRILL PIERCE CONTEMPLATED why another early morning meeting and more so, why the secrecy? Marissen wanted the meeting held in yet another conference room, much smaller and located in the far northeast corner of the complex, two levels below ground. Pierce hoped it wasn't that "Let's go in and get her out" foolishness again. Out of breath, he entered the small room and found Ed already seated at the end of the table. Four others were seated that he did not immediately recognize.

"Come in, Merrill, come in! Sorry to make you cover so much ground this morning, but we have some important visitors."

The two men in uniform sat to Marissen's left and two suits to his right. Pierce thought the two suits appeared familiar. As he stepped up to the small group, he realized just who the suits were just as Ed began the introductions.

"Gentlemen, this is our project manager, Merrill Pierce. He runs the whole show; everything happens because he makes it happen. Merrill, these two men are Ralph Atkins, Secretary of State, and Tom Gagnepaign, the Secretary of Defense. The men across the table are General Robert Townsend and General Gary Forsythe, United States Air Force."

Pierce maneuvered around the table, greeting each with his proper title.

"Have a seat, Merrill. We're here to discuss the Sonora Project and I think General Townsend would like to say something before we begin. General."

As Marissen sat, the General rose to begin. "Thanks, Ed, for holding this meeting on such short notice." Turning his attention to Merrill, he continued, Mr. Pierce, we've requested a confidential viewing of your Insertion Vehicle, Orbital Vehicle, and the XM Fighter simulator flights as a preliminary step towrd possible government contracts in defense and space exploration. I cannot express how impressed everyone is, from the President on down. You are to be commended for your management of the project."

A proud moment, indeed, for Merrill Pierce, the proudest of his career, and he recognized none of this would be possible if not for the brilliant and preservering members of his team, every one of them. Pierce, in his usual soft-spoken demeanor, informed the four guests of the importance of every person involved.

Townsend spoke again, "Ed, your business has absorbed the research and development costs for every aspect of this project. The only job left for us is to view a live test of the three craft once the simulation flights have been accomplished today.

"It is my understanding that an actual test of the IV, OV, and XM is scheduled for this Wednesday. We would like to remain here until then if all goes well today."

Marissen leaned forward, hands folded. "That will be fine, sir, but I must point out there is nothing fancy here; all quarters are identical in size and function. He wanted them to understand there would be no preferential treatment.

Gagnepaign spoke up, "Mr. Marissen, I don't see a problem with that. I did a tour on an aircraft carrier; I'm sure this will be fine."

"Leave it to the Secretary of Defense to be Navy,"

joked Townsend.

Following an hour or so discussing the results of the most recent simulation tests, the meeting broke for a coffee refill and another Danish or donut. After small talk about nothing in particular, General Townsend suggested the meeting resume. Everyone sat but the General.

"Gentlemen, let's begin our discussion of the real reason we are here."

Pierce's ears perked up with that statement.

Townsend continued as he paced alongside the table. "We are aware of the Samantha Marissen situation. It now appears tensions between the United States and Russia have risen to a very dangerous point. Ralph, would you explain what is going on with the Russians?"

Secretary of State Atkins stood to address the group. "The situation in Russia, we believe, is at the boiling point. There are two distinct factions: Those who, in the beginning, campaigned to maintain the status quo but quickly showed themselves as a group wanting a return to the glory days of the U.S.S.R. and communism. Then, there are those who want to overthrow this current government in the hope of establishing a true democracy.

"Those for democracy view the Marissen incident as a means of discrediting the government in the eyes of the world to increase their chance for revolt. The United States has not taken a position one way or the other, nor will we. That's a tough decision but we must let those cards fall where they may.

"We view the current government as highly unstable and dangerous. Members of their own party have no idea whom they can trust. Any information we have been able to gather, points to the Kitai-Gorod bombings being carried out by the government, not the rebels, to lay blame on the rebels and discredit them. This and the whole spy situation is causing such internal strife that we believe Miss Marissen is in very grave danger. Her life is in the hands of a grossly irresponsible and untested group. We truly don't know what their next move might be. I'm sorry, Ed, to be so blunt about her situation, but we must face reality in order to make sound decisions.

"Now, we do know her location thanks to an imbedded informant and that there are no immediate plans to move her again after her relocation several nights ago. They are pushing forward plans for a trial, which we fear will be held before the Constitutional Court of the Russian Federation, but, unfortunately, influenced by the President of the Russian Federation. Can everyone see where this is heading?"

Secretary of Defense Gagnepaign rose to speak. "As stated before, The United States will not take one side or the other, nor will we take aggressive action against the Federation… however, a suggestion was voiced several weeks ago regarding an independent force to slip in, find, and bring Miss Marissen home. After much deliberation, it has been determined the independent force will be one man. The remainder of the group would be Russian revolutionaries working from the inside to free her."

Merrill had an inclination the Secretary of Defense would turn to this course of action, but this was also the first he had heard of the internal strife going on within the Federation. His mind searched for a logical solution to the dilemma but found none. There would be no easy way. The United States could not do nothing and hope for the best. Was the only answer to send a rescue mission…of one man?

Pierce heard Gagnepaign continue, "We have reached the point of frustration; we cannot allow the Russian Federation to drag Miss Marissen through a trial, a farce at best, find her guilty, and imprison her for a crime she did not commit.

We cannot!

"All this, in a vain attempt to free their very guilty spies. A simple swap cannot be allowed until we know for certain the amount of damage done…and that may take a very long time. How these men got as far as they did is mind-boggling. We're not sure how they even accomplished it. At least, the operation was broken before any data was lost…we think. We keep them here and the data remains here…forever, if necessary.

"As far as everyone at Sonora is concerned, we are here to witness the simulator testing today and the actual test flights Wednesday to determine if the government would be interested in a bold, futuristic move in defense and space exploration. No one need know differently. What happens after that will be known by a very select few.

"Therefore, Mr. Marissen, the mission to get your daughter out of Russia rests solely on the results of today and Wednesday."

Gagnepaign addressed Merrill, "Mr. Pierce, what are your thoughts on this?"

Ed watched Merrill with anticipation, aware of Pierce's earlier objections.

Merrill cleared his throat, searching for the right words. "I have heard reports this morning much graver than I knew of Samantha's captivity. I believe I am a peaceful man…but this cannot be allowed to continue and must be done while we know where she is, the quicker, the better. I will back this with everything I've got."

"Thank you, Mr. Pierce. With your record, I feel certain we're looking at a good chance for success. What do you say we get a tour of this place?"

Five of the most prominent men in the country prepared to exit the room along with Merrill Pierce. Ed approached him from behind and placed his hand on Merrill's shoulder,

"Thanks for your support. This couldn't be done without you."

"I just didn't know the depth of what is going on. I honestly thought this could blow over, you know?"

Ed sighed, "We were all hoping for that. I truly appreciate your being on board."

WASHINGTON, MISSOURI

SAMANTHA RECLINED IN Jim's front porch rocker, lazily gazing over the distant hills humming an old childhood song, while Scott sat on the step leaning against a support post, one knee raised. Since she, Scott, and Jim were to visit Rose, Samantha stayed the night to simplify logistics. As promised, Rose dispatched a car to pick up the weary troop, which had spent the last evening taking advantage of Jim's telescope viewing of the moon and a few of the planets and stars. Samantha envied, at times like last night, Jim's seclusion: the peace, the quiet, and the night sky.

Her overnight stay evolved into something a bit more complicated than before. Normally, when she stayed she slept on the couch, but not while Scott shared quarters with Jim. Samantha, or Queen Sam, as she became known the previous evening, inherited the bedroom by default. Scott took the couch and Jim, the recliner.

Suddenly, the grinding of spinning tires straining to reach the peak of the steep gravel grade interrupted her humming. She trotted down the slope stopping at the driver's window.

The tinted window lowered; the driver inquired in an uncertain tone, "Is this the Gordon residence?"

Samantha laughed, "Residence may be a bit extreme but 'a Gordon' does live here. Wait here, we'll come to you."

Walking briskly toward the cabin, she called Jim, then

prompted Scott, "You ready?"

"Yeah, but are you sure you want me to go with you guys?"

Jim overheard Scott as he closed the cabin door. "Yeah, I want you to go. Like it or not, you're a part of this now."

Placing his hand on Samantha's shoulder, he ventured, "And I believe Queen Sam would appreciate your attendance."

Striking a royal pose, she acknowledged, "Yes, the Queen does not suffer fools."

"All right then, lead on m'lady."

Several steps from the car, Jim laughed, "Poor guy probably wonders, who could live out here? May even think I'm a real country boy. Just think, he may think the same about you!"

"But," Samantha retorted, "maybe he thinks you're with me and you have some class!"

How many times had Jim figured she inherited her father's off-the-wall humor? Somehow, she managed to keep him occupied, especially during this difficult time, in conversation or some activity, like the stargazing of the night before. He reached for the front car door handle knowing the young couple would rather sit together, although he had considered sitting in the rear only to see their reaction.

The driver experienced some difficulty backing down the hill, the car repeatedly sliding on the loose gravel. Taking a steep downhill curve on gravel in reverse can become a hair-raising adventure.

Once on the paved road, Jim remarked, "If we do this again, we'll meet you down here!"

The driver smiled, "Sounds good to me!"

Sitting in the back seat, Samantha and Scott agreed the tinted windows, crushed velvet upholstery, and plush carpeting positively added to the already deluxe ride. Samantha made an intentionally quiet comment regarding the fastidiousness of automobile air-conditioning in this current day and age.

Jim's only recourse, "Hey! I like my jeep. It's not like I have somewhere classy to go."

Samantha quickly inquired, "What about your business flights? What about then?"

"Usually, it's early morning when I leave for those. If not, I spend the night before at a hotel near the airport. Cheaper than a car."

Dismayed, she admitted, "You never told me that. Never mind; doesn't matter, you're still impossible. Sometimes I think you keep that jeep just to irritate me!"

"And if I got rid of it, you would have nothing to complain about."

Scott, without hesitation, interjected, "Nothing?"

The conversation reminded Jim of the verbal sparring with his Samantha and how, many times, the banter would turn an ordinary discussion into something humorous, especially regarding a completely unimportant matter. At times, they appeared to have a routine to perform for their friends, who found their act entertaining. He closed his eyes and thought of the comfort and the…never mind, too many years since then.

Gazing at the passing scenery, Samantha wondered aloud, "Everything is going so badly over there right now, with those bombings and protests. Mrs. Marissen has to be in a lot of pain, you know, emotional pain, worrying about her daughter. I wonder what's happening with Samantha right now. What time is it there now?"

Jim figured, "I think they're either eight or nine hours ahead of us, pretty sure. So, it's evening already."

He then responded to her concern, "Rose knows we're here for her. That's really all we can do, just listen and be a comfort to her."

Several miles passed in silence when Samantha shared,

"You know, if I didn't know better, I would guess Scott is pretty nervous about our visit." Shifting her attention to him, she noted, "In the time I've known you, I've never seen you so pensive."

"Pensive!" Scott straightened up, "What do mean pensive?" He paused for effect, "No, really. What do mean pensive…? Do you mean…am I being thoughtful…or reflective…in a sad or melancholy way?"

Pointing his finger at her, he proudly declared, "Ha! You thought I wouldn't know, didn't you? I got you. This round goes to me!"

Laughter filled the car, including the driver. Jim knew that was one to file away for a future story. Yes, Scott did appear to be a worthy addition to the group, and maybe to the family, the Reynolds family.

"Scott," Jim called. "Don't worry. Just be who you are, and for reasons beyond my comprehension, Mrs. Marissen will like you."

"You know what?" Samantha poked Jim's arm. "Mom and Dad are right! They say you and Scott are the same!"

To which, both vehemently denied, "No way!"

NORTH OF MOSCOW, RUSSIA

"NIKOLAI, DO YOU know where we are?"

Stepping her direction in a grassy area, hands behind his back, Nikolai answered, "They tell me 350 kilometers from Moscow. I think in middle of Vologda and Tver...north of Moscow."

"Why didn't they tell you before we left?"

Nikolai appeared stressed as he responded, "I not know. Is strange, or is nothing."

Samantha walked a short distance from the dacha, an aged Russian summer place, small and fairly run-down. Must be used by Federation officials now; the place accessed water from a pond, pumped in with the aid of a gas-powered generator. Any light was also supplied by the same generator, with additional power stored in batteries, which did not appear that reliable. The building did have a primitive bathroom and a tub to provide an occasional, warm bath. The conditions convinced Samantha her stay here would be short.

Her new countryside location meant she had outdoor privileges as long as accompanied by a soldier, normally Nikolai. Relieved he remained her full-time guard, she felt reasonably safe. However, she feared every morning may be the day to travel to Moscow for her trial.

She shivered. A soft, cool breeze blew through her hair as she wandered the property, finally experiencing sunlight, inspecting the gray, cracked, worn wood exterior and shingles of the dacha. Nothing of the dacha brought to mind any image westerners believed to exist. She found the interior far less than imagined, consisting of a cooking area, two sleeping quarters, a bathroom (obviously added at a later date), and a sitting room with a fireplace. Again, Nikolai bunked in the corner of her room. Never did Samantha fear sharing quarters with Nikolai; his presence provided a sense of safety and some peace-of-mind.

During conversation, Samantha mentioned she had thought of a dacha as a summer home or cottage. He explained it is not necessarily a comfortable symbol of affluence or a picturesque image of country living. Most are poorly constructed and unsanitary structures. The term 'summerhouse' is true only in the strident sense that most lack heating and are unusable during the winter. As far as Samantha could tell, her new 'holding cell' would be extremely difficult to reach.

"What are you doing, Nik?" she exclaimed. "You're not watching, I could run off and escape."

"Not to worry," he answered, as he swept his extended arm around the rugged surroundings. "Where would you go?"

"Nik, is something bothering you today? You seem sad."

"Is nothing."

"Yes, it is something! Tell me."

Looking down to the ground, he fumbled for words, "When we talk…I think of Anechka. I…I miss her."

"You will see her soon. Soon you will finish guarding me and be able to return to her. And, you know she will be waiting for you."

Squatting to pick a blade of grass, Nikolai raised his eyes and asked, "How are you this day, Sam?"

Shielding her eyes from the sun, she scanned the area, sighed and quietly addressed his concern, "I don't know anymore. I'm scared every day, scared so much I can't stand it. I want to be home; I want to be with the people I love. I'm afraid I will never see them again. I don't understand why nothing has happened."

"Is to be OK. U.S. not to release spies. Russia not release you. But…good will happen. You to return home…I know." His heart went out to her; he wanted to raise her spirits without giving false hope.

Not wanting to appear too friendly, Samantha turned slightly away before asking, "Why do you call the Russian agents spies, but you believe I'm not?"

His response surprised her, "You…you cannot lie. Russian Federation…they do, I know."

She remarked softly, "You sound like you are not a supporter of your government."

Nikolai straightened up and turned away.

SONORA COMPLEX, ARIZONA

THE SUCCESSFUL SIMULATED test flights of the IV, OV, and the XM absolutely amazed and astounded Secretary of State Atkins, Secretary of Defense Gagnepaign, General Townsend, and General Forsythe. As a result, the high-level group remained for the live flights of the three craft. Although the temperature registered 101° at 6:00am, Merrill Pierce transported Ed Marissen and his four guests to the outdoor viewing platform from which they would observe the launch of the IV/OV craft followed by the mostly unseen flight of the XM.

As performed in simulation, the Insertion Vehicle would piggyback the Orbital Vehicle to the max altitude for separation and ignition of the OV thrusters for the burn into low-earth orbit. While in orbit over the Philippines, The XM would disengage from the OV; drop into the atmosphere; rocket to the mid North Atlantic; and return to Sonora, where the IV and OV had already landed.

The increased duration of the XM test flight allowed time for a thorough testing of its components. The XM, as a pilot-only craft, carried a substantial fuel supply for extended flight. To accommodate a second passenger, Samantha Marissen, the XM faced extensive refitting upon completion of today's test.

Removal of nearly one-half the fuel capacity would necessitate a considerable reduction of flight time.

The first half of the rescue mission would initiate over the North Atlantic and terminate at a predetermined rendezvous point near Moscow. Far more dangerous would be the journey home, requiring a takeoff from the Russian countryside to an orbit 200 miles above to dock with the OV. To attain a 200-mile altitude required far less fuel than to fly the thousands of miles to the continental United States. Rendezvous with the OV was expedient due to the fact the XM would be dangerously low on fuel by that time. An XM reentry alone would not be possible; similar to today's jet fighters, the craft did not have the capability to glide to an airbase. The United States also desired no foreign involvement in order to prohibit the Russian Federation from taking action against any country aiding the rescue mission or participating in any way, thereby protecting the lives of innocent populations.

At this point, all U.S. military installations remained unaware of the existence of the Marissen AeroSpace aircraft. Other than Ed Marissen, Merrill Pierce, and the four high-level guests, only President Burton had knowledge of the rescue mission. True to Ed's word, the rescue would not happen without government approval. Officially, among the small group, the project would now be known as Operation Lightening Strike.

Not since WWII had such a level of secrecy been demanded. Total secrecy assured those present that the tests were an accurate portrayal of stealth; a radar image registered anywhere across the United States would prove failure of the system. The Secretary of Defense stood prepared to halt any retaliatory action taken by the military to bring down the 'unknown' aircraft.

Employees of Sonora Complex, aware of the test flights but not the mission, assembled in three dining halls, each furnished with four large flat-screens. Marissen would not deny those who labored tirelessly on the project the opportunity to participate in the day's excitement.

The IV and the piggybacked OV holding the XM in its belly, positioned one-half mile to the north of the viewing area, awaited final countdown. Tensions mounted as Marissen and Pierce fathomed the importance of the flights; today was all or nothing. Without a complete success, his daughter's rescue mission would cease to exist. His dream of major government contracts no longer mattered; Ed wanted Samantha home.

The six observers inserted their earpieces to listen in on the communications between ground and aircraft. The prelaunch checklist continued as they viewed the craft resting on the airstrip through binoculars. At its conclusion, came the words all had been awaiting, "Launch sequence to begin…10…9…8 (final electromagnetic alignment check executed)…7…6 (ignition sequence begun)…5…4…3…2…1 and launch of IOV."

The IV ripped down the runway building incredible velocity with each passing .10 second. The craft lifted off the surface at the exact mark, streaking upward at the prescribed 40° angle, climbing to an altitude of 263,000 feet amid constant chatter between the IV, OV, and ground control in preparation for separation of the OV and burn, boosting the spacecraft to a 200-mile altitude. Two Earth orbits were required: one orbit for the XM to undock over the Philippines and drop away from the OV; the second for further systems tests of the OV, followed by reentry and landing at Sonora.

The calm voice of the mission coordinator came through the earpieces once again, "OV launch sequence to begin in 7…6 (pre-electromagnetic release check performed) 5…4…3…2 and 1. An electromagnetic reversal of polarity instantly repelled the OV from the back of the IV as the IV dipped down and away.

With precision timing, the OV's powerful thrusters kicked in with tremendous acceleration, boosting the craft to 17,250 miles per hour toward orbit. Upon OV thruster shutdown, the three-man crew of Commander Webster, Captain Malone, and XM pilot Glen Blakely marveled at the blackened sky outlining the blue atmospheric shell visible along the horizon curvature.

Captain Malone reported, "IV/OV separation flawless, a slight lurch at separation but expected."

Commander Parker and Captain Moore of the IV added, Moore first, "A spectacular launch! Thrust was astounding, separation a piece of cake. A flip of the switch and the procedure complete. Followed the simulation to the 'T'."

Parker reported next, "This vehicle is beautiful! Nothing will outperform this marvel for the next century! I hope all of you saw this on your screens, although I'm sure it didn't do it justice."

Communications between Sonora and the three craft passed through a scramble and digitize process, not once but hundreds of times per second as the program recoded itself at random. The code may eventually be broken, but not today. That and minimal transmission was the rule.

Commander Parker and Captain Moore initiated a wide southern arc over the East coast, starting just above New York State at 240,000 feet and crossed westward over the South Carolina coast at 90,000 feet on its return to Sonora Base. ETA of the IV was one hour, twelve minutes at 2,000 miles per hour, far less than its maximum speed.

Webster, Malone, and Blakely prepared for the initial orbit of the OV. Webster inspected the onboard systems analysis as Malone corrected the orbit to nominally circular. Blakely, outfitted in a newly designed spacesuit, maneuvered from the flight deck of the OV through the bay access airlock to the cockpit of the XM. The bay area could be fully pressurized if necessary, which reduced the size of the working area. Compromise became the key word when searching for the maximum space available since a pressurized bay provided the ability to work without bulky, motion hindering spacesuits. The area surrounding the bay stored the pressurized oxygen tanks. Today's test would leave the area unpressurized, requiring a full spacesuit worn by Blakely.

The present orbit carried the OV across the North Atlantic, cut between Iceland and Norway, skirting northern Russia. If the camouflage or stealth features failed, the result would be catastrophic. However, up to this point, no radar installation had detected the OV.

Once Webster verified the system analysis, the sequence for opening the bay doors and Blakely's undocking began. Depressurization of the airlock was necessary since the bay was not. An airtight seal prevented the flight deck from depressurizing during any flight, especially during a transfer of astronauts in or out of the bay.

Controls to the bay doors, docking equipment, and other procedures were located in a clear bubble capsule off the side of the airlock. From this vantage point, Webster had full view of the bay and bay doors. Slipping into the bubble feet first, he strapped himself into the control seat. A panel swung around from the side and locked into position, all controls illuminated. This was the bay command center.

The XM could be pressurized but not during this test. Blakely, strapped in the fighter, calmly awaited the release countdown activated by the opening of the bay doors. Commander Webster initiated the procedure, "Bay lights off. Bay door sequence to begin in 10…9…8…7 (bay doors slowly slide open/XM docking clamps release)…6…5…4…3…2…1."

The maneuvering thrusters responded to Blakely's touch and the XM drifted from the bay. Webster observed in awe, as the Philippine Islands, under wispy stretches of clouds, slipped past below.

A safety margin of 100 feet between the OV and XM was required prior to Blakely firing the reverse thrusters, lowering the XM through the atmosphere on his way to the North Atlantic. An electromagnetic force field dutifully repelled the heat of reentry. Upon breaking through the atmosphere, Blakely excitedly reported, "This is breathtaking! I can see ships and the wave patterns left behind on the ocean surface. Amazing!"

Leveling the XM at the predetermined altitude of 100,000 feet, he streaked across the sky at 3,850 miles per hour with no sensation of speed. Blakely set his sights on the middle of the North Atlantic where he was to perform an inverted loop for his return to Sonora. Distraction always loomed as a danger, but he was a man of silence on any test flight, reporting only necessary data. Glen Blakely, the ideal test pilot, never allowed emotion to interfere with work. His eighteen word exclamation of his first sighting of ships and their accompanying wakes during reentry, shocked the flight controllers. So many words spoken at one time! As he neared the West coast, flight data informed him the XM would reach the North Atlantic in fifty-five minutes. Now, **that** amazed him.

Dan Malone, following the flight plan, performed a set of test maneuvers as Commander Webster remained strapped in the bubble with the bays doors open. First, a 360° counterclockwise roll followed by a 360° clockwise roll. Next, a 360° counterclockwise flat spin followed by a 360° clockwise flat spin. The final maneuver consisted of a 360° forward tumble, ending with a 360° reverse tumble. Webster joked that he thought he might lose his breakfast on that last set.

Once Captain Moore completed the maneuvers, the most important procedure would end the OV's part of the test mission. Commander Webster closed and sealed the bay doors and returned to the flight deck to prepare for reentry and landing at Sonora. During the OV landing, Blakely would continue the XM test flight without docking and returning with the OV. Another flight was scheduled for testing the undocking, landing, and re-docking with the OV after which the rescue mission would take place as planned.

Cockpit instruments alerted Blakely to bring the XM to the required airspeed to avoid blackout from excessive G-forces during the inverted roll. Just moments before taking the controls for the roll, the XM thrust abruptly failed. Checking the gas mixture percentages, he found one of the three at 0%.

Blakely broke radio silence with a subdued yet strained message: "Mayday, mayday! Failure of propulsion…one gas mix 0%…can't tell which…violent vibration…sudden cutout…no explanation. Craft in flat spin…now…tumble. Losing altitude fast…airspeed over 900…might break up… before crash. Crash site…North Atlantic…possibly 5…700 miles south of Greenland. I repeat…experiencing complete failure of…" Transmission ended, smashing into the cold, harsh ocean at 875 miles per hour, guaranteeing no remains of him or the XM.

Marissen, Pierce, Atkins, Gagnepaign, Townsend, and Forsythe, along with project leaders ran from the air-conditioned vans to the observation deck. Why? The XM would not return to Sonora. Not only had a billion dollar craft been lost, but more importantly, a very good man, a husband and father, lost to his family…and the Sonora family. A grief-stricken Marissen leaned on the deck rail as the IV flew overhead to slowly arc around Sonora Base to the landing strip. There would be no congratulations, no excitement over the successes of the day, only deep mourning of the death of Glen Blakely.

At some point, a debriefing of the flight crews, project support teams, Merrill Pierce, and especially Steve Hamilton, scientist and designer of the propulsion system, would take place…but not now. Time for mourning, for grieving was necessary. Ed left that afternoon for Seattle to be with Glen's wife and family. Marissen would do everything possible to provide for his family.

The project and the mission were finished…the chance for Samantha's rescue died with the project.

ABOARD AIR FORCE I

DIPLOMATIC RELATIONS WITH the Russian Federation, like brittle metal, snapped under pressure. The current weak and unstable government, attempting to save face in the eyes of the world, used their trump card with the declaration the Samantha Marissen espionage case would go to trial. Once relocated to Moscow, any hope for her rescue would be futile; open revolution even appeared imminent. Any attempt to free her at such a time of instability would place her life and the lives of potential thousands in jeopardy. If a feebly planned revolution failed, the results would be horrific for all involved. An obvious addition to the crisis was the recent loss of the XM, placing the bold extrication in a momentary state of chaos.

For security reasons, Secretary of State Atkins briefed President Burton aboard Air Force I of the two fronts facing the United States: First, the imminent transfer of Samantha Marissen to Moscow for trial; and second, the drastic need to resurrect the rescue plan, especially since the Kitai-Gorod bombings. Such an attempt must be made before her move. Defense Secretary Gagnepaign and General Townsend, on the other hand, sensed futility in any attempt of a rescue operation with the tragic death of the test pilot and loss of the XM in the North Atlantic. The multi-faceted dilemma cast a dark shadow over the rebirth of the mission. Could the second, and last, XM be completed in time? Could the cause of the failure be found with no wreckage to investigate? Could a capable and trustworthy pilot be recruited…quickly? Could he learn the intricacies of the craft and details of the mission in six weeks, or more than likely, less? Far too many questions.

NORTH OF MOSCOW

SAMANTHA, NOW A very light sleeper, rolled over as soon as she heard the light knock on the door. Oh, thank goodness, it was only breakfast. She feared every knock, every outside movement that might signify the time for her transfer to Moscow.

Nikolai insisted she receive the same meals as he, not wanting to face reports of mistreatment of the prisoner. At least, that became his explanation to others. He also demanded she be treated with respect for similar reasons. Samantha truly wanted to put her trust in him, but why? Once transferred to Moscow, all hope would be lost.

After eating, she washed in the tepid water, brushed her teeth, and attempted to do something with her hair. Totally unimportant, she knew, but managed to put a face of civility on the situation. By now, any concern regarding her appearance had faded into obscurity, satisfied only with her personal cleanliness and, thankfully, a steady supply of clean, orange or yellow jumpsuits. She supposed the bright colors would ensure easy recapture if she attempted to escape. Why would she try to escape; where would she run?

When Samantha entered from the makeshift bathroom, she requested time outside, something she felt would not be denied. Nikolai trailed her to the sunny side of the dacha where she sat in the grass with her knees under her chin, her arms wrapped around her legs; the same protective position she assumed when Igor had been terminated. He wanted to console her. Samantha's emotional state seemed to deteriorate since the move; she was lost and deeply depressed. He had to be very careful. No one must know he watched over her more than guarded her. So far, his actions, or lack of, registered well with those observing. He proved himself to be cold, hard, and unfeeling, a heavy, impermeable display that ultimately worked in his and Samantha's favor.

"Sam, let us go to table. We talk at table."

Nikolai took a position between her and the dacha and dropped a clean handkerchief into her lap.

"Maybe you need," he stated with hands on hips.

She clutched the handkerchief, chuckled slightly, then wiped her eyes and blew her nose…several times.

"I guess you don't want this back?"

Appearing tough, Nikolai responded, "No, I do not."

Rising from the grass, Samantha made her way to the table, blowing her nose again. She sat with her back to the sun; it felt warm, soothing.

"You're getting very good with your negatives. Our conversations improve your speech. You should be proud of yourself." Even her compliments carried a tinge of sadness.

"We do not talk much now," he explained. "After move, you be…quiet? Yes, quiet."

"I'm sorry," she softly answered. "I just want this to be over. We can't stay here very long; we're pretty far north and its August. Its already cool at night. September will just be cooler and there is no heat here. Something will have to happen soon, don't you think?"

SONORA COMPLEX, ARIZONA

"MARISSEN, CONDITIONS ARE such that, if at all possible, the project must move on. After a great deal of deliberation, the President has given the order to proceed…under the same order; the United States is not seen as involved. That's the word from the State Department. We must find what went wrong with the XM; complete and prepare the second craft; and to recruit and train a capable pilot to handle such a mission. Intelligence reports we have five to six weeks before your daughter is moved to Moscow for a trial."

"Ralph, the second XM is a long way from completion and prep; we have no aircraft to investigate the failure; and there is no pilot to take over the mission." Marissen pointed at the Secretary with each negative. "Those are three real-time responses to our three needs."

Townsend inquired, "Pierce, what's your take on this? Is it possible to accomplish this by September 1? Can the mechanics of the project be complete by this date?"

Pierce nervously responded, "Regarding the completion of the second XM, the interior must be revised by removing 45% of the fuel tank assembly to accommodate Miss Marissen; the chromatoskin must be applied; but, most importantly, the cause of the failure must be found. The entire operating system must be gone over with a fine-tooth comb. Finally, and I know this is not a part of the mechanics, but has anyone considered where and how a more than capable pilot can be found? And one who is willing to undertake such an assignment."

"Merrill, you haven't answered the question. You've only brought up issues already questioned."

Tapping the tabletop, Pierce surveyed the individuals awaiting his answer. Finally, "Yes, sir. We have the best people here; I believe it can be done."

Marissen nodded to Pierce, "Are you sure, Merrill? A lot needs to be done."

"I know," he responded, "But we have to try…and I do believe we can do it."

Ed shook his head in a positive approval. "All right, make it work!"

Pierce gathered his notes, cordially excused himself and left the conference room.

Marissen rose from his chair and paced before the high-level group. "Gentlemen, I want my daughter out of there, but I will not endanger the life of anyone to meet my personal needs."

"But what of National interest?" Tom Gagnepaign argued. "What if I informed you the President and the State Department demands this as a means of demonstrating to the Russians, once and for all, they must back down and cease threatening the world with their foolishness…downright stupidity, actually. If not, there will be severe retribution for their actions.

Shaking his head in the negative, Ed argued, "Maybe so. Let's say we move ahead with this, what about a pilot? He will not have the time to train for the mission. There is too much to digest in such a short period. He would barely have enough time in just the simulator."

"Tell you what, Marissen," retorted General Townsend, "I

personally know several men who, I believe, can do this…one in particular. He is the one I would approach first, an excellent pilot, a good man. Miss him since he retired. It's a longshot but we could possibly have our pilot."

Ed rubbed the back of his neck, "And he can accomplish this in the timeframe we're talking?"

"If he agrees to this, I have every confidence he could."

"Who is this guy?"

"You'll know as soon as he's onboard.

Ed pushed a bit more, "You think he'll do this?"

Townsend answered as a matter of fact, "If he's needed, he'll do it."

*   *   *

During the return flight, Townsend confided to Atkins, Gagnepaign, and Forsythe, "I hate doing this, but we need a complete background check on our man. He's got to be squeaky clean. We have to know everything."

MARISSEN ESTATE, ST. LOUIS, MISSOURI

ED MADE IT home for the weekend to be with Rose who had been alone far too much. He also needed the solitude of home after visiting with Glen Blakeley's wife and family. He felt certain it to be of no consolation to speak of her husband's contribution and his heroism. It was also of no consolation to Ed.

He and Rose spent Friday and Saturday together, just together. He apologized for his absence, explaining his time away unavoidable and offered to take her to Sonora. He wanted to wrap things up in Arizona, seriously believing the mission dead, not accepting a project completion in the time remaining.

Although many years had passed since Ed had been so attentive, Rose understood his need for activity and productivity. His daily work routine kept him occupied, kept his mind from dwelling on his daughter's plight. She explained she now had plenty of support from the Reynolds family, a renewal of friendships Ed gratefully appreciated. He would return to Sonora for a brief period.

WASHINGTON, MISSOURI

SCOTT, COFFEE MUG in hand, rocked from one foot to the other at the cabin's open door, glumly looking over the rain-soaked property. Pointing upward, he called to Jim, "So, this is that beautiful music you were talking about? Rain and tin. Who would have thought those to be your favorite musical instruments?"

Pouring another coffee, Jim muttered, "Yep."

"You're a man of few words in the morning, aren't you?"

"Yep."

"Especially when you don't get your run in."

"Yep."

"Where you heading?"

"To the porch…listen to my music."

"I'll join you, nothing like a little geezer activity on a Saturday morning."

"Careful, watch who you call geezer. There are ten-year-old kids who think you're a geezer."

"Point taken." Scott eased into the gray plastic yard chair Jim purchased the day before at a bargain store. "This is fine. I just needed my morning whine. And hey! Thanks for the chair…beats the porch floor any day."

"Only the best for my guests, no expense spared."

Thunder echoed in the distance. "Listen…that is a beautiful noise." Leaning back, he sipped his coffee.

Scott nodded approval. "This place frees your senses; you see and hear things taken for granted elsewhere. I could get used to this."

"Don't get too used to it. You'll want your own place. Staying with me is like living with your parents, right?"

The fresh clear sound of nature transformed slowly into the noise of the internal combustion engine climbing the gravel grade to the cabin. Jim stood as the black vehicle pulled onto the crushed rock drive alongside his estate, as he referred. Four men exited the car into the rain and splashed across the soggy ground toward the porch.

Standing next to Jim, Scott asked, "Who are they, boss? Anybody you know?"

"Actually, I do…I think. But what are they doing here?"

As the visitors approached, Jim realized he did know two of them and thought he recognized the two others. What the heck was going on?

"General Townsend, General Forsythe! What brings you here? And so early yet! It's good to see you!" Surprise could not describe Jim's reaction.

"Good to see you too, Jim." Townsend opened, "I believe you recognize these two: Secretary of State Ralph Atkins and Secretary of Defense Tom Gagnepaign. Gentlemen, Retired Colonel Jim Gordon and, who is this young man, Jim?" He already knew but wanted Jim to introduce the 'young man'.

"He is my new co-pilot, Scott Larimore. We fly for a small airline. Keeps me in the air, you know?"

"Good to meet you, Mr. Larimore." General Townsend greeted him with a firm handshake, as did the others. Scott remained speechless during the process, not believing his involvement with such main players.

Ralph Atkins spoke next, "We're sorry to interrupt your

morning but we need to speak with you…in private."

In defense, Jim stated, "He's a family friend, I'd like for him to stay."

"But—

"I'd like for him to stay, he's good. Besides, he would just have a bunch of questions later. He's good."

"He's good?" Townsend repeated.

"He's good." Glancing to Scott, he asked, "You good?"

Scott shrugged his shoulders, "I'm good."

Jim pleaded the case, "Look, he's good. I'll vouch for the guy! You know me; I wouldn't do that for just anyone. Why don't we go inside? Do we want people to think we don't have sense enough to come in out of the rain? It's dry and I'll get you some coffee."

Mild laughter trickled from the group as Jim and Scott allowed first entry to the brass. Scott looked quizzically at Jim who responded with one raised eyebrow, his half-smile, and a shrug.

Noting the coffee pot just about empty, Jim stated matter-of-factly, "Gentlemen, if you do want coffee, I'll have to make some."

"I'll do it; may as well make myself useful."

"Thanks, Scott, I appreciate it." Jim pulled a chair out from the kitchen table, sat down, crossed his arms, and, after looking the four men over, asked, "All right, gentlemen, what gives? Why the secrecy? What do you need?"

Forsythe responded, "Pretty astute, Jim. Obviously, we are here for a reason and we've come to you because of your qualifications and…you are already a part of this."

Jim appeared confused. "A part of what?"

Atkins took control of the conversation. "Let me cut to the chase. I understand you're a man who prefers information short and sweet. OK, I'll open with a question. Are you familiar with the Samantha Marissen incident?"

Jim froze, not visibly but in his head. Rain on the tin roof, the only sound heard at that moment. Suddenly, questions raced through his mind, trying to understand the point of the visit. Samantha? Why would they ask me about her? Has something happened to her? What would that have to do with him?"

He calmly declared, "Of course I do. Who doesn't?"

"All right, whatever is said here, remains here. Am I right, Larimore?"

Scott turned from his coffee making duty, surprised a response was necessary. "Yes, sir. Absolutely, sir!"

"And you're vouching for him?"

Jim smiled; Scott returned to the coffee making.

Atkins continued, "Once you know why we're here, you'll understand the need for secrecy. We didn't have the time to catch you alone. No offense, Larimore."

Without looking, Scott responded, "None taken, sir."

Jim scanned the faces of the four, looking for any evidence of what was to come. Positioning his elbows on the table, he demanded in a strong but calm voice, "All right, sirs, how about someone explaining what's going on? You're right, I like the info short and sweet. So, why the mystery?"

Secretary of State Atkins stressed, "I'm pretty sure you aren't fully aware of all the details. There's a lot that hasn't been on the news."

Atkins reported every detail of the past four months, explaining the diplomatic attempts at a resolution, every Russian rejection, and every veiled threat of a trial and possible imprisonment of Samantha Marissen. Several times Jim had to choke back an emotional reaction to what he heard.

"Has she been injured, hurt in any way?"

"From the information gathered, she was physically abused

in the beginning but that threat was removed. She is now guarded by a Russian soldier sympathetic to her situation."

"Where?"

After receiving an affirmative nod from Gagnepaign, Atkins continued, "At a rundown place north of Moscow. As of now, she is being treated OK, nothing more, nothing less. Our informant reports she is emotionally, mentally, and physically drained…it's not good. This is a matter of grave concern. We are speaking of the need for expediency due to her overall poor condition. That, and now we have the danger of bombings and the blame game."

"Expediency? What expediency? I'm already a part of this? What are you looking for from me?" Jim remained calm despite his need for answers along with the news of Samantha's health.

Taking a deep breath, Townsend took control of the explanation, "Jim, we want you to be a part of a plan to get Samantha Marissen out of Russia. Any questions?" Abrupt, to the point, Townsend simply stated the purpose of the meeting, leaving the rest to the retired Colonel.

Jim stared at the men in disbelief. Scott stopped with the coffee making, unsure of what he heard.

"What?" Jim could only come up with the one word question. Nothing else registered. At least, now he would have to listen to their explanation. Townsend's blunt approach worked beautifully.

Tom Gagnepaign, Secretary of Defense, spoke, "I understand your shock, maybe even skepticism, but we do have a plan… we want you to carry it out. We believe you are the best man for the mission. Not only are you good at what you do, you're calm under pressure.

"Like your mission to take out a large, well-guarded fuel depot to cripple enemy advances severely during the Mid-East conflict which, I might add, was successful. Returning to base, a rogue missile out of the hills hit and you lost a portion of the wing and sustained tail damage. You brought your jet in after significant portions of its flight control surfaces were destroyed. You assessed the damage to your plane and saw the entire outboard section of the left wing was gone. All the while, you kept a lookout for any other missiles coming for you.

"I have your report from General Forsythe; allow me to read from it." Gagnepaign pulled the papers from his inner suit pocket and began, "After inspection, I selected flaps half and could feel the jet change configuration but had no indication of flap position on my display. Next, I selected gear down. With 3 down and locked indication, I continued to slow the jet in 10-knot increments and determined the jet was stabled at 180 knots at 15,000 feet. However, due to some light turbulence down low and the feel of the jet, I made my approach at 200 knots and coordinated a landing on Runway 5B-11 at Wilderness Base Delta Z. Unable to perform flyover for ground based visual inspection of landing gear, I utilized a $3°$ descent on approach for about 13 miles straight in. At approximately 0835 hours, I experienced wheels down without failure and made a successful landing which concluded the event."

"That took one cool head to perform such a critical operation under such extreme conditions. That, right there, explains why you were chosen. Hear us out. This mission is a necessity. We want you. So, if you don't mind, may we continue?"

Atkins then stated the obvious, "You do want to help her Colonel Gordon. We know that. This is not an international crisis to you…its personal."

The coffee was ready but Scott paid no attention. So many things he didn't know: Jim almost losing his life during deployment; Samantha's situation deteriorating so quickly; and a one-man attempt to go into Russia and bring her back. His head spun with the overload of information.

Jim realized a complete, deep background check had been performed, but he didn't care. He lowered his eyes to the floor, thinking of Samantha, her pain, her fear, her health, and her despair. For these months, he had wished, hoped, and prayed he could do something…not just sit and wait. He would listen to the plan; he would not back away, not ever again.

He forced himself to return to the conversation, to conceal his emotions. "I'm listening."

Townsend explained the plan, describing as best he could in the brief time available the overall design and function of the three craft, including the XM's ability to maneuver virtually unseen with tremendous airspeed. He reported the bad with the good: the XM had drastically diminished flight duration due to the fuel tank reduction necessary for the second seat installation.

Anticipating his question of, why not fly into a neighboring country and avoid all the science fiction drama, Atkins emphasized the instability of the Russian Federation power structure and the fear of excessive retaliation against a country that would assist the United States.

"We do not want to endanger another country in the rescue of Ms. Marissen. The world appears to be behind us, but we do this under the guise of a private operation. We have a man with the power and financial resources to accomplish this. However, I must stress the narrow window of opportunity and how it grows narrower daily."

Awed by the enormity of such an operation, Jim's only reply, "You can't be serious."

Atkins solemnly added, "Colonel, a good man died preparing for this mission, a civilian test pilot…a husband and a father. The craft experienced what appears to be a massive instant thruster failure…he died as a result. This plan is real, Jim, very real."

Scooting his chair back from the table, he leaned forward and folding his hands between his knees responded, "I'm sorry, I didn't know. Any idea what the cause of the failure was?"

Forsythe, surveying him cautiously, returned the only answer, "No."

Out of curiosity, Jim probed further, "I didn't realize the government was involved in this type of development. I mean, this is so drastically different from anything I've ever heard. When did the project begin?"

Townsend stressed the point, "The government was never involved in the project. This is how we can label the mission a private operation. We were not aware of the project, not until the CEO came forward with the plan which we found, as you did, outrageous…until we witnessed it for ourselves."

"Yes, but you said the test pilot died in the first major test. Did you witness that?"

Forsythe replied, "We were at the home base at the time of the fatal crash; we heard the pilot attempting to describe the failure as he went down in the North Atlantic at nearly 900 miles per hour reporting as much detailed information as possible. I'm sure you know of a few test pilots who lost their lives in the testing of something new."

"Yes sir, I have. I've been lucky. Never had to do any test flights. Those are for the guys with guts."

Townsend disagreed with Jim's assessment, "No, not a test flight…you're right. But, you were never lucky; you were good…and still are. Your Mid-Eastern experience speaks for itself. We need you, Jim. Time is running out. We may have only four weeks max to pull this off."

Jim rose from the table and deliberately passed through the living room to the open door where he spent several long minutes gazing over the rolling hills of his Washington 'estate'.

He wasn't contemplating a thing; he simply had to step away a moment to collect himself, to gather his thoughts. He knew what he had to do and returned to the kitchen to find the brass waiting restlessly.

Scott had turned to face the table as he leaned back against the counter. He nervously straightened up as Jim pulled out his chair, spun it around, and straddled it resting his forearms on the back.

All eyes focused on him as he spoke, "Last question. What is the private enterprise that developed this aircraft?"

Gagnepaign motioned to Townsend, "Go ahead, Bob. But I don't think he will be surprised."

Before Townsend could respond, Jim answered his own question. "It's Marissen, isn't it? Marissen AeroSpace."

His conclusion did not require genius, he reasoned. Ed Marissen is the only man in the country with the resources and the power; he also has the necessary audacity and ego. Jim knew if he held that power, he would demand the same for Samantha. In a sense, Jim did have the power, but he would not resort to such a low blow. Now is not the time for foolish games.

Rubbing his forehead with his fingertips, he began to answer when Townsend interrupted, "I hope you will not allow personal feelings to interfere with your decision."

Jim stood, flipped the chair around, and sat again leaning forward with his elbows on his knees, hands overlapped. Quietly, yet confidently, he replied, "I have no problem with Ed Marissen. There would be no problem."

Jim scrutinized the men at his kitchen table, then Scott. The air hung heavy with anticipation of his response. He straightened up and with a half-smile gave the long-awaited answer, "Gentlemen, I will join your mission."

General Townsend stood, hand extended, "Your mission, Jim. Thank you."

After the handshake, Jim reached for his mug and a refill. The decision made, the pressure released, the business portion of the meeting could commence. Scott passed full cups of coffee around the table and returned to his counter position.

Gagnepaign returned from the bathroom, drying his face with a napkin. "Is it me or is it humid? I didn't pay any attention to it until now. I'll pass on the coffee."

Secretary of State Atkins motioned to Scott, "Pull up a chair, Larimore. You may as well take a load off. Won't make any difference if you're standing or sitting at this point. You're up to your tailbone in this."

Unnerved by the Secretary's offer, Scott slid a stool from the kitchen corner to near the table and took his seat. As he observed Jim taking in vital information, the more he learned. He hoped to be that type of man someday; a man who did what was necessary when necessary, a man of strength and courage.

Atkins rapped the table with his knuckles, "Gentlemen, we have one very important matter to discuss, and Mr. Larimore, this pertains to you as much as anyone here."

Focused only on the Secretary of State, Scott responded seriously, "Yes, sir."

Atkins continued, "We are well-aware of the sensitive nature of this operation, which means certain precautions must be taken by order of the President. Whether the mission a success or failure, nothing must ever be spoken of it. Jim, if all goes as planned, you may never divulge any knowledge of the mission. Same goes for you, Larimore. Can you do that?"

After witnessing Jim's acceptance of the mission, the depth of his strength and courage, Scott wanted nothing more than to prove the depth of his own character. "Yes, I understand and I can."

Gagnepaign reported the immediate schedule for Jim and the mission. "You will depart this afternoon for Sonora Complex in Arizona to begin the first phase of training tomorrow 0700. I forwarded your affirmative response; your cover has been established and already implemented, which is: You have been approached by the Air Force to fly to an Israeli air base as a consultant in the initiation of strategic…"

Scott sat through the entire scenario, mesmerized by the casual attitude of those involved in such a magnificent plan, setting the stage for the rescue of Samantha Marissen. He could not fathom his involvement in such a world event as a result of responding to a simple need for a co-pilot. What possible plans did God have in store for him? Whatever they were, he knew he was involved with the best 'family' to see him through. God had placed him in the right place at the absolute right time.

"…and for those reasons you will be out of the country approximately 4-6 weeks. That will cover the time frame required for the Marissen mission." Gagnepaign completed his explanation of the cover mission and additional details to which Jim acknowledged understanding and agreement.

"Mr. Larimore!"

Scott jumped to the commanding voice of Ralph Atkins. "Sir?"

"Don't forget your agreement! You are not here this morning; you heard none of this; and you will not speak of this…ever!"

"I promise you…I can do that, sir." Of that he was certain. He would not betray Jim, or Samantha Marissen. He prayed he would have the opportunity to meet her, that she and Jim would be together someday…soon.

"I hope so." Atkins finished. "There will be severe repercussions if you do, but I don't believe you would. Colonel Gordon said you're good, and you seem to from the same stock."

Scott reassuringly heard Jim voice, "He won't, he is good."

*   *   *

Thirty minutes later, serenity returned to the cabin. The steady rain kept beat on the tin roof; a fresh pot of coffee stood ready; and Scott sat on the porch, dazed by the visit. Within the span of one hour and a half, he witnessed the rebirth of a rescue plan that would amaze the world if successfully pulled off, and neither he nor Jim could ever speak of it.

"Wait a minute, what do I mean 'if'? He'll make it work… he has to."

Jim leaned out the door and asked Scott to come in to talk over the details of his Israeli trip.

"Close the door behind you. I turned the air on. It's too humid, too hot. It was fun watching those guys sweat, wasn't it?" He paused to change the subject. "OK, have a seat. I've taken care of the necessary items for when I'm gone—

"Jim, slow down, take a breath. This has been one heck of a morning. You're racing a hundred miles an hour. Let's just talk…for a few minutes."

Jim stopped pacing, "Yeah, yeah, you're right. Sorry."

He eased himself into a chair near the table. Scott poured a cup of coffee and joined him, both staring ahead in silence for several minutes.

"Look, Jim, I don't know what to say—

"You don't have to say anything. This whole thing is crazy! I don't know what to make of it myself but I do know I will do anything I can for her. She's in danger; she's not well; and I will not desert her this time. I abandoned her once…never again."

"I understand. I think…at least once in a lifetime, a person makes a decision that marks the purpose of his life. This is yours. I'm just concerned; so many things can go wrong."

Speaking softly, Scott admitted, "Before you leave, and I don't say this easily, I want you to know…I've come to think of you as…a father. In the short time I've known you, I see you as a person I want to be like. You have helped me through a very rough time…thank you."

Jim had to smile to himself. He never thought of himself as someone to be admired. He appreciated the young man, maybe even thought of him as a son, the son he never had. A lot of responsibility goes with admiration. "I know you had a tough decision to make before you came to St. Louis…but you made it…and it was right. Everything will work out, you'll see. Just hang in there…and pray about it. Give your family time; give them a chance. God will never let a good decision go unrewarded. I promise. I appreciate you telling me about all that. We've shared a lot over the last few weeks. Thanks."

Shifting back to an earlier comment, Jim explained, "A minute ago you said, so many things can go wrong. You're right, but when something appears that complicated, you can't look at the whole picture at one time; it'll overwhelm you in a heartbeat. I do my part one step at a time; the guys in the suits and uniforms handle the theirs. Finally, it all comes together."

"You learn that in the Air Force?"

"Had to. When you're in the heat of things, you have to make moment to moment decisions. You have the whole book in front of you but, for that moment, you're only on one particular page."

Scott made the connection, "Like when you were flying in the Mideast; you turned the page and you were hit by that missile. Didn't know that was going to happen. Everything you did from that point completely changed from simply returning to base to returning alive."

A clip of the memory flashed through Jim's mind. "Yeah, pretty much."

"You know," Scott shared, "Samantha told me she prayed for you every day during your deployment."

"That young lady has gotten me through a lot. I've been blessed with good friends and her…and, now, you. You treat her good; she's a winner. If things don't work out, don't let it be over something foolish. You guys look good together. Just remember, you have to like each other first. And not to sound one-sided, I think she has a winner too."

Grinning, Scott responded, "Thanks, I was beginning to wonder! And, just so you know before you leave…I do like her…very much." He rose from the table and leaned against the kitchen counter. "OK, so what are these details you want to go over?"

"Yeah, I better get in gear; got a lot to do." Jim stretched in the chair before beginning. "Here's the story: you just got here and I told you about my unexpected Israel assignment. I'll be gone about six weeks, maybe less, advising on some Air Force stuff. You know, just be very general. You're not supposed to know what I'm doing, so you really won't have to explain anything.

"To make things easier, while you were on the porch, I called Rich and Gina and kind of explained the assignment to them…no details. They were surprised but understood…sort of. Gina said it would be sad if Samantha, uh, Marissen, was released and I wasn't here to see her. If she only knew, huh?"

He brought his coffee cup to the sink and poured out the remainder before continuing, "I called SBA and gave them the same explanation. I recommended Bill Everdin to replace me during my absence. He's a good guy and a good pilot. You'll get along fine. Last thing, you'll stay here while I'm gone. Obviously, don't try to contact me. They probably wouldn't like that.

"Any questions?"

RICH AND GINA'S HOME– KIRKWOOD, MO

SCOTT STEPPED UP to the Reynolds' front porch and rang the doorbell, still awed by the day's events. A car had been dispatched to deliver Jim to Chesterfield Airport for the flight to somewhere in Arizona aboard Ed Marissen's private jet. Was Ed Marissen on the same flight? Scott didn't know but thought how awkward that would be for both men. An upside to the afternoon materialized when the Reynolds invited him to dinner once Samantha learned of Jim's mission to Israel.

Saddened she had been unable to speak with Jim before he departed, Rich and Gina thought it good the four of them spend the evening together. Samantha feared another call to the Mideast for Jim. Why now? With everything going on, why now? Touched by her parents' inclusion of him in their desire to comfort Samantha and his own desire to be with others tonight, made his decision easy. He liked them and they seemed to enjoy him.

Just several hours earlier, Scott sat in on a meeting with the Secretary of State, the Secretary of Defense, and two Air Force generals discussing with Jim the rescue of Samantha Marissen, daughter of the wealthiest man in America. Add to that, the fact he had spent an afternoon several days earlier with Rose Marissen, mother of Samantha who, by the way, did like him as Jim said she would. And now, Scott knew everything…everything.

He almost rang the bell a second time when Rich opened the door. "Scott, come in. Good to see ya!"

"It's good to be here. Thanks for having me over. Kind of a strange day…with Jim and all."

"I'll bet! Samantha will be here soon. She wanted to get her grocery shopping done before she came. I think she's doing something special for our guest tonight, like a microwave pie or something."

They both laughed at the fatherly joke. Over the short span of time, Scott found Jim to be right on the mark with his analysis of Rich, the antagonist, yet a teddy bear. He had a serious side mildly interrupted by 'splatters of humor' as Jim called it.

As they made their way to the kitchen, Rich gave fair warning, "Samantha is upset by how quickly all this came up with Jim. You know how concerned she is about him; she didn't get a chance to talk with him before he left. She's not mad; she just missed saying good-bye."

"Jim's a lucky man," Scott acknowledged. "He has a great family."

"Don't tell him I told you this," Rich stated in a purposely loud whisper, "But we kind of like him."

Laughing, Scott affirmed, "OK, I'm pretty sure that was serious!"

"You're learning," Rich revealed. "You're learning."

Nearing the kitchen, he bellowed, "Honey, Scott's here!"

Only feet away, Gina shouted back, "Really? Where? Good grief, don't do that, I almost dropped the pizza and I haven't gotten it to the oven yet. Sorry, Scott, we were going to barbeque but I didn't think it would ever stop raining. Did you get much in Washington?"

"Pretty much rained all day! Stopped just before I left.

Anything I can do, Mrs. Reynolds?"

"I'm just going to put the pizza in—wait, there is. Would you open the oven door for me? Please."

"You bet!"

Rich didn't resist, "Way to get in good with the daughter's mother."

The back door opened, Samantha entered carrying a pie. "Hellooo! I thought I would bring a little something special tonight. And no, Dad, I won't need the microwave…it's apple and it's fresh!"

Gina reached for the pie. "Baby, you just burst your father's sarcasm bubble, but appeased his appetite in one shot! Well done!"

Rich turned to Scott, "You gotta be pretty thick skinned around here. Thanks for balancing the gender scale this evening."

Scott laughed at his comment, "Yeah, but I don't think I'll be much help until I know everyone better."

Handing him a piece of cheese, Samantha touched the tip of his nose announcing, "You will."

He smiled as she moved to the counter to slice off a few more pieces. Her positive attitude of their future delighted him. The longer he knew her, the greater his feelings grew. She inherited her mother's beauty and grace along with her father's wit and outgoing personality. Gina fed the inner soul, Rich the outer, and Samantha…both. She carried the cheese and crackers plate to the table.

As they sat around the table, Gina informed Scott the pizza was not one of those frozen ones from the store but her own special deluxe pizza made from scratch. Rich and Samantha filled him in on just how much she liked to cook, constantly trying something new. As he chuckled, Rich let Scott know how good it was to have a new guiney pig around for the taste testing. Gina simply responded she never heard him complain, to which Rich admitted he never would; a further lesson these were good people, and…good friends. He had a hard time believing how at ease he felt with them after such a short period.

The conversation naturally turned to the subject of Jim's surprising consulting trip to Israel.

Samantha opened, "I don't understand how he can be gone so fast. Why didn't they give him time to say good-bye? I just wish I could have talked with him before he took off."

Rich attempted to console her, "Look, Hon, that's how the government works, hurry up and wait. When their ready, there is no waiting. This must have been pretty important to pull it all together in one day."

"I hope it's not dangerous; his Mideast tour scared me. I just don't want anything to happen to him."

"Samantha, he'll be fine. This is Jim we're talking about." Gina stressed, "He's there as a consultant, nothing more. If his smarts don't keep him out of trouble, his good looks will."

"Oh, brother, please," Rich laughed. "Don't give him any more credit than necessary. He'll be fine. I've known him for a long time. I just can't believe he's become so high profile. I owe him a lot more credit than I've given him. I must say…I'm impressed."

Gina mentioned what Rich and their daughter also wondered. "Well, I'm just sorry that he may not be available if Samantha is released. He would be so disappointed. Rose would be. And what about Samantha? It's all so sad."

Scott listened to the table talk, absorbing a deeper understanding of family. These people knew the true value of friendship, not the superficial "Hey, wassup?" baloney. Jim's friends truly cared for one another; Rich loved him as a brother; Gina had grown, over time, to love Jim; and Samantha, she simply loved Jim for Jim.

Scott wrestled with the knowledge of Jim's true mission. Should Rich, Gina, and Samantha remain blissfully ignorant? How could they pray for him if they didn't know? It also meant not praying for Samantha Marissen's health and safety before and during the rescue attempt. And, what would happen once they became aware that he knew of the mission? Would they be upset? Finally, if he shared the information with the Reynolds, it would mean he could not be trusted to maintain secrecy during the deathly important rescue.

"Scott…Scott," Rich nudged his arm, "You with us?"

"Yeah, sorry. Got a lot on my mind."

"I said, it's too bad you didn't hear any of the conversation. You might have had some inside scoop about this."

"Oh, you know Jim. I probably wouldn't have heard a thing."

After a long pause for a decision, Scott folded his hands under the table and looked at the three, one at a time. "I'm going to take a risk…a huge risk here. I was told there would be some severe repercussions if I divulged any information. I shouldn't do this, but I believe you guys should know…but, I need your complete silence on this. Do I have it?"

"Of course," Rich consented. "But what are you talking about?"

Shifting his focus to Samantha, he hesitantly admitted, "I do know something…

Silence filled the kitchen as Rich, Gina, and Samantha awaited the remainder of his statement.

"I was at Jim's this morning when four government people showed up. I'm not going to say who…for now. Just hear me out. There has been a planned rescue of Samantha Marissen that is completely outrageous, but I was there, I heard it."

Rich interrupted, "How did you get to hear this? What's this got to do with Israel?"

"Please, let me tell you what I can."

Scott continued, "Israel has nothing to do with this; that's just a cover story. They want Jim to take over part of the rescue—

"What?" came a unified exclamation.

"Please wait. I'll get to that."

Searching the eyes of the three, he returned to his explanation. "They need a pilot to take over that part of the mission. The original pilot…

Scott quietly relayed the details of the morning meeting, including why Jim was asked to take over, Samantha's physical state, the reasoning for the rescue, how it would be accomplished, and the timing of the attempt. Everything top secret. Jim's part or name would never be made public. That is why he needed their full cooperation. None of the information was to ever leave the confines of the Reynolds' home, or Scott would suffer the consequences.

"Oh, my gosh," Samantha whispered. "No wonder you didn't know what to do. I'll never breathe a word of this to anyone."

Gina and Rich promised their silence. The two couples sat in silence as the information gradually took root. Different thoughts formulated as the newly acquired knowledge slowly grew into a reality.

Samantha voiced her greatest fear, "What if something goes wrong…like the first pilot."

Scott shared Jim's thoughts, "Samantha…Jim told me this afternoon this was something he had to do. He was not going to abandon her again. He still has very deep feelings for her." The young man took Samantha's hand. "I think I'm beginning to understand. I hope to experience that depth of feeling in my life.

"Look, I'm sorry. I honestly didn't want any of you to worry, but I thought you should know."

"I may worry, but I appreciate you telling us. I want to know. I just…" Her eyes filled with tears as she attempted to continue. Scott stood, Samantha followed to his open arms, sobbing. He wished different circumstances to hold her but thanked God she turned to him for comfort.

Rich also held Gina, reassuring her all would be well. A pang of paternal jealousy struck without lingering, as he witnessed his daughter consoled in the arms of, not him, but a young man of good character, hand-picked by another man of exceptional character. Rich felt blessed to know the men Samantha chose to admire, one of which appeared to mean something special to her.

"Oh, my! The pizza!" Not that Gina cared but she certainly didn't want it to burn. The oven smoked a bit as she retrieved the not burnt but extra crispy pizza and placed it on the stovetop and returned to the table.

"It'll do, if anyone's interested."

But they weren't. Conversation soon drifted back to Scott's revelation.

"And this is within the next four to six weeks?"

"Yes, that sounded pretty definite. No matter what, seems the whole thing will be over soon."

Gina shook her head, tears forming in her eyes again. "We lost Samantha years ago, and now, we may lose Jim. This is a lot to take. I don't know if I can handle this."

"Yes, you can," Rich emphasized. "We all know Jim. If anyone can pull this off, its him." Rich heard himself speak words of false support for an impossible mission. He feared for his friend.

As the evening wore on, the pizza grew cold.

27,000' ABOVE OKLAHOMA

AFTER YEARS OF piloting, the role of passenger quickly grew tiresome. Jim opened his small travel bag and retrieved his Bible, laid it on his lap and closed his eyes. He attempted to pray as he did prior to reading Scripture but his mind would not settle, knowing he would soon shift into an intense learning mode. The magnitude of his decision had not yet been fully absorbed; much unknown awaited.

Thoughts of the mission invaded his Scripture time: The mission consisted of five men, drop to three, and at the time of landing, one…him. Failure never entered his equation for success before; one minor failure among many successes resulted in a hardly noticeable statistic, a blip. However, one failure out of one chance would be disastrous for the United States…and Samantha. For him, failure would be meaningless; he would be dead.

He pushed back the seat, crossed his ankles, and closed his eyes. He would think of nothing so negative as returning without Samantha or not returning at all; she would come home, diplomatically or as his backseat guest. The mission, tentatively scheduled September 12th through 15th, could be moved up as early as August 30, dependent upon the Russian Federation's hunger for a trial. Within one month, by sometime September, the crisis could be over. A lot to learn…a lot to do.

The flight to the Sonora Complex provided his final opportunity to do nothing, to simply kick back, relax, and reminisce. The month of September triggered a memory of long ago, a float trip taken by Samantha, him, and their full complement of friends, always scheduled after Labor Day to avoid an overcrowded Huzzah River. Rich and Gina had married late that spring, while Samantha and James had become an 'item'. The float seemed an excellent opportunity to close out a perfect summer.

Jim had just picked up the cooler of food and refreshments for their canoe when Samantha called him aside. As he set the cooler at her feet, she nervously began to explain she had never been on a float and she didn't want to embarrass him. She went so far as to apologize for being a country girl with little outdoor experience. She did this to be with him.

"Really? You've never done this before?" He took her arm and escorted her several feet from the group. "Do you know what this means?"

Removing her sunglasses, she most seriously asked, "No, what?"

"It means…no problem. I just want you to have fun. We're going to have a good time. I kinda like that you've never done this. I'll show you what you need to know. I get to act like I know what I'm talking about. You're going to do fine."

She smiled, then added, "I, uh…don't know how to swim either. How deep does it get?"

"You know, it can be about one to three feet…but mostly less. You'll laugh when you count the times we have to push the canoe across the gravel bottom."

Turning from their friends, he placed his hand on her back to guide her a step or two further away. "You've been afraid to say something, haven't you? Don't ever worry about talking to me, promise?"

"I promise. Thank you for not making fun of me, for not laughing. I know y'all did this before. I want to be a part of your life, a part of what you enjoy."

"You are a part of my life, and I enjoy being with you. This…this is just for fun. You'll see. Keep an eye on Bob and Liz, or better yet, an ear. You'll find you're pretty good, real quick." He kissed her forehead and said, "Stick with me, Hon… one hour and you'll be a pro."

Unknown to Jim was what that one short conversation accomplished. She watched as he carried the cooler to the canoe and recognized a man who cared, truly cared about her. He would never embarrass her over something as insignificant as her lack of 'outdoor' experience…the thought never entered his mind. She wanted to rush to him, to hold him, to tell him…

Jim reached for her hand as she stepped into the river to the front of the wobbling canoe. Although a warm day, the cold water registered quite a shock to the system. Samantha increased her grip when the canoe rocked as she attempted to sit. He steadied her into position and extended an oar to her.

"I probably should have warned you, you really can't stand in one of these things. You have to kinda squat and hold the sides to balance yourself as you get yourself situated."

She laughed nervously, "Anything else before we begin?"

"I think we're good to go! Ready?" Jim splashed to the rear and pushed the canoe from the gravel bank into the current of the shallow river. Their fellow canoeists were already well ahead but Jim felt confident he and Samantha would eventually catch up.

"I think you're going to like this. Peace and quiet, only the sounds of the river. If you do enjoy it, we'll do it again."

With her back to him, she held up her oar, asking, "Can you

tell me the right way to do this? I don't want to just sit here!"

"OK, watch me. When you row on the right side, your left hand should be up here, on the upper end of the oar. Your right somewhere in the middle, wherever is comfortable. Try spacing your hands about 18 to 24 inches apart."

"Like this?"

"Yes…that's it. Now dip it in the water and pull back with your right arm. Good, good, that's it! After two or three times, change to the left side but reverse the positions of your hands. Go ahead, give it a shot!"

She did and after a short time found herself enjoying her first float. Jim handled the steering as he kept an eye on her progress, occasionally instructing her to "Keep doing this" or "Change to that."

"See, look how good you're doing! I think we're gaining on the others."

"All right, James, this is a challenge now! I don't want them to think you were held back by some weak little girl!"

He laughed to himself. Here sat the southern girl, normally 'the lady', dressed in a swimsuit, blue jean shorts, and old tennis shoes excitedly proclaiming, "We're going to catch them!"

She and James did slowly gain on the others, enough to witness a Bob and Liz moment from twenty yards behind.

"Other side, other side! Row on the other side!" Bob yelled, as their canoe slowly angled 90°, striking a log protruding from the center of the river.

Liz shouted back, "I am, I am!" using her oar to splash Bob who willingly returned the favor, drawing laughter from Samantha and Jim.

"See how good you're doing? Bob and Liz have been doing this for years and it's the same every time…but I do think they might exaggerate it for us."

"So, they're not arguing?"

"Oh, no, that's just their way of coping. Early on, they weren't going to come anymore, but we kept forcing them until now they have such aggravating fun, they wouldn't miss it."

Managing to straighten out their misguided canoe, Bob and Liz floated on as Jim taught Samantha how to maneuver around the same log with little effort. She promised she would not tell what he had shown her.

The river settled into one of its less shallow lengths of imperceptible current where the calm surface sparkled with dancing diamonds of scattered sunlight working its way through the heavy overhanging branches. Fish darted back and forth beneath them as each stroke of the oars eased the canoe serenely across the still, smooth water. Birds and crickets carried on multiple conversations with their partners, never noticeable near the shallower, rocky areas of the rushing river. Jim appreciated not passing through the tranquil stretch with everyone. The natural solitude struck him with a sense of peace he felt Samantha also experienced; she had grown so very quiet.

"James?"

"Yeah?"

"I…I love you, James."

"Samantha?"

"I said…I love you."

She said it not once but a second time. Stunned, Jim carefully yet quickly stepped into the two-foot deep water and made his way to her. She sat motionless, oar on her lap, biting her lip.

"Samantha?" He slowly removed her sunglasses revealing misty eyes. Squatting in the cold river, he held the canoe in place.

"Samantha, I love you. I love you so much."

With his hand on her shoulder, he drew her toward him and kissed her. As he inched away, she smiled that smile, her smile.

"James…I've wanted to tell you. I was afraid…afraid you didn't feel the same."

"I do love you, Samantha. I've wanted to tell you too. There's something about you, about us, something permanent."

She took his face in her hands and kissed him. Running her finger down the bridge of his nose, she advised, "Why don't you climb back in? We can talk and you'll be a little more comfortable."

He kissed her once more, then straightened up. "You're right…this river is cold."

She laughed as he took her hand. "What?" still chuckling at his cold-water comment.

"I would like if we sat closer, we can talk face-to-face then. Besides, I like looking at you. Is that OK?"

She responded shyly, "Yes, it is."

"So, swing around, stay low. I'll keep the canoe steady. Hold on."

"You know, we won't catch them if we don't both row."

Giving her hand a gentle squeeze, Jim calmly answered, "That's OK. I'd rather talk with you. We can catch up later."

Once settled, Jim climbed in and began to row. Samantha opened the cooler and pulled out two bottles of water.

"What's this?" Jim asked.

Handing him an open bottle, she smiled, a little embarrassed. "You may think this silly, but I thought we could toast this new love of ours."

He took the bottle from her. "There's nothing silly about this. I'd like that. You first?"

"Me first." She raised the bottle. "To my James and our everlasting love!"

He raised his. "And to my Samantha, my love forever."

They tapped the bottles and sipped the cool water. Leaning

together, Samantha and Jim kissed. He would never forget her kiss, always so soft, always so loving, always followed by the smile. And she loved his manly, military ways, while aware of his kindness, his gentleness. He had just expressed his love for her in a romantic, yet masculine manner.

From that point, the two talked and laughed as if the only couple on the river. His world had changed dramatically; he experienced a true happiness, a joy never before known, having voiced a commitment to the woman he cherished, the woman who loved him. Nothing would ever change that.

Samantha found herself in a state of exuberance, a newfound eagerness to live for God, to continue to share her faith and life with James. Not since the loss of her family had she felt so alive. She requested they take a moment to thank God for bringing them together.

He placed the oar across his lap and took her hands. "Lord God, Samantha and I thank you for the love you have given us for each other. We will always respect the other as we move forward in our relationship. And I thank You that she brought me to You. I will never take that lightly. I love her, Lord."

"And I love him, Lord," she added softly, with bowed head.

Together, they closed, "Amen."

She watched as he began to row once more. Exactly as she thought; the Air Force pilot trained to defend his country just prayed to thank God for her and their love. God truly blessed her after the many years without her family.

Drifting around a wide lazy bend, the shouts and calls of their friends roused Samantha and James' attention.

With everyone standing at the water's edge, Bob called out, "Where have you guys been? Are you so embarrassed Liz and I are ahead of you that you're ashamed to show your faces?"

Jim steered the canoe onto the gravel bank amid the torrent

of heckling and razzing. Gina hurried Samantha from the boat to the group of women. Bewildered by the rush for Samantha and the call for quiet, Jim stepped out of the canoe and joined her.

"What's going on? Something happen?"

Rich took over, "Although we knew it would be a struggle who got here first, Bob and Liz or Samantha and you, we figured there would be some delay."

Samantha laughed to herself; she knew Bob and Liz were ahead by default. She would never trade what occurred between her and James for reaching the rest stop first.

Rich continued, "Got some news for you guys. Gina, why don't you tell—

"We're going to have a baby!"

An eruption of joy swept over the riverbank. Surrounded by her friends with Samantha at her side, Gina laughed and cried. Rich accepted the hearty backslaps and congratulatory handshakes from his friends culminating with a firm shake from a beaming Jim.

"Rich, I'm so happy for both of you! This is fantastic!"

"You know," Rich nudged Jim toward Samantha, "Maybe the same for you someday."

"Maybe sooner than you think!"

Surprised, Rich managed, "What?"

"Jim, come here!" Gina excitedly gathered everyone. "Papa Rich, get over here! Jim, you stand with Samantha. OK, now we're ready.

"The baby is due in May." Another cheer. "If the baby's a girl, we want to name her Samantha, and if it's a boy, James… Jim. See what you started, Samantha?"

More laughter and congratulations filled the air as Jim watched Samantha hugging the mother-to-be. When he caught her eye, he smiled and winked, but this time felt completely different, especially when she returned the smile and wink…as if everything had new meaning.

"Jim!"

"Hey, Rich, thanks for the honor! This is great! You gotta be happy!"

"Yeah, I am. This changes everything…it should. I can't wait. I can't tell you how much I love her. I hope we have a dozen kids. She's terrific!"

"You are one happy man…but I think I might understand what you experience with Gina."

"What do you mean?" Rich asked as he kicked in the gravel.

"I mean, believe it or not, I have someone who loves me… and I know you warned me, but I told Samantha I love her. I know what you said…but I meant it…I wouldn't hurt her, ever."

Rich gripped his friend's arm. "I know. This is different. You're different. I know. So, this is what you meant a few minutes ago?"

"Yep, that's what I meant."

"Oh, man, I thank God for this! We've prayed you and Samantha would, you know, fall, uh, fall in love. Man, why do I have such a hard time saying stuff like that?"

Laughing at his friend's fumbling with romantic 'stuff,' Jim declared, "That's nothing! I'm shocked Gina would pray I'd fall in love with anyone!"

"Yeah, there was a time. She always liked you; didn't trust you…yet she liked you. But, she sure didn't want you near her friends, especially Samantha. She kept a close eye on you but, you turned out to be the best thing to happen to Samantha…and Samantha, the best for you. I was so happy to hear Samantha led you to Christ after our reception. You know, had you not told me that morning you wanted to talk to me, I may have questioned your motives with her…but, you were ready. It was time. Now, you seem to be ready for something else. Maybe you two should let everyone know where you are in your relationship today."

Jim grinned. "No, Rich. This is your day, enjoy the moment." Choosing a couple of smooth flat rocks, he skipped them across the river.

Rich matched Jim's rock skipping prowess plus one. The sound of another happy commotion resonated from the circle of women. They turned to see Samantha and Gina hugging again, surrounded by the others.

Placing his hand on Jim's shoulder, Rich jokingly lamented, "Sorry, pal, I think the word is out."

*   *   *

"Colonel Gordon, we'll be landing at Sonora shortly. Merrill Pierce, the Complex manager will be there to pick you up."

"Yeah, thanks. I must have drifted off. Who did you say will pick me up?"

Taking a quick look about the cabin, the co-pilot responded, "Merrill Pierce, sir. Complex manager. Nice guy, dry, wound a little tight, but a nice guy."

"OK, thanks."

And so, it begins, he thought, the mission of his life now set in motion; he would bring Samantha Marissen home safely. He would not fail her, not this time.

Jim angled his head against the seat for a comfortable view of the Sonoran Desert as the Lear descended toward the Complex. Cacti, shrubs, and trees survived in abundance having adapted to the harsh environment of less than 10 inches of rain per year during the winter and mid-summer months, combined with extreme temperatures often as high as 120°. He remembered the desert as home to a variety of animals and birds but, humorously, only the roadrunner and coyote came to mind. Cartoons will never lose precedence over good hard schoolwork, he mused. Scanning the horizon of the rugged terrain, he considered how most thought the desert a vast, lifeless expanse, not the eerily beautiful living panorama below.

Closing his eyes, he prayed,

"Oh, Lord, help me through this time. Give me the ability to learn and retain all I need to accomplish what needs to be done. Grant me patience…patience with myself to perform my duties successfully. Keep me focused on the objective, not my personal feelings. Keep Samantha safe, watch over her, bless her. Somehow, let her know she will be home soon, home with those who love her. I ask this in Jesus' name. Amen."

As the jet banked toward an east to west landing, Jim opened his eyes to see…nothing, no structures, no roads, nothing. However, before the approach straightened, he observed what might be a camouflaged runway, only because of the sheer flat immensity of the airstrip, both width and length. Suddenly, the runway seemed to disappear with the change in approach angle. How is something like this built without public knowledge? With Ed Marissen, anything is possible.

A knot tightened in the pit of his stomach; he would finally meet the Ed Marissen face-to-face, a never before event. The entire time Jim and Samantha spent together, Ed held Jim in such disdain he made no effort to meet. Sad, Jim thought. Had they met, Ed would have grown to either accept him or reject him based on sound reasoning, not the mindless egotism that destroyed their relationship. Their meeting would be…interesting.

Once the jet taxied to a complete stop, the co-pilot prepared to open the exit. As Jim rose, he grabbed his bag and straightened up. He had to remain slightly hunched over in the smaller confines of the Lear, and he was not an extremely tall person. He looked out the window while waiting and noticed a Hummer pull up very near; probably that Pierce guy the co-pilot mentioned, Jim speculated.

The driver of the Hummer rushed into the plane as soon as the door opened straight to Jim. "Colonel Gordon, Merrill Pierce."

Jim reached to shake his hand. "Merrill, Jim. Call me Jim."

"Welcome to Sonora…Jim. As you can see, there's not much to see…from here. Got your bag? Good, it's already hot in here. Made it to 115° today. Maybe some storms tonight."

Merrill hustled out the exit. Jim followed, pausing a moment to acknowledge the pilots for the good flight. Pierce took Jim's bag and tossed it in the back seat of the Hummer. "Hop in. I've got the air on full. Should be cool."

A hot, dry wind burned into Jim's face as he turned a quick 360° survey of the desert. "So, this is home for the next month." He climbed into the passenger seat of the Hummer. Bless Pierce; it was cool.

Pierce drove down the airstrip in silence, having no idea what to say to this Colonel…Jim. Who was he? Why would he accept a mission like this? Was he as good as General Townsend said? Too many questions without answers.

His need for answers exposed a Pierce dilemma; he didn't appreciate, nor could he tolerate, a lack of answers. Nevertheless, his drive for answers made him the successful Complex manager of today. The lack of answers regarding James Gordon would be placed on a back burner; he required answers to why the XM crashed into the North Atlantic not yet a week past. He could not bear to witness another man flying to his death.

Pierce pulled the Hummer off the runway onto a pad the size of a three-car garage and pressed a button on the center of the dash. Without warning, the entire pad lowered slowly below ground to a large staging area for the transfer of materials or people. Merrill had yet to initiate any conversation.

Jim broke the silence. "This is quite a structure…looks like something special effects people would put together."

Pierce responded, "Yeah, it took a lot of years to get this in place. It's an ongoing project; we expand when needed." He parked off to the side next to a battery-powered cart for the ride to Jim's underground suite. Merrill threw the travel bag into the rear of the cart while Jim climbed aboard. They departed through opening double-doors down a long, two-lane hallway toward the residential quarters of the Complex.

Another stretch of dead air.

"Look, Merrill, I know I'm coming in at the tail end under extremely difficult circumstances for you and your people. I will not interfere with your work. I won't be one who thinks more of myself than the mission. I'm here to pick up wherever I can."

"Colonel…Jim, I apologize for my silence. It's not you or the circumstances. I just don't understand what drives someone…you…to take on something like this without fear of the consequences. I'll be honest with you Colonel; this scares me. How do you…no…why do you accept a challenge of this magnitude?"

Jim nodded and smiled, "Heh! I understand. This scares me too. Scares me that I won't be able to do it. Scares me that I could fail. I could die…don't want to, but I'm not afraid to die. I realize now, I've trained my whole life for this."

"You're not afraid to die?"

"Like I said, I don't want to die, but I don't fear death, and that's not some macho, hero, wannabe thing."

Pierce stopped the cart. "Well, someday you'll have to explain that to me."

"I can, just let me know when."

"I'll get back to you." The ride resumed. "Do you have any

questions for me, Col…Jim?"

Without hesitation, Jim asked, "Is Ed Marissen here?"

Pierce seemed to ponder his response, "Yes…yes, he is. He spent the last several days with his wife. No one thought this would go this far. He has a sensitive balancing act going on. Mrs. Marissen isn't aware of the real dangers her daughter faces, nor does she know of the mission. He doesn't want to leave Mrs. Marissen alone too long, not now. Somehow, he has to forge ahead without appearing as uncaring.

"People can say what they want about Ed Marissen but, he is willing to sacrifice all he has for his daughter." Pierce hesitated before continuing, "He's changed since this happened; he has many regrets about his life before."

"How do you know that?" Jim needed to ask.

Pierce slowed down and visually scanned his passenger before sharing such private information. "We've known each other for a very long time. I see that he is in great pain right now. He told me many things that happened prior to his daughter's abduction. He feels responsible for what has happened to her. He loves his wife and daughter.

"I'm sorry, I've said far too much…given out too much of Mr. Marissen's personal information."

"Don't worry about it, Merrill. This conversation goes no further. I appreciate your honesty."

Wow! Never did he think he would hear anything like Pierce had shared. What will happen when Marissen finds out Jim is the pilot chosen to take over the mission or, does he already know?

"Merrill, has Marissen been told who is the replacement pilot? Does he know who I am?"

"Yes, he knows. General Townsend informed him immediately after you consented and I spoke with him shortly before you landed. You should know…he is very grateful for your decision, which reminds me, Mr. Marissen requests a private meeting with you first thing in the morning. Should I let him know that's good for you?"

Two words reverberated through Jim's mind, 'grateful' and 'requests,' words of civility, both used for Jim's benefit. He decided no assumptions today; wait and see what tomorrow brings.

"Yes…it's good for me."

"Excellent. I'll arrange the meeting for 7:30. After that you'll meet with the Insertion Vehicle and Orbital Vehicle crews, then the remaining people directly involved with the mission. Not everyone at Sonora is aware of the scope of the next few weeks. You'll find out who is and who isn't at tomorrow's meetings. The safest thing to do is not speak of the true reason for being here unless I'm with you, and that will be for the next twelve hours. I'll pick you up at 7:00.

"All right, end of the line. Your quarters is down this hall. We'll get you settled in, grab some dinner, and show you how the necessities operate. By tomorrow evening, you'll be one of the regulars."

Before exiting the cart, Pierce extended his hand. "Colonel… Jim, thank you for taking this on. I will do everything in my power to make this a success."

Jim shook his hand. "Thank you, Merrill. "We will make this work."

SONORA COMPLEX, ARIZONA

HE PROMISED IF he rolled over once more, he would surrender and get out of bed. As his eyes adjusted to the dimly lit clockface, the all too early time of 4:30 glared into focus. Four-thirty! He didn't get to sleep until after 1:00, so many emotions, too many feelings racked his mind.

That's all right, just stagger into the kitchen, he thought, and put on the coffee, different place, same coffee. While the coffee brewed, Jim clicked on the satellite TV and began flipping through the channels. Infomercial…infomercial…infomercial; 500 channels, 495 infomercials. Unless looking to purchase some inane item in the middle of the night, don't plan to find a decent movie or TV show. Wait a minute! He laughed out loud…a Roadrunner cartoon; perhaps the Coyote had it filmed outside the complex!

The coffeemaker, spitting and sputtering, signaled completion of his morning caffeine fix. Jim filled a cup and carefully carried it to the couch where he eased back and enjoyed the old cartoons without volume. Obviously, he chuckled when the Roadrunner dropped an anvil on the Coyote's head and when the Coyote strapped a rocket on his back and blasted himself into a cliff face. All the money the Coyote spent on products to catch the Roadrunner would have supplied many a fine meal.

As he sipped his coffee, visions of the float trip, pleasant and humorous memories, popped into his mind; memories almost forgotten. He allowed himself to drift back to the Huzzah; Samantha and he no longer held last place in the parade of canoes. Bob and Liz had a firm grip on that position.

Looking over her shoulder, Samantha proudly declared, "We did it, James! We're second from last!" Words spoken too soon.

A quarter mile remained; the final bend of the trip still to come, soon. A fast-flowing stream fed into the Huzzah at that point and, unknown to them, had gouged a deeper, turbulent stretch in the normally shallow riverbed along the far bank due to several heavy rains during the previous week. The clamor of the two waters rushing together heightened the degree of difficulty in communicating.

Jim called out that they must stay to the inside of the bend to avoid crashing into the opposite bank where a large fallen tree lay. By the time Samantha made out his instructions, she could no longer fight the stronger current and they failed to hold the inside of the bend. Lacking control, they were swept to the far bank into the fallen tree. Several large branches of the dead tree extended over the water; the current of the incoming stream forced Jim and Samantha directly through them.

Jim shouted, "Get down as low as you can!"

She did, as he attempted to push away from the downed tree with his oar. Unfortunately, he focused on pushing off instead of paying attention to the branches, one of which caught him square in the chest, flipping him from the rear of the canoe into five-foot-deep churning water. The reaction to his backward fall caused the canoe to tip to the right and Samantha, looking back for James, rolled into the river.

As the current swept him toward her, he grabbed her arm, then the canoe. She hung on until back in shallower water.

Winded, they shoved the canoe onto the bank. Both stood, hunched over, hands on their knees, trying to catch their breath.

Jim raised his head. "Well…that was exciting!"

They laughed hard at their end-of-float misfortune. Playfully, she smacked his arm. "I thought you said the deepest parts were only three feet!"

"I sure missed this one!"

Samantha gave James a quick hug and a kiss. "You rescued me, my hero!" Locking gazes with him, she softly stated, "You are my hero, in more ways than this."

At times, he displayed embarrassment with an 'aw shucks' look. This was one of those times.

Samantha skipped to the canoe and dragged it back into the water. Jim steadied it for her to climb in as Bob and Liz drifted past backward, serenely waving good-bye.

With hands cupped to his mouth, Bob called out, "Hey! We'll have to do this again sometime! Thanks for the memory!"

* * *

"Well, still have time for one more cup. Don't want to miss my one-on-one."

The meeting with Ed Marissen…two hours away. Why would Marissen want to meet alone with him? What could they possibly have to discuss? Seems like nothing good could come from this. His mind raced with memories of the pain and the damage done to two lives as a result of Marissen's egotistical, power-driven mindset. Anger flared in his gut, a more intense anger than before. Why now?

Setting the cup on the kitchen counter, he began to pray: "Lord, take away this anger. Now is neither the time or the place to give in to it. I need your strength to put this anger aside, not to say anything I would regret later. The mission is of far greater importance than satisfying my ego. Give me the peace of mind to do your will."

* * *

As expected, Merrill Pierce knocked at Jim's door at exactly 7:00am. "Good morning, Merrill. Come in. I'll be ready in a couple of minutes."

"Take your time, Col—Jim. I apologize. I misspoke yesterday; it won't take thirty minutes to get to Ed's office. We're early but I spoke with Ed; he's in his office. I checked to see if we could come by early. Every bit of time is important. Mind if we do this now?"

"No, that's fine. We can do this any time he wants."

"Colonel…Jim. He wants only to meet you…something he says he should have done many years ago."

Pierce's statement stopped Jim in his tracks. "What are you talking about?"

"Look, Jim, I want all the cards laid on the table, no secrets, nothing that will adversely affect the mission. You two have a history…not a very pleasant history. I know that you know, for this to succeed, we must be a team. That's why I'm the manager. I can be your greatest supporter, or your worst detractor. I see you as an obvious integral part of the team.

"Ed and I spoke earlier this morning. He shared openly with me of your association, or lack of in the past. He acknowledged many mistakes he made which, more than likely, eventually led to his daughter's current situation. I'll tell you this, he deeply regrets his past actions. I know Ed very well; we're close friends after so many years. All I ask is…go easy on him. He is a strong man, but right now, he is fragile. Know this: only Ed, myself, and you share this information. He felt I should know this because…he just felt I should know. Actually, I think he wanted someone to talk to about the past without admitting it."

Jim could only nod in agreement. The trip to Marissen's office amounted to a mass of jumbled thoughts. What had just happened? Had Marissen indirectly apologized for the past? Was this an answer to his earlier prayer to take away his anger?

Merrill parked the cart to the side of the double-door entrance that opened to a lengthy hall to Marissen's office. The office door slightly ajar, Pierce knocked softly.

"Mr. Marissen, Colonel Gordon is here."

"Ah, good. Send him in, please."

An involuntary shiver crawled up Jim's spine; this was the first time he ever heard his voice. Merrill passed a knowing wink and patted Jim's shoulder as he entered. Pierce then stepped into his office next to Ed's to pull together the next meeting.

Ed sat on the edge of his desk situated in the corner of a large, yet not ostentatious, room. The simple layout and décor surprised Jim; not the power look one would expect. Marissen rose and approached Jim displaying strength and confidence, measuring in at 6' 3" with a wreath of white hair adding to his distinguished image.

"Colonel Gordon, thank you for coming this morning." He paused, motioning to the coffee pot. "I understand you like coffee. Can I get you a cup?"

Jim chuckled to himself as he thought, Ed Marissen serving me coffee. "No thanks, I'm fine."

Ed fumbled for words, "Well…have a seat, make yourself comfortable."

"I'd rather stand, if you don't mind." A strong distrust and dislike of the man swelled in Jim's chest as he struggled to hold the negative feelings in check.

"All right, son. I'd like to—

"Please…just call me Jim."

Marissen sighed, dropped his head, and turned away. "Colonel, I understand how you must despise me…I do."

A tinge of sympathy pricked Jim's conscience. "I don't despise you, Mr. Marissen. I don't know what I feel, but I don't despise you. My feelings should not stand in the way of accomplishing our goal."

Ed faced him again. "You're right, Colonel. We both want the same thing; we want Samantha home. I'm putting everything on the line to bring her back, but you are willing to risk your life, a far greater sacrifice. You must believe…I am deeply indebted to you; I will always be grateful. You could have turned this down…you didn't. I…I see what I refused to see twenty-five years ago."

Moving to his desk, Ed picked up an 8 x 10 frame and returned to Jim. "Here, take a look. These are the two most important people in my life; I should have let them been yours too. Selfishly, I did not."

Jim took hold of the frame containing a studio portrait of Rose and Samantha. They appeared so happy together. Ed's absence came as no surprise; he doubted any pictures of the three existed. Samantha's image managed to capture her smile, that wonderful, beautiful smile. Hesitantly, he handed the frame back to Marissen.

For a moment, Ed stood silent, then reached out, "We can do this?"

Jim responded with the slightest grin, "We can."

Resting the picture on the small conference table, Ed notified Merrill to bring in the IV and OV crews. Jim stepped to the table, picked up the frame and examined Samantha's face. In his mind, she hadn't changed since that Saturday morning in the church parking lot.

Ed smiled when he noticed Jim holding the picture. He

asked, "Are you sure you won't have a coffee?"

Jim pulled out a chair, but before he sat answered, "I think I will have one. Thank you."

WASHINGTON, MISSOURI

THE TOAST POPPED up, the microwave and coffeemaker beeped, and his cell phone rang. Snatching the phone from the table, Scott caught 'Samantha Reynolds' on the caller I.D. No contest which device received his attention.

"Samantha! Hello."

"Scott, hi. How are you this morning?"

"Couldn't sleep last night. Kinda strange being here without Jim. I'm going to his church; fill people in about his 'Israel consulting' assignment. You know?"

"Mind if I go with you? I've been up all night too. Would that be OK?"

"Are you kidding? I wanted to call but…I don't want to be a nuisance."

Softly, she responded, "You're not." Then silence.

Thinking he lost connection, "Samantha…you there?"

"Yeah…I'm here. Thank you for being with us last night… with me. You really helped."

"That's OK. Being with you was good for me." Thinking for a moment, he explained, "I want to get there early enough to tell those closest to him. What if I pick you up in about an hour? That should give us plenty of time. Maybe lunch afterwards?"

"I'd like that. See you at nine!"

"Nine it is!"

* * *

"Jim told you to drive this thing just to make me crazy, didn't he?"

"Actually…he did. Seems I owe him that."

"He's had this jeep for years; kept it at his uncle Dave's He'd work on it when he'd come into town. He didn't start driving it until he retired from the Air Force."

"You do know, Samantha, you're the reason he keeps it… just to give you reason to give him trouble. You don't know how much he enjoys your wisecracks."

"Oh, I think I might. I know he wants me to give him trouble. He loves it…and so do I. There are times I intentionally say something just to get the ball rolling. He is such a great guy; I do think of him as my uncle. He's closer to me than any of my real uncles." She grew quiet.

"What are you thinking?"

Samantha placed her hand on his forearm. "I honestly believe I'd be disappointed if he did get rid of it."

"If it reminds you too much of Jim, I can drive my car, OK?"

"This may sound strange, but I think I would like if you drove this when we go out."

"Are you saying you'll continue to go out with me?"

"As long as you continue to ask."

* * *

Although Scott had accompanied Jim only twice to the church, people recognized him immediately and inquired of Jim's whereabouts. Before explaining Jim's absence, Scott introduced Samantha, who quickly became an honorary member of Jim's family. She soon felt as important in Scott's explanation of the Israel consulting mission and the length of time Jim may be out of the country as Scott. Although distressed about Jim's mission, most felt it best for him during this time of Samantha Marissen's imprisonment in Russia.

Once they had informed everyone of Jim's current special assignment, Scott and Samantha spent time in the rear of the church simply talking. Over the next hour, a deeper bond of friendship took hold, a bond that would return Samantha and Scott to Jim's church many, many times.

SONORA COMPLEX, ARIZONA

PIERCE KNOCKED AND entered Marissen's office in one motion. "The teams are ready, Ed. You ready?"

Marissen handed a black coffee to Jim. "Yes, let's get this started. Time you met the crew members, Colonel; I believe you will blend well with them."

Jim rose from the table. "Mr. Marissen, call me Jim, please. No sense in too much formality."

A look of relief washed over Ed's face. Extending his hand, he asserted, "Well…Jim, I am just Ed…thank you." The two men shared a firm handshake.

As Ed returned to his desk, Merrill paused at Jim's side before bringing in the crews and said in a hushed tone, "Well done. Thank you."

Jim remained standing, awaiting the arrival of the four crewmembers. A sense of calm and serenity enveloped him; he knew only the strength of Jesus carried him past his early morning anger. God does work in mysterious ways, he thought, and thankfully so.

The two crews entered Marissen's office, Pierce followed, closing the door behind him.

Stepping to Jim's side, Ed began, "Mornin' guys. Thank you for the early rise. I want to introduce Colonel Jim Gordon, the pilot selected by General Townsend to replace Glen Blakely as pilot of the XM.

"Jim, I'd like you to meet Dan Malone, Captain of the Orbital Vehicle, and Kyle Webster, Commander. And, over here is Tim Moore, Captain of the Insertion Vehicle, and Mike Parker, Commander."

Greetings and handshakes exchanged among the men, except for Malone who remained silent. His lack of camaraderie failed to pass unnoticed.

"What's the problem, Dan?" Merrill demanded.

Malone didn't hesitate, "I still don't understand why we had to go to the outside for the XM pilot. I requested that position but you turned me down. Give him the OV! That would work fine!"

"Dan!" Marissen stepped in, showing no patience for what he considered insubordination. "Merrill didn't turn you down...I did! Not because you're unqualified...we don't have the time to train two positions. You know the OV; you're good! If you took over the XM, both of you would start at ground zero. Think about it! Leave your ego at home for once!

"Colonel Gordon is qualified. He's a thirty-year Air Force veteran; he's flown F-15s, F-16s, and the F-22. I think he knows what he is doing!"

Grasping for the last straw, Malone went for the emotional reaction. "Yeah, but you want to risk another family man?"

Jim calmly responded to the irrational argument, "I have no family, Dan. That is a non-issue."

Although thankful for Jim's initiative to respond, Ed grimaced at the answer, a valid reminder of his refusal to honor the love his daughter and Jim Gordon possessed for one another. The straightforward statement silenced Malone, who stepped back from the semi-circle of pilots, obviously embarrassed by his juvenile outburst.

The awkward moment broke with the buzz of Pierce's phone. "Yeah, everything ready? OK, we'll be right there. Thanks."

"Ed, they're ready for us in the presentation room. Not everyone will be there, just the core group for today."

Pierce addressed Jim, "Colonel, you're going to meet those in the inner circle of the mission, those aware of what we're doing. You'll meet the others over time. Everyone else has been given time off due to the death of Glen Blakely. We will be the only personnel here until the completion of the mission. Of course, I'm speaking of just under seventy-five employees."

Surprised, Jim replied, "Seventy-five! You can trust seventy-five individuals?"

Pierce didn't blink. "Yes, I would trust these people with my life."

The IV/OV crews entered the presentation room with Merrill through a side door, passing through a supply room before reaching the stage. Ed stopped Jim in the hall.

"Mmm…Jim, I apologize for Dan's behavior. He's one of the cocky ones; likes to think he's the alpha dog. He's not… never was. Don't get me wrong, he's good, real good. That's his problem. If we didn't have this schedule, he would no longer be part of the mission."

Perplexed, Jim asked, "Why are you telling me this?"

"I want to give you a heads-up on what to expect from him. Actually, I'm glad he had his little tantrum. You got to see firsthand his attitude—not a team player. Don't let him pull any of his nonsense on you."

Somewhat surprised by Marissen's candor, Jim flatly stated, "I've handled his type before; I can take care of it."

Ed broke into a wide grin, "I figured you could. Let's go show 'em who you are."

Taking a deep breath, Jim preceded Ed through the door onto the stage and immediately noticed Generals Townsend and Forsythe sitting to the right. As Ed reached the podium, he motioned for Jim to join him on his left.

After clearing his throat while surveying the remaining employees, Ed spoke softly into the microphone in his distinct southern baritone. "I want to thank you all for staying with us at this critical time. You have been with the project from the beginning and I know of your pride in what we have accomplished through your dedication and hard work."

He paused briefly to gather his thoughts and to hold his emotions in check. "Glen Blakely was a great man…a great pilot, and a good friend. He is missed by all…and will not be forgotten. That is what makes this so difficult. The President has deemed it necessary to continue. To do so, General Townsend and General Forsythe have highly recommended a pilot to take over the XM."

Placing his hand on Jim's shoulder, Ed announced, "My friends, Colonel Jim Gordon."

During the polite applause, Jim stepped to the podium scanning the many faces of Marissen's dedicated people. What could he possibly say to ease their acceptance of him, to get a solid, safe working relationship off the ground? All eyes focused on him as he swallowed hard, grasping for words.

"Oh, Lord," he prayed, "Give me sincere words to let these people know I'm here to work with them, to learn from them, and to help bring their dedication and labor to a successful end."

He began, "Good morning. As Mr. Marissen said, I am Jim Gordon, a retired Air Force pilot. I did not know Glen Blakely but I've known men like him; men who routinely strapped themselves into an experimental aircraft to test what others had figured out on paper. These men would help transform a brilliant design from that paper into a magnificent, beautiful, powerful aircraft.

"Tragically, a time arrives when one of these brave men does not return. Then, angered by his death, we blame everything possible, including ourselves. Finally, we understand his death should not be in vain. Then, and only then, can we properly mourn the loss of a friend by honoring his life with a firm conviction to complete the work with success. We investigate, dig for answers, search for a cause until a solution is discovered. Glen Blakely deserves that success."

Pausing, Jim looked over the silent gathering. "I am not here to replace Glen Blakely…but to carry on his work, to learn from him, and you. My goal is to help bring your dedicated hard work to completion, and to successfully bring our objective home. I do consider being chosen to work with you a privilege and an honor."

As he backed from the podium, mild applause slowly escalated to a higher level of enthusiasm and excitement as Jim's words infused the downcast, downhearted souls with new life, a fresh desire to move forward. Many approached to shake his hand, welcoming him into the Marissen AeroSpace family. The stage filled with personnel looking simply to meet the man who stepped into such a dangerous position, yet pleased he had. Ed drifted to the background, allowing Jim's acceptance to unfold, very confident in General Townsend's choice.

Project Manager, Merrill Pierce, addressed the rejuvenated crowd, requesting they return to their seats, a lot of ground needed to be covered. Slowly, the employees returned to the floor leaving one man standing before Jim.

"Colonel Gordon?"

"Hey, yeah, nice to meet you. You're…?"

"Sorry, Steve Hamilton, designer of the propulsion system.

You know…the system failure that killed Glen."

"Look, Steve, don't blame yourself." Merrill looked for them to resume their conversation later. "Can we talk after Pierce is finished?"

"Yeah, I'd appreciate that. C'mon, sit with the rest of us."

Jim followed Hamilton off the stage and took the vacant seat next to him.

With remote in hand, Pierce plunged into the timeframe and schedule of every phase of the mission for each craft, including a comprehensive investigation of the second XM in an attempt to uncover any hint of the fatal flaw. The manner he spoke of the investigation led Jim to suspect Merrill of taking blame for the propulsion failure also. Neither he nor Hamilton should. Merrill kept track of everything and kept everything on track. A deadly error of such magnitude producing so disastrous an effect without warning after years of designs and tests boggled the mind.

A little more than an hour later, Pierce wrapped up his presentation and recommended everyone take a break but meet thirty minutes later in the XM assembly area. There, Jim would view the XM and be briefed by the people responsible for his aircraft. Although the schedule called for Monday morning as the start time, Pierce hinted that any preliminary 'getting to know you' work should be taken care of today.

Without hesitation, the crowd resumed about Jim, wanting to find out more, just the type of attention that made him uncomfortable. He remained calm and answered every question asked, reminding himself these brilliant people were his lifeline and any success relied on strong bonds with one another. And that is the reason they now mourn the loss of Glen Blakely; one of the bonds had been broken.

From beyond the crowd, Jim heard his name called. Looking up, he saw Marissen motioning for him. He excused himself from his audience and made his way to Ed.

"Yes, sir."

"Jim, I want to take a minute to thank you for your words to these people this morning. They are reinvigorated, ready to resume. I also appreciate how you sat with them during Merrill's presentation. You didn't hesitate to be part of the team. I know they appreciated your joining them. They're a good group. Someone had to come in to pick up the pieces and…I'm…I'm pleased it was you. I won't keep you, but I…umm…I hope we can talk sometime soon, you know…talk."

Somewhat confused by Ed's statement, Jim responded, "Yes, Ed…talk."

He didn't know what to make of Ed Marissen who appeared to be making overtures of friendship toward him. But why? Did Marissen fear Jim would not make every effort to rescue his daughter if he didn't? Did he regret his interference in Samantha's life that doomed her to the present international crisis and didn't know how to express it? Or…was he simply fearful of displaying vulnerability? No matter, Jim thought, whatever he wants to say, he will eventually say.

Steve Hamilton approached Jim from behind. "Do you think we can talk before we move to the assembly area? It will only take a few minutes."

"Sure, what's on your mind?"

"I need to tell you that I honestly don't know what happened. I don't think anyone understands how I feel. I can't figure out why or how the XM failed. For three years, there was never an inkling of this type problem. I've been over this so many times since it happened…and nothing. It just should not have happened. I want you to know, I won't let this happen to you."

Jim grasped Hamilton's shoulder. "I know, Steve. I've been involved in R & D and testing aircraft. This kind of failure doesn't pop up without a hint of some kind…usually. I believe what you're saying and I'm sure everyone else does too. If I run across anything in my training, I'll come to you. I'll keep my eyes open. Sometimes another pair can help."

"Thanks, Colonel. Your safety and the success of this mission rely heavily on locating the problem. After the assembly meeting, my assistant, Cole, and I are going to run a full overnight diagnostic of the second XM propulsion system: the programming, the mechanics, everything. The design is identical to the original XM as well as all the components. You will not climb into a deathtrap like Glen did."

"Blakely did not climb into a deathtrap. You'll figure it out; we'll figure it out. Don't worry, we have a month."

Six scientists, Pierce, Marissen, and Jim Gordon stood in the dimly lit corner of the assembly area looking into the darkness of the massive space. Anticipation ran high as the scientists, Pierce, and Marissen awaited Jim's reaction. Jim stared into the blackness then at the faces of those involved in the project wondering how difficult this moment must be for them. He could feel the pride these people had in their accomplishment, yet subdued by the death of their pilot, their friend. Their one desire this moment was for him to be impressed by the futuristic aircraft. Jim hoped that to be true.

Ed moved to the front of the group. "Colonel…Jim, you are about to see what may be the future of military aircraft. These people put their blood, sweat, and now, their tears into the XM. I am extremely proud of their accomplishments, how they made the whole project a reality. With your background, I think you will be able to appreciate what you will see. So, Nate, why don't you give us some light."

Nate Garcia, at the electrical panel, flipped a series of switches, systematically lighting the entire assembly area.

Situated on the far side of the room, the XM rested on its landing pods, the arrowhead wings drooping slightly, and twin tails angling majestically into the air. If animated, the XM would appear as a strutting rooster showing off in the barnyard.

Jim approached the aircraft with the remainder of the group staying behind. What he observed was far beyond anything his mind had imagined. Nothing…nothing had ever impressed him like this; the beauty of the design alone could win awards. The rippling rainbow effect dazzled his senses; a full explanation of that would be necessary. Circling the XM, he hardly breathed as he attempted to absorb the concept. Who could possibly dream up the aerodynamics of this sci-fi masterpiece? Was that Thurmond? Dave? Got to get these names down, he heard himself say.

The upper arc of the cockpit canopy measured no higher than maybe five feet off the floor and blended sleekly into the body of the craft, the tips of the angled tails no more than nine feet. With no visible engines and the 'alien' rear thruster/exhaust system, Jim found himself utterly baffled, yet mesmerized, by the design.

Stepping away from the craft, his eyes absorbed the full view. He anticipated the day he would lower himself into the cockpit to begin a departure to bring Samantha home. Amazing, he thought, where God had led him. How many years had he wondered what purpose his life served. Now he knew…and was thankful.

Running his hand along the wing, Jim turned to his audience as they anxiously awaited his thoughts. "She is… absolutely beautiful, remarkable. If she flies as good as she looks, you've really got something here! I'm sorry, I can't put into words my impression of this aircraft. I'm in awe of your results. This is amazing! I'm honored to be a part of this!"

With those words, the onlookers converged on him in semi-celebration; an odd feeling of loss with a renewed spirit of determination, a desire to continue their march toward completion of the mission. Merrill approached Ed, and in a low voice stated, "I really believe he is the man for the job. They would fight for him… and he will give them all he's got! Don't you think?"

Ed stuffed his hands in his back pockets. "I don't doubt that for a minute, Merrill, not one minute."

"Colonel Gordon! Dave Thurmond. Want to look inside, see what she's got?"

Jim turned to face a young aeronautical engineer. "So, you designed this? This is yours?"

"Yup, but Steve put her in the air. If needed, he could make a rock fly."

"Steve? Steve Hamilton? Yeah, I met him earlier."

"C'mon, let's get you in there!"

Thurmond pulled a small remote from his pocket and pressed a button causing multiple canopy locks to snap distinctly, releasing the canopy to rise from the locked position. Aided by hydraulics, the canopy was now free to lift forward easily.

"Go ahead, step up on the wing; she won't break. The interior's not complete yet. We have to get the second seat in and adjust the controls for you. The shortened fuel tanks are in but recalibrating the center of balance for the sensitive systems is a bear."

Jim agreed. "I get it; sometimes a minor design change causes major headaches trying to put it all back together. Sounds minor…but it's not."

"You understand the problems I'm facing?"

"Yeah, I'm an aeronautical engineer myself."

"That's great! I can bounce some questions off you, get some discussion going."

"About what?" Their conversation carried Jim into the involvement he needed.

Thurmond continued, "This is only a temporary change on a relatively small aircraft, so I need to have a weight range to maintain proper weight distribution. If we don't figure all the in-flight changes properly, there could be control issues. Not in space, but in atmospheric flight."

Jim backed up a step. "So, now that the internal weight will change from what was based on a single pilot aircraft to a two-person craft, you need to compensate?"

"On an aircraft this size, yes. Not to the ounce but a fairly narrow range. To figure in the absence of a portion of three tanks is simple…just add the weight of what was removed in the same area. What about leaving without an additional person but returning with the added weight. That will make a difference. Not insurmountable but it needs to be done in the simplest way. See what I mean?" Thurmond sat on the edge of the wing, his foot keeping beat to an imaginary tune.

Jim joined Thurmond on the wing. "What if you had an approximate weight of Samantha, uh, Marissen? Couldn't we just throw in some extra weight, you know, secure it, before we left and I would leave that behind when we return…if you can work with a small weight range."

"I can work within a small range. Like I said, this doesn't have to be down to the quarter-of-a-pound, but the closer we get to the actual weight, the better. Your solution could be so simple, I overlooked the possibility. I think I'll start there; see what happens."

Thurmond wrote himself a couple of notes before returning his attention to Jim, familiarizing him with the XM cockpit including flight control, guidance, and the weapons system, which he called G-BoF. When asked what G-BoF stood for,

Thurmond laughingly referred him to Charlie Rice, the weapons designer. Sitting in the cockpit, Jim expressed satisfaction with the area available for freedom of motion, but Thurmond reminded him of the necessity of a spacesuit since his portion of the mission began and concluded in earth orbit, facing the hazards of space. Although the newly designed spacesuit was not as large or bulky as those in the past, the possible stiffer motion would be an adjustment, something Jim would practice.

"The pilot will always wear the full spacesuit, even though the cockpit will be pressurized. This action protects the pilot from two potential failures. First, if the suit fails, the pressurized cockpit becomes plan B for the return to base. Second, if the cockpit pressurization fails, the suit with the emergency air supply becomes plan B for the return to base." As usual, Thurmond presented a thorough explanation.

"So, Sam…Ms. Marissen and I will be fully suited for the return flight."

"Yep, fully suited."

Steve Hamilton interrupted from the opposite side of the XM. "Hate to bother you guys but I gotta get rolling on that diagnostic. It's going to take hours to complete and I need to know everything is good."

Thurmond glanced up. "Yeah, no problem. We'll get out of your way. Anything I can do to help?"

"Not right now," Hamilton responded as he looked over his notes. "Cole and I can handle it, mostly nerd work."

Jim climbed out of the cockpit on Hamilton's side. "Who is Cole? I'd like to meet him."

"Cole? He's my assistant, really good. Has a mind like a computer. I think he may be the offspring of one. If you stick around, you'll see him."

"That's OK. I don't want to get in the way. We'll meet."

As if on cue, Merrill Pierce approached holding a small object. "Sorry, Jim, I almost forgot. This is your radio. Carry it at all times…and respond at all times. We're down to the wire and every second counts. We gotta be available for anything. That goes for everybody."

Pierce motioned to his left to a dark-haired, medium built man. "Jim, here is someone you need to begin with today. This is Nate Garcia, your flight instructor. Actually, he is the man behind our simulators and he will transform you into our ace XM pilot.

"Nate, Colonel Gordon, but I believe he prefers Jim. I think you will make a good team. Show him everything he needs to know, so he can begin training tomorrow morning. I want everything running by 7:00am."

NORTH OF MOSCOW

SAMANTHA STOOD AT the dacha window staring forlornly toward the rise behind her gray wooden prison wondering what lay on the other side. Freedom? To where? Didn't matter, she resigned herself to the fact she would be held in Russia a very long time. Her family and the friends she deserted many years before, would be only memories if something didn't happen soon.

Remorse over her mistakes, her loss, and her loneliness threatened to bring her to the brink of a suffocating depression if not for Nikolai, her only respite. Yet, she did not understand him, asking herself the same questions day after day: Why does he care what happens? Why is he so protective? Why does he share personal stories with her? He expressed belief she was not a spy but never explained further.

She knew in her heart that Nikolai would allow nothing to happen to her; he would protect her from physical harm. He held very few options to aid her emotionally and mentally. The best he could offer was communication, which would temporarily ease her mind.

Samantha jumped at the sound of a vehicle pulling alongside the building, nervously stepping to the side window in time to see Nikolai and the driver climb out. Relief at the sight of Nikolai and another week's supplies brought tears to her eyes, knowing that meant another week at the dacha, another delay in a trip to Moscow. She listened as his footsteps thumped across the floor to her room, pausing long enough to unlock the door with the only key, which he controlled.

Nikolai entered, closed the door with his foot, and set a box in the corner, more than likely her weekly changes in clothing. He removed his weapon from its holster and ejected the magazine, replacing it with an identical magazine from his footlocker. Samantha thought it odd; he repeated the routine before and after every task away from the dacha. Fear prevented her questioning his action.

Returning the gun to the holster, Nikolai finally spoke, "Sam, look in box. Maybe something you need."

Cautiously, she knelt before the box and raised the lid. Jumpsuits as expected. She looked to him.

"Look," he announced. "Something there."

She removed the horrible jumpsuits one at a time until…she could not believe what she saw, her Bible…her very Bible. She clutched it to her chest, as if hugging a long-lost friend.

"Nikolai, you don't know what this means. This book is my life! Thank you, thank you. How did you do this? Why?"

"No matter…you are happy."

He watched as she turned through the pages, not believing she had her dearest possession. She soon stopped and gazed intently at something wedged in the center of the Bible. Gently, she removed and carefully unfolded a small worn paper. Nikolai could see she was reading to herself. Samantha refolded the paper and sat on the edge of the bed as she pressed it to her heart. Closing her eyes, a single tear trickled down her cheek.

Nikolai moved quietly to the window until he heard the paper being unfolded once more. He faced her and softly asked, "What is paper? You tell me?"

Samantha straightened up and wiped her eyes. "Remember the man I told you I hurt so badly. He wrote this for me shortly after we met. He didn't give it to me right away, but when he did, I kept it in my Bible. I thought it was beautiful."

Nikolai stepped closer. "He was…good to you?"

"Yes, he was. I know thinking of him after all this time is pointless, but…

"Nikolai, if I ever get out of here, I'm going to look for him. If he is married, he will never know I looked for him, but if there is the slightest chance he isn't…but I'm sure he is, he must be.

"But…you will try?'

"Yes." Her answer…tired, weak. "Yes, if I ever get back home."

"You will, Sam, you will."

How could he be so confident, she wondered. No, he was only being a supportive, sweet boy.

"Sam, you cannot…stop. You must be…strong. Do not…give…up.

"Tell me of this man. What is name?" He pulled a chair toward Samantha to maintain quiet. He desired the conversation to continue, to strengthen her, keep her going.

"Nik, you are very kind but you don't have to do this."

"Yes…but you hear about Anechka. You tell me what to do. And I will do what you say. Now…is your time." Nik looked as though he meant what he said.

Displaying the slightest smile of appreciation, she straightened the paper on her lap.

"Are you sure I can read this to you? I shared this with only my best friend."

He responded quickly, "Gina, am I…right?"

"Yes, you are." Samantha showed surprise he remembered Gina's name from earlier conversations. "She is another person I lost. I wonder if she remembers me. I made some horrible, stupid mistakes. I let the wrong people lead my life. I failed to do what I should have done."

Perplexed, he asked, "Persons make you not do what you want?"

"Yes…but that was my fault, no one else."

Nik leaned back in his chair. "Please…read to me."

She began, "His name was…is, James…

> *May it be the smile of sincerity*
> *What I always see*
> *Praying for those she loves.*
> *God knows why we found one another,*
> *I think, the smile of true sincerity.*
>
> *Time passes, I begin to understand*
> *In my thoughts of her,*
> *A still, small voice within says,*
> *"Wait, my time…not yours."*
> *And so, I wait.*
>
> *For as I wait,*
> *The more I learn of her.*
> *I see her loving care,*
> *Her arms gently caressing*
> *The shoulder of her mother.*
>
> *Again, her smile, as she*
> *Warmly comforts others.*
> *And at times, laughter*
> *From one in her own pain,*
> *Suffering her own emptiness.*
>
> *Many questions surround me,*
> *Why has God placed her in my life?*
> *May it be I have the chance*
> *To someday experience her love,*
> *And, I pray, to heal her heart.*

Her voice faltered as she read the final stanza through tears, one dropping to the worn page. Speaking James' writing aloud gave him presence, as if he stood next to her. Sadly, the personal expression of his feelings reinforced her knowledge that she and James should have been together forever. God determined their relationship before time, before He formed them…and she rejected His plan.

"Sam, you OK? You stare at paper." At the last moment, Nikolai added, "He loves you."

Samantha rose from the bed and stepped to the window. "Oh, Nik, how could he?"

He answered quickly, "A man…writes…only if…love is. James loves you…yet."

Returning to the bed, she did not sit. Instead, she pointedly asked, "I have a question you must answer." She lowered her voice to a whisper, "Why do you always say I will get out of here?"

She caught him off-guard with her direct inquiry, yet her look of desperation brought the only response he could offer, "A feeling…a feeling. Please, be strong."

SONORA COMPLEX, ARIZONA

PULLING THE DOOR to his quarters closed, Jim hustled down the hall to Merrill Pierce and his electric ride to the XM simulator.

"Merrill, do you ever sleep? No matter the time, you're always available."

"Without all the drama, this is very important to Ed and I'm responsible for every aspect. I set a rigid time schedule and I want to keep it. His daughter's freedom, and maybe her life, depends on it."

"I know you were against this but, at least now, it's under the auspices of the President and his cabinet. You must respect Ed Marissen a great deal."

"I do, but now I see the need for this. Negotiations are non-existent and their threatening us with a trial sometime soon. Who knows just how dangerous that renegade government is?

"I have family, and at this point, I would do the same. Those clowns in power, and I use the term lightly, those clowns are young, immature, very radical and unstable. Logic is out of the question for them. Fear of losing their foothold has taken over. Just get her out of there and be done with it.

"We have the technology to pull this off. Then, we can support those who want to bring the Russian Federation back into the fold. Our success in freeing Ms. Marissen may guarantee that."

Pierce glanced toward Jim. "Everyone here has the utmost confidence in you. Your record speaks for itself. Morale has taken a huge jump and Ed feels he has an immediate partner in this mission…you. And I sense you are grateful for the chance to do something. You're not the type who wouldn't. You have something at stake here…or someone. Don't forget…I know. Both you and Ed have someone in common in this mission… and I can't think of a more powerful combination than you two."

Merrill changed the subject, returning to the matter at hand. "Did you and Garcia get together about this morning?"

"Yeah, we spent several hours checking out the simulator; even that is amazing."

* * *

Nate Garcia paced the stretch of floor surrounding the simulator anxiously awaiting his student. Merrill pulled alongside.

"All right, you're here!" Garcia chided. "I was about ready to radio both of you. Got your radios?"

Jim patted his right side, radio clipped to his belt.

"All right, Nate." Pierce moaned. "I'm not that bad, am I? I think I still have two minutes."

Nate laughed. "No, you're not! But, I am disappointed. I thought I might catch you this morning. Do me a favor. Just once, be a minute late just so I know you're one of us."

"You know I can't do that; sets a bad example."

Jim smiled at the exchange; listening to the rapport Pierce had with those he managed. Although a stickler for promptness, accuracy, and details, Merrill maintained a deep sense of camaraderie and respect for his employees; small wonder the Complex ran like a fine piece clockwork.

Merrill patted both men on the back. "Good luck. I know all will go well today. Pace yourself, Jim. You don't have to become an ace this morning. If there are any problems, give me a call; I've got my radio, Nate."

*   *   *

While Nate made his way to the IOS (Instructor Operating Station), Jim climbed into the full-scale XM mounted atop a multi-hydraulic cylinder motion platform, which simulated acceleration in the six degrees of freedom, providing, under state-of-the-art computer control, the three rotations of Yaw, (left and right motion of the nose), Pitch (up and down motion of the nose), and Roll (one wing up, the other down). The platform also accommodated the three linear movements of Heave (up and down motion), Sway (left and right sideways motion), and Surge (longitudinal acceleration and deceleration).

From the IOS, Nate could create normal or emergency conditions in either the internal craft or external environment, ranging from XM system failures, to weather conditions, to intercepting aircraft, and various innumerable obstacles Jim would need to be familiar and ready to respond.

Jim situated himself in the XM cockpit, inserted his communication earpiece, and notified Nate he was ready to begin. Immediately, his view through the canopy jumped to life; the XM sat on the sun-drenched Sonoran airstrip prepared for flight, the computer-generated images so convincing, Jim felt as though instantly transported from the simulator room to the arid desert floor.

"Nate, this is fantastic, absolutely amazing!"

"Thanks, I hope the scenery isn't the best part. So, as you can see, once the canopy is closed and locked, the XM performs its own checklist and records each as complete by a small flashing light located on the left side of the front control panel. When the sequence is finalized, all system lights will flash in unison. If launch is not activated within twelve seconds, you will be asked if you want to continue. A third request without response will shut down the XM as a safety precaution. The launch sequence must be manually restarted at that point.

"Just remember, no one expects immediate success; this will take time. Relax and let your pilot instincts take over."

Jim wrapped his right hand tightly around the joystick, visualizing each maneuver. He loosened his grip on the stick, thinking he didn't have to choke it to death. Gazing across the simulated desert runway, he repeated his first assignment, "OK, I'm going to raise her 25 feet and return to the ground. Let's see what happens."

He pulled back slowly on the stick, activating the lower thrusters, lifting the craft off the airstrip. The sensitivity of the stick made stability difficult to maintain, causing the XM to wobble slightly as it rose. Jim figured to compensate for the sensitivity while the craft continued to lift, still wobbling, to 18', when the instability increased beyond the tipping point, sending the craft sideways into the ground. The realism of the simulator gave Jim's mind reason to brace for the crash, sensing he had truly hit the runway.

"Sorry, Nate."

Garcia chuckled, "That's OK, I'll get you a new one."

With Nate's touch of one key on his laptop, Jim found himself on the airstrip in an upright position, the XM finalizing the pre-launch checklist. Jim eased the stick back once more, the XM rising slowly but at 12' slipped backward, crunching the twin tails into the hard surface.

"One more time!" It had been quite a while since he experienced this level of frustration. Never before had he flown this advanced a craft, but 12'. C'mon, he thought. The XM lifted slowly but steadier, 10'-12'-15'-18'-21'—then, suddenly, a sideways roll into the airstrip.

"Again!" Another wobbly crash.

"Again!" One more.

"Another!" Crash! Nose first.

"OK!" Thump! Belly flop.

Unfortunately, the crashes continued until Jim, exasperated, called out, "Enough! Garcia, is there a way to decrease the sensitivity of the stick?"

"That can be done. Right now, its set at the level Blakely preferred. Sorry about that."

"He certainly had a nice touch if he could handle this."

"Let's get you out here and make it work." A few adjustments to the program and to the physical simulator and all would be well. Nate wanted this to work. He knew Jim could fly the XM; he simply wanted the learning process as frustration free as possible.

Ed Marissen, Merrill Pierce, General Townsend, and General Forsythe observed the simulator trial run in the private confines of Marissen's office. Merrill spoke first, "I hope the fix is as simple as those two think. If he can't get it off the ground, we have a problem. Time is the issue here; we don't have much. If too many of these minor problems crop up, we will run out of time through no fault of Colonel Gordon. There may be just too much to learn in such a short period."

Tapping his pencil on the arm of his chair, he continued, "Perhaps we view flying the XM as simple since Glenn sat in the pilot's seat from the beginning. Maybe there were things we took for granted because he handled the problems in his own private way, ways Jim doesn't have access to."

General Townsend responded, "Mr. Pierce, Colonel Gordon is the best man for the mission. He knows how to think on his feet...or should I say, ahem...in a sitting position, and rise to the occasion of a pressure situation."

Townsend rose from his chair. "Let me tell you about an incident he survived in the Mid-East conflict and later went on to instruct fellow pilots how to handle similar catastrophic events."

He proceeded to explain the bombing run Jim flew and the missile that struck his jet while returning to base which blew off a sizeable portion of wing and severely damaged the tail section. Townsend minced no words when he said, "The maneuvers that pilot had to pull to get his plane back was beyond remarkable. He could have bailed...but didn't. He was bringing his bird home no matter what. When we saw the condition of that aircraft, we knew he was lucky to be alive. But, luck had nothing to do with it. His cool, collected skill did it. That...and he credited God completely for his safe return. Not only is he good, he will not act like it. Personally, I've great admiration for that man. If there's anyone I would want on my side, it would be him.

"Don't sweat it, Merrill. Let him show you what he can do. He's entered a whole new era of flight. We all want this to go like clockwork...and it will, but there's going to be some glitches to overcome."

Merrill paced across the room. "I know you're right, General. I didn't mean to sound like an alarmist. I just want everything to go well for him. He stepped right into the middle of this; I want it to be easy for him. He's a good man and I don't want him to falter for any reason."

"He won't. Besides, you have put a challenge in front of him...that's when he is at his best. He won't falter, and he certainly won't fail. I guarantee you; he's back in his environment. He's lovin' this."

Ed leaned back in his chair as he viewed the screen, listening to the two men discuss the modification of the control stick.

"Do you hear these guys? They are calmly addressing the problem at hand together. This interaction tells me Jim is an integral part of this mission. I have faith in his abilities. Let's get these nuisance problems out of the way and the preparation can move on."

While conversation continued in his office, Ed thought back to General Townsend's account of Jim's harrowing near-death flight. Not of what a skilled pilot he was, but what a pity Jim went through the ordeal alone. While protecting his daughter from life, he had doomed Jim to a life of solitary confinement, a life alone. Of course, Ed was not aware of young Samantha Reynolds' constant prayers for the safe return of her uncle.

Ed recognized Jim wanted nothing to stand in the way of a successful mission, noting that Jim felt no need to work around a problem but, rather, fix the problem and move on. He also realized Jim would allow nothing to interfere or halt the rescue of his daughter.

Sadness gripped him over his past desire for control and protection of Samantha. What good came of it? Her marriage to an evil man destroyed whatever dignity she possessed. She is now a prisoner in a hostile country. His personal selfish drive negated the life of Jim Gordon. Even though Ed had not been a loving, giving, supportive husband or father, he did have his family; Jim did not. He could have been a part of the Marissen family. Rose certainly hoped that to be. His daughter would be happily married…very happily. There would be grandchildren. Everyone's life would be full. But…no.

The remainder of the morning involved the reconfiguration of the XM controls to match Jim's specifications. A test of the changes would take place after a quick lunch. Word spread fast, which drew a crowd anxious to observe the results and to support Nate and Jim in their quest to remedy the problem.

"OK, Jim, ready?"

"Ready, let's do it."

While Merrill and the Generals viewed the test in Marissen's office, Ed stood quietly off to the side, hoping the best result for Jim and Nate. No one breathed as the simulated XM rose steadily from the computer-generated airstrip to a height of four feet and hovered.

Jim's voice announced over the speaker, "Nate, I'm hovering to get a better feel for the control. I'm experiencing no wobble whatsoever. The stick feels good. I'm gonna take her up another four."

Ed stepped closer to the screen as the craft rose to eight feet hovering again but only for a moment. Jim kept the XM rising until reaching 25'. Would it suddenly tip and crash on the runway? Not this time.

"Yes, yes! Way to go, son…Jim." Marissen excitedly clapped his hands. "Yeah, I know, minor stuff but he took her right up, no problem. He's gonna be fine."

Very cautiously, Jim turned the XM 360° midair before gently returning to the ground.

Nate burst out laughing, "Hey, what was that?"

"I don't know, just a sudden urge. What's all the commotion out there?"

Garcia replied, "I think everyone's happy with the results. It's been a good day."

Rubbing his face with both hands, Ed exhaled heavily and mentioned, "Merrill, I need to make an important call."

With that simple statement, Pierce politely escorted Townsend and Forsythe from the office to the simulator. Ed stared at the phone a couple of seconds before punching in the number. Hearing an answer after one ring, "Rose, baby. I love you…"

During that afternoon and the remainder of the week, Jim spent every waking moment learning and simulating the basics of XM flight, stepping out just a little further every day. The mission pressed on.

MARISSEN ESTATE-
ST. LOUIS, MO

ROSE WELCOMED SAMANTHA and Scott to the tree-covered stone patio adjacent to the sun-drenched pool. The tranquil sound of water babbling through a narrow, man-made, rock-strewn stream into the far end of the pool conveyed a sense of serenity and peace, although none existed.

"Oh, Samantha, Scott, it's so good to see you. Please sit. Tell me what's happening in your lives. Y'all getting along nicely, I see."

"Mrs. Marissen, please! We're just getting to know each other. You might embarrass Scott."

"Me? Mrs. Marissen, really, Samantha is the one who doesn't want to admit—

"Admit what? Mrs. Marissen, he—

"Wait just one minute, you two. First of all, if you don't stop referring to me as Mrs. Marissen and start calling me Rose, you may inflame my southern ire...and you don't want that. Second, you're both so afraid to just enjoy what you might have, you may miss it."

Reaching for Samantha's hand, Scott announced in a semi-serious tone, "Rose is right, *sweetheart*. Perhaps we should—

"Perhaps you should what?" a voice boomed from behind.

"Dad! How do you always manage to be in the wrong place

at the wrong time?"

"Sorry, baby, it's a 'dad' thing. Scott, go on, finish what you were going to say."

"Richard Reynolds, leave them alone. They are fine and don't need your assistance."

"Sorry, Rose," Gina apologized. "I hoped after all this time to make a better entrance."   Rose stood immediately. The long-lost voice of her daughter's best friend released a burst of joy. "Gina! Oh my, Gina, it is you! Come here, honey." Rose took her in her arms, laughing and crying at the same time.

"Oh, Gina, it is so good to see you." Turning, she added, "and Richard."

"You know, dear, he hasn't changed a bit…and I'm glad."

Rich stepped to Rose with arms spread wide. "OK, Rose, I'm gonna hug you whether you like it or not, so don't fight it."

"Richard, you know I'll like it. You were always the 'good little bad boy'."

"Richard," Scott egged. "Please do tell us of the 'good little bad boy'. Sounds interesting."

"Yes, Father, do tell, please." Samantha joined in the playful attack.

With mock shyness, Rich declared, "Rose, you have disarmed me with a few simple words. I surrender."

"Sorry, Dad, it won't be that simple. We're not going to press for an explanation now. It'll be much easier to ask Rose when you're not around to lie about…umm…defend yourself."

After Rose's forewarned hug and a good laugh at Rich's expense, everyone settled around the table centered in the gazebo off to the side of the pool; a ceiling fan circulated the muggy air.

"My goodness, it's so good to see y'all. Samantha promised you would visit soon. I'm happy it's today."

A young lady arrived with a pitcher of tea and five ice-filled glasses. "I thought the next time Scott and Samantha came for a visit, we should have some tweet tea. So, Gina, Richard, you must have some too."

Gina moaned, "Oh, just what my waistline needs. But…you know what? I'll risk it."

Rich chuckled, "Yeah, as if she needs to worry. I'm the one who needs to watch it!"

Samantha and Scott receded to the background as Gina and Rich shared much news of family and friends with Rose. The conversation brought much-needed relief to Rose, providing an opportunity to rediscover and rebuild another lost relationship. Gina, Samantha's best friend for many years, brought Rose's daughter closer to home with her mere presence.

"Gina," Rose wished aloud, "I hope with all my heart you and Samantha can continue the beautiful friendship you had before her…her disastrous marriage to that awful man. I hope and pray Jim will come back into her life. Do you know how wonderful that would be?"

Gina touched the back of Rose's hand. "I do, Rose, I do. I pray for that too. We all do."

A thought-provoking discussion ensued regarding Jim's refusal to open his heart to anyone since Samantha, drawing the conclusion that he unconsciously avoided the pain of a failed love by filling the void with his career, burying his 'cowardly' non-action against the powerful Ed Marissen.

Rose felt Samantha's fear wasn't living without wealth but, rather, a fear of Ed who forced his plan on her as a sense of duty to his sister. Each had abandoned the other because both felt weak and ashamed.

The analysis brought about a time of quiet thought, broken when Gina asked, "How is Mr. Marissen? Is he doing OK?"

Rose sipped her tea. After setting the glass on the table, responded, "He's good. His work keeps him occupied…very occupied here of late. Ed has been different, especially this week; he's been…very attentive to me."

Rich leaned toward her. "How so?"

"Well…starting last Monday, he called, told me he loved me. I'm sorry, you don't mind me sharing this with you?"

"No, not at all," they agreed.

"It was so strange. Last weekend, he had to rush back to Arizona for some special project. I don't know what could be so important right now. I really wish he could be here…with me. He calls, tells me he loves me, but then, remains in Arizona. He's there and Jim is in Israel. Both of my men are gone.

"If any news about Samantha broke, I'd be here alone. That's what I don't understand; he won't be home because of that project, or whatever it is. Sometimes, that business of his make me so angry. Despite everything, it still comes first."

"I'm sure there's a reason for that, Rose." Rich weakly suggested.

"What could possibly be more important than bringing Samantha home?"

Scott's mind wrestled in turmoil over Rose not understanding Ed's actions regarding the Arizona project and Jim's sudden trip to Israel. As the conversation around him continued, he debated whether he should share what he knew with her. He recognized how distraught Rose was, thinking she bore the brunt of concern for her daughter, believing her husband cared more for his business than his family. He could not allow her to be swept up in such untrue thoughts. As wrong as he knew it to be, he could not bear to see Rose in such pain; he would tell her the truth and leave the rest to God.

"Rose," Scott interjected.

She stopped speaking mid-sentence. "Yes, Scott."

"I'm going to tell you something and you must promise me

you will not repeat this ever, to anyone."

Samantha squeezed Scott's hand. Rich turned to him. "Are you sure?"

Determined, he answered, "I've never been more sure. This is right."

"What are you talking about?" Rose begged.

Scott insisted, "You cannot repeat this. Promise?"

With a perplexed look, Rose declared, "I promise. Now, what are you talking about?"

"There is a plan to rescue your daughter…

As Rose sat in utter amazement, Scott related how Marissen AeroSpace, under the auspice of the President, the Secretaries of State and Defense, and two Air Force generals, devised a plan to fly into Russia to rescue Samantha. Marissen AeroSpace had developed a new futuristic aircraft and required a pilot to fly the aircraft into Russia. Jim Gordon was chosen as that pilot one week ago and was now in Arizona training for the mission. Scott did not go into detail regarding the method used to get Jim's aircraft from point A to point B; he would wait for any questions Rose may have. He did not bring up Samantha's physical, mental, or emotion state, nor the fact the initial pilot died in training for the mission. Both facts seemed unnecessary for the moment.

While continuing with his explanation, tears filled Rose's eyes as she began to understand the tightrope her husband walked attempting to rescue his daughter and protecting his wife at the same time. Her tears also fell for Jim, the man of Samantha's life, who would make the attempt to free her. She regretted not seeing him before he left for Arizona, where he would be working directly with the man who had interfered in their lives so many years before. How much did Jim love her daughter if he would risk his life for her? How much, if he would respond to a need of Ed Marissen? And what about Ed? What has he been through over the last months.

"Oh, my Ed, my poor Ed. All I've done is complain all the while he was worrying and working to bring Samantha home."

Gina came to her side, holding her as they cried. "How were you to know? Ed was doing what he had to do. He couldn't tell you."

"And Jim, my wonderful Jim. I can't believe what is happening. I knew it then…he truly loved her…and he still does. This is so very dangerous, I'm sure. I certainly hope the people in charge know what they're doing. I will pray for him every day; I'll pray for every one of you. I will thank God for bringing us all back together…and, He even added a couple of young ones." Rose smiled as she nodded toward Scott and Samantha.

"Thank y'all for telling me. Scott, thank you. I promise you, I will not breathe a word of this to anyone…ever. I understand so many things I couldn't see before. God certainly answers prayers!"

Rich leaned forward to address the small group. "We all know Jim. We know he's a good pilot. He will learn what he needs to do and he will carry it out as best he can. What we need to do is pray for him and Samantha and for the success of the mission. We must put this in God's hands."

Several minutes later, Samantha broke the post-prayer silence when she whispered, "Just imagine, Rose, Jim and your husband working together. Did you ever believe that possible?"

Sipping her tea, she pondered a moment to collect her thoughts. "You know, those two headstrong men could make an impressive combination. Neither will allow this to fail. You know the old saying, 'The enemy of my enemy is my friend.' If they are enemies, they will bind together as partners against their common foe. If they find they are not enemies, there will be no stopping them. That is what I believe; I believe this will work for good."

For the next hour and a half, the small group discussed the past, the present, and the past once again before Gina suggested returning home. Rose agreed; Ed would call soon and she passionately needed to talk with him. She would not tell of her knowledge of his work at Sonora but deeply desired for him to know of her love for him, to free him of any guilt he felt for leaving her alone so often. Knowing the background of his circumstances changed everything. She wanted to hold him, to express her love for him; Ed was truly her hero, her knight in shining armor, willing to sacrifice everything for the safety of his family.

Samantha and Scott hugged Rose good-bye, promising to call or visit throughout the following stressful weeks. She held their hands, reminding them, "Do not forget what I said. Do not deny what you think you have. Oh, you remind me so much of Jim and Samantha. You could just see that special something when they were together."

Kissing both on the cheek, she whispered between them, "Do not let love slip through your fingers."

Turning to Gina and Rich, Rose revealed her deepest gratitude for their visit, presenting an undeniable opportunity for the renewal of a long-lost friendship.

"I look forward to the day Ed and I can share time with y'all, and I mean all of us. Please keep Ed and Samantha and Jim in your prayers."

Gina embraced her, "We will…we must."

Turning her attention to Rich, Rose smiled, saying, "Richard, I do thank you for being here. You were always a joy to me…and now, I find you still are."

Out of character, Rich took Rose in his arms as her eyes began to fill with tears and comforted her. "I love you, Rose."

A CLANDESTINE COMMUNICATION

"EXCELLENT WORK."

"Maybe, but I never wanted him to die."

"Shut up, you fool. Never say…just shut up!"

"What about my money?"

"Been a change in plans."

"What? We had a deal!"

"The deal is still good, just some bonus work."

"What?"

"The XM project is still moving forward?"

"Yes, the second one is almost complete."

"Why is Marissen continuing with the project?"

"I…I don't know. Ego maybe?" The accomplice would not divulge the Marissen AeroSpace involvement in the plan to extricate Samantha Marissen from Russia from a deep fear of crossing the government. Odd, how an individual will justify one action without acting on another.

"I want the second XM destroyed."

"But why? Isn't one man's life enough?"

"I want Marissen AeroSpace destroyed. Kill the project and the losses will bury Ed Marissen."

"So…this is personal?"

"There is three times the money in it for you. You will be

one wealthy man."

An agonizing silence while the saboteur wrestled over his need for financial gain. Finally, he responded, "No, I won't do it. I can't bear to see another man die no matter how much you offer."

"Then you leave me no choice."

"Choice? What choice?"

"Do you realize the danger you will put your family in?"

"You wouldn't harm my family!"

"Don't try me."

"Why? Why do you need to do this?"

"I've lost everything. I want Marissen to feel that pain. He must go down."

"What if I go to the police right now? You wouldn't have time to arrange anything."

"Everything is already in place; all I have to do is give the word. You want to see that happen?"

"You're a sick man, you—

"Call me what you want. All I have to do is transmit the OK…and it's done."

"Comes your time, you'll burn in hell!"

"Hmmph! There is no hell, no God…only today. So, what's it going to be?"

Beaten, scared for his family, and alone, he gave the only answer he could, "OK! After this, no more! I'm finished!"

"Correct. No more…after this. But I need to know: How did they replace the pilot so fast?"

"Really? A man dies and you casually ask how he was replaced so fast! I don't know! How would I know?"

SONORA COMPLEX, ARIZONA

"950 – 960 – 970 – 980 – 990 – 1000! Hold her right there; you're doing great!"

"Roger that, Nate, but I'll feel a lot better when I'm in the real thing."

"I know, I know, but we can't rush this initially. Much better to crash the simulator than our last XM."

"Yeah…I don't like it when you're right. I'm impatient; I just want to keep this moving."

"We are, Jim. We're on schedule. Let's not rush it. The mission depends on coordination between you and the XM. She has to be an extension of you. You gotta be one. When that happens, you'll be ready."

"Well…let's do it. What's next?"

No doubt he was anxious, probably too anxious. The morning kicked off with slipping into the spandex mesh, one-piece, temperature maintenance garment, which went relatively easy. Donning the upper and lower torso of the spacesuit consumed a great of time and energy, only to be followed by the boots, gloves, and helmet attachments. The bigger problem might be getting Samantha Marissen into the assembly with her questionable ability to physically support the almost forty-pound suit, lightweight compared to earlier models.

"You know the controls," Nate explained. "This exercise will put it all to use. A holographic jet will display in front of your craft. All you have to do is follow it. This portion should be essentially no different than flying a jet fighter, just get a feel for the thrusters in direction changes. No flaps, all thrusters for control. I hope you're surprised by the quick reaction to the stick movement. In real flight, you'll need to be concerned about how many Gs you're pulling. Don't try to catch the object in front… just follow. It'll lead you back to Sonora. No fancy stuff."

"Fancy?"

"Yeah, you know what I mean. Get a little comfortable at the wheel and you add some personalized flair."

"Me? OK, I'll play it conservative this time…no funny stuff…play by the rules…be a stand-up guy." He chuckled as he heard Garcia mutter a statement in mock disgust about pilots.

An image of a generic fighter pulling into a steep climb instantly appeared about a mile ahead of the XM. With reflex action, Jim shot after him with a burst of thrust, reaching 40,000 feet where the image leveled off, cruising for a minute before diving sharply to the left, sweeping back toward the area of the initial climb. The next twenty minutes involved a most intense chase Jim ever experienced, testing maneuvers so extreme he instinctively came to rely on the constant, yet unobtrusive, critical data display on the canopy. At one point, Jim pulled out of a 1200mph dive 100 feet above the desert floor prior to screaming to an altitude of 32,000 feet. He momentarily lost visual of the jet but maintained its location on the radar display and instinctively veered back behind the bogey.

Just as Nate had said, the object slowed to a respectable 800mph returning to Sonora Complex where he brought the XM to a pinpoint landing at the designated mark.

Garcia reached Jim as the canopy locks released, allowing Jim to stretch his arms outside the confines of the cockpit. "Congratulations, that was outstanding. I pushed it to the limit but you hung in there. Thought I lost you once but you got right back on my tail. You came awful close to blacking out when you pulled out of that dive at max Gs, but you must have been keeping an eye on the data. You changed your angle of descent and airspeed enough to neutralize the danger. I'm sure your fighter pilot experience has benefitted you."

Jim strained an "ugh, yeah" as he unlatched and removed his helmet while Nate detached the umbilical line from the XM.

"How was the suit…too heavy…too hot…too stiff?"

Holding the helmet in his gloved hands, Jim exhaled a long sigh. "No, no, it was good. Once I got into the chase, I forgot about it. It's actually pretty flexible—not bad at all…and the temperature was good throughout the flight… and the oxygen flow good. I think my only concern will be getting Samantha…Marissen prepared, and getting my helmet and gloves back on."

Handing the helmet to Garcia, Jim asked, "Who manufactures this? How'd it get here?"

Nate grinned. "I can give you an overview, nothing more. Not because I can't tell you, I just don't know the whole story myself. Parts for our suits are constructed by several businesses and shipped to St. Louis, where they are inspected, then sent here for assembly. Only Pierce and Marissen know the whole story. I'm willing to bet many of the suppliers don't know what they are making; they just make it and ship it. The suit's designer is a contractor, a consultant, who likes the secrecy of the whole thing. He probably gets a thrill out of not telling anyone what he works on. Bottom line is, nothing is tied directly to Marissen AeroSpace or Sonora."

Jim held out his arms for Garcia to remove the gloves. "I hope I deserve one free ticket to have you help me out of these.

"I can't believe the level of secrecy here. Marissen covers all the bases; leaves nothing to chance."

"What do you mean?"

"I mean, the one thing not handled in-house is done by manufacturers who don't fully understand the big picture. Only one person, an outsider, knows—the designer of the suit. That's quite an accomplishment in itself."

With some effort, Jim managed to exit the XM without damaging his ego. The last thing he wanted was to stumble out of the craft or tumble off the wing to the floor in front of two onlookers, Lisa Kerrick and Steve Hamilton. His self-respect good for another day.

Placing Jim's helmet and gloves aside, Nate exclaimed, "Great! Glad you guys showed up; you can help. I'll disconnect the upper torso from the lower while you hold up his arms. Jim, I want you to lower yourself out of the suit while we lift. Then, we'll get you out of the bottom half."

With the assistance of three people, Jim experienced no problem dropping free from the upper portion, nor in the removal of the boots and lower torso, once he lowered himself into a nearby chair. Entering the upper torso and locking the two halves together would be the problem.

Jim speculated, "Since this is an issue of speed, I suggest I remove as little as possible once there. Just the helmet and gloves… no reason for any more. If our window-of-opportunity is as narrow as forecast, why even consider removing more than that?

"We should concentrate on Samantha. Getting her in the suit may not be the easiest task. I have to get in and out of there quickly. I need to work on suiting her up." No one seemed to catch the first-name reference to his passenger.

Dr. Kerrick spoke, "Well, Colonel, I'm here as Samantha Marissen's double to help you practice getting her in the suit. I understand we're close to the same size; she might be just a little taller. Perhaps then, you will be able to instruct her in how to help. I know nothing about the suit, so teaching me will be the same as instructing her."

Garcia wondered aloud, "Who's idea was it for you to fill in for Samantha Marissen?"

"Who else?" Kerrick responded. "Merrill. The man thinks of everything. Kind of scary sometimes."

"Dr. Kerrick," Jim interrupted. "Are you the one responsible for the special covering on the XM?"

"Yep, that's me. I call it Chromatoskin."

Always Lisa's biggest supporter, Nate raved, "Wait until you see this stuff, Jim. You won't believe it. I mean, it's right out of science fiction, absolutely fantastic…a brilliant discovery."

"Oh, Nate, you give me way too much credit," Dr. Kerrick shyly maintained. "You always make me smile."

She further addressed the issue of the suit and Samantha Marissen. "Colonel, once her suit is here and fully assembled, we can practice getting outfitted as quickly as possible."

"Sounds good." Jim turned his attention to Nate. "Since you're very familiar with suit, you should probably be there."

"Sure!" He smiled in Lisa's direction. "Be glad to."

Of course, he would. Jim suggested the arrangement because of the obvious attraction between the two scientists.

"Any idea when the suit will be ready?"

"Last I heard," Lisa shared, "the manufacturer is waiting for delivery of a couple of components. Shouldn't be too long."

"Meanwhile, I'll learn as much as I can about my suit, to help…umm, Ed's daughter when the time comes." Jim fumbled again with the name. He was going to have to come up with a generic title for Samantha.

Steve Hamilton raised another issue, "Jim, there is something I want to try…something I think we need to do."

Jim motioned to the chairs around Garcia's console, "Have a seat. Sounds like this may take some time."

Pulling a chair into the group, Hamilton looked over the three before beginning, "I haven't been able to figure out what went wrong with Glen's XM; that failure just shouldn't have happened." He paused, watching for any reaction but, saw only the concern of friends. He continued, "I want to program into the simulator a propulsion failure. Maybe, without understanding the failure, we may devise a method of restarting proper gas flow after failure."

Leaning forward, Jim rubbed his forehead with his fingertips, elbows on his knees. "So, you want a proactive approach, see if the XM will fire after failure?"

"Yeah, sounds crazy, I know, but I'm at a complete loss. I'm sorry, I don't know what else to do. Maybe, at least, we can be better prepared if it happens again."

Jim looked at Nate, Nate glanced at Lisa, and Lisa at Jim who broke the silence, "I think your idea makes good sense. It sounds logical."

Nate agreed, "Yeah, I think it's good. Everything in the simulator is identical to the XM. I say we do it. Let me know what you need."

"One thing," Jim broke in, "I don't want this to be a test just to find if the XM can be re-initiated mid-flight. I want the failure to happen without warning during one of my simulated flights to test me, my response. Make it as realistic as possible."

"You got it I'll get on it immediately. Nate, what do you think? When do you want to do it?"

Leaning back, Nate thought a moment before responding, "I don't want to do this right away. I want Jim to have more time in the simulator. The test should happen when he knows the XM inside and out. Not now, but when he's there. I'll know. Fair enough?"

"Fair enough," they concurred.

NORTH OF MOSCOW

"NIKOLAI?"

"Da…yes?"

"Do you hear that?"

"Yes, trucks."

"Trucks? Do you think it's time? My transfer to Moscow?"

"I do not know. Nothing told to me."

He grabbed his boots and gun and quickly pulled himself together.

"Stay, I will learn what it is."

"Nikolai—

"I let nothing happen."

"I know." Calmly, Samantha sat on the edge of the bed with her hands on her lap."

"Do not worry."

"I won't…go."

He opened the door. A young soldier who had been with him since St. Petersburg stood prepared to knock. Samantha had seen him many times but he never acknowledged her, let alone speak. She thought it might be that he didn't know or understand English since she had seen him speaking only Russian. She did not know his name but eventually learned he and Nikolai alternately picked up supplies, ensuring one or the other always on site. Four additional soldiers, she later learned, reported to Nikolai and guarded the perimeter of the dacha grounds.

The soldier at the door nervously questioned Nikolai in Russian about the arriving trucks. The conversation bounced back and forth as neither appeared to know what was taking place. The increasingly frantic discussion halted as soon as one of the two vehicles pulled to a stop just outside the front entrance to the dacha.

Turning to Samantha, Nikolai emphatically commanded, "Open door to no one but me!"

She simply looked up and nodded. After he pulled the door closed and locked, she prayed that she face her accusers with courage and strength, that she would show no fear.

"Take this fear from me, Lord. I am afraid; I am scared. I know You are with me, and if You are with me, who can be against me." She repeated the Bible quote over and over.

Suddenly, angry shouting interrupted her prayer. She recognized Nikolai's voice rising above the others. A gunshot, then silence.

She sat motionless, wanting to investigate the disturbance but her body refused. Every nerve screamed RUN, but where?

Footsteps approached; a key entered the lock; the door opened. Samantha stood. Still gripping his gun, the gun he had fired, Nikolai entered looking every bit as one in charge. That changed quickly as he slumped in the chair and laid his head back staring at the ceiling.

Samantha returned to the edge of the bed without a sound, choosing not to do or say anything. The faint smell of gunpowder residue from his firearm slowly reached her. What had occurred out there? Why?

A sharp knock startled them. Again, she stood and faced the door. She would show no fear, her time of weakness, she decided, was now over. With weapon drawn, Nikolai cautiously unlocked the door and with relief, exhaled "Alexei," motioning his fellow soldier to enter. He glanced toward Samantha, nodded, and began to speak with Nikolai in Russian…as usual.

"Nikolai, what is happening? Do you know?"

"I know nothing of this!"

"Why did you fire your weapon?"

"They wanted to take over, take charge. They could not show any papers, no proof of their orders. I could not let them do that. I do not believe they are legitimate."

"What do we do?"

"I'm not sure. We don't know who they are. Are they Federation troops? We do not know." Slipping his gun back in its holster, Nikolai took a quick look out the window and seeing nothing blew out a long breath.

"Bring the men in from the outer perimeter. Position two of them at opposite corners of the building. Two will rest. We will stagger the shifts. No one, except our men, is to enter this building. Use force, if necessary, to prevent entry. How many are there—twelve? We must maintain control, at least until they can prove who they are. I want papers—nothing else, papers! The responsibility of proof rests on their shoulders. I cannot explain, but I do not trust them."

"What do you want me to do?" Alexei asked as he lit a cigarette.

"You and I will guard from the inside. We will split the time to stand watch."

What about supplies?"

"We are almost out. One of us will have to pick up fresh supplies in the next day or two." Stepping closer, Nikolai added in a whisper, "Whatever we do, we must be very careful—trust no one. Get the men off the perimeter and up to the building. We must begin immediately."

"Yes, sir."

"Alexei."

"Sir."

"Thank you for standing with me."

Alexei departed to carry out his orders. Nikolai turned to Samantha, who remained standing during the Russian strategy session.

"Sam."

"Without moving, she asked, "What's happening? What was that about?"

He motioned for her to sit, then began his explanation of what had taken place; why he fired his weapon and the orders he gave because of his distrust of the officer and twelve men who had so abruptly arrived without papers. He admitted neither he nor Alexei had prior knowledge of the morning development and, as far as he knew, she would not be departing for Moscow. He did speculate that the unrest in Moscow may have convinced his superiors to send additional protection in the event of some rebel activity.

"So, what does this mean—I'm confined to this room now?"

"Yes."

Angrily, she stood and kicked the bed. "Great! That's just great! I hate this, I just hate it!"

The hint of a smile crossed his face.

"What? What's the smile for? Do you think this is funny?"

"No...no," he stammered. "Is good...you are mad...you fight. You are stronger."

Samantha paused her outburst, "Nik, I'm sorry."

He refused her apology, "Do not be sorry."

"No, I'm not sorry for my anger. I'm sorry for having been so weak. You have been so patient with me. My Lord God has been very patient with me. He has protected me. You've protected me. He has helped me in so many ways. I promise… you won't have to babysit anymore. I've been afraid my whole life. No more!" Turning to the wall, she meekly declared, "I'm forty-eight-years-old. I should have grown up a long time ago."

Nikolai felt her anguish. He wanted to say something to ease her guilt. "Sam, you have been hurt much. You have seen much. You not know what is to happen next. I see, your faith brings you to now; you are not weak."

Samantha vowed, "Well, they will not see me scared. I may be, but they will not see it."

Nikolai spent the next several hours in thought, pacing, sitting, standing at the window, and pacing again before finally dropping his tired body into the chair. "Sam, time is now…I want to give my life to Jesus."

Breaking into the widest smile, Samantha knelt with him next to the chair. "Nik, I thank God for your decision. Let's pray…"

SONORA COMPLEX, ARIZONA

SPECIAL AGENT ZYGMAN completed the necessary connections for the highly classified presentation his boss, CIA Director Allen Jamieson, was about to make to a select few at the Sonora Complex. Present were Secretary of State Ralph Atkins, Secretary of Defense Tom Gagnepaign, Air Force Generals Gary Forsythe and Robert Townsend, and Ed Marissen. Since the meeting was unannounced, Merrill Pierce left to retrieve Colonel Gordon, whose attendance Ed had insisted.

As the clump…clump…clump of heavy boots approached, Ed opened his office door giving easier entry to Merrill and Colonel Gordon, Jim outfitted in his spaceflight suit minus the gloves and helmet. Ed welcomed them with a handshake.

"Thanks for joining us." He motioned to those already present. "Jim, you know everyone here but CIA Director Al Jamieson and Special Agent Ray Zygman."

Director Jamieson approached, hand extended. "Colonel, it's good to meet you. We appreciate what you're doing. We'll do everything we can for your success."

Shaking Jamieson's hand, Jim responded, "Thank you, sir."

Zygman, a younger man in his early thirties, stood a step behind the Director, almost in awe. Jim raised his arm. "Mr. Zygman, thank you."

Zygman inched toward him. "Sir, it's an honor to meet you, really, sir."

Embarrassed by the attention, Jim shook his hand and asked what the meeting was about. Zygman glanced to the Director but the Director merely responded, "Go ahead, Ray. Fill 'em in."

"Er…yes, sir. Right away." He returned to his laptop and, typing in a series of commands, he began, "What we will have here in a moment, is satellite images over the past week showing the area where Ms. Marissen is presently detained, about 350 kilometers north of Moscow. At the time of the mission, we will provide the most accurate data available for her location and sites available for landing."

The screen leapt to life with a satellite view of the Russian countryside from what appeared to be no more than 500 feet.

"These images were taken a week ago and, if you look closely, you can see guards stationed some distance from the building. Two individuals can be seen outside the building, one of which may be Ms. Marissen."

Ed strained to see. "Samantha?" He placed his hand on Jim's shoulder. "Do you think that could be her?" Very difficult to tell, viewing straight down.

Jim could only nod, numbed by the thought of her held prisoner by a bunch of wannabees in a hostile country. A mixture of anger toward her captors and despair over her enduring such a dilemma alone tore at his gut. He wanted to get back to his training; he wanted to leave tomorrow to bring her home to those who love her.

Zygman pressed the remote and a new image flashed on the screen. "As you can see, the situation has changed. Last Thursday, two trucks carrying thirteen men and weaponry arrived, disrupting reports from our informant. Doesn't mean we're not getting information—just not on a regular basis…for the moment.

"At the present time, it's not known for certain whether these men are government supporters or rebels. Best guess says they're government supporters. The rebels will not make a move for the rescue unless based on information from our contact—nothing has been relayed to date. The government supporters are reckless, dangerous. We feel strongly the supporters are committing the acts of terrorism and placing blame on the rebels to draw on the anger of the Russian people. If that's true, then why have they suddenly arrived at this place? Our informant tells us the situation is tense but stable...so far."

Jim clumped forward. "So, what you're saying is, we've got to get her out of there...soon."

Director Jamieson took over, "Very soon. The longest we figure we can wait is ten days from today. Any longer and we lose any control over the mission organization or timetable we might have. September 5 appears to be the necessary launch date. Can you do it?"

Highly agitated, Merrill sprang from his chair. "Do you realize what this requires? We can't just throw Colonel Gordon in that machine and expect him to fly like he's been flying it for months. This will take more time! We owe him that!"

Jamieson shot back, "Understood, Mr. Pierce. But keep in mind—our intel could dry up without warning! Then, we'd really be flying blind."

Before the argument could intensify further, a voice confidently interjected, "I'll be ready! Ten days? I'll be ready!"

All eyes turned to Colonel Gordon. Ed attempted to speak, "Jim, how—

Raising his hand, Jim cut Marissen off. He looked to Jamieson. "Mind if I speak with Mr. Marissen...alone."

Jamieson nodded approval.

Ed opened the door and stepped into the hall. Jim followed. "Look, Jim, I know you—

"No, there is no waiting," Jim interrupted. "I can do this. We don't have time. We do what training is absolutely necessary and move on. I need to fly the real thing. If the simulator is anywhere near the XM, I'll be OK. Garcia assures me it is."

"But, Jim—

"No buts. Look, I don't blow my own horn, but then…I've never had to. I'm good at what I do…that's why I was chosen for this, isn't it? We both want the same thing, but only if done professionally. I won't let it happen any other way. I'll be ready. I give you my word."

Grasping Ed's upper arm, Jim solemnly vowed, "I won't fail you. I won't fail Samantha."

Ed closed his eyes and sighed…a long, anguished sigh. The two locked eyes as he quietly confessed, "Jim, I'm so sorry for what I did to you and Samantha, so very sorry." His voice trailed off.

A rush of sympathy surged through Jim as he observed a man on the edge, a man who feared he would lose the daughter he promised to protect. "Ed, we're going to make this work, the mission, you, me, Samantha."

"Yes, yes we will." He turned away for only a moment, allowing emotion to pass. "You're right, we will make this work."

Both returned to the meeting as a team, forcefully explaining their agreement with the ten-day timeframe until Merrill grudging consented.

* * *

Pierce drove Jim to the simulator without uttering a word. He wasn't angry, only worried, too many questions still unanswered regarding the crash. Nothing had yet to be resolved—no reason, no cause…no solution. The mission appeared destined for failure.

An animated discussion between Thurmond, Hamilton, and Garcia was taking place as Merrill brought the cart to a stop several feet from the simulator.

"OK, everybody, gather round. We have a definite date for the mission…September 5." He checked his notepad although he'd written nothing. "Ten days…we have ten days to pull this together. We've got to get Jim into the XM for real air time. When will she be ready for flight?"

Thurmond fired back, "She'll be complete day after tomorrow; the skin application is just about finished. Final inspection starts tomorrow morning—flight ready in two days."

"How about weapons?"

"Weapons ready."

"All right, here's the schedule—pretty straightforward. Jim, you spend as much time in the simulator as possible. Friday, you take up the XM…the real thing. Evenings spent with the suit; Ms. Marissen's should be here tomorrow. You will begin training with Dr. Kerrick getting her into the suit. Sometime during this period, Charley Rice will train you on the weapons system.

"Unfortunately, you will not have the advantage of an actual spaceflight prior to the mission. All undocking and docking procedures and atmospheric reentry maneuvers must be practiced in the simulator only. However, you will have an extended flight of the XM, putting it and you through the paces. Any questions?"

The magnitude of his training would have overwhelmed him if not for the years of experience in taking each responsibility one phase at a time. Jim grinned, responding, "I don't think there's time for questions. We'll make it. I'm surrounded by good people. What can stop us?" He knew. They all knew.

"OK, let's keep it moving then. Carry on with the simulator

training this morning. I'll work up a loose schedule to cover as much training as Jim needs. We'll add or cut as necessary. OK?"

Nate threw in a bit of humor as he answered, "You're sounding kind of flexible, Merrill. I really don't know how to react."

"Good! This will keep you on your toes. Maybe I should have run the project like this all along!"

Joking aside, Nate understood Merrill would have everything under control by that afternoon. Nothing happened at the Complex without a plan.

*   *   *

Once settled into the XM, Jim took the gloves and helmet from Nate and after some difficulty, sealed himself into the suit. He plugged in the umbilical line and waited the few seconds for the fresh oxygen to fill his lungs and the cooling to take effect. He regretted not removing the suit during the short interruption. Jim and Nate exchanged "thumbs up" as the canopy closed and locked.

Returning to the IOS, Nate activated the training program for that morning which had brought about the earlier discussion just prior to Merrill and Jim's arrival at the simulator.

"Did you tell him?" Hamilton inquired.

"No I didn't. Remember, he emphasized he didn't want to know."

The moment the LEDs flashed in unison, Jim raised the XM to a height of fifty feet before initiating thrust to power him to an altitude of 110,000 feet. Every aspect of the simulation mimicked perfectly actual flight—except thrust, something he would experience Thursday during his first experience in the actual bird. The old excitement coursed through veins, just as in his early Air Force days, imagining himself at the controls of the XM, performing the maneuvers learned in the simulator.

No longer would he remain in contact with Nate during a training flight, beginning today; the flight in Jim's complete control. Leveling off at 110,000 feet, he set course due north and prepared to execute a tight northeasterly turn. To the northwest, the Rockies rose out of the shadows in glorious splendor to the morning sunrise.

The planned maneuvers would test his ability to accomplish a high-speed, high-altitude change of direction in the ultra-thin atmosphere. Banking into the first turn, Jim nearly lost himself in the beauty of the deep blue horizon against the blackness of near-space when, without warning, silence, complete silence. Thrust had come to a halt; this was the test.

The XM began a sideways slip in the thin atmosphere, while dropping in altitude. Jim raced through a mental checklist as he systematically shut down his aircraft. "OK, Lord, let this work."

Nate motioned for Thurmond and Hamilton as he brought the XM up on the screen. No other Sonora personnel had access to observe this test. The frightening view, the identical view Jim experienced, popped onto the screen displaying the craft tumbling as it encountered the thicker atmosphere. Their pilot fought for control.

"He's shut it down, like we discussed…and, he's begun the system startup. Wait…wait, OK, it's ready!"

Although a simulated disaster, Jim's heart raced, his mind flooded with frantic thoughts of "Had he done everything correctly…and in the right order?" The tumbling motion of the craft magnified the horrible view of sky…horizon…ground… horizon…ground…sky, as the XM plummeted earthward. His neck tightened as he squeezed the control for ignition. Immediately, thrust fired full force, sending the craft seemingly every direction, similar to releasing an inflated balloon without the end tied off, no stability whatsoever.

Unable to gain any control, Jim could only stare straight ahead as the XM screamed into what would have been a twelve-story office building in downtown Ottawa at nearly 2200 miles per hour.

The three men raced to the simulator. Garcia remotely released the canopy. Jim sat motionless, numbed by the catastrophic incident. Never before had he experienced such a lack of control. He realized had the flight been real, he would be dead. He had just experienced his simulated death.

RICH & GINA'S HOME– KIRKWOOD, MO

"SCOTT, WELCOME BACK! Have a seat. How was the trip?" Rich stood to shake his hand.

"Mr. Reynolds, I didn't expect to find you alone back here. Usually, you and Mrs. Reynolds are both out here enjoying your garden, or complaining about it which, I guess, goes hand in hand. Good to see you. Where are the ladies?"

"They're inside putting together some snacks or something. Samantha got here just a few minutes ago. They'll be right out.

"So, how was your dash around the southeast these past days?"

"Scott! You're here...good!" Samantha placed the refreshments on the table, kissed his cheek, and sat in the chair next to him, reaching for his hand.

Rich broke in, "Yeah, I was just asking Scott about his—

"Scott, it's so good to see you," Gina excitedly expressed. "How was your trip with Mr. Morelli? Did it go well?"

Scott looked to Rich, chuckling at the convoluted manner he would finally hear the answer to his question. "Yes, it did, although Joe...yeah...he wants me to call him Joe, is a real dynamo—never stops. He's go, go, go. We picked up Joe and Shari in Naples on Sunday, flew to Chicago, then Charleston, Jacksonville, Miami, and back to Naples...and here I am. Got in around 4:30 this afternoon…but I love it, and Jim was right—that Bill Everdin is a good guy, a good pilot. I enjoy flying with him and I think he's OK with me."

"I'm glad the transition is going well for you."

Samantha added a dig, "You seem to have added to your already good tan."

"Don't forget, when I'm not flying, I've got some spare time on my hands…except when Joe asks Bill and me to join him and his wife for dinner. I gotta tell you, he has a good, dry sense of humor, and she's a riot. They're like…a perfect combination."

"Like us?" She squeezed his knuckles together.

"Yeah…yeah…like us! You do know I would have agreed without you breaking my fingers."

"I had to make sure with Dad here."

"Whoa, what? I'm the easiest going guy you know. I wouldn't give you any trouble. Besides, it does seem to me that you two are…hmmm…you know…OK…together. If you know what I mean."

"Dad, you and Mom are a perfect combination. You have this constant 'stuff' going, even when it's just the two of you. Experience tells me it's time for Mom to throw in some funny comment right about now."

"Oh, baby, you put too much pressure on me. I'm at a loss; I have nothing. Rich! Help!"

"Sorry, Hon. We knew this day would come. Our little girl has finally figured us out."

Laughing at her parent's playful jabs, Scott tossed out a question he had wondered, "I've heard hints of Jim and Samantha's own brand of quips and teasing. What's that about?"

"Oh, my," Gina giggled, laying her hand on Rich's. "I haven't thought of that for so long." She tapped her finger on her husband's hand. "Remember how they would work on each other until the rest of us would be rolling. And heaven forbid if they decided to turn on one of us, nothing hurtful—just plain, simple fun.

"What surprised everyone was Samantha's ability to turn her *sweet lil' ole southern charm* into a setup followed by *the dig*. I'm sure Jim helped fine-tune that. They gave us all fits; we could hardly ever get the best of them but, if we did, they would laugh with the rest of us. Talk about a team; they were good." Gina paused in thought. "I can't tell you how much Samantha changed after she and *James* met."

Scott and Samantha leaned forward. "What? James?"

Rich and Gina both chuckled. Gina explained, "Jim and Samantha talked in the greeting line at our wedding. Neither knew the other's name. Unbelievably, they were both so unsure of themselves. When she overheard me call him Jim, she immediately decided she liked 'James'. I don't think I ever heard Samantha refer to him as Jim, only James.

"I never thought of this before, but when she called him James, it was like a new name for a new man; the old Jim no longer existed.

"But someday, you'll have to hear the story of how they met, and from them. When they get home, you can ask them." She grew quiet recalling the memory of the evening. Tears welled up. "I know Jim will bring her back…and they'll be together again…like they should have been." Gina dabbed her eyes with a tissue.

Rich attempted to steer the conversation another direction. "You know," he mused, "the funny thing is, neither of them was loud or forceful, yet people listened when they had something to say. I mean…well, Gina, you know how well the Foundation flourished when Samantha took charge of her idea for fundraising."

Turning to Scott, he verified, "And I think you already know Jim pretty well. He's really a soft-spoken guy but you can tell when he expects you to listen. I would imagine that comes from his time as an officer in the Air Force…but I think he always had those leadership qualities."

Scott stretched out, crossing his legs at the ankle. "Tell me, I have to ask—what was Jim like as a younger guy?" He glanced at Samantha before continuing, "Better yet…what were the two of you like before you and Mrs. Reynolds got together? I've only heard bits and pieces from Jim. It almost sounds like he's embarrassed to talk about it."

Not offering an immediate response, Rich lit the citronella candle in the center of the table. Samantha scooted her chair closer to her father. "OK, Dad, I can only speak in generalities; you can talk from experience. I think this would be fun. Tell us something I've never heard before."

"All right…maybe I will." Interlocking is hands behind his head, he leaned back looking to Gina for approval.

She giggled again. "Oh, my! Thinking about back then makes me laugh…now…not then though. For a while, I didn't know what to think about Jim. If you're thinking the same as I am, go on, tell them."

Rich cleared his throat. "Let me preface this by saying everything we did was Jim's idea, always."

Groans rose from around the table, including Samantha's, "Yeah, right."

"Hey! I had to give it a shot. Now that that's out of the way, I can go on with the real story." He reflected a moment before going on, "But I want you to hear this first so you know what kind of friend Jim really was." Looking to Scott, he set the stage, "I'm going back to when I met Samantha's mom."

He smiled simply recalling the day. "Jim and I were cruising one Saturday afternoon when we drove past this church and noticed something in the back parking lot. Turned out to be a church fall festival, wasn't it? Yeah, it was. Anyway, we parked about a block away and walked back. Once we got closer, Jim said, 'Hey, there's some good-looking girls over there.' He was right, so we decided to check it out.

"No sooner had we walked into the festival than my eyes fell on the most beautiful woman I'd ever seen." Gina smiled at his recollection. "She was playing with a bunch of little kids, laughing and running around chasing them, and when she caught them, she'd give them these big hugs. They'd squeal and laugh. I couldn't take my eyes off her. Then suddenly, she looked over to me, and she smiled."

"Yeah, Dad, I know—

"But you don't know this. Jim nudges me and says, 'OK, I'm first.'

"We had a deal whenever we went somewhere: We'd alternate who got first pick...to eliminate any argument."

"Oh, Dad, that's awful. You didn't!"

"Hey! That was then. Yes, we did. So, I asked him who he had in mind. Imagine my shock when he pointed to Gina and said, 'That one'."

Scott straightened up, "Oh, no! This is priceless! You know, I can picture you guys doing that."

Chuckling, Rich continued, "I looked at Gina and decided I just couldn't let that happen. He was set to walk over to her when I grabbed his arm, 'Jim, look, how about I go first this time? She smiled at me.

"He says, 'I don't think so. She smiled at me. Besides, I'm first'."

"Dad...that is awful!"

"Sorry, baby, just trying to get the true flavor of the story in here. Anyway, I said, no way, man, she smiled at me. I don't know why, but I gotta meet her. C'mon, how 'bout it?"

"Well, Jim looked at me and…I'll never forget that look, he said, 'You're right, she did smile at you. I think you should go first.'

"Funny how God works in our lives. Had that day been any different, look how our lives would be changed…or never have happened at all."

"Wow, Mom, you might have dated Jim!"

"No, no way!" Gina declared. "That would have never happened. In the beginning, Jim really irritated me. I didn't dislike him; I just didn't trust him. I tolerated him because I liked your father and he was his friend.

"Your father was so sweet that day. I tried to act nonchalant when he came over but I was so glad he did. He was so much fun to talk with and he helped me with all those kids. I must admit one thing—I was impressed when Jim offered to come back later to pick up Rich; of course, that was after he struck out with all my church friends. But, I did see from that small gesture that he and your dad were good friends, but I saw something in your father that couldn't be seen in Jim."

"That's a great story!" Scott exclaimed. "What changed your mind about Jim? When did you finally accept him?"

Gina smiled knowingly as she rubbed Rich's arm. "I think our relationship made Jim stop and think about his life. He saw changes in Rich, and in me, and knew he was going nowhere in his life. And, I think he knew he was going nowhere in his spiritual life either. Rich was growing closer to God; our relationship was also growing closer. I believe Jim realized he wanted more than just superficial gratification. He wanted to experience real love. But, he still clung to his old ways, probably because he didn't know any other."

Rich picked up the explanation, "Jim was an only kid. His

mom was an alcoholic and his dad a…well, let's just say he wasn't a good husband; not a recipe for a loving, caring family. I really believe that's why his mother turned to alcohol. She was a very sweet lady who loved Jim very much. It's just that the family environment was almost toxic.

"Jim was really unsure of himself and early on faced a lot of social rejection. Seemed to harden him; he dated, but only on a win/loss basis. Occasionally, someone would crack open the door but he would get scared and run. Later on, to add to his troubles after he was in the Air Force, there would be those who wanted only to brag they were dating a pilot. Whom could he trust? He gave up any thought of dating anyone seriously. I knew he was hurting; he was so alone. He always acted like it never bothered him, but I knew better. There were times when Gina and I were dating that I felt so bad for him.

"I was a follower. In the beginning, his life looked pretty cool; I wanted to be like him. Yeah, I let myself get sucked into it, but there were plenty of times I steered him the wrong way. My family was so large that as long as I was OK, they were OK. Since I came from an all-male family, Jim was well-liked, even admired at my home, but they only knew the superficial Jim. Still, they were relieved when I brought Gina to meet them."

"The moment that changed my relationship with Jim," Gina pointed out, "was when I explained to him that he could not hit on any of my friends. I didn't want any one of them used or hurt by him. I would not stand for that. So, I demanded, 'Do you understand me? I don't want you with any of my friends!'

"And, you know, he looked at me with such an expression—I don't know if it was a sadness or what, maybe it was the same look he gave Rich at the festival, but he looked at me and told me, 'That was pretty gutsy, Gina. I respect that. I like you. I promise…I won't approach any of your friends.' He kept that promise until he met Samantha at our wedding."

Rich quickly added, "And I know it was the same for Jim as it was for me when I first saw Gina; something drove him to pursue Samantha. He even asked Gina at the church about her. But he was very sad that morning, wasn't he?" Gina nodded agreement. "When Gina asked him not to hit on Samantha, she had enough pain in her life, he promised he wouldn't and stepped away more depressed than I had ever seen him. He even cut the morning short with Samantha; told her it was nice to meet her and walked away. I remember Samantha watching him as he did. She looked so very sad. I didn't know what happened after that.

"But for some reason, he later changed his mind. At the reception, it became obvious they were together for the evening. Towards the end, I questioned him about what he was doing. He told me in no uncertain terms, 'If Samantha agrees, I'm not going to stop seeing her, Rich. Not for you, or Gina.' His lack of fear convinced me of his sincerity." Rich laughed at the outcome.

"After that, he explained everything that happened earlier. Later that evening, Samantha brought Jim to Jesus. I mean… it was almost like a fairy tale. I can still get a little…umm… choked up just talking about this."

"So, Mom," Samantha asked, "were you pretty strict about your rule with Jim?"

"Very!" Gina stressed, "For him it was a good rule. But after he and Samantha met, the rule deserved to be broken. They were so good for each other. I know they truly loved each other. It didn't take long before I was certain he would never do anything to hurt her. What happened in the end was just awful, something no one expected. Just shows what too much power in the wrong hands can do to harm innocent people."

Scott questioned a statement he caught in Rich's explanation, "You mentioned Samantha had enough pain in her life. What was the pain?"

Rich pointed to Gina, indicating she should be the one to explain. Gina recalled, "Oh, my, I haven't thought of that in a long time. Samantha, I never told you this; it just didn't seem necessary. I think you'll understand why, especially since you didn't really get to know her."

Gina related the tragic event of Samantha's past so many years ago, the loss of her family at twelve years of age and her move to St. Louis from Chattanooga to live with the Marissens. She explained her friendship with the young girl, so sad, so lost. Gina worried about her to the extent she, finally, secretly, spoke with Rose, who filled her in regarding that horrible evening.

"Samantha recovered, but not completely. She never spoke of her family or what happened. She did suffer from depression; who wouldn't, after something like that. At least, when we were together, she showed some signs of enjoyment." Gina stopped momentarily to maintain her composure. "Many years later at our wedding, she met Jim. That very evening, she told him everything; she broke down for the first time and just wept in his arms. He held her, consoled her…" Placing her hand over her mouth, Gina fought back her own tears.

"At last, she was able to let go of that deep depression; she could start to rebuild her life. She felt so safe with Jim. The miracles God performed were amazing. He not only freed her from the past, He rewarded Samantha by giving her the opportunity to bring Jim to Christ and, He rewarded Jim with His gift of salvation, all on our wedding day. I think we were every bit as happy for them as we were for us!"

Scott bent over and rubbed his forehead with his fingertips for several moments. Sighing heavily, he straightened up. "Wow! I don't know what to say. I never met Samantha and, yet, I feel I know her better than myself. I hope she's all right. I pray they can be together. This whole time has been awful for both of them."

He turned to Samantha, tears trickling down her cheeks. She managed to express, "I never heard that. I didn't know she lost her family. I didn't know Jim played such a major role in her life. There are so many things I…."

She rose from the chair, went to her mother, and hugged her tenderly. "I never realized just how good a friend you were to her. You were there for her for all those years. God had you watch over her until Jim was ready."

Gina responded softly, "Our friendship was not one-sided, by no means. She was a good friend to me too. I miss her. I hope we can have that again…someday."

"You will, Mom. You will."

Shifting in his seat, Rich stated the obvious, "Gets to you, doesn't it?"

"Seriously, yes." Following a brief moment of thought, Scott cautiously broached a different matter, "Jim hasn't spent the last twenty-five years with no one in his life, has he?"

Rich settled back to best explain his friend's life after Samantha. "When the break happened, it must have been six months before we saw him again. I think that not only was he hurting, he was…oh, I don't know…embarrassed, maybe? But it was our little girl who got him back. He showed up at our door one Saturday…wanted to see Samantha, he said.

'Well, we were able to talk with him, convince him we cared about him, and didn't want him to stop being a part of the group. It took a bit, but he finally started coming by when he was on leave. But then, he was deployed to the Middle East for thirteen months; built up quite a distinguished record over there; almost got shot down once—

"Wait, you never told me that either!"

"Samantha, you were very young, just a child," Rich confessed. "At that time, we felt it would serve no purpose to tell you. We didn't say anything because that could happen to him on any given day. I know we protected you but we didn't want you to be afraid every day that something bad could happen. It could, but we would wait until it did, if it did. I worried about him every day; he was my friend, like a brother to me. No sense in all of us worrying."

"Oh, Dad," Samantha moved behind her father. "You get a hug too. You are a great friend to Jim." As she returned to her chair, she asked, "What happened when he was almost shot down?"

Rich related as best he could Jim's harrowing experience of the missile striking his jet and the massive damage it did, almost downing him in enemy territory. He also told of a few of the many missions he flew. He didn't have a lot of details since Jim never spoke of his active time in much detail. That was just like Jim, Rich explained, not to have much to say about his own skill.

"Are you worried now?" she asked, reaching for his hand. He realized his daughter awaited an honest answer.

Taking her hand between his, he searched for the words, finally settling on, "Yes…yes, I am worried. I'll be honest, Samantha, this may well be the most dangerous mission he's ever undertaken."

An uneasy silence enveloped the four until Rich worked the conversation back to Scott's question. "Jim didn't go out with anyone except for those times he needed someone to accompany him to an official function of some sort. He pretty well cut out what he considered unnecessary social activities; he didn't even have a guest for any of his retirement stuff, official or otherwise.

"We had a big party for him…he came alone. Gina, Carol, Liz, Sue, and Nancy wanted to set him up, but we convinced them—if he wants to bring someone, he will. Once this is all over, I hope they can be together again, I do. We'll just have to wait and pray."

Casual conversation filled the remainder of the evening until Scott finally gave in, "I guess I better get going. I didn't realize how tired I am. Thanks for everything tonight."

Concerned, Rich inquired, "Are you OK? You're able to drive?"

"I'm fine. Just need to stretch my legs, get moving. Jammed a lot of travel into this week. Got a long weekend off, gonna rest up."

"Don't forget next weekend, Labor Day," Gina reminded him. "We're still going to have everyone over on Monday, try to keep things as normal as possible. You can make it, can't you?"

"Sure! What can I bring?"

"Steaks!" Rich quickly answered

"Deal…but why don't you, Mrs. Reynolds, and Samantha come out to Jim's this Saturday. Give me a chance to show you a little Idaho hospitality."

"On one condition," Rich demanded. He draped his arm around his wife's shoulders. "Our friends call us Rich and Gina. You should probably start doing the same."

"Yes, sir…Rich…and Gina. Thank you."

"Good, Saturday it is!"

"You know, while traveling this week, I thought, I want to tell you my story—what brought me to St. Louis. You've shared so much of your lives with me, I figure, it's my turn."

SONORA COMPLEX, ARIZONA

JIM HUDDLED WITH Thurmond, Hamilton, and Garcia near the open cockpit of the XM simulator reviewing the procedure for the Emergency Ignition Override (EIO) Hamilton had feverishly devised within the previous twenty-four hours.

The propulsion scientist nervously repeated his instructions on the location of the EIO, "OK, Jim, the activation button for the EIO is at the base of the joystick slightly beyond the reach of your normal hand operations. At the moment the thrust fails, shut her down and activate the EIO. The quicker you activate the emergency ignition, the less work the stabilizing thrusters have pulling the craft from flat spin, minimizing potential tumble.

"Instead of all systems powering up simultaneously, the EIO will transmit to the onboard computer a command to initiate stabilization before activating thrust. It's up to you to apply thrust when you feel she'll best maintain stability. Your last flight results were due to the computer matching the rate of descent without stabilization taking place first, sending you on an out-of-control trajectory—and an impossible recovery. I thank God it was a simulation.

Jim was aware he already had.

"Ready?" Garcia asked.

"Ready as I'll ever be," Jim affirmed as he climbed into the simulator. "Let's do it."

The canopy lowered and locked. The airfield snapped into view. Cool oxygen flowed into the suit as the XM worked through the systems check. All LED's flashed in unison. Jim wrapped his hand around the stick and brought the craft to a height of twenty-five feet before blasting into the brilliant blue on a 30° angle toward the north until attaining an altitude of 110,000 feet. He eased back, tensely setting in motion the identical maneuvers as during his ill-fated sim-flight.

Thurmond, Hamilton, and Garcia uneasily observed as Jim successfully executed each test as ordered, impressed by his ability to take to the new-age flight. Dr. Kerrick stepped behind them, engrossed in what she observed.

"Amazing how he's learned this so quickly; I wonder what drives him." She waited, but no response. The intensity of the test blocked any interruptions.

"OK," Garcia exclaimed. "He's at max altitude heading due south, time to go into thrust failure." Looking at the laptop, he slowly tapped the key.

Jim's body tensed upon recognition of the failure. He hadn't realized just how fast the XM deteriorated into a flat spin on the previous flight. He quickly shut down the craft and slid his hand down the stick until coming to the EIO activator. He squeezed. The XM had just begun a slow tumble.

The instruments lit up once more, vital data streamed across the lower canopy as the stabilizing thrusters struggled to level the craft, losing altitude dramatically. As near as he could tell, he was screaming southeast toward the confluence of the Ohio and Mississippi rivers.

The moment of decision: at what point would stability hold when he fired thrusters? The responsibility was his. He had to rely on his gut, his flying experience.

Keeping one eye on the canopy readouts and the other on the fast-approaching rivers, he decided 3—2—1, now! He eased into the thrust, his decision. Sweet relief…thruster response. As he fought to maintain control and pull out of the dive, he had only 15,000 feet to work with. Airspeed and the number of G's became uppermost in his mind; excessive G's meant blackout, ultimately slamming into the water.

"C'mon, Jim, c'mon," muttered Hamilton. "Make it work."

Garcia voiced concern, "Man, it's gonna be close."

From that point, the four observed Jim's struggle to 'survive' in silence. Complete stability remained elusive until Jim's mind and manual actions meshed with the computer's efforts, slowly resulting in smooth control and thrust—normal flight. Pulling out of the dive at near max G's, he banked hard to the west while climbing in altitude, leaving the rivers behind.

"Whoa," Nate exhaled. "He just about pulled max G's clearing the river surface by forty-two feet. He's on his way home."

A minor celebration of simple relief ensued.

Glancing down upon the digitized landscape, Jim executed a full thrust spiral to 85,000 feet for the forty-minute return flight. He and the machine flew as one.

"He is ready!" bragged Garcia, the proud instructor.

Steve Hamilton fell limp in his chair as the tension of the past weeks and lack of sleep left him drained.

Thurmond slapped him on the shoulder. "You did it, Steve. You came up with a solution!"

With barely a smile, Hamilton bemoaned the fact, "We still don't know the cause of the failure."

"At least, we have a remedy, a way out!" Lisa countered. "Enjoy this success."

She joined the three celebrating until Jim 'landed' on the

Complex airfield and popped the canopy. Immediately, the exuberant group surrounded him, congratulating him on his handling of the simulated crisis.

Hamilton assisted Jim with the removal of the gloves. "Thanks, Jim. You made this happen."

"Hey!" Jim corrected him. "You came up with the plan; you put it all there. All I had to do was use it."

Nate joined the conversation, "Really, Steve, what you came up with is extraordinary." Patting Hamilton on the back, he reminded him, "Look at the difference between the crash in downtown Ottawa the other day and Jim's recovery in southern Missouri today, a world of difference!

"By the way," Nate veered another direction, "Are you going to install the EIO in *Sojourner* for Jim's flight on Friday?"

"Sojourner?" everyone asked. "What in the world is that?"

Nate appeared to be somewhat embarrassed as he explained, "I just thought Jim's ship should have a name, something simple, yet dignified." He looked around for someone to agree.

Finally, Lisa stood with him, "I think Nate has a good idea. The OV, IV, and XM have all had their drawing board designations from the start; time to give them a little personality. 'Sojourner' is good! I think it means a traveler who stays somewhere for a very short time, doesn't it?"

"That it does, my very smart friend!" Nate didn't hesitate to compliment the young scientist. Their interaction didn't escape Jim's attention.

Hamilton grinned, "Then Sojourner it is, and the fix will be installed for Friday's flight. It's the least I can do for the guy that made it work!"

"Let's tell Merrill about the fix," Thurmond enthusiastically suggested, to which Kerrick and Garcia wholeheartedly agreed.

"Wait!" Hamilton cautioned. "I don't think we should mention this to anyone, not yet anyway."

"But why, Steve? This is great news," expressed a disappointed Thurmond.

Motioning them closer, Hamilton shared his concern. "Look, I know this sounds crazy, even paranoid, but I think we should sit on this a day or two. It worked—today; but will it work the next time. I don't want to give the false impression that the problem is solved. We took this upon ourselves…and I think we should keep it that way…for now."

Dr. Kerrick turned her attention to Jim. "What do you think, Colonel?"

"I think, at this point, there is nothing to be gained…or lost. Steve is correct about the reliability of his solution. It won't hurt to respect his request."

Hamilton appeared relieved by Jim's response, especially when Thurmond, Kerrick, and Garcia joined in their approval.

NORTH OF MOSCOW

SAMANTHA PACED ACROSS the room and back, awaiting Nikolai's return with the week's supplies. Although the grounds were occupied by thirteen additional soldiers, he was forced to retrieve the supplies…alone. She would not breathe easy until his safe return.

Her nerves jumped like an electric shock upon hearing a light knock at the door. Oh, Lord, why now when Nikolai is not here? She did not answer.

"Miss Marissen, it is Alexei. I must speak with you."

Alexei? He doesn't speak English. What should she do? Doesn't really matter, does it. Whoever is on the other side will just break it down if they want in. He doesn't need me to open the door.

She approached the door warily, turned the lock, and cracked it open the tiniest bit. It was Alexei.

"Miss Marissen, come out, please. We must talk." His English perfect with only the slightest Russian accent.

Cautiously, she widened the opening and stepped into the kitchen. "Alexei, your English, it's very good. Why haven't you said anything before?"

"Quiet, please. I don't have much time to explain. Please sit."

Samantha sat uneasily on one of the kitchen chairs. "What? Can't this wait until Nikolai returns?"

"No, this cannot wait. I must tell you now. Please, just listen." After checking both windows, he pulled out a chair and sat across from her.

"Nikolai was ordered to protect you; that is true. I am here as a contact for the rebels. They take my information and relay it to your country."

Her hand covered her mouth as she gasped. "They know where I am? They know I'm here?"

"Yes…they do. Everything is now so tense, the world fears harm may come to you if this goes on any longer. I am telling you this to prepare you."

"Prepare me…for what?"

"A plan is in place to rescue you. You will be taken from here to an American who will get you home."

"How? When? Those soldiers out there aren't going to let me just walk out of here!"

"No, they will not. Our country could soon be in the middle of a civil war. It will be too dangerous for you to be in Russia. You are known by the whole world now. You would be very valuable to either side. You must not be here. It will take a fight to get you out, but you must be ready…and you must not be afraid. We will get you out."

Her mind buzzed with the reality she had not been abandoned; her country planned to rescue her! The thought, however, of escaping in the midst of weapons fire shook her to the core. Couldn't there be another way? Now, she wished she hadn't been told.

"When will this happen? Soon? What will happen to Nikolai?"

"You have many questions. This will take place very soon, within a week depending on the actions of the Russian Federation. The time could be moved up…but it will not be delayed.

"Nikolai backs the government; he is not aware of the plan

and I cannot guarantee his safety. He has chosen his side; he may die with that decision. I'm sorry."

Samantha swallowed hard, understanding Nikolai may lose his life. He can't! He has done so much for her. She bit her lip; she would not cry—not before anyone.

"Miss Marissen, nothing must be said of this…to anyone, especially Nikolai. I will inform you of anything you need to know. Until then, any contact will be no more than before. We must be very careful. I hope you understand what I'm telling you."

"Yes, I understand."

"Good. I must insist you return to the room."

Her eyes locked on Alexei's, she rose slowly and retreated to the room closing and locking the door behind her. Gradually, she lowered herself to the edge of the bed, buried her face in her hands, and wept, not for her but Nikolai.

*   *   *

An hour passed as she prayed for Nikolai. Was there anything she could do or should do to keep him alive? Should she tell him of Alexei? Would that bring an end to her rescue? If she remained quiet, would Nikolai die? She thought of Anechka. Memories of her own emptiness tore at her heart as she realized she might be the fault of another's loss. "Oh, my Lord God, what do I do?"

Reaching under the mattress, she pulled out her Bible and fanned through the pages until coming to Psalm 102. She laid the open book on her lap and looked to heaven. "Lord, give me an answer…please."

She read through her tears,
    Hear my prayer, O Lord,

And let my cry come to you.
Do not hide your face from me in the day of my trouble;
Incline your ear to me;
In the day I call, answer me speedily.

Before closing the Bible, she flipped to the folded poem of James. She held it for only a moment knowing now was not the time to revisit the past; that time must draw to a close. She should halt her delusional thoughts and focus on the present. Her decision was crucial.

The sound of boots on wood startled her; she had been so engrossed in prayer she failed to hear the arrival of Nikolai. She laid the Bible down and quickly attempted to hide her despair, a futile task, as he unlocked the door and lugged in another week's supplies. She said nothing.

After setting the crate in the corner, he turned and immediately noticed a difference in her countenance. Pulling up a chair, he sat and asked, "Sam, what is wrong? What happened?"

At that moment, she understood what she must do. His honest concern overwhelmed her. Softly, she spoke, "Nikolai, we must talk. Be very quiet." She picked up her Bible and caressed it in her arms.

"Warily, he whispered, "What, Sam?"

"Alexei spoke to me while you were gone."

"How? He talks no...speaks no English."

"Shhh. But he does...perfectly."

"I do not understand. What does he talk...say?"

Placing her finger to her lips to silence him, she urgently whispered, "He told me there is a plan for my rescue. He said he is a contact for the rebels. My country knows where I am."

"He say this?"

"Yes, there is going to be a raid or something to free me.

They will take me to an American who will get me out of Russia. He didn't know how, but he said this will happen within the week, no longer."

Nikolai stoically listened as she continued, "He said there would probably be a fight, which I took to mean gunfire. It would have to be." Motioning to the window, she went on, "Those soldiers won't just let me leave; they're here to make sure I stay until the trial. People will die trying to get me out of here.

"He told me you are with your government. He could not guarantee your safety when this happens." She fought to maintain a whisper, "Nikolai, I do not want you to die! Not for me! Please, you are my friend, tovarich…you cannot die!" Tears streamed down her cheeks, not for fear for her life, but for another's.

Struggling to maintain her composure, she barely breathed the words, "I don't understand why he told me. For what purpose? He told me I could not say anything to you, nothing!"

Distressed by what he heard, he remained strong. "Thank you…for what you say. I will let no harm to you…or me. We do not say word to Alexei. We wait."

She nodded a hardly noticeable 'yes', although to what she was unsure. What should they wait for…next Friday? Saturday? When? She feared for his life, yet informing him of Alexei's talk could possibly destroy any rescue attempt. Who was telling the truth?

Nikolai sat with his hands folded and head down for several minutes. Samantha felt unsure of what to say. Finally, he straightened up, looked directly into her eyes, and stated clearly, "Sam, I am not with government. Hear only me…I get you out, not Alexei. I do not know what he does. We wait, please."

All Samantha could do was to hold her Bible up and pray, "Oh, thank you, Lord, for hearing my prayer. I will trust Nik with whatever he wants me to do. Thank you. Please help us with whatever happens. I ask this in my Lord Jesus' name."

Nikolai smiled as he added, "Amen."

SONORA COMPLEX, ARIZONA

"COLONEL, REALLY, I'M not joking; I can't support this suit for an extended time. I need to rest!"

"Sorry, Dr. Kerrick. This isn't your fault. As frustrating as it seems, it's good to know this ahead of time."

Jim rolled a chair over and carefully eased her into a sitting position.

"Ahh, this is better. Sorry, I can't carry the weight that long. At the beginning, it's not heavy, but the longer I stand, the more strain it puts on my back and legs. Thanks for the seat."

"No problem. This is just a guess, but I imagine you can support this suit longer than Samantha. She may be in a fairly weak state by now."

"Yeah, that's a distinct possibility. We have to plan worst case." Dr. Kerrick hesitated, then asked, "Look…Colonel, you call the other guys by name; can't we do that too. You're way too formal with me. Is there a reason?"

"You're quite observant, Doctor. Yeah, there is a reason."

"With a perplexed expression, she pressed on, "There is? Tell me, so I can defend myself."

"No, no, you have nothing to defend. It's probably just me…and maybe I'm looking at this all wrong, but I admire what you've done in your career, no small achievement. I've seen, too many times, very accomplished women taken for granted only because they're women. I see the others respect your position and your opinion. I wanted to show a professional respect for you so they would know I felt the same. That may sound foolish, but that's why. If I've kept it too formal, I'll loosen up."

As an afterthought, Jim added, "Just like Nate, I regard you as a very impressive scientist."

Quickly, Dr. Kerrick's face turned at least three shades of red. "What do you mean?"

"I mean, the compliments, the looks, the innocent smiles. It's all there. Nothing wrong with that, unless you're letting it all go to waste."

Immediately, she slipped into denial, "Me and Nate? Please."

"Oh, don't give me that, Lisa," Jim chuckled. "It's so easy to see. He cares, and he respects you. And you seem to feel the same. When this is over, you should pursue that option; you probably won't be disappointed."

His forward statements momentarily left her speechless. Finally, she managed, "OK…but, OK, I will."

Jim smiled at her soft response, hoping she would speak to Nate, get the ball rolling. The time he had spent with Nate proved he would never make the first move. There were moments, he knew, when he wanted to prevent others from regretting a lack of action, more deadly than direct action.

Rising from his chair, Jim stretched. "Just let me know when you're ready to try again. No rush…you've already done this four times. No wonder you're tired! You don't give yourself enough credit. Thanks to you, Saman…Samantha Marissen will have to do this only once."

'So, I'm about her height, her size?"

"Yeah, pretty much. Works in our favor, doesn't it?"

"How do you know?"

"Know what?"

"If I'm the same size, same height. How would you know that?" she playfully asked. "And why do you keep fumbling over her name? Do you know her? C'mon, you can tell me."

Jim lowered himself back into the chair, studying Lisa's face, which faded from the impish smile to one of knowing realization.

"Oh, no! I thought I was turning the tables on you, have a little fun like you did with me." She paused to make certain she wanted to continue. She did. "Do you know her? That would explain a lot."

"Explain what?" he calmly inquired.

"Well…if you do know her, it would explain your drive, your persistence, and your need for perfection…for starters." Lisa spoke more as a friend, "This is personal, isn't it? I'm sorry I brought it up."

Leaning forward, Jim stared at the floor. "No, that's OK." He exhaled a cleansing breath. "I do know her…did know her, not now, but…many years ago."

"Were you…

"We were…involved, but it didn't work out. I just want to make sure she gets home safely.

"Listen, Lisa, don't say anything to anyone about this. I don't want this to turn into a circus. Please, keep this to yourself. That's…that's all I ask."

Reaching toward Jim, she touched his arm. "I won't. I…I won't breath a word of this. And I won't ask you anything more."

"Thank you." He rose quickly. "You ready to get back to the suit?"

Surprised by his quantum leap to the issue at hand, she stuttered, "Yes…yes, but…I had an idea." Lisa gathered her thoughts. "What if we try with me sitting? Then, I won't have to strain with the weight of the suit."

"Yeah, but," and he smiled when he noted, "there won't be a chair to roll up to *Sojourner* in the Russian countryside."

Lisa shot him a look of "well…duh!"

"Oh, yeah? You'll have the next best thing—your XM, *Sojourner*…and I do like the name."

"Good! Now the other guys want to name their ships. Gives them a little personality, brings them to life, something military pilots are good at. What's the word for that?"

Without hesitation, Lisa answered, "Personify or personification, giving human attributes to an inanimate object, thinking of it as a person."

"Wow, you're good!"

"Well," she laughed, "I minored in English Comp in case I needed to write papers."

Jim relaxed. He felt he had a friend in Dr. Lisa Kerrick. Kyle Webster, Mike Parker, and Tim Moore checked on him daily to see how things were going; how was he doing; was there anything he needed? His cohorts worked at making a connection, building a mutual respect. Dan Malone—nothing. Jim didn't worry about Malone; if they could work together, no problem. Not an ideal situation, but tolerable.

"Before we were sidetracked, I said you had *Sojourner*. Use your ship for, can I refer to her as Samantha? Easier than both of us fumbling for a name."

"Yeah, fine…when it's just us."

"OK, use your ship for Samantha to sit on while she gets prepared."

"I assumed the skin, the outer covering was fragile. That won't be a problem?"

"Chromatoskin! Silly name but you've got to call it something. Anyway, not at all! It is a war machine." Lisa defended her finding with zeal, the same zeal required to convince her fellow scientists of its durability. "It's somewhat difficult to apply, but once it's on, it's good to go!"

"Think we can use it to test your idea?"

"I don't see why not. We're trying to see what works best for the mission, right?"

"Right! Let's get you out of that suit and over to assembly. I haven't seen the completed ship yet. Looking forward to it!"

"It's no longer in assembly. They hauled her over to the sub-hangar for your flight tomorrow."

With the suit carefully removed and loaded onto a flatbed cart, Lisa and Jim began the lengthy trek to the sub-hangar. Along the way, he inquired how she came up with the idea of 'Chromatoskin'.

She was only too happy to explain. "Have you ever heard of cuttlefish?"

"Cuddlefish?"

"No, not cuddle, cuttle...c-u-T-T-l-e, cuttlefish."

"Oooh, that cuttlefish—let me—no, I haven't."

"All right, Colonel—

"Please, not so formal."

"You are one smart—

"Don't say it!"

"Say what?" she laughed. "OK...Jim, prepared to be bored."

"I doubt it. This could be good."

"You sound like Nate. He always encourages me to talk about my work, like he's interested."

"He is interested. I'm telling you—

"Yeah, yeah, I know."

"OK, so what's this fish story of yours?"

"Cuttlefish...Jim, are found off the coasts of Indonesia and Australia. Their survival depends on their ability to blend in with the surroundings. Blending in, protects them from predators and helps in catching their meals. Remind me to show you a video sometime. You won't believe what you see… or don't see.

"You can look as close as you want, you will not be able to see the fish on the seafloor, only coral, seaweed, and other fish. Suddenly, a portion of the seafloor moves then rises and remains suspended several feet above. The creature will slowly morph from its seafloor appearance to its own brownish-gray coloring. It even changes shape, which your ship can't do…obviously.

"You'll see it cruising the ocean floor, stalking a fish. Once it determines who will be dinner, the cuttlefish slowly sinks into the coral while changing its shape and color to match the surrounding area. Moments later, the intended victim swims too close to investigate and is immediately slurped into the mouth of the cuttlefish."

"How does this fish do that? How in the world did you ever figure it out?" Jim began to understand Nate's interest in this brilliant woman.

"I've spent a lot of years researching the cuttlefish, probably too many. I was married during this time…I lost my husband." Lisa stopped the cart and faced Jim.

Jim's first thought: her husband left because her work became the dominant factor in her life.

"Don loved the ocean and he loved research. We were on a dive to film cuttlefish." She suddenly faltered. "You don't want to hear this." She turned away.

He didn't know what to do or say. He needed to do something, but what? "Lisa, you don't have to tell me, but you can…if you want." Jim opened the option door. She didn't have to, but if she wanted, she could.

Lisa faced him. "I haven't told anyone about this. I've kept it inside the whole time I've been here."

Jim placed his hand under her forearm. "Lisa, tell me what happened."

She held tightly to his arms. "He…Don…he was not old! He was eleven years older than me but he was not old enough. He suffered massive heart failure while we were setting up for the underwater shoot. By the time we reached the surface, he was gone."

Before Jim knew what was happening, Lisa fell into his arms, sobbing. Images of Samantha releasing her anguish in his arms swept through his mind, awakening still other feelings from long ago. He freely allowed Lisa the time she needed. The death of her husband—such a loss, a permanent loss! Nothing could be done. His loss, minor by comparison, seemed insignificant; he still had possibilities where she had none.

Her sobs slowly transitioned to soft crying, then to tears and halting breaths. She backed away, wiping tears from her eyes. "I'm so sorry. I never meant for this to happen. I have wanted to be strong, for him. He was my love." Lisa pulled herself together. "He was a good man, a good husband. Thankfully, he was a Christian man; we were both Christian. I don't know where I would be if it wasn't for that. I know he is with our Lord."

Jim cautiously approached the subject, "How long…has he been gone?"

"Almost five years; I can't believe it's been that long." She wiped her eyes again.

As Jim watched the hurting young woman, he thought of Nate and deeply regretted his feeble attempt to push them together, how hard that must have been for Lisa.

"Lisa?" he had to let her know she was under no obligation to pursue Nate; she should not get involved in something she's not ready for yet, and she certainly shouldn't listen to him.

With her back to Jim, she responded, "Yes, did you

say something?"

Closing the short distance between them, Jim stood behind her. "Yeah…I want to apologize for earlier, you know, the stuff about Nate. I didn't mean…I mean I would have never done that had I known…I'm sorry for butting in; I was really out of place."

Facing him, she quickly asserted, "No, I like Nate; he's so good to me. He treats me like Don always did, not the same ways…but for the same reasons. Don always looked at me, worked with me…laughed with me…with respect. Nate treats me the same. I know he is sincere. I know he respects me. And I think there could be something. I've been afraid. There are times I feel I would be cheating on Don if I did. I know that's ridiculous."

His heart went out to Lisa. "I don't think that's ridiculous. I think that is something only you can decide. Does Nate know any of this?"

Without hesitation, she responded, "Nate doesn't know anything about this. No one here does. Funny thing, I know you the least and, yet, I shared this with you first." She sighed. "Go figure."

"Maybe I'm not threatening; you know, I'll be gone in a week or less."

"No, but as old guys go, you're nice, you're kind. I guess that makes you easier to talk with."

"Hey, thanks…I guess."

Finally, a smile crossed her face. "I'm just kidding. I feel as though some weight has been lifted off me. I guess they're right, talking is the beginning of healing."

Giving Lisa his half-smile, he admitted, "I suppose we both learned something about each other today. I will keep this to myself." Jim waited a second or two, "May I suggest something…that you don't have to listen to."

"Sure," as she joined Jim pushing the flatbed down the long hall. "You haven't been that far off the mark!"

He focused fifty feet ahead as he spoke, "What do you think about telling Nate, just as you told me? Tell him everything, even your fears. What do you have to lose? You see…I think he may be ready, you may be ready. Preparing for this mission has put a lot of things on hold. Time to move ahead. There are some things to work for, to fight for."

"You may be right, Colonel. I'll give it some thought." A long period of silence ensued as Lisa wondered how best to approach the matter. "But…I'll need to know where he stands with Jesus before anything else. That is very important to me."

At first, Jim said nothing as they continued down the hall until he uttered agreement, and more, "I think that is very wise. A similar situation happened to me many years ago, except in reverse. We spent the evening together at a wedding reception. I was already searching; I was so lost. By the time the evening was over, she had led me to Christ, even given me her Bible; she…gave me her Bible. Went to church with her and her mother the next morning. Finally, I understood what had been missing in my life, what I was searching for. I had a relationship with Jesus… and I was beginning a relationship with her. What a wonderful young lady…she was." His reflection faded into silence.

Turning left into another hall, Lisa softly raised the question, "Was that wonderful young lady…Samantha Marissen?" She felt, if so, maybe he wanted to talk about it. After all, he is risking his life for her. She awaited an answer.

Pushing their way through a set of double-doors, they traversed another forty feet before Jim responded, "Yes…the young lady was Samantha Marissen." He offered nothing more; Lisa asked for nothing more.

"Are you sure you want to continue with this today?" Jim attempted to sound out her feelings after revealing such a personal tragedy.

"Yes, I do. It's better when I keep busy. Besides, we have to keep on; you only have days before you depart." Strong or strong-willed best described Dr. Lisa Kerrick. Nothing would stand in the way of her duties.

"We don't have much further to go. Let me finish that overview of Chromatoskin; it'll be quick since we don't have time for a full explanation of the process, so I'll just tell you this. There are red, yellow, brown, and black pigmented chromataphores, reflective iridophores, leucophores, pigment cells, xanthophores, erythrophores, and melanophores, which used in any number of combinations, can produce unlimited colors.

"The Chromatoskin was applied by hand to the XM, or Sojourner, in three layers, each layer having its own function yet, all three working in conjunction with one another. Sensors installed opposite the side you are viewing controls the appearance of that side. If the craft is above you, the underside of the craft appears as the sky. If the craft is below you, the upper portion of the craft looks like the ground below. The same principle applies to the sides and front and back views. A low-level electrical charge is required to activate and maintain the Chromatoskin." Jim continued to push the flatbed as Lisa grew more intense with her delivery.

"On an initial test, we covered a small plane with Chromatoskin and discovered by accident that a Chromatoskin clad aircraft cannot be detected by radar. Radar seems to be absorbed by Chromatoskin; there is no return. I can't share those details with you right now."

Jim simply shook his head. "And I'm helping a genius learn how to get dressed. How did Marissen get you out here?"

"Here's where my English classes paid off. I wrote a paper on my work with cuttlefish and my belief that the camouflage effect could be reproduced in the lab. Unbelievably, my paper was published, and in a matter of three weeks, or so, Marissen AeroSpace contacted me and asked if I would be interested in joining a special project. We had several meetings before I was flown out here for a full disclosure interview and I was amazed by what I saw. And, at that time, I just wanted to run away. I went from very little to having everything at my disposal for my work."

Curiosity regarding Ed Marissen peaked his interest, he had to ask, "Did you speak with Ed Marissen personally? Did he have anything to do with your hiring or was it Merrill?"

Lisa chuckled before answering, "Surprisingly, Merrill had little to do with the interview process; Ed hires whom he wants and Merrill takes over after that. He's a pretty hands-on person but he had no choice in your case. You volunteered for the job; probably not too many applicants."

"Yeah, probably not."

"I don't know much about what you have done in the past, but you sure have come in and continued the project without missing a beat."

Deflecting her compliment, he raised the question, "Of the thousands of papers written, how did Marissen find yours… and so quickly."

"You know, I wondered that myself, so I asked. His answer shows, I believe, why he has been so successful. Years ago, he developed a group whose sole purpose was to investigate newly written papers and a group who researched older, forgotten papers. Steve Hamilton and Charley Rice were discovered by that group. One wrote a paper on propulsion and the other weapons, that some thought too sci-fi. Ed brought them on-board and look what we have."

"I haven't seen Charley's work yet."

"Oh, you mean G-BoF? Since you were a fighter pilot, I'm sure you'll love it!"

Jim stopped the flatbed. "What is G-BoF? I've asked, but everybody says I have to see it to believe it!"

Lisa smiled. "You'll have to see it."

He simply shook his head and returned to their trek. As they finally approached the entrance to the sub-hangar, Lisa's radio vibrated.

"Give me a second; this might be Nate," she assumed.

While waiting for Lisa, Jim reflected on the mission, the training, and the individuals involved. The life lessons the Lord placed before him during this period revealed a darker reality, a side he rarely took into account. His friends, his 'family' had led relatively simple, uncomplicated lives. Although he experienced quite an exciting, active life, he had remained blind to the countless examples of personal pain experienced by many. Rose came to mind, struggling through the agony of her daughter's unjust arrest and detention, and now, Lisa's loss, the sudden death of her husband, a microcosm of the tragedies he had unknowingly ignored. Jim's self-evaluation revealed an arrested development of close relationships outside his immediate friends, setting up a barrier between himself and sincere empathy for others. He prayed for change; an awareness of others' pain. Perhaps change had already begun.

"That was Nate," Lisa shared. "I asked him if he wanted to help with the suit training. Hope you don't mind."

"Nope. Is he coming?"

"Yes! He said he'd be here as soon as he can."

Extreme security existed to enter the sub-hangar and beyond, requiring both a thumbprint and an optic scan. The doors opened revealing the completed XM, or Sojourner, her official designation. The inactivated Chromatoskin provided a wavy rainbow effect to the body surface, shifting color shades as Jim and Lisa approached. Oddly, the canopy was open, a body leaning into the craft, which straightened immediately upon the sound of the sliding entry doors.

"Dr. Kerrick, I wasn't expecting anyone. Just running a diagnostic for Dr. Hamilton before tomorrow's flight."

"Cole, you startled me. I didn't know you would be here. I wanted to show Colonel Gordon the Chromatoskin feature of the XM. Have you met Colonel Gordon?"

"Just a second. OK, finished. Let me disconnect this." Unplugging a device from a computer module in the cockpit, he stepped down from the craft. "No, we haven't met."

"Jim, this is Cole Chambers, Steve Hamilton's assistant. Cole, Colonel Jim Gordon."

Shaking Cole's hand, Jim expressed, "Good to meet you, Cole."

"Same here. Let me get out of your way. Got to run through this data before tomorrow." Cole gathered his materials and departed just as Nate arrived.

"So, the sub-hangar is now a dressing room?" Nate joked, "Pretty expensive piece of furniture, isn't it?"

Laughing at his opening line, Lisa turned to him and softly requested, "Would you like to get a coffee when we're finished?"

Nate smiled, and with no hesitation responded, "Yes, I would."

SONORA COMPLEX, ARIZONA

THE RAPID BEAT of his heart contradicted the cool pilot exterior as the mobile lift transported Sojourner to the center of the Sonora airstrip. The decisive moment had arrived, except today held greater significance than any other of his life. The most dangerous mission of his career hinged on the results of this flight in the single remaining aircraft available for a one-time rescue attempt of the woman he loved, a woman who may no longer feel as he, a thought he unsuccessfully attempted to push to the side. One mistake, one error in judgment would terminate any hope of completing the mission.

The lift rolled slowly to a stop; a voice came through Jim's earpiece, "Your landing gear is fully extended. Lowering to the surface in 5-4-3-2-1." A slight thump could be felt. "You are now resting on the surface. Sit tight—backing away. I'll let you know when you're clear."

"Roger that," he responded in typical pre-flight monotone.

The remaining Sonora personal readied for the test in the main auditorium where several large, hi-def widescreen monitors focused on Sojourner awaiting take-off, the celebratory atmosphere of the previous fatal test flight noticeably absent. Ed Marissen observed the tense proceedings with Merrill and the high-level assemblage of Atkins, Gagnepaign, Townsend, and Forsythe. Also invited to the large conference room viewing were Hamilton, Chambers, Thurmond, Rice, Garcia, Burchfield, and Kerrick; along with the IV and OV crews: Webster, Malone, Parker, and Moore. Dan Malone and Cole Chambers, however, chose to observe in the main auditorium.

All eyes studied Ed as he paced nervously about the room, stopping occasionally to pat an employee on the back or to accept some word of support. An unspoken fear haunted the entire complex; the cause of the fatal flight never found. Only Garcia, Hamilton, Thurmond, and Kerrick had knowledge of any possible chance of survival if the failure occurred again.

Because the elite conclave required access to real-time data, General Townsend requested all information exchanged between Sojourner and flight control be displayed in the conference room as well. As Ed retreated to the rear of the room, he solemnly noted those present, thankful for their hard work, dedication, and friendship. Great success had been attained as a result of these fine individuals. Now, the final success rested in the capable hands of a man he, at one time, disliked and mistrusted without reason. He choked back emotions brought on by thoughts of the pain he caused his wife and daughter. He could never repay this man for his courage and willingness to place his life on the line for Samantha, his sister's daughter.

"Sojourner, you are clear for take-off."

"Roger. Thanks for the ride. Pick me up when I get back?"

"Yes, sir, Colonel Gordon." The final exchange, one of respect.

With that, Jim initiated power-up, his eyes scanning the cockpit displays as Sojourner came to life. She was beautiful, a work of art. Sounded ridiculous, he knew, but once in a great while, an object comes together perfectly, deserving of admiration...nor worship, just appreciation. Sliding his hand down the stick, he felt for the EIO. Yep, there it is, location same as in the simulator. Good man, Steve, good man.

All systems flashed in unison; he gripped the stick, thumb at the ready.

"OK, Sonora, this one's for you…in 5-4-3-2-1."

As Sojourner rose majestically from the airstrip, everyone seemed to slide to the edge of their seats in anticipation… of what they didn't want to think. Jim maneuvered a slow clockwise spin, then counterclockwise as he climbed, getting a feel for the controls.

At one hundred feet, he announced, "Going to warm her up; see if she reacts like the simulator, then on to the flight plan."

Jim attempted to ready himself for the thrust required to propel Sojourner to an altitude of 18,000 feet. Set for a heading of west-southwest, he brought the nose of Sojourner up 47°, took a deep breath, and initiated thrust.

"Whoa…wow! What a ride! After the simulator, I wasn't ready for this! What a blast!"

Ed smiled, the room chuckled at Jim's comment, but tension took precedence. The tracking cameras attempted to follow Sojourner, and for the most part did so, capturing his deliberate figure eight at 18,000 feet followed by an intentional gradual dive to the desert floor turning into a graceful counterclockwise banking sweep along the distant low hills just prior to activating the Chromatoskin and disappearing into the southwestern sky to an altitude of 117,000 feet.

The flight plan called for Sojourner to fly to San Diego, then on to the north along the coast to Oregon, east over the Rockies to Minnesota, south to Mississippi, and west to Sonora. Multiple maneuvers had been scheduled throughout the flight, testing Sojourner and the new-age spacesuit. For now, Sojourner would be pressurized, as well as Jim's suit; test both but rely on one.

The several thousand miles per hour flight up the coast granted Jim an overview of God's creation—the blackness of space suspended above the blue atmospheric shell enveloping his world, wrapped heavily with puffy wisps and ribbons of clouds. Far to the northwest, still over the Pacific, loomed an oncoming weather system, a massive dome of moisture preparing for entry over the North American continent.

The sole purpose of the west coast fly-over lay in the testing of the Chromatoskin and the exhaust ports stealth ability with focus on the Defense Support Program operated by the Air Force, using reconnaissance satellites with sensors to detect infrared emissions from intense sources of heat. The design of the low-heat thrust and concealed exhaust ports would be tested again, the second counting Blakely's failed flight, of which not one report surfaced, neither satellite nor air/ground-based radar. Public visual sighting tests had been deemed off-limits; civilian safety remained foremost and a low altitude flight was not to be part of the plan. As before, General Townsend stood ready to call off a scramble resulting from discovery.

At an altitude of nearly twenty-two miles, with the Pacific Ocean stretching to the west and America to the east, Jim appreciated the privilege of flying Sojourner. Without doubt, he was the only man to sit at the controls of such an outstanding machine. If not for the seriousness of the time and the urgency of the mission, he could classify the flight as breathtaking, exciting, thrilling...but he wouldn't, not until Samantha occupied the seat behind, safely on her way home.

Operating under manual control, Jim noted the latitude and longitude readings for crossing the coast between Portland and Eugene, Oregon and on to Great Falls, Montana. Performing flawlessly under his control, Sojourner banked hard east providing a view through spotty clouds of the west coast to the south. After leveling off, he viewed the Columbia River to the North, the very river Lewis and Clark traveled to the Pacific. Amazing, he thought, the journey took them months; I'll make it in minutes.

The northern portion of the flight entailed the bulk of the maneuvers he was to put Sojourner through. Regardless of technological advances, Jim studied the list he had prepared and taped to the back of his left glove to double-check the upcoming tests and times.

Microbursts of encrypted data reached Sonora at predetermined intervals informing flight control of Sojourner's location, systems, and real-time maneuvers—information fed directly to Marissen's conference room.

"What do you think, Merrill? How do you think he's doing?"

Merrill smiled as he responded to his boss' query, "So far, the only negative is Colonel Gordon is 7.3759 seconds behind schedule, but I don't believe that to be a hindrance to the mission." A very rare occasion for Merrill to offer humor to a serious inquiry, alleviating some of the tension in the room, allowing everyone time to breathe, time to converse.

General Townsend stood as the screen data detailed Sojourner's hovering at 117,000 feet. Colonel Gordon rotated the craft 360° while decreasing altitude by 2,500 feet. Upon reaching 114,500 feet, he fired thrusters, returning to the original altitude.

As reports reached Sonora of Jim's success through each maneuver, the community collectively exhaled a sigh of relief knowing their craft and their pilot performed beyond expectation. Beginning at Grand Forks, Jim banked Sojourner into a wide, lazy turn to the south, the third leg of the flight to Mississippi and an unheralded near-return to Columbus Air Force Base. An expansive, thick cloud cover prevented a view of Lake Superior but half of Lake Michigan and its southern tip urban giant, Chicago, stood out plainly from his twenty-two-mile-high vantage point.

Glancing to the backside of his glove, he noted the first of three final tests before heading west to Sonora Complex and completion of the 6,500-mile flight in little more than two hours. Suddenly, a new sound, a digitized, monotone voice from his earpiece, "Warning, thruster shutdown, thruster shutdown. Warning."

He listened…they had.

As the shocking data scrolled across the screen, breathing ceased. Steve Hamilton slumped in his chair. "How can this be? It's not possible!"

Nate offered consolation, "Hold on! He still has a possible solution. Just hold on!"

Marissen's voice boomed across the room, "Steve, what's happening?"

Hamilton faced Marissen. "I don't know. I just don't know! This should not be; a failure like this does not just come out of nowhere."

Methodically, almost robotically, Jim shut down the XM as it fell from the sky, beginning a slow clockwise spin and slight tumble. The shutdown caused an immediate break in the data feed, startling all at the Complex.

"What happened to the feed? Where's the feed?" Townsend yelled across the room.

Jim slid his gloved hand down the control stick and, reaching its destination, activated the EIO. All instrument panels jumped to life and, again, vital data flashed across the lower portion of the canopy as the stabilizing thrusters fought to bring the XM under control, the sky no longer black.

"LOOK! DATA! He's back online! He activated the EIO!" Kerrick excitedly shouted.

The what?" Marissen demanded.

"There's a plan Please, we'll explain everything later. Jim's trying to implement the plan! This has to work! It has to!"

Quickly, yet calmly, Jim kept a visual on all readouts, waiting for the moment to initiate thrust. On his current doomed trajectory, the computer projected impact between Friars Point and Mayersville, Mississippi. He certainly wanted to avoid crashing near a populated area.

"Check his rate of descent. He may not be able to pull out." Forsythe paced the room. "C'mon, Jim, keep calm…you can do this."

"I've got to go for it, get the nose up, use the full underside as boards out…one large speed brake. No time…do it…now!' Jim fired the thrusters; the XM reacted erratically, barrel-rolling while screaming earthbound. Fighting the roll, Jim gained partial stability, enough to pull back, bringing the nose up but not enough to flip the XM over.

"Please, Lord, keep me conscious. I can't black out now."

Maximum G-forces pressed him down and back into the seat as the XM decelerated dramatically. As the Sonora people watched data fill and refill the screen, each took on a look of horror as they noted Colonel Gordon pulling a hair less than 9 Gs, which would push the blood in his body to his lower limbs, blocking the heart's attempts to pump it upwards. If his suit operated as it should, continuous air flow would apply pressure on his abdomen and legs to keep blood from accumulating in those areas and starving the brain, as long as he maintained less than 9 Gs.

As the streaming data tracked his severe deceleration, Colonel Gordon resolutely struggled to achieve stability and slow the craft from its maddening descent. His fight for flight continued; at times, the XM uncontrollable, as if alive, kicking and screaming to their death. Not checking the altimeter, Jim fought with sheer determination to diminish the velocity of his fall. With pilot instinct, he looked—was enough altitude available to pull up the plummeting craft or was impact imminent? One last effort—lower landing pods, fire landing thrusters full, damn the G-force.

Seconds later, the screens at Sonora appeared to freeze, all zeros displayed across the board…but they did not go blank. No one spoke; not a word emanated from any area of the complex. Did the XM slam into the Mississippi countryside?

Ed lowered himself into the nearest chair and buried his face in his hands. "Jim…are you there? Please…be OK."

A numbness settled into the room as the silence grew unbearable. No one knew for certain what had happened. While Flight Control frantically attempted to determine the status of the aircraft, Sonora observers could only stare blankly at the screens. Once more, the project seemed to have taken a life.

Both Dan Malone and Cole Chambers left the auditorium, exiting different doors.

A weary, yet steady, voice broke over the com, "Sonora…we have landed. Last second decision to go for landing. It worked. She appears to be all right. Computer says we're northwest of a town…Rosedale…I think. I'm probably no more than a hundred yards from the river in a clearing. I'm not sure, but I don't think I was noticed. Chromatoskin still activated. Take-off in a few minutes; I need a break. Steve, thanks for that E-I-E-I-O thing. I owe you…big time.

"ETA…one hour. Sure glad I didn't lose her."

One concise calm message, that's all.

General Forsythe offered words everyone already knew. "That's the stuff I knew he was made of. He's the man I would bet my life on!"

Several minutes later, data displayed the XM climbing nearly vertical to 90,000 feet with Chromatoskin activated. Only now did everyone fully understand Colonel Gordon, Jim, their pilot, was on his way home. He had survived. The Complex celebrated with tears, cheers, laughter, and more tears.

Mentally exhausted, Ed remained seated as the celebration carried on around him. Steve Hamilton, perplexed that an unknown, undetected problem resurfaced in a most destructive manner, as if on cue, also remained in his chair.

Suddenly, he jumped up. "Stop! Not yet! He is not home free!"

Abruptly, all laughter, conversation, and celebration came to a halt. Thurmond called out from the center of the room, "What are you talking about? He's on his way back. He survived this thing. Your plan worked!"

"No! The failure could occur again. What's to stop it from happening again before he gets here?"

One more, the conference room grew deathly quiet with the realization Hamilton was right. Nothing guaranteed a safe return flight.

Having leveled off at 90,000 feet, Jim scanned all readings for anomalies, anything to show a recurrence of thruster failure. The chilling thought he was not in the clear invaded his mind. "I'm bumping her back up to 117,000. Without the additional 27,000 feet, I wouldn't have survived back there."

What should be done; he no longer had any faith in its reliability? Something had to be in common with the two XMs. One, yeah, but the second experiencing an identical failure? Doesn't make sense. He found he no longer referred to the XM by its new name. Maybe Cole can find a clue as to what happened; he has the diagnostic from last night. At least, Jim reasoned, we still have this model to check out…for now, anyway.

After contacting Sonora regarding his concern, he settled in, although uncomfortably, for the return, reflecting on his harrowing experience. "You must have something for me, Lord, to protect me like you do. I know this mission is important… but I see now there is so much more I should have done with my life. Yeah, I'm a Christian, but what have I done for you? From here on, I'm listening. I just ask that you tell me…plainly. And Lord, thank you for flying with me today. You are not my co-pilot; You are the pilot, the One in charge. Thank you for my life. I will not waste it."

*   *   *

Lisa Kerrick moved next to Hamilton. "Steve, Jim will get the XM back here; he'll make it. He's aware of another possible failure. He won't be caught by surprise. This is not exactly like the last time. We have the XM to analyze. And Cole ran that diagnostic you wanted last night. That may tell us something, don't you think?"

"What diagnostic? I didn't ask for a diagnostic."

*   *   *

Colonel Gordon cruised into Sonora fifty-four minutes later, having experienced no abnormalities or malfunctions, setting her down 250 feet from the main hangar. No sooner had he shut the craft down that the above-ground hangar doors opened and, despite the heat, the Sonora team flooded toward him, surrounding the XM. Although Jim experienced satisfaction with the results of the emergency landing, he was not one for adulation.

"Colonel, Flight Control here. Please remain in the aircraft. It's too hot for you to exit in your suit. The lift will bring you in."

"Yes, sir! I'll be right there to pick you up. Need to get these

406

people out of the way. Keep cool, keep your air on. One more thing, Colonel. Bravo Zulu!"

The excited crowd made space for the lift operator to position himself above the XM for the lower, lock, and transport operation. Jim remained concealed behind the tinted canopy during the short ride to the hangar. Once inside, the lift lowered and released the craft. A path cleared for Ed Marissen and Merrill Pierce, who remotely released the canopy latches, allowing access to the cockpit. Merrill assisted with the removal of the helmet and gloves, chuckling at the list taped to the back of the left.

Jim looked into the faces of the two men, as he made the necessary disconnects. "It's good to be back. That was quite a ride."

Ed grinned as he offered assistance. "Short and to the point, as usual. It's so good to have you back, son…sorry…Jim."

Clutching Ed's hand before he climbed out of the cockpit, he responded, "That's all right, Ed. Thanks."

"Cmon, let's get you out of there; your public awaits."

Ed carefully guided Jim onto the wing. No polite applause today; the Complex exploded immediately into cheering, whistling, and shouting, anything that added to the decibel level.

"I know you don't want this but they're happy to see you," Ed hollered over the din. "Give them the moment!"

With that, Merrill vigorously shook Jim's hand. "Welcome back, Colonel!"

Cracking a smile, he faced the celebration. Generals Forsythe and Townsend stood off to the side and saluted. Jim returned the salute. For a moment, he gave in to his emotions, swallowing hard the lump in his throat.

Finally, Ed raised his hands, asking for quiet. "Please, I don't want to dampen your enthusiasm, but I'm sure Colonel

Gordon would like to get out of that suit, grab a shower and a little down time before debriefing."

Jim cleared his throat and, looking over his audience, managed to express, "Thank you. Thank you for your support. You are the greatest." His simple statement brought on another bout of cheering.

As the exuberant crowd slowly dispersed, the core group of Kerrick, Garcia, Hamilton, and Thurmond approached, each smiling broadly.

Stepping directly to Hamilton, Jim wrapped him in a bear hug. "Thank you for that emergency program; worked great! You saved the mission!"

Flustered by his gratitude, Steve smacked Jim's back with both hands. "I'm just glad you're here; we all are! I thank God above it worked."

Ed approached Lisa from behind. "Dr. Kerrick, you said you would explain that ignition override thing to me," Marissen probed. "Now might be a good time."

Glancing at her fellow scientists, she began, "Well…here's how it worked…

As Ed and Merrill listened intently, Lisa and Steve filled in the details of the Emergency Ignition Override, or EIO, implemented just the day before and apologized for not telling them earlier, hoping it would not have to be used. Unfortunately, it did. Jim's shower and down time would wait; the unofficial debriefing had begun.

After thirty minutes, Ed determined, "All right, we'll continue this evening with Townsend, Forsythe, Atkins, and Gagnepaign. I want every bit of data there and, Steve, I want you to go over everything in this aircraft, everything."

Jim interjected, "That diagnostic Chambers performed last night might shed some light on today." He paused, then added, "Something has to be there; this doesn't just happen out of the blue. Something had to cause the problem. At least, we still have the XM to study."

Searching his memory, Steve reported, "I didn't ask for any tests yesterday; I wanted to get the EIO installed. I'll look into it. Maybe there is something we can use."

*   *   *

Leaning forward on his palms, Jim rested his forehead on the back wall of the shower allowing the warm water to pulse rhythmically over his neck and back. Deeper thoughts returned following an afternoon in survival mode. Only by the grace of God had he come back alive. His many past mistakes and poor choices had determined the path of his life, reminding him of the despised desertion of Samantha and, whether he accepted it or not, how he lived in the shadow of that decision… alone. His conversation the day before with Lisa Kerrick had exposed his blindness toward others in thinking himself to be the only person suffering personal pain. Lisa had lost her husband, been alone for five years. Who else had he ignored? Not since Samantha exposed such deep grief over her loss had Jim allowed another person to enter his heart, to experience his care and concern.

Dropping to one knee, he broke down; the final realization of his near death, his loneliness, and his selfishness released an emotional logjam. "Oh, dear God, my God, forgive me, help me, please help me to be the man you made me to be."

NORTH OF MOSCOW

There is therefore now no condemnation for those who are in Christ Jesus. For the law of the Spirit of life has set you free in Christ Jesus from the law of sin and death.

Romans 8:1-2

"WHAT PAUL WAS instructing the Roman in his letter is—no sin a believer commits, whether in the past or future, can be held against him. Jesus paid the penalty on the cross and righteousness was given to us, the believers."

"So...I am not guilty today for past?"

"No, Nik, you are not. You are a new creation in Christ, a new man, a Christian. But, someone cannot sin repeatedly, or again and again, and think he is forgiven, that God will continue to pour out His grace on him. At some point, continuing in the same sin can show a person is living in sin or, maybe, that person did not make a true confession of faith; never truly gave his life to Jesus. He did not really invite Jesus into his heart. When we do ask Jesus into our hearts, God fills us with the Holy Spirit, changing our nature by giving us strength to overcome our sinful weaknesses and show our adoption as His children.

"When the Holy Spirit changes us, that doesn't mean we become sinless. He convicts us of our sins; we know we have sinned and we must repent, which doesn't mean we simply say

'I'm sorry' but we turn away from our sin, we reject our sin."

Samantha suddenly stopped; a commotion outside the dacha sent a chill down her spine. Nikolai rose slowly, checked his weapon, and slipped it into his holster as he quietly stepped to the door. Carefully, he turned the knob and pulled until he could see through a narrow slit. While checking the kitchen area, the Russian officer Nikolai did not trust barged through the outer door into the dacha.

Loudly, in Russian, he barked, "We have taken your men prisoner. They threatened to shoot several of my men…for what, I do not know! They are a threat to the operation."

Nikolai threw open the door and charged the officer, stopping inches from his face. "No, my men would not without provocation. Let me speak with them!"

"NO! They will be transported to Moscow for questioning. They may be part of an attempt to free the American."

Glaring at the Captain, Nikolai growled through clenched teeth, "Ridiculous! We are guarding her for the trial."

"NO longer! You are confined to this building. Your weapons and ammunition will be confiscated." The officer snapped his fingers and three soldiers swept into the dacha demanding Alexei and Nikolai's guns.

"You cannot do this!"

"I can…and I have." He then ordered the soldiers to search the building for ammunition and other weapons.

Nikolai's eyes followed the soldiers as they searched each nook and cranny of every room, finding nothing. Completing the outer rooms, one of the soldiers investigated the room opposite while another entered Samantha's room, Nikolai's footlocker an obvious point of interest. Samantha moved to the bed, calmly sitting near the head.

After removing personal items and clothing, the silent young soldier found several boxes of ammunition, placing them in his canvas bag along with Alexei and Nikolai's guns. He secured the bag, straightened up, and began to depart when he suddenly stopped, turned, and inspected Samantha. Although her heart pounded, she remained calm, returning a look of "don't even think about it!"

Placing the bag on the floor, the young soldier dropped to his knees and cautiously examined the floor under the bed. He rose slowly, pulled Samantha up from the bed, searched under the pillow and patted the mattress down for anything hidden within. He gave her a cursory look of disgust, picked up his bag, and left the dacha with his commanding officer and the other three.

Left with no weapons and no men, Nikolai brimmed with anger for the treatment received and the fact they were left with nothing. Alexei suggested Nikolai explain the situation to the American woman and reassure her of her safety, which was humorous in itself. No weapons, no men, yet assure her of her safety. Maybe Alexei should do the explaining.

Nikolai returned to the room seething, with no means of venting his frustration. He wanted to slam the door, to do something, but he did not. Rather, he quietly closed and locked the door. Head down, he sank to his cot.

"Captain arrest my men. He send to Moscow for questions. I worry for them."

Focusing on Samantha, he asked, "You OK?"

"I'm still shaking, but OK," she whispered, then reported, "He…a soldier, took boxes of ammunition from your trunk…locker."

"Boxes? Not more?"

"No, nothing more. He even looked under the bed."

Signaling for her to remain quiet, he crossed to the bed, stooped to the floor, lay on his back, and slid partially under, where he carefully removed an object, a 9mm GSh-18, wired to a mattress support. He wriggled from beneath the low bedframe and rose to one knee.

Smiling, he reported, "He look at floor, only floor. Not good, he thinks you have nothing."

Shocked, Samantha asked in a hoarse whisper, "Is that your gun?"

"I hide gun when first here." His smile faded. "Is good, but no ammunition."

Knowing he would find nothing, Nikolai inspected his footlocker, then repacked his belongings, muttering in disgust as he did.

"Nik." She stood as he turned to her, knowing for certain she did trust him fully. Reaching into her yellow jumpsuit pocket, she withdrew a slender gray object. "Is this what you're looking for?"

Still shaken, Samantha placed the object in his hand, the very object he would interchange on days he left for supplies.

His eyes opened wide, "How…Sam…how?"

"I…I was watching when they took your gun and were searching out there. I figured they would look in here too. I don't know why you do what you do…but I know where you keep that thing. I took it before they came in here."

Holding back laughter, Nikolai grabbed her shoulders. "Sam, you are brave!"

"No, Nik, no. I'm scared."

"Ahh, but you are brave. Brave is to do right when scared. We have small protection because you are brave."

"What do we do now?" She bit her lip.

"We wait."

Wait…she understood he meant to wait the week out for validation of Alexei's information.

SONORA COMPLEX, ARIZONA

"STEVE HAS SOME very disturbing news." Ed stepped around the desk to take his seat. "That's why I called y'all together." He motioned for Hamilton to pick up the explanation.

Weary from the stress, strain, and a lack of sleep, Steve Hamilton rose deliberately from his chair at the rear of the room to address the same group as the previous day with the addition of Dan Malone. "Let me first state the facts, then I'll follow up with any explanations necessary. Plain and simple—I have found the failure of Jim's XM to be a direct result of sabotage; sabotage committed right here by someone at the Complex. What happened to Jim probably also caused Glen's death."

The meeting broke into chaos, disagreement over who would do something so detestable, but more importantly, why! Why take one life and almost another to destroy a project so massive and necessary for the future and security of the nation?

Jim didn't know which emotion hit him the hardest, disgust that one individual would destroy the earnest work of these dedicated people, or anger that someone thought so little of his life that killing him was of minor importance. Anger, it had to be anger. When facing a foreign enemy, death may be a consequence, but death simply because a person is in the way is unacceptable and must be dealt with. Yes, it was anger he felt.

He wanted the man who did this.

Near the front of the room came the charge, "Knowing you and your envy, I'd put my money on you being the guy," directed firmly at Dan Malone who leapt to defend himself against the accusation.

Ed demanded silence. "Stop! Stop this now!" An ugly, smothering pall permeated the room.

"We believe we know the individual based on eyewitness accounts…which does not conclusively prove guilt. As soon as Steve informed me of his findings and suspicions, security dispatched a search team that quickly found this person missing from the Complex and appears to be out in that desert environment. I apologize for this, but a room-to-room search was to be conducted while work went on this morning. Right or wrong, we felt a search of the premises without anyone's knowledge would be the most effective method.

"Turned out to be mostly unnecessary. The individual under suspicion was the first quarters searched. He was already gone. Everyone else is accounted for; we believe this person acted alone."

General Townsend took a moment to address the small assembly. "Since no one is certain, the saboteur is regarded as armed and dangerous. You were not called together until the all-clear had been determined for the internal Complex. A search of the surrounding desert area is taking place as we speak. If you notice anything suspicious, notify security immediately. The work on this project must continue despite what happened. Time is running short and much remains to be accomplished."

He turned the briefing back to Hamilton, "Dr. Hamilton, thank you for your diligence in uncovering the cause of the failures. Your findings are disturbing, yet a relief to know the XM is a reliable aircraft. Please…continue."

Tired, but boosted by his overnight success, Steve returned

to his summary. "I found Sojourner's computer," she earned her name back, "had been reprogrammed to a predetermined elapsed time at which one of the three feeder lines would cease supplying the combustion chamber, bringing about complete propulsion failure. Thankfully, we came up with a method to override the shutdown."

"You came up with the solution!" expressed Garcia.

"Absolutely!" all agreed.

Maintaining humility, Hamilton went on, "Nevertheless, we caught a break. When Jim shut down the computer, everything shut down, but the program failure was not cleared, merely reset. Once the same amount of time passed after the emergency ignition override, the failure would recur. Let's say the failure had been programmed at twenty minutes into the flight—a failure would occur twenty minutes after each recovery. Failure was based solely on elapsed time, not fuel consumption."

"Steve!"

All heads turned to Colonel Gordon.

Jim took one step forward. "I need to know…how much time did I have before the next failure?"

Hamilton blew out a long breath as he studied the faces of his audience. "You returned to Sonora approximately 800 miles per hour slower than earlier. You had about twelve minutes remaining before the next failure."

The gravity of the failure settled over the group; the reality of the near disaster hit home. Not a word, not a sound.

Merrill interrupted the quiet contemplation, "All right, everybody," he commanded, "time to roll; we've got a busy week ahead, a lot of ground to cover…but we're on the home stretch.

"Nate, you Webster, and Malone prepare for the OV/XM docking simulations with Colonel Gordon. He has a few days to learn all about docking and undocking in space—the basics, only the basics. Give him what he needs.

"Steve, show Jim how the XM handles motion in zero-gravity, its action-reaction, Newton's three laws of motion. Jim, are you familiar with them?"

"Yes, I am. Force, mass, acceleration; force equal in magnitude and opposite in direction. I remember. Just need to put it in practice."

"Excellent, we just gained a day in training. You'll grasp action-reaction with the XM in zero-gravity conditions—

"Sojourner," Malone barked, "Sojourner, Merrill! Don't forget the name."

That was enough, the final straw. After weeks of that attitude, Jim stepped within inches of Malone, causing him to bend backward, Jim calmly, yet forcefully whispered, "You've been on my case since I've been here, griping and complaining because your little boy ego is bruised."

Pausing to drive the point home, he gripped Malone's upper arm and, applying pressure, continued the low, gruff whisper, "Do you think I don't know what you're doing? You're angry, you're pouting like a ten-year-old because you didn't get the call for the XM. That's your game, but I don't play games. I don't owe you any explanations, but I will say this—the people you have been blessed to work with all exhibit class and strength, traits you sorely lack."

"Hey! You can't—

Colonel Gordon tightened his grip on Malone's arm. "You've got the world by the tail, and yet, you think you deserve more. I've been around and I've served with your kind. The beauty of your type is, I don't have to do anything. The more you attack, or insinuate, or lie, the better I look.

"Grow up, Malone. You're a coward."

Flashing a look of disgust, he warned, "One more word behind my back and we'll talk again, alone. Got it!"

Muttering a barely audible affirmative, Malone left the office whipped. The schoolyard bully suffered a severe beating at the hands of the new kid. Jim offered a faint smile as he returned to the immediate group.

"Sorry about that, Merrill. I was probably out of place."

Merrill gathered his thoughts before responding, "No, I'm sorry it had to come to this. Dan is a royal pain. We all know that. You taking him behind the woodshed may be just what he needed. I'm sorry you're the one who had to pick up my responsibility. I should have taken care of him some time ago."

"Well," again a slight smile, "it's done. All we can do is move on. I hope he joins us. He's good, and he has that ego of his. He'll be back. He's not going anywhere."

Merrill shifted back into his business mode. "Alright, let's get back on track. I have just been informed the undocking for re-entry is now an automated process and should decrease your training time. The OV and Sojourner will run the procedure through a coordinated computer program; the return rendezvous and docking must be performed manually. You'll have the radar guidance system and multiple cameras offering every view necessary. You'll see…Nate's simulator does a great job.

"However, I also want you in the tank before the mission."

Baffled, Jim questioned, "Tank? What's the tank?"

"Oh, yeah," Pierce chuckled, "you haven't seen the tank. It's a huge pool containing a full-scale mockup of the OV and bay including a docked XM. It's the closest simulation of weightlessness available. I want you to practice transferring from the OV, through the airlock, and into the XM. Kyle Webster, the mission commander, will work with you. He's been in the tank and in orbit."

Webster nodded agreement.

Merrill looked for the next person on his list, "Lisa?"

"Yes, sir."

Pierce swung around to find her just off to the side. "Oh, there you are. How are you doing with the suit? Any problems I should know about?"

"I think I'm doing OK. Jim and I have worked out a routine that is efficient and allows me to conserve strength. Initially, the suit doesn't feel like much weight but, after a while, maneuvering in it can be tiresome. We don't know Samantha Marissen's physical condition, which could affect her ability to do this. One thing we haven't considered…will she actually go through with the flight or will she panic? I honestly don't know how I would react to this situation."

"She won't have a problem."

The calm, confident voice of Colonel Gordon reassured them, "I am going in to get her; she will return with me." Lisa saw the sincerity in his eyes. What had happened between the two so long ago?

Pierce continued, "Jim, when you're not working with the docking simulation, I want you to keep practicing the suit-up… and I want you to get with Charley Rice and Mark Burchfield. Charley, as you know, is the weapons expert. Sojourner packs only one weapon but it is one unbelievable weapon, the only one you'll need."

"You mean G-BoF? Seems no one can say it with a straight face." Jim wanted to see it now. All he hears is how fantastic this weapon is.

"You'll understand. The name is so fitting. You'll have no need for any other weapons."

"Nate," Pierce called out.

"Yeah, over here!"

"Nate, we have a sim for G-BoF, right?"

"Sure do. Charley and I will get Jim into that too."

"Mark," Pierce continued down his list. "Get together with Jim. Fill him in on the re-entry force field."

"OK, everybody, we've got a lot going on; let's not get sloppy in the last days. Any questions?"

"Got one, Merrill." Kyle Webster, Mission Commander of the OV stepped forward. "What do you want to do if Dan doesn't show for the docking simulation?"

"I'll give him the first one. I'm sure his bruised ego needs some time to heal but he'll be there for the remaining runs. If not, I'll drag him there myself. OK? Then this meeting is over. I'll check in with you in about three hours; we have to keep this tight."

During Merrill's planning session, Atkins, Gagnepaign, Townsend, and Forsythe gathered at Ed's desk. Before Jim left for the simulator, a voice boomed, "Colonel Gordon, would you remain?"

Jim turned at Forsythe's request. "Sir?"

Once the office door closed, the General explained, "We've a few things to discuss, Jim, and we want you in the loop, but first I have to tell you that was some intense flying yesterday," to which everyone agreed. Ed remained quietly behind his desk awaiting a private time with Jim, a time most difficult. However, that time would have to wait, but before Friday, the scheduled launch date.

Atkins placed his hand on Jim's shoulder. "Have a seat, Jim. There's new intel you should hear."

Reaching for the nearest chair, he fired off one question, "Is Samantha all right?" Absent was any effort to refer to her formally.

"We've lost contact with our man at the dacha but we did receive one short signal burst signifying he's still there. There's been a change in routine. Four of the soldiers guarding Ms. Marissen are no longer present. That means only two remain.

We classify the recent additional thirteen as enemy combatants."

"But has she been harmed?"

Pained expressions swept over the faces of Jim and Ed as they heard Atkins response. "We don't know. At this time, there is just no way to know. This we know: the mission must be next Friday. We know she is definitely scheduled to be transferred to Moscow that day. One other fact we know for certain— the Russian government plans to make her arrival in Moscow public. But we believe that works in her favor…and ours. They will not want to parade an injured American before the world. For that reason, we believe she is OK."

He paused that all could absorb the news. "So, Colonel, will you be ready?"

Heavy in thought over Atkins report, Jim hadn't acknowledged the question.

"Colonel…you will be ready Friday?"

The forceful repetition snapped Jim's attention back to the group. "Yes…yes, I'll be ready. We just went over the schedule for the week; it'll be intense…but, I'll be ready."

Atkins studied each man before continuing. "The terrorists, who in reality are pro-government, detonated a series of bombs again today across Moscow killing several hundred innocent citizens, which has really fired up the Russian public bringing out a fresh hatred of the United States. The average citizen believes we are the cause of their political turmoil resulting from the Russian spies we are holding.

"We fear the final scapegoat will be Ms. Marissen when… when everything breaks loose over there, and it will break loose. The people in power have accomplished what they set out to do—get themselves out of the spotlight and turn the focus to us. The inexperience of their political leaders presents a dangerous scenario; they don't understand power and its potential hazards. The Russian population wanted change; voted in the good-looking slick people selling the most unrealistic promises."

"Kinda like here…except we do have a few checks and balances." Ed never held back when the truth begged to be stated.

Shifting in his chair, Jim raised his hand slightly with index finger extended. "How is it, we know this but we don't know what happening at the dacha."

"Fair question," Atkins declared. The resistance in Moscow have cell phones, laptops, and tablets which they use as sparingly as possible under extremely cautious conditions. Those thirteen soldiers keep a tight lid on the dacha—no one in, no one out… plus they patrol a very wide perimeter. We don't want to chance tipping anyone off. The schedule calls for solid recon beginning Monday. We will know, and I emphasize 'will', what is taking place at the time of the mission. Timing is everything. The raid on the dacha should take place before Ms. Marissen would begin her transport to Moscow. Timing is the key.

General Forsythe took over. "You'll fly in, pick her up, and get out. Your time in Russia should be no more than two hours. What's your time on getting Ms. Marissen suited up?"

"Right now, Dr. Kerrick is in the suit in about thirty minutes."

"Can you get it down to twenty?"

"You said we had two hours."

"Max. You'll want to get out of there long before two hours. The quicker you're out of there, the better. The longer you take, the more opportunities for something to go wrong. They have pulled every Russian diplomat from the United States, expelled ours from Russia, and, as suspected, threatened any country who assists us in any way. We just never expected they would murder their own countrymen to save face."

An obsessive fear of losing power and prestige activated the tongues of egomaniacal Federation politicians to lash out at an innocent world, lie to their own people, and obscenely order the deaths of hundreds, forcing the international situation to such an extreme point that the world teetered on the brink of disaster, as not seen for decades.

The Letter of James spoke of the tongue. "And the tongue is a deadly fire, a world of iniquity. It is an unruly evil, full of deadly poison."

Marissen's phone rang, jarring the men from the intense briefing.

He answered, "Yes, what is it?"

He listened, acknowledging each statement, "Yes…yes…I see…I don't understand. Yes, OK, hold on…"

Passing the phone to Atkins, Ed leaned far back in his chair and stared at the ceiling until Atkins handed it back several minutes later.

"That was Sonora Security. They found the body of Cole Chambers about a mile from the Complex with a self-inflicted gunshot to the head. This is now a matter of national security; the FBI and CIA have been called in to investigate further. We can't have the mission unravel, not now."

Atkins did not divulge a note found in Chamber's shirt pocket: "I am not alone." He hurriedly departed, urgently contacting Washington on his secure line.

WASHINGTON, MISSOURI

"HELLOOO! ANYBODY HERE?"

"Mom! Dad! Hey! We knew you guys were here. We could hear Dad complaining about the gravel drive. Scott, honestly, every time we came out here, it was the same 'you know what' hill!"

With palms up, Rich pleaded, "Am I that predictable?"

Samantha and Gina turned to Rich in mock amazement that he need ask.

"OK, OK, I guess I might be, but that's not always a bad thing, right?"

Shaking her head, Gina sighed, "To a point, Richard, to a point," then laughed.

"Mrs. Reyn—Gina, what have you got there?"

Samantha interrupted, "Mom! That's not a string bean casserole, is it"

"Oh, Samantha, you know everybody always enjoyed Aunt Louise's casserole."

"String bean casserole? I love string bean casserole. Do you know how long it's been since I've had string bean casserole?" Scott enthusiastically took the dish from Gina's hands and placed it in the oven.

"Now you've done it," Rich moaned. "This means string bean casserole for another twenty years."

Laughing at Rich's humor, Scott motioned to the kitchen.

"Grab something to drink and have a seat. I'll fire up the pit."

Five minutes later, Scott returned showing the effects of St. Louis summers. "Man, it's hot. Love that St. Louis humidity. Isn't that what we're supposed to say?"

He snatched a soda from the fridge and joined the others in the living room. "Ahh, feels good."

Rich sniffed the air. "I have noticed something odd but I can't put my finger on—

Wait a minute! The air conditioning is on. Yeah, that's it!"

Hanging his head, Scott confessed, "You caught me, I'm in trouble now," but then clarified the point, "Jim does use the air, just not at the first sign of a temperature rise. I kid him about it but he just laughs. He's a pretty good guy."

Setting her soda on the coffee table, Gina had to laugh. "We kid Jim about a lot of things, but he expects nothing less from us. I suspect he does a lot of things just to get a reaction."

"Like his jeep, Samantha?"

"Yeah, Dad, like his jeep."

With an air of seriousness, Rich shared his thoughts, "I wonder how he's doing. I mean, we have no contact, we don't know anything, like when is this mission going to happen? I worry about him."

"Richard, you know he's OK. I'm sure he's doing fine. He has a job and he'll do it. He's always been that way."

"Yeah, I know, but this is more than a job. It's not a matter of clocking in and clocking out. What he's doing has got to be difficult and…dangerous, if not outright impossible." He paused, then looking at Samantha, continued, "I know you don't want to hear this but…we should be prepared for whatever may happen."

Gina broke in, "I know you're right. My casual attitude is my way of coping with all this. I can't bear the thought of losing Samantha or Jim. This…this huge mess brought Samantha to the forefront of my thoughts, but, in my heart, both of them are family. I love them."

"Dad, I know I…I don't want to face the reality of this. I," Samantha fought her emotions, "I just don't want anything to happen to Jim. It's like…if I don't think something bad will happen, it won't."

Rising from his chair, Scott took control, "Hey, hey, what is going on here? This is a very dangerous situation; something could go terribly wrong with his training or the mission. But, we know this: Jim is very capable, very dedicated, and will do everything he can to make it work. All we can do is turn this over to God."

Scrutinizing the three, he searched for signs of any holes in his argument and found none. His words appeared to place Jim's mission in a proper perspective.

He moved on. "So, on a different subject, I promised you the story of what brought me to St. Louis, and today I will tell you.

"It all began in the State of Idaho…Boise, Idaho to be exact. Born there, raised there, and I swore I would die there, but I didn't. OK, all seriousness aside…no…wait, I'm just nervous. I shared this with Samantha after I picked her up this morning so there'd be no surprises.

Rich and Gina glanced to Samantha, to which she responded with a smile.

"Rewind several years when I was engaged to an up and coming corporate executive, Rachel Westoff. We were to be married a year and a half ago. But, you know, I noticed changes in her, changes that bothered me. Like, she kept talking about when I would get a real job and quit this foolish flying thing. Flying was something I wanted my whole life, and it was not foolish. Then, close to the wedding, she told me she needed to wait before we had any kids; she wanted to make sure her career was on track. I asked her how many years." Scott stared at the floor a few seconds. "She told me at least five, maybe more. Depended on what happened."

No one spoke a word, waiting patiently for the remainder of Scott's history.

"I asked her, point blank, if she really loved me. She said yes, but she had to think of her future. I thought, well, yeah, but that's not a future I want. Problem was…I didn't have the courage to say something until the day of the wedding.

"I was getting ready that morning when I honestly told myself I couldn't go through with it. I just couldn't. I left the tux at my place, drove to the church, and barged in where she was with her bridesmaids. I asked them to leave so Rachel and I could talk. I don't know how I did it, but I explained everything and told her I couldn't marry her."

Gina covered her mouth with her hand. She'd never known of an actual wedding called off at the church. "So, what happened? I mean, how'd she take it?"

Picking at an imaginary piece of lint on his shorts, he assured them, "Oh, she was mad, real mad. I don't blame her. I should have spoken up a lot sooner." Then, chuckling, he added, "Her brother punched me right in the jaw, knocked me to the floor. I figured I had it coming."

He pulled a chair up close to finish. "I took my savings and paid back the cost of the wedding to her mother and father and her bridesmaids. Everybody was angry with me, including my own family. What I did was a major disappointment and a shame, but…it was not wrong! I finally had to get away…and that's how St. Louis came into the picture. SBA had Jim contact me after I sent my resume. And here I am."

Nodding toward the back door, Rich reached out to

Scott, "Let's say we throw on those steaks. Maybe some quiet conversation would be good about now."

"Sounds good! Let me grab the steaks."

Before the men headed out, Gina and Samantha overheard Rich state, "I'll bet you could have taken her brother."

"Yeah, probably."

WASHINGTON D.C.

RALPH ATKINS CALL to Washington ignited a firestorm of action. The National Security Agency, the Central Intelligence Agency, and the Federal Bureau of Investigation formed, at the insistence of President Burton, a combined effort of a limited, but supremely effective task force to investigate, find, and bring in the other or others involved in the sabotage of the Marissen AeroSpace aircraft.

Their efforts uncovered small man with large gambling debts who faced divorce papers his next trip home. Such a simple man was Chambers that the thorough investigation seemed preposterous until the task force discovered an unknown bank account, opened only days earlier at another bank, to receive predetermined deposits from a foreign bank. Red flags shot up immediately and the hunt was on.

Initially, the decision came from the top that the mission would continue although the accomplice, or accomplices, could still be at Sonora. All communication with the outside ceased with full approval of the Complex population. When the existence of the bank account and planned foreign deposits surfaced, the suspicion of a major leaked leapt to the forefront.

Detailed checks were to be run on those who had voluntarily left positions at the Complex or had been laid off. Only seven individuals came to light and all had left for family reasons.

Current Complex employees offered that their backgrounds be reviewed so as not to jeopardize the mission and to remove further suspicion from those who struggled the many years on the IV/OV/XM project. In-depth reviews were conducted, revealing no surprises. The expansive Sonoran workforce investigation proved the population of that particular Marissen AeroSpace sector loyal far beyond normal parameters.

From there, the systematic inquiry spread internationally. The NSA monitored all electronic communication for key words that might sound alarms of a questionable or peculiar transmission. The CIA and FBI investigated national and international connections, rumors, and past corporate espionage attempts—any and every avenue for possible leads. Running in the background were checks on the remainder of the Marissen AeroSpace Corporate giant employees within its plants, subsidiaries, customers, and suppliers. The magnitude of the investigation grew exponentially as the task force introduced additional variables in their attempt to capture the missing 'other.' Two final possibilities existed: the 'other' has no idea of the mission; or, there is no 'other.'

KIRKWOOD, MO

AS SEPTEMBER OPENED, Gina's exasperation grew. She found herself constantly flipping through various cable news channels each day awaiting some newsflash that Samantha Marissen returned home safe and sound, rescued by her long-lost knight in shining armor. Instead, one day dragged on longer than the last. How many times had she paused, thinking the attempt may be happening at that very moment?

Rich and their daughter handled the strain much differently: he kept busy working on *Foundation* needs in his upstairs office; Samantha relied heavily on the quiet of her apartment and prayer, much as she practiced when Jim had been deployed earlier in the Middle East. She never knew of Jim's return flight in his severely crippled F-16 or how Jim felt certain her prayers saved him. Her father worried every bit as much about his friend but working with numbers calmed him.

Rich could not fathom how Gina could subject herself to such punishment with worry. Gina, in turn, wondered about his sudden lack of concern, considering several weeks earlier, he had voiced the opinion that the mission proved to be far too dangerous. But, in the end, Rich would join her downstairs to watch the news…all the news.

Scott Larimore had been a rock, easing Samantha's fears and worries with calm conversation, prayer, and the comfort of a friend, although 'friend' no longer fully described either. The crisis had drawn them closer without either understanding just how their relationship grew so quickly. But now, of all times, SBA scheduled Scott with Bill Everdin on a three-day business flight to Lansing, Michigan. Samantha and her mother and father leaned heavily on one another for strength during, what they prayed, Samantha Marissen's final week of captivity.

Gina abruptly announced she didn't want to have their *end of summer* party; she felt it wouldn't be right. Everyone had been invited, Rich explained, and it might be good for everyone to get together. Besides, if they did cancel, there would only be questions. Samantha promised she and Scott would handle things. The get-together should go on. Finally, Gina conceded, knowing she should trust her husband's and daughter's judgment.

Sonora Complex—Arizona

Jim had run on automatic since his arrival at Sonora, blocking out anything that might detract from his training, until his very personal conversation with Lisa Kerrick, exposing her deep, permanent loss, followed by his near-death plummet in Sojourner, singeing every nerve, intensely reminding him of his mortality. Subsequently, his response was one of fervent gratitude and the realization that his multiple survivals over the years meant God had some plan for him; of what, he hadn't a clue. Too long had he existed in the depths of loneliness, burying his feelings for Samantha in the pit of his soul. Only since her illegal confinement had he guardedly allowed himself to think of her and even then, he'd smother any emotional reaction…that is, until the shower.

Jim had no recollection of the length of time he knelt in the shower, only that, afterward, he threw on a robe, clicked on the TV, and called Merrill to request the remainder of the day off, to which Merrill was happy to oblige. Stretching out on the couch, he flipped through the channels, settled on one and soon fell into a deep, much needed sleep.

He awoke refreshed, invigorated and prepared a pot of coffee to enjoy during his quiet prayer and Bible time after which he closed the well-worn book, thanking God for the peace that filled his heart, soul, mind, and body. He had come to a solid, definite decision: no longer would he ignore his love for Samantha, nor would he fear the possibility she no longer held similar feelings after the many years. Rose expressed the belief Samantha loved him, but he would patiently wait for Samantha's own words of verification. Until then, he would freely allow his love for her to fill his empty heart. He would release everything to God, no longer would he attempt to bury the past, no longer would indecision rule him. His love for Samantha filled him with hope, a hope not felt for years. If their future together dissolved, it would result from her decision. No more mind games; no more self-inflicted pain. His near death gave birth to a new day, a day of hope.

Once Jim resolved peace and hope with himself, his schedule screamed into overdrive with training of every sort: OV/Sojourner separation and rendezvous simulation with Webster and Garcia; underwater weightlessness training with Webster, continued suit-up practice with Lisa Kerrick; electro-magnetic re-entry force field instructions with Mark Burchfield, and, finally, his introduction and training of G-BoF with Charley Rice.

As suspected, Dan Malone did not show for the initial simulated separation of Sojourner from the OV and re-entry through the Earth's atmosphere. The mission commander, Kyle Webster, handled his responsibilities but only for the day.

Kyle had been a Navy pilot aboard the carrier Abraham Lincoln, a fact that created a bond with Colonel Gordon. He shared that he could have flown the XM but the difference between him and Malone was he understood the ramifications of training another individual for his commander position. Not only that, he felt unsure whether he could have recovered the XM as Jim had. Jim reassured Kyle that we truly don't know what we're capable of until placed in that position. Kyle admitted the rescue mission came about so quickly, an allowance for additional crewmembers never materialized and he appreciated Jim coming on board so quickly.

The initial simulated separation from the OV proceeded well as Steve Hamilton's talents shone brightly, automating the undocking, thereby reducing Jim's need of learning the manual maneuvers originally required. His taking control began 100 feet below the OV when he fired reverse thrusters, dropping Sojourner out of orbit.

Mark Burchfield explained his development of the electromagnetic locks between the IV and OV before and during launch along with the force fields surrounding the OV and Sojourner at re-entry, based on the principles of electromagnetism. Sojourner would charge as it sat locked in the OV bay, supplying the power necessary to create a re-entry force field, preventing annihilation. At this early stage of the project, Sojourner was good for only one re-entry without recharging.

Prior to firing reverse thrusters, Jim studied his digitized surroundings astounded by the view of the Earth from the 225-mile altitude, the arc of the horizon greatly magnified. Tilting his head back as far as possible, he observed the OV bay doors coming together. His aim was to drop through the atmosphere to an altitude of 50,000 feet, then return to the OV.

Once into his descent, he understood the necessity of experiencing re-entry, for the moment, a simulated re-entry. The fiery, eerily blinding glow of overheating atmospheric molecules surrounding Sojourner convinced the mind of imminent destruction. The canopy darkened, reducing the extreme brightness to a manageable level.

At 50,000 feet, Sojourner ripped across the sky at 3000 miles per hour. Under real-time, the OV would have traveled far ahead of Sojourner due to the 14,500mph difference, but in simulation, the OV showed itself to be thousands of miles behind Jim, but one orbit ahead. Webster signaled his lock on Sojourner; Jim fired thrusters for orbital insertion, bringing the craft within approximately one mile of the OV, initiating visual rendezvous. Instruments marked the OV one-half mile ahead and one-quarter mile above.

The slightly lower orbit allowed Sojourner to catch up with the OV, eventually suspended directly below the open bay. Instruments lit up images and data on the canopy as aids for docking completion. Commander Webster began a distance callout to Colonel Gordon, ensuring a synchronized operation under one man's authority, leaving no room for ego.

"Minus twelve, one-left, minus twelve, go two, minus ten, go one-half, stop, check alignment…go two, minus eight…" Webster calmly specified order after order, reading after reading until Sojourner settled firmly into the docking locks. The bay doors closed, the initial simulation complete…not perfect, not bad for the first but hardly the last. Three additional run-throughs took place that day.

Despite the full day, Webster and Gordon resolved to manage one excursion into the tank, the massive pool housing the OV flight deck, crew quarters, airlock, and bay area holding the docked XM. Both men, fully suited minus their helmets, stepped onto a non-metallic platform which Webster motored across a truss suspension track to the center of the tank and lowered through a five-foot diameter tube into the dry flight deck of the OV. Stepping from the platform, Jim noticed his boots adhered slightly to the deck. Webster explained the magnetic boots would allow him to walk carefully across the deck and crew quarters passageway to the airlock in the weightless environment of space.

He and Webster entered the airlock at the rear of the passageway, sealed the entry hatch, and donned their helmets. Webster instructed Jim to take an oxygen umbilical line and connect it to the left front of his suit just below the ribcage as he did. The Commander then reached above and flipped a series of switches causing the airlock to fill with water.

As water began to cover his helmet, Jim instinctively took a deep breath in the event of a leak, but to his relief—nothing. He did find, however, he had to maintain a grip on the rail to keep from floating aimlessly. Webster chuckled, explaining that is exactly what would happen in space. Magnetism worked only on those surfaces covered with a thin metallic film.

At a future date, the bay would be pressurized requiring only the sealing of the hatch to guard against sudden loss precious air. But for now, suits and umbilical lines remained the rule of the day. With the airlock water-filled and the pressure equalized, Webster opened the hatch to the bay. The cumbersome portion of the transfer began. The Commander exited the chamber and, grasping a well-placed handle, reached for a second line and connected it to the additional valve of his suit. He disconnected the first line, allowing it to rewind into the airlock. Jim floated from the confines of the lock, grabbing hold of another handle. Webster handed a second umbilical to Jim, who quickly made the connection then disconnected the first, letting it slip through his glove as it also rewound into the airlock.

The tank could not present an exact replication of weightlessness, but certainly offered fair warning of motion, and what to expect of 'neutral buoyancy'—today's buzzword for creating the effect of weightlessness. Special tank test suits, worn by Kyle and Jim, maintained a zero-gravity effect through systematic monitored regulation based on individual weight, depth in the tank, and actions performed.

Webster sealed the airlock hatch then instructed the first-timer to follow his procedure to reach the docked XM easily. As Jim continued to grip the handle for stability, he soon realized that, although weightless, telltale signs of gravity surfaced: if upside down, blood still flowed to the head, and when upright, a sense of standing in the suit could be noticed; the body did not float in the suit. Yet, the simulation proved more than adequate.

Proceeding downward, head first, Webster grasped, hand-over-hand, a series of rungs molded into the sidewall of the bay toward a catwalk stretching alongside the XM. Cautiously, he pulled himself along the catwalk until reaching the craft. Although Jim could hear him in his earpiece, Kyle still turned and motioned for him to follow.

Jim released his grip on the handle and stretched for the first rung, momentarily floating free. He lunged awkwardly and grabbed the handle he first held, causing his body to collide with the airlock. OK, he thought, let go of one object only after the next is in hand…always maintain control. Webster withheld comment, understanding Jim was one who would pick up the method through observation and hands on experience.

Relax…relax, Jim told himself as he took several deep breaths to settle before reaching down to grab hold of the rung just below, then the next, and the next, until at the catwalk rail where he slowly and cautiously joined Webster next to the simple mockup of the XM. Kyle patted Jim on the shoulder, giving him a thumbs-up as they laughed over the first stage of his weightlessness lesson.

Commander Webster explained to Jim the need for care in entering the XM. The position of the catwalk could give the impression one could vault into the cockpit, close the canopy, and be off. The valuable lesson learned at the airlock and ladder served him well; move from place to place always holding on to something secure. Floating free is not a good idea. He pointed out that in the tank there is resistance—water. In space, there is none; push off in one direction and nothing would halt the forward motion.

Webster pressed a simple release and the XM canopy opened. He pointed out another oxygen umbilical line required to transfer into the XM requiring the same procedure: connect the new line before removing the one already connected. He suggested Jim perform the switch after settling into the cockpit.

Carefully using the catwalk rail as his starting point, Jim guided his body into the cockpit and, bracing himself with his feet, pulled the padded restraints over his shoulders and secured the straps that crisscrossed his upper torso, firmly holding him in place. He then connected the umbilical line from the XM and detached the original, handing the line off to Webster. Colonel Gordon was ready to depart the OV.

Webster had Jim return to the exterior of the airlock and perform the procedure alone an additional four times before stopping for the evening, satisfied Colonel Gordon could handle the maneuver in real time.

Exhausted, yet satisfied, Jim rested well that Sunday night. Monday, Tuesday, and Wednesday proved much the same with simulator time, weightlessness training, and dress rehearsals with Lisa Kerrick. Lisa and Jim developed a routine to prepare Samantha Marissen for takeoff with speed and efficiency. During one of the practice sessions, Lisa confided she told Nate of her interest and elatedly shared that Nate expressed a similar feeling. She laughed as she declared nothing would have ever come about had she not said something; he was such a quiet man. Lisa also told of the lengthy conversation regarding their Christian background, each now aware of their precious similarity. Jim realized he would never have known based on conversations with Nate during the simulator sessions of the past few days.

And...Dan Malone took part in the exercises Monday, Tuesday, and Wednesday.

North of Moscow, Russia

The situation at the dacha had grown more tense, if possible, during the week prior to the transfer of Samantha Marissen to Moscow for the trial. Only Alexei and Nikolai remained as her legitimate guards, the four perimeter guards arrested and taken to Moscow for questioning. In retrospect, the original number of guards at the dacha was laughable, although the current inept government had blown the crisis disastrously out of proportion.

Ironically, no longer was Samantha the sole political prisoner, Nikolai and Alexei now joined her under house arrest until the trial. Why they were allowed to remain puzzled Nikolai. Wouldn't matters have been simplified to ship both he and Alexei to Moscow with the others, leaving only Sam? Somewhere lay a deeper reason.

Perhaps, behind all the political and military maneuvering lay a dark plot, a plan to use the two remaining guards as scapegoats for a failed prisoner transfer. Perhaps the plan calls for the death of Samantha Marissen, thus ending the five-month standoff, albeit tragically. Blame would be assigned to two young soldiers who lost their heads in the heat of a failed rescue attempt, losing their lives in the process, a tragic outcome...but an end to an otherwise hopeless situation for the hapless men in Moscow.

Alexei had earlier informed Samantha of an attempt to free her and hand her over to an American, who would get her out of the country Friday, possibly sooner. Today is Wednesday, Today? Tomorrow? Friday for certain…if Alexei spoke the truth. Nothing left to do but wait. Without weapons or manpower, their lives were in the hands of the Russian resistance.

Supplies no longer an issue since they barely ate or slept and only quickly washed so as not to be caught unaware when the time arrived. Nikolai made no mention of his gun and one magazine to Alexei nor did he pursue Alexei's ability to speak perfect English. Too many secrets. What had Alexei not told him? Lack of trust only breeds deeper distrust.

The only person Nikolai trusted fully—his fellow Christian. Her situation pained him so; an innocent victim, undeserving of the previous four months, the beatings, the conditions, and total separation from her family and country. In spite of her wealth, she had nothing, her life in shambles. Nevertheless, he witnessed her growth in strength and courage…and although forty-eight-years-old, maturity. Individuals under intense pressure and strain, either break or grow—she the latter. He prayed for her safe return home to begin anew, with James, if he was willing. Nikolai wondered if James ever thought of Samantha.

The more Samantha mulled over Alexei's divulging information of a rescue, the more she drew the conclusion his motivation meant to strike fear, to terrorize, yet her faith and prayers kept fear at bay. If Alexei's attempt was to convince Samantha to confide in Nikolai, as far as he knew, she had not. Every sound, every voice of every moment set her on edge.

Samantha spent a great deal of time in her Bible and prayer; Nikolai joined occasionally, preferring, wisely, to remain alert for any sign of attack. If the resistance stormed the dacha, he must know the very moment the attack began in order to protect Samantha, taking every measure to ensure a successful rescue.

A change had taken place over the past two days, the Captain and men had ceased checking on the three, deciding instead to position five men around the dacha at varying distances. Nikolai observed the Captain did not have the resources necessary to guard the area responsibly if attacked; only a matter of time before peak efficiency would suffer. To push so few men so hard meant Samantha's transfer must be near.

SONORA COMPLEX, ARIZONA

HE REFILLED HIS mug a final time before situating himself between Commander Webster and Nate Garcia. Jim accepted he'd grown quite close to these people, a dedicated group, proud of their accomplishments, yet humbled by the magnitude of the mission and their desire to aid Ed Marissen in his quest to bring Samantha home. Jim's role as the one to bring closure utilizing untold hours of blood, sweat, and tears, bore heavy responsibility.

CIA Director Allen Jamieson stepped to the front of the semi-darkened room, revamped as the staging area for the remainder of the mission, equipped with state of the art technology recently flown in and installed. His assistant, Ray Zygman, dimmed the lights further before flashing an aerial view of the Russian dacha on the full-wall screen.

Jamieson cleared his throat and began, "What you're looking at is the building the holds Samantha Marissen. This is real-time so, Moscow is ten hours ahead of us, which makes it a little after six this evening.

"Back out a bit, Ray."

Using a telescoping pointer, he went on, "OK, from this altitude, we can observe the perimeter guard, which has been pulled in considerably. There are now five guards rotating around the building at all times. No one has gone in or out.

The latest intel reports the two original guards appear to have been placed under house arrest and held with Ms. Marissen. Thankfully, one of the arrested guards is our contact. If nothing else, we have a man on the inside, but we don't know how much good he'll be at this point."

Zygman backed the view further out. Jamieson continued, "Colonel Gordon, here are three small clearings where you can land. You'll choose the site based on GPS readings from a homing device carried by our contact. Once Miss Marissen is freed from the dacha, the device will emit a signal denoting her location. You are to land as close as possible to her location, prepare her for departure, and get out, ASAP. Any questions so far?"

Shifting in his seat, Jim pointed to the screen, "Yes, sir, one. Can I get a hard copy of these views? I want to familiarize myself with the target area."

"Not a problem, Colonel. We have prepared a manual of information for you to study—data, photos, anything you need…I hope. If something is missing, let me know."

Zygman reached back, handing the inch-thick manual to Lisa, who passed it to Nate, who presented it to Jim, who flipped through the multitude of pages before returning his attention to Jamieson.

"I notice the landing sites are northwest of the building. What's the background on that?"

Jamieson smiled, "I was coming to that, Colonel. The attack will come from all sides but the men who extricate Miss Marissen will proceed through the trees over a rise behind the dacha to the northwest. None of this happens until key targets are eliminated—munitions, transports, personal. They must traverse several miles to reach the clearings. By that time, the signal should be broadcasting, allowing you to locate your passenger. You do not leave the clearing you land in; they will find you. Recon shows no nearby troops, giving you a brief window of opportunity to get in and out. Chaos and confusion should work in your favor.

With a grim look, Jim presented a needed question, "What if there is no signal?"

Jamieson answered straight up, "The only reason there would be no signal is if…if the mission failed. If there is no signal, you are to return to the OV immediately."

"But what if—

"Immediately, Colonel."

Glancing to Marissen, Jim noted his head, although down, nodding in the affirmative. Every mission has a hard side, a side difficult to accept.

"Yes, sir. Got it."

"Good. Now, Dr. Hamilton will address fuel allocation for the mission. You have a tight timeframe, Colonel, and must maintain a strict schedule. Dr. Hamilton?"

Steve Hamilton approached the front to begin his explanation of the extreme caution required when using the XM as a two-seat fighter. After comparing facts and figures, he cut to the chase: bottom line, even if Jim could orbit back to the U.S., insufficient fuel remained for a powered-flight landing, leaving them stranded in orbit or crashing on re-entry. The only solution—return to the OV.

"The last item—you must adhere to a precise departure vector to ensure subsequent orbits do not put you above Russian airspace. Your windows of opportunity for liftoff will be configured by Sojourner's computer the moment you depart the OV. Lifting off from Russia at one of the predetermined times at the correct vector will place you within 500 miles for eventual rendezvous. I know I'm repeating what you learned this week but I want to make certain we've covered everything. And, just a reminder, since you will be flying manually, you will receive periodic notifications of fuel consumption, airspeed, and elapsed time."

The briefing extended until nearly noon when Ed suggested a short lunch before Charley Rice introduced Jim to the long-awaited, mysterious G-BoF. Ed watched with satisfaction and yet, a sense of sadness, as the dedicated group left for the dining room. The small assembly had proven themselves the best and were balancing on the cusp of immense success or the brink of interminable failure. Everything they had worked for, struggled through, rested on the shoulders of James Gordon.

James, the name that angered him so many years before, now the name of the man he relied upon, a man he admired greatly. Deep remorse surged through him once more as he imagined the pain he had subjected his daughter. "Oh, Samantha, my baby…I'm so sorry." Lowering his head into the crook of his elbow, he prayed for forgiveness and the safe return of his daughter. He also prayed fervently for the man who would lay his life on the line for her. He thanked God he could pray.

In mid-August, before his last return to St. Louis, Ed contacted the church Rose attended until the day he drove the deadly wedge between Samantha and Jim. Rose never worshipped at the church she loved again, once Samantha stopped attending due to sheer embarrassment and the pain of her loss. Ed spoke with the pastor, a recent replacement for Mark Rogers, who retired but continued to serve as an assistant, and asked if he had time to speak with a man who, at one time, thought himself a Christian, but realized he lived a lie. He had never truly given himself to Christ. Without hesitation, the pastor agreed to see him as soon as he arrived in St. Louis. Imagine his surprise when he asked for his name; he promised

Ed confidentiality, not because of the subject matter but the circumstances of the day. He and the pastor talked for more than two hours after which Ed tearfully, earnestly gave his life to Christ. He did not share the event with Rose; he would, but he had to set many things straight before he could. He deeply desired her to believe his sincerity when he did.

Eerily sensing the presence of another, Ed raised his head to see Jim.

"Are you OK, Ed?"

"Yeah, just a little tired."

"C'mon, let's grab a bite. The break will do us good."

As Ed rose from his desk, he asked, "Jim, would you have supper with me tonight?"

Laying his hand on Ed's shoulder, Jim smiled and responded, "Sure, your place or mine?"

Ed laughed, "How about my place, after your G-BoF training?"

"Sounds good. I'll finally find out what G-BoF is all about."

With a feeling of genuine contentment, Ed shared, "Son, you will be amazed."

1:30pm

The final lesson at Nate Garcia's simulator—G-BoF, the unknown weapon system. The last month passed swiftly; each day filled with training of one sort or another. Most of his time had been spent in the simulator, a fascinating piece of equipment. Transitioning from the simulator to the XM flowed seamlessly, far smoother than imagined. As Jim thought many times, this period would be a wonderful experience had it not been overshadowed by the seriousness of Samantha's plight. No longer a matter of weeks or days, the crews' departure now possibly only hours away.

Jim shifted into his "I'm ready, let's roll" mindset, a nature he adopted during his Mideast duty. No time for second guessing, no time for doubt, which should not translate to ignorant cockiness, only steady confidence. Charley Rice, a six-foot average-build guy with thinning black hair stood before the group with Jim at his side.

"I could go into a lengthy explanation of what makes this work, but time determined you learn how to use it first. That's the important factor today."

Rice appeared forced with his delivery; he was a researcher, not a teacher, which made the fact that he came up with the name G-BoF more humorous. Jim grew more anxious as he listened. Rice handed Jim a pair of gloves and a helmet with only a visor for the simulated run.

"Wear the gloves to get a feel for the weapon. This helmet enables you to see the laser. Your helmet for the mission has the identical feature built in."

"Laser? The weapon is a laser beam?"

"No, no, not quite. A laser is used to conduct or direct the G-BoF to the target." Rice chuckled, "Sorry, I'm rather proud of the name I came up with. I'm normally not a very funny guy but with this, I made my mark."

The group appreciated his light hearted self-deprecating demeanor.

"Anyway, Jim, the basic explanation—electricity is generated by minute protrusions extending from your craft in contact with air molecules you fly through and stored similar to a high-voltage capacitor. Think of it as friction causing a static charge except you decide when and where you want to release the charge. The moment you fire the weapon, silicon is shocked by the released charge and the resulting 'ball of lightning' traverses the laser that has locked onto the target at the speed of light and either disables or destroys the bandit. That is the correct vernacular, isn't it?"

"You bet it is!" Seeing the majority of the group had no idea of what they spoke, Jim explained, "A bandit is Air Force talk for an enemy aircraft." Turning to Rice, Jim laughingly asked, "Do you know more of the slang?"

"Oh, I probably know them all." He laughed at himself, "At one time, I thought of enlisting in the Air Force but I chose this instead. I guess I'm living vicariously through you this month."

Jim smiled, "I hope I don't disappoint you."

The brief levity lightened the strain of the day and relaxed Dr. Rice.

General Townsend took several steps toward the front. "To be sure, Jim, you have, if necessary, the right to defend yourself or whatever you determine to be defended. Your hands are not tied. You are well-respected, having proven yourself to be level-headed and decisive, always making the decision that needs to be made. And, this is the word from the top."

Never before had Jim been complimented in such a manner. He had received commendations and promotions but General Townsend's words of trust moved him.

"Thank you, Sir."

Unsure of where to go from here, Rice stammered, "Umm, OK, I guess we can…umm, get this moving. Ready, Jim?"

"Yeah, Charley, I'm ready. Let's do it."

Jim climbed into the simulator for the final lesson; the canopy closed. After strapping on the helmet and slipping on the gloves, he spoke into the mouthpiece, "I'm ready in here."

"OK, the simulation will begin mid-flight," Rice warned. Don't want you to be surprised when you find yourself at 15,000 feet."

"Thanks!" Instantly, the craft was flying over mountains

with enemy aircraft fore and aft.

"All right, pull the red lever located in the right wall."

He did and a handgrip with a trigger mechanism and a large button on top extended from the wall near the control stick.

"Now squeeze the trigger and you'll see the laser. Toggle the handgrip until the laser is near the target. You don't have to be on target, just close."

"You mean bandit, don't you?"

Rice laughed. "Yeah, the bandit. Squeeze the trigger again and beam will lock on. Ready?"

"Yeah, ready. Now what?"

"Squeeze again."

Without warning, a brilliant ball of white light blazed across the beam to the target, instantly burning a hole through the skin, transforming the aircraft into an intense ball of fire. No explosion, only the flaming craft falling to Earth.

Wide-eyed at what he witnessed, Jim blurted, "Great balls of fire! What just happened?"

"Exactly!" Rice declared. "G-BoF—Great Balls of Fire! You nailed it first time! You just blew a plane out of the air with a bolt of lightning. Let's try it again, only this time, lessen the power of the strike."

"OK, how do I do that?"

"Slide your hand from the handgrip onto the extension arm. There's another grip. Got it?"

"Yeah, what now?"

"See the number **3** on the upper right of your visor?"

"Yep."

"That tells you at what power level you're firing. Squeeze the grip again and it will lower to **2**; again, **1**. Level **2** will neutralize the craft, completely frying the circuits and components, leaving it useless. Perfect for eliminating aircraft still on the ground.

Level **1** destroys all instruments, allowing the pilot to fly, but only manually. Not many pilots could pull that off. They'd probably wind up ditching their plane. The weapon resets itself to level **3** after each firing.

"Want to try level **1**?"

The original scenario flashed on the screen. Jim quickly aimed the laser in the vicinity of the bandit and squeezed to lock. Excellent, no need for a direct mark to lock the weapon. Taking the power level to 1, he squeezed the grip to fire. A smaller, yet just as brilliant ball of light streaked across the beam, striking the target, which momentarily appeared to sparkle blue before struggling to remain airborne.

"This is unbelievable, right out of science fiction! What else can this do?"

I think you'll like the next feature. Hang on; I need to change your battle scenario…ahh, there it is."

"Hey, what the—

"Sorry about that. Should've let you know."

"That's OK. What do I want to do here? I see six, uhh, bandits ahead, slightly above."

All eyes on the screen as Dr. Rice talked Jim through the lesson. "Aim the laser to the center of the enemy formation, but when you squeeze to lock, maintain the squeeze until you see what happens."

"OK, here goes."

Jim squeezed the grip, locking the laser onto the center aircraft of the formation. As he continued his squeeze, the beam split apart; each separate beam locked onto an individual craft. With the power level at 3, he fired. Six G-BoFs streaked to their targets, destroying each simultaneously.

An audible gasp could be heard across the com as Jim

experienced the relative ease of taking out six enemy aircraft in one instant.

"Charley?"

"Jim?"

"Sorry, it's…it's just that I've never seen anything like this… obviously. How in the world did you—

"Just an idea…a lotta time, a lotta work. I read about ball lightning when I was a kid. Always wondered if it could be reproduced. You know, just like anything else, you want it you do it. Well, now we have it."

The group chuckled at Jim's remark, "I'm glad you're on our side."

The surprises weren't over. Rice demonstrated the weapon's ability to strike from the aft; no enemy aircraft was safe. The difference lay in viewing the target and locking in the laser with the assistance of a rear camera viewed in the cockpit very much like a video game. Many scenarios played out over the course of the afternoon as Charley trained Jim in the use of his 'awesome' weapon. It may well be his ticket out of Russia.

The small group remained to follow the training session if only to be with their pilot for the final time. All that had to be accomplished had been accomplished…and within the required month. Ed's group were amazed by Jim's abilities, while Jim gave all credit to Ed's group. The next forty-eight hours would thrust years of research, development, training, and skill to the forefront of testing. Great success or dismal failure lay in wait.

5:45pm

Stretching out on the couch with eyes closed, Ed contemplated all that had occurred in the past month. Although Samantha was still a political prisoner, she could well be home in twenty-four hours. He had come to know and respect the man who should have been a member of the family these many years. This man, Jim Gordon, had agreed to take over a rescue mission when success seemed darkest and kept the mission alive. Greater than these was his realization and admission he had never been a believer and had taken the steps to give himself to Jesus Christ several weeks back. Now, he had one final wrongdoing to rectify. He asked God to bless him with the right words, the best words to do so. A light knock stirred him from his thoughts. He rose from the couch, made his way to the door, and opened it to Jim in the hall.

"Ahh, Jim. I'm so glad you accepted my invitation to supper. I hope you don't mind; I took the liberty of ordering dinner for both of us. Nothing fancy…steak, baked potato, corn, green beans, and biscuits…and a fresh pot of coffee. That all right with you?"

Jim stepped into the room. "That sounds great! Thanks for doing this. A good meal and a little free time is just what I need."

"Please, have a seat. I'll get you a coffee, black." Ed laughed. "Everyone here knows how you like a good cup of coffee. You have really fit in well in such a short time." He brought a cup to Jim and sat across from the couch with hands between his knees.

Both began to speak at the same time. Jim stopped to apologize, "I'm sorry, Ed, go ahead."

Ed coughed in nervous anticipation. "Jim, there are some things I need to say. I regret it took me so long to do this." He cleared his throat again. "There are many things I did wrong… or handled wrong during my life. The most blatant of these was my treatment of you twenty-five years ago."

Staring at the floor, he continued, "Straight and simple, I was jealous. Rose and I, well…mostly Rose, tried to help Samantha recover from the loss of her family. I was so afraid; I overprotected her. I thought I was doing right…making good on a promise I made to my sister. But nothing seemed to help."

Raising his eyes to Jim, Ed confessed, "Then, one evening… one evening with you opened the door to the rest of the world for Samantha. I was afraid for her…for me. I feared losing my sister's little girl, my little girl. I felt I was supposed to be the one to rescue her. I was so wrong."

Now pleading with his eyes, he finished, "I am asking forgiveness for forcing you and Samantha apart, for robbing you both of many years together. I am sorry, Jim. I am truly sorry."

Stunned by what he heard, Jim finally understood the reasoning behind Ed's actions of the past. There was nothing to do but forgive him. Not because he should, he wanted to forgive Ed.

Rising from the couch, Jim stepped to Ed with hand extended. "I forgive you, Ed. I do. I have learned much this summer and I want nothing more than to make all things right between you and me."

Ed stood slowly, face-to-face with the Air Force pilot and grasped his hand in a firm handshake. "Thank you, son." He paused momentarily, "It is OK if I call you son?"

Using both hands to grip Ed's, Jim smiled broadly and replied, "Definitely, Ed, definitely."

8:30pm

Jim crossed the airstrip in the light of a near full moon, glad to be free of the confines of the Complex; grab a breath of fresh air, warm, dry air. For a month, Sonora had been his all; his only outdoor venture the test flight, the nearly fatal flight that would have rung the death knell for the mission.

Since the report of Cole Chambers' note became known, a thought haunted him: who was the person behind Chambers' attempt to sabotage the project? Why? If the reason was not to prevent the mission, what then? Whoever called the shots must not be aware of the mission or work for the Russians; otherwise, the Russians would have exposed the plan by now.

Better to let the Feds figure it out, he thought. He had enough on his mind. With the photos of the dacha and potential landing sites seared into his memory, a time of peace and reflection seemed appropriate.

What an experience after twenty-five years; a wonderful dinner with Ed, beginning with an amazing apology and Jim's forgiveness, followed by conversation that led to greater respect and understanding of one another. Before Jim left, Ed shared his experience of accepting Christ several weeks earlier at the church he and Rose first attended and how, despite the strain of Samantha's ordeal, God gave him the strength and peace to carry on. Jim asked if Rose knew what he had done. Ed conceded he had not; he needed to make things right with Jim Gordon first. Jim gently reassured him that he could tell Rose, now that things are right. The reconciled men prayed together before Jim departed.

And what of Rose? Was she well? She must be; Ed would have told if she wasn't. Rich, Gina, Samantha, and Scott are with her; she's in good hands. He remembered, this was Labor Day weekend; he would miss the Reynolds' end-of-summer party. This year would be different, definitely.

The important question remained: how is Samantha? Is she safe? Inexplicably, the memory of Samantha leading him in his prayer of salvation that first night flashed into his mind. She… wait a minute! He quickly grabbed at his waist, searching for his radio. Whew, it's there. He hadn't left it in his room!

Jim stepped from the airstrip onto the immense desert, pleased he hadn't forgotten his only means of contact. The recollection of her elation after he prayed his prayer of salvation in front of her home that cool spring night continued. When he finally looked up, he noticed her smiling with tear-filled eyes. She welcomed him to God's family as she ever-so-softly held his face and kissed him lightly. He remembered the one tear that rolled down her cheek to her lip, crossing to his as their lips met.

Touching his lip where her tear had fallen, Jim stopped in his tracks and prayed. "Lord God, watch over us all tomorrow; keep us safe. Give me the courage and strength to pull this off. Help me to bring Samantha home safely. I cannot believe I will see her after all these years…and half a world away. I cannot believe how things worked out between her father and me. I know it is your sovereign work, Lord, and I thank you. Whatever your plan is for us, Lord God, I will follow your will. I love you, Lord…and I love her. I ask that she still loves me.

An early rise tomorrow morning to determine their time of departure; his arrival in Russia could not be too soon…nor too late. Time to get back and get some rest. All the training, intel, and planning boiled down to a last day decision. Lord, make that decision a good one!

Strolling back to the Complex, he observed the preparation crew working feverishly to have Sojourner secured in the Orbital Vehicle, magnetically mounted atop the Insertion Vehicle, ready for liftoff. Once assembled, the massive joint aircraft could lift off anytime. From the corner of his eye, Jim caught a glimpse of a lightning flash beyond the southwest horizon followed several seconds later by muffled thunder.

Suddenly, a radio transmission disrupted the golden solitude of the night, "Colonel Gordon, please clear the airstrip. An unscheduled arrival is due to land in seven minutes."

NORTH OF MOSCOW, RUSSIA

OVERCAST AND NOT yet sunrise provided little sight for the three captives. Forty-seven degrees and damp, Samantha attempted to sleep in the corner of the kitchen wrapped in a blanket, but restful sleep not possible. Nikolai positioned himself on the floor next to the door, alert for any outside activity. The cold afforded him the opportunity to wear his heavier military jacket, concealing the only weapon they held for defense. Alexei positioned himself in the corner opposite Samantha, awaiting the supposed rescue attempt, more than likely that afternoon he surmised.

Slowly, quietly Nikolai rose and eased his way to the window nearest Samantha.

"What?" she whispered. "Do you hear something?"

"No. Is quiet."

Scanning the area behind the dacha in the dim pre-dawn light, he observed no activity in the tents of the soldiers, the only light in the command tent of the Captain. The two vehicles remained stationed near the rear of the small clearing. The soldiers on guard duty close by the building were barely visible; the perimeter guards still in darkness.

Samantha joined Nik at the window.

"No. Do not. Is too dangerous," he chided. "Keep on floor."

"Just a quick look, then I will."

She strained to see over his shoulder just as one of the guards trudged into view obviously weary from his long shift. He stopped long enough to light up a cigarette, a foolish mistake. The red tip marked his position. As he pulled his first drag, intensifying the glow, his head forcefully snapped back; he fell into a crumpled heap. At the same moment, a loud CRACK, the sound of a bullet impacting the dacha sharply permeated the dawn air, then another, and another. Nikolai threw Samantha to the floor, protecting her with his body as best he could.

One shot, then a second, broke through the windows striking the walls opposite. Samantha squeezed her eyes tightly shut and scrunched into a fetal position, realizing the attack had begun.

Her mind screamed, "Oh, my Lord God! This is really happening! Protect us, please!"

Alexei yelled from across the kitchen, in Russian, "Nikolai, we must get out of here!"

Nikolai commanded, "No...we stay! We leave...we die! Stay!"

As he lay over Samantha, Nikolai stretched back and pulled the table by the leg and, straining, tipped it on its side. He crawled low into the makeshift barricade dragging Samantha with him. Reaching into his jacket, he withdrew the gun, their only protection, checked the magazine and slammed it back into the handle.

Bullets ceased striking the dacha but the three were not prepared for the incoming ground-launched grenades that took out the tents and trucks with speed and precision. The supply truck packed with munitions exploded violently blasting shrapnel all directions, ripping gaping holes into the dacha walls while breaking out any remaining windows.

The horrific sounds of battle—munitions blowing, machine gunfire, screams of dying men—all invaded the innocent mind of Samantha Marissen. Although she did not fear death, the ear-piercing, terrifying stimulation of auditory nerves initiated a massive adrenalin rush, igniting the 'fight' or 'flight' reaction, neither of which possible.

Erratic, heavy footsteps approached, thudding over the wood porch. None dared breathe as Nikolai, Samantha and Alexei awaited entry of friend or foe. Kicking the door open, the Russian Captain, appearing as a drunken man, staggered into the opening, eyes darting non-stop left to right to left to right again, waving his weapon wildly searching for Samantha Marissen.

Residual munitions explosions from the burning truck and rapid gunfire bursts continued as the severely injured soldier swayed in the doorway. Weakly, he attempted to shout out; instead, blood spewed from his mouth onto his already bloodstained uniform. In a moment of final desperation, his eyes locked onto Samantha huddled on the floor.

Leaning on the doorframe, he haltingly aligned his gunsight on Samantha's body. Then, a shot. The Captain, so focused on killing her, had not seen Nikolai quickly raise his weapon and fire. The bullet entered below the left cheekbone, passing through his brain, before blowing chunks of skull from the back of his head.

A look of utter surprise contorted the Captain's face before his lifeless body dropped to the floor. Samantha stared in silent shock as she witnessed the final moment of life slip away from the dead Russian blocking the exit. The sound of boots running across the porch electrified them once more. Not waiting, Nikolai raised his gun to the center of the opening, anticipating his next shot.

Only a hand, slowly waving, extended across the doorway. To Nikolai's relief, he heard in broken English, "Do not shoot! We are here for woman! Do not shoot!"

Samantha began to sit up; Nikolai pulled her back to the floor. Slowly, he stood, weapon still aimed at the entrance.

"Remove weapon," he shouted, "and put where I can see."

"No, I—

"Do it!" he snapped. In no mood to negotiate with only a handful of rounds remaining, Nikolai commanded again, "DO IT!"

He heard movement on the other side of the wall and strengthened his grip on the gun while adjusting his finger on the trigger. An arm extended across the opening holding an assault weapon by the shoulder strap and slowly lowered the weapon to the porch floor. A young mid-sized blond soldier stepped to the entrance with hands interlocked behind his head and stopped for inspection.

"I must speak with Nikolai."

Moving to the center of the kitchen, Nikolai responded, "I am Nikolai."

"We must move quickly." The soldier rapidly explained in Russian, "This was not to be until tonight, but the plans for the woman changed this morning. They are on their way to take her to Moscow. Security, they said. Who knows? They are all crazy!"

"How many men do you have?"

"Thirty, but half have left. Once the woman is gone from here, another half will leave. The moment she departs, we all disappear...no trace."

Nikolai thought a moment, then asked, "What of the American who is to meet her? If this was moved up, when will he be here, and where?"

"The change is being transmitted as we speak…and we can tell them the woman is safe, for the moment. They must make changes on their end."

Nikolai hesitantly inquired, "You mean…we can walk out of here…now?"

"Yes, everyone is dead; we made certain of that. No one and nothing is left. Only this building remains, barely."

Surveying the surroundings, Nikolai wondered, how did they survive?

Ignoring Alexei, he turned to Samantha and extended his hand, "Time to go."

"Home?" Tears filled her eyes as she stood…every blink causing tears to fall down her cheeks; she wiped them away with her sleeves. "I'm ready."

Motioning to the corner, Nikolai advised, "Take blanket, is cold morning."

Grabbing the blanket from the corner, she rolled it up under her arm as she cautiously stepped over the dead Captain lying in the doorway, glancing at the massive chest wound and the fatal gunshot below his cheekbone. Blank eyes stared back. Samantha quickly looked away.

Alexei called to Nikolai as he stepped over the Captain, "Where did you get the weapon?"

"Never mind that! Why were you shouting for us to get out? We certainly would have been shot! If I didn't know better, I would think you were trying to get us killed!"

"No…Nikolai, I—

"Shut up!"

Walking briskly to a mangled, dead soldier, Nikolai removed the young boy's assault weapon and slung it over his shoulder. He checked the soldier's pockets, found a small handgun, probably a personal weapon, and made his way quickly to

Samantha's side. Unknown to him, Alexei had also confiscated a military handgun.

When the small group reached the woods, Nikolai shouted out, "Stop! I need to explain to the woman the change in plan and what to expect."

The leader turned to Nikolai, stating forcefully, "No, we must keep moving!"

He fired back, "We will move better if she knows what has happened and what is to come!"

"Thirty seconds…that is all!"

Nikolai steered Samantha several feet away and stood behind her so as not to be observed easily by the leader or his men…or Alexei.

"Wrap blanket around you."

"But why?"

Nervously, he replied in a sharp whisper, "Do it…please."

She unrolled the blanket and swirled it around her shoulders pulling it together in front. It draped below her knees.

Reaching into his jacket, he withdrew the small handgun. "Have you shot gun?"

"A long time ago."

"Watch and hear." He held the gun for only her to see. "Safety here—off, here—on, off, on. Yes?"

"Yes, but…why?" Now frightened, she took the gun.

"We need to—we do! Put in pocket, keep blanket on."

OK, Nik, I will. Why shouldn't I trust you now?"

As the fugitives methodically worked their way deeper into the pine-wooded, low-rolling hills, several resistance fighters remained at the dacha, dragging three dead Russian soldiers into the shrapnel-torn building, stripping the bodies and placing them in the kitchen as Nikolai, Samantha, and Alexei had been. After strategically planting a number of incendiary devices, they barraged the structure with grenades launched from a distance causing massive explosions followed by an intense fireball rising horrifically into the air.

The resulting conflagration would leave nothing more than bones and ashes which authorities would assume to be Samantha Marissen and her guards…at least initially. Regardless, if later she was not identified as one killed in the attack, she would be long gone, the mission a success.

SONORA COMPLEX, ARIZONA

REACHING THE HANGAR, Jim decided to await the incoming flight, to check out the unscheduled flight when Merrill's voice exploded over the radio, "Jim, come to the hangar; we have a situation."

"Roger that, Merrill, I'm right outside."

Inside stood the six scientists the flight crews, Atkins, Gagnepaign, Townsend, Forsythe, and, of course, Ed and Merrill. CIA Director Jamieson and his assistant, Ray Zygman, joined the emergency meeting as Jim arrived.

Jamieson addressed the group, "We just received word—approximately two and a half hours ago resistance fighters stormed the dacha to free Ms. Marissen. The mission had to be bumped up; intel learned she was to be transported to Moscow earlier—9:00am, Moscow time."

Ed immediately broke in, "Is Samantha safe; is she all right?"

Jim stepped to Ed's side.

Jamieson continued, "That portion of the mission was a success. She is safe and on her way to a pickup point. Problem is...that point is unknown. The rescue team must position themselves further from the original site since the Russian military will be crawling around the dacha...probably already there."

Tension hung heavy. Samantha was on the run, but to where? And the mission hadn't begun at Sonora.

Zygman carried on the briefing, "We've got to get Colonel Gordon in there ASAP, meaning," he pointed to Jim, "you must depart immediately." Assembly of the IV/OV is complete. We are waiting on the arrival of two NASA astronauts, doctors who will accompany the OV in a last-minute decision, to tend to Ms. Marissen should she require medical attention. We will have to stow their suits and equipment aboard the OV prior to liftoff."

Neither Jim nor Ed had considered Samantha's possible need for medical attention, a highly likely scenario.

Merrill stepped up, "Gentlemen, suit up. We're getting you outa here."

"One minute, Merrill." Malone spoke from the rear of the group.

What could he possibly want, Jim thought angrily. Just shut up and get in line with everyone.

He heard Merrill ask, "What is it, Dan?"

Malone hesitated briefly but went on, "What if…what if, to get Colonel Gordon there ASAP, he rode in the XM while still docked in the bay. All he would have to do is drop out over the North Atlantic and fly into Russia. That would knock one orbit, about ninety minutes, off his ETA. Ninety minutes could make some kind of difference…wouldn't it?"

Ed pressed Merrill, "What do you think? Could it work?"

Merrill looked to Hamilton, "Steve, you think it's good to go?"

Hamilton considered the pros and cons before answering, "As near as I can figure, that should work. The XM, or Sojourner, is locked in position; there hasn't been a problem yet on launch. Jim will have his own oxygen supply. Essentially, he won't be using more oxygen than before, just earlier. It should work. Ninety minutes is a bonus. I'd say, it's up to you, Jim. You wanna try something we've never done?"

Jim studied Hamilton and his calm concern; then Malone and his youthful optimism; and, finally, Marissen, a man fatigued by months of fear and worry.

"Dan's right. If we do this, we can knock off ninety minutes. While the Docs and their medical supplies and suits are secured, I can get situated in the XM, probably easier than in zero gravity."

Merrill performed his usual hand clap. "All right! Let's roll!"

Before Malone could rush off, Jim gripped his shoulder. "Good idea, Dan. Nice work."

Malone cracked a smile. "Thanks." Looking Jim in the eye, he reassured him, "You'll be OK in Sojourner. Hamilton's right, there hasn't been any problems in the bay during launch. The OV has been flawless."

NORTH OF MOSCOW, RUSSIA

BREATHING HEAVILY, SHE dropped to the forest floor immediately upon the squad leader calling for a short rest; they had been on the move for two hours over hilly, forested terrain, which proved her no longer as young as she once thought. Samantha kept securely wrapped in the blanket to conceal the handgun Nikolai had entrusted to her, although she continued to wonder why. Perhaps his philosophy revolved around "Trust no one." Lord God, bless him, she prayed; he protected her, saved her life. Anechka should be very happy to have someone like Nikolai.

The leader spoke low in Russian as he circled the outfit. Nikolai translated for Samantha, "We stay here short time. Wait for report from dacha. We move where American pick you up. Half leave now. Half at pick up."

Nikolai reiterated his promise, "I stay until you leave."

Samantha touched his arm. "I will never be able to repay you. Thank you."

He smiled and whispered, "Thank you, Sam."

The morning chill remained; the day would not warm much with the partial cloud cover. She pulled the blanket tighter about her shoulders. Images of Rose and Ed drifted into her mind as she rested against a tall evergreen. Soon after, memories of her brother and sister, her mother and father followed. Closing her eyes, she sighed. What a life she had experienced; what a shame she had wasted so much. No more, she promised. When she returned home, she would correct as much of her past as possible.

Thirty minutes later a lone resistance fighter ran stumbling to the fringe of the rescue party and immediately began an animated exchange with the squad leader, pointing in the direction of the destroyed dacha and to the sky. The leader listened patiently before turning his attention to his team. Stooping beneath the low-hanging branches, he explained the report.

Again, Nikolai translated the information for Samantha, "Troops at dacha, find burned. They think we are killed…but, not sure. They want…umm," he performed a spinning motion with his index finger as he looked to the sky.

Samantha guessed, "Helicopter?"

"Da…yes, helicopter to check forest for you…we…us. We find American."

Pausing briefly, the squad leader knelt on one knee before Nikolai and, in Russian, informed him, "There was never any intention of taking her to Moscow. You and the American woman were to be killed today. We were to be blamed for her death."

Glancing to Alexei sitting twenty feet away, Nikolai quietly inquired, "Alexei was to be killed also?"

Not looking from Nikolai, the leader mouthed, "Nyet."

Rising from his knee, the leader pointed out several men and those selected disbanded without a sound. The remaining men picked up their weapons, ready to complete the mission.

As the smaller assemblage moved on, Samantha whispered to Nikolai, "What did he say to you back there?"

Thinking she would ask, he gave a prepared response, "We stay under tree cover; cannot be seen from air. Not to walk in open."

She nodded understanding. He did not want her to know the truth, or to fear the possible danger ahead.

SONORA COMPLEX, ARIZONA

"SONORA, ALL SYSTEMS go. *Operation Lightning Strike* set to move forward," noted Tim Moore, Captain of the IV. And none too soon. Intelligence had reported multiple acts of violence sporadically across Russia, but mostly within Moscow and still believed to be the responsibility of the Russian Federation government itself.

However, the latest information indicated the Resistance or Revolutionaries were responding in like manner, wiping out government offices, killing corrupt officials. Soon the violence, acts of desperate men, would spill into innocent parts of the country. The unofficial position of the United States, known by a handful of individuals, stood at, "We will extricate our innocent American citizen using any force necessary. The rest is up to the Russian resistance."

Colonel Gordon, secured in Sojourner, docked firmly within the OV, electromagnetically locked to the back of the IV, had to smile at the operation name *Lightning Strike*, since his Air Force call sign had been *Flash*, only a result of his last name. The unusually dry desert, lit by a full moon in the east and glimmers of lightning beyond the western horizon, anticipated a possible late summer rain within the next several hours according to the latest satellite forecast. Although plant and animal life relished the chance, Sonora Complex performed the impossible without rushing the launch.

A slight lurch alerted Jim the towing of the massive assembly to the launch strip had begun. His cockpit screen jumped to life displaying the OV's view of the airstrip.

"You got the screen, Colonel?" sounded the inquiry from launch control.

"Roger that. Thanks. I thought I would miss the launch."

"Glad to serve. Good luck, Colonel. Good luck, all! See you back here!"

Not in unison, the three pilots, two commanders, and two NASA physicians, Fran Benoit and Jake Brinker, acknowledged the farewell as the 'mule' disconnected from the OV and returned hastily to the hangar.

From Mission Control, "Launch in 30—25—20—

Making a last moment adjustment in his seat, Jim readied himself for his first launch to orbit in a craft no prior NASA astronaut had ridden.

The slightest vibration passed through Sojourner as the Insertion Vehicle built up thrust. Next, the clear enunciation of the countdown, "IV, you will be at full thrust in 10-9-8-7-6-5-4-3-2-1 LAUNCH!"

Colonel Gordon's body instantly pressed into the contoured pilot seat as the IV acceleration took effect. Without blinking, he observed the screen as the dimly outlined airstrip passed beneath at ever-increasing speed. A sudden burst of extreme energy raised the aircraft off the runway to a 40° angle on its journey transporting the OV to orbit. The power of the IV surprised Jim as the increasing acceleration buried him deeper into the cushioned cockpit seat. No longer watching the screen, he closed his eyes allowing his body to experience the sensation of a lifetime. Held captive within the belly of the beast made for an odd journey to space until, opening his eyes, he caught the ever-beautiful blue-rimmed slight curvature of the horizon onscreen.

"Flash, how're you holdin' up?" The voice of OV Commander Webster startled him.

"I'm fine…what? Wait! Where did you get that?" Jim questioned.

"What? Flash? Figured you needed a call sign; seemed to go well with Gordon!" Webster laughed, believing he had come up with something new.

Jim said nothing about his past call sign. Hearing it again felt right. "You know, it doesn't take much to come up with that!" he joked.

"And you wonder how I thought of it?" Webster laughed again, more than likely the last laugh of the departure.

Jim resumed the communication, "Smooth ride…all things considered. How long until separation from the IV?"

No sooner had he voiced the question than the IV Commander Mike Parker announced, "OV…separation sequence to begin in 6 (final electromagnetic check performed)…5…4…3…

2…1. Without warning and to Jim's surprise, the reversal of polarity repelling the OV from the back of the IV came as a jolt locked in the confines of Sojourner. A sudden sensation of falling off the edge, immediately followed by the pressure of extreme thrust lifting the OV upward once more to orbital insertion.

His cockpit screen, blacked out at separation, sprang to life with the majestic expanse observed by the OV—the darkened planet slowly illuminating into sunrise as the crew raced over the eastern United States toward the brilliant blue-shelled curved horizon. Jim gazed steadily and intently at the screen as the ship pushed forward and upward until the intense thrust ceased.

"Be with you in a minute, Colonel," the calm voice of Commander Webster reported as he made his way to the 'bubble' command center. "Sorry you didn't get to see the launch firsthand but, soon you'll be out there taking the ride of your life."

"Yeah, it all comes down to this, doesn't it?"

All that transpired the past month now seemed unreal, a dream at best. Yet, here he waited to embark on the ultimate, possibly final mission of his life in an aircraft advanced far beyond any known. Glancing upward through the canopy, Jim observed Webster's preparations for his embarkation. Oddly, only now did he note the sensation of weightlessness.

"Colonel, we are currently at the 175-mile altitude, climbing toward apogee. Your screen should now display our location over the Atlantic along with the countdown to your departure. Sojourner will control the exit from the bay to the determined clearance before turning the controls over to you… just as we practiced. The remainder of the mission is yours. Godspeed, Jim."

"Thank you, Kyle. Leave a light on. Flash, signing off."

Concealed by the activated Chromatoskin, the OV's bay doors cracked open, methodically revealing the Earth below. From the cockpit, Jim beheld a most awe-inspiring view, the partially shrouded southern coastline of Nova Scotia and Newfoundland to the north with the Gulf of St. Lawrence snuggly between. As he awaited the locking clamps release, he gave a final prayer requesting a safe and successful mission.

At mark, the clamps simultaneously released the nose and rear wingtip sections, signaling the craft to initiate descent with micro-bursts from maneuvering thrusters, nudging Sojourner free of the bay. Streaking more than 17,000 miles per hour through the silence of space at eight times the altitude of his near fatal test flight, Jim devoted a moment to God's creation before shifting to his mission driven mindset. Any thought of the beauty beyond his spacecraft or of the woman he was to rescue dared not interfere.

Once the automated egress system determined Sojourner's required distance from the OV, downward thrust ceased and control of the craft handed over to Colonel Gordon. From this point, all contact with the OV terminated; he flew alone, accountable to no one. His ability to track Samantha hung on the reliability of one GPS in the hands of one escaped prisoner.

His eyes drifted to a small keypad, a last-minute addition, fastened to the lower left sidewall of the cockpit. The CIA demanded, and he understood, that if captured or killed, Sojourner must not fall into the hands of the Russian Federation providing a means to reverse engineer the most sophisticated weapon devised to date. A powerful explosive had been rigged to detonate twenty-four hours after landing, ensuring Sojourner's total destruction should he not return.

Colonel Gordon's instructions determined that within two minutes of raising the canopy, he must **CLEAR** the keypad three consecutive times, then enter the numbers **4-2-7-9-5-6** followed by* and +. He had three chances to punch in the correct sequence. If not, Sojourner would violently cease to exist at the fourth attempt or two minutes after opening the canopy with no solution.

Analysis showed that a steady constant descent would best conserve the limited fuel carried by Sojourner. Also, the resulting sonic boom of re-entry over the North Atlantic would be little noticed. The Chromatoskin offered the ability to fly virtually unseen to St. Petersburg at 3850mph then on to the south between Vologda and Tver, approximately 218 miles from Moscow where he should pick up the signal.

Taking control, Jim initiated a gradual descent, firing reverse thrusters to slow Sojourner, all the while anxiously anticipating the fiery furnace of re-entry. The planned flight path placed him over the North and Baltic Seas once he crossed the Atlantic. He shook his head in disbelief, aware the 6900-mile flight would be accomplished in less than two hours—1 hour, 48 minutes to be exact.

Sojourner continued its nose-up deceleration until Jim observed the first sign of re-entry—a faint thin orange ring surrounding the electromagnetic field. The downward glide grew increasingly bumpier as the craft began to collide with the ever-thickening air molecules of the upper atmosphere. The faint orange ring flamed into blazing fire-like streaks, darkening the canopy for continued visibility.

"OK," he thought. "This does NOT match the simulator… how could it? There is no way to experience re-entry through simulation."

His suit took over as the G-forces steadily increased, but not to the 9 G's experienced during his earlier flight and fight for control of Sojourner. As the flame of an acetylene torch diminishes, so too the flaming streaks that enveloped Sojourner, soon followed by the sonic boom created as the craft broke fully into the atmosphere faster than the speed of sound. The resulting shock wave seemed to pass over the ocean waters without notice; Colonel Gordon's sub-orbital flight had ended.

Reviewing his instruments, double-checking the activation of the Chromatoskin, he nosed down for the continuous descent. Sunrise arrived quickly as his course carried him from the North Atlantic across central England, over the northernmost tips of Netherlands and Germany, the Baltic Sea just south of Sweden, Latvia, Estonia, and into Russia near Pskov, all the while decreasing in altitude. Not once had any alert or warning been activated by his invasion of a national airspace.

The plan called for Sojourner to hook south between St. Petersburg and Novgorod in order to face head-on any possible military response from Moscow. Suddenly, the screen jumped with activity announcing the signal had been acquired, briefly displaying the location. Despite his training and hard-core mission demeanor, he allowed the realization that Samantha Marissen was at the opposite end of that signal. Jim initiated a broad, sweeping descending circuit toward Moscow to lock onto the signal…then…it was gone…lost. He was flying blind.

NORTH OF MOSCOW, RUSSIA

"GET DOWN! EVERYONE down! They must not see us!"

Although concealed beneath a thick evergreen cover, Nikolai desired to take no chances. As near as he could tell, three Ka-50 Black Shark helicopters had been deployed to sweep the area for any sign of escaped survivors. The Sharks appeared to be fitted with laser-guided Vikhr anti-tank missiles under-wing, capable of penetrating armor up to 900mm thick; and armed with a 2A42 rapid-fire 30mm gun equipped with high-fragmentation, explosive incendiary, and armor piercing ammo, any of which the pilot could select in flight. Moscow or the Russian military took the escape seriously—no survivors.

Nikolai and Samantha scrunched as low as possible next to the trunk of a tall pine to avoid detection from the air. In the distance, angry, growling machine gun fire echoed through the woods forcing the group of seven to press deeper into the evergreens, aware future rounds could be for them. Nikolai prayed the resistance fighters who broke off a short time earlier were safe, not victims of the rage now terrorizing the escapees.

As the exhausted company hid in the undergrowth, the powerful, forceful sound of coaxial rotor blades viciously beating the air passed sixty-five feet overhead. The three Black Sharks split the area into equal segments, with the remaining two preparing to fire blindly into the forest as the first had, splintering any hope of survival the escapees might possess.

Nikolai turned to Samantha; her eyes wide with fear as she clutched his arm.

"What's happening? Why are they circling around? They want to kill us, don't they?" She shouted her questions, the thundering reverberation of the Ka-50s drowning out all normal tones.

He knew it best to be straight with his response. "Yes! Russian military! Take no survivors," he shouted in return.

Turning next to the rescue leader only feet away, he yelled in Russian, "We must move! Once they start firing, we are dead! What direction?" Exceedingly aware of their hopeless plight, he screamed for an answer, "WHICH WAY!"

Running on adrenalin, the leader shouted, "To the west…there is a stream…and rock. We may find cover there. GO! NOW!"

He signaled three of his men to lead Nikolai, Samantha, and Alexei west to possible protection from the inevitable hail of machinegun fire; he would follow, although, he surmised, they were running to their deaths. Weaving through the trees beneath the low-hanging branches, they hadn't covered much ground when the sheer calamity of 30mm rounds broke out, ripping, tearing, and shredding bark and branches, mindlessly seeking victims. The seven raced to the, as yet, unseen stream aware of nothing but the need for shelter. The heart-pounding combination of machinegun fire and rotor blades beating the air generated such fear in the minds of the runners, nothing else mattered.

Samantha diligently followed Nikolai, who positioned himself as her lead, frantically dodging trees and low-hanging branches, occasionally slipping or sliding on the damp, musty ground cover. As the intense pounding of rotor blades and constant barrage of ammo grew closer, Nikolai suddenly found both he and Samantha tumbling down a steep embankment, sliding to a stop at the edge of a shallow stream.

Jumping to his feet, he quickly noted Samantha and the others stunned but essentially uninjured. Surveying the immediate area, he discovered a narrow rock overhang in the side of the hill not more than fifty feet away. Yelling and motioning to the others, he grabbed Samantha's hand and bolted toward the formation as the Ka-50's destruction grew ever nearer.

Samantha's lungs burned as she gasped for air; her only salvation—Nikolai's death grip of her hand as she stumbled behind almost every step of the way. Reaching the rocks, he flung her back against the wall, the five others crowding with them under the 18-inch wide overhang which, because of the helicopter approaching from the rear, would protect them on this pass, not so of a probable frontal approach.

The ground above virtually vibrated with the impact of every round; ripped or torn tree fragments and bits of ground cover shot in every direction. Seven bodies pressed deeply into the rock as the Ka-50 roared overhead firing indiscriminately, shattering chunks of the rock ledge, remnants blasting wildly about. The ear-piercing cacophony of the turboshaft engines and rotor blades passed. If the pilot turned back at this point, Nikolai, Samantha, Alexei and the four others crammed under the ledge instantly became a highly visible target. With nowhere to run, they stared at the helicopter through the clearing, awaiting its impending return.

* * *

As he broke through the partial cloud cover, Colonel Gordon descended in an ever-tightening spiral, hoping to locate and lock on to the signal again. There must be a valid reason why the signal broke off, he thought. His order had been, if no signal, return to the OV. A signal had been transmitted but cut short. She was out there; he could not turn back, not now.

Scanning the Russian countryside to the east, he immediately understood. Within seconds, Sojourner identified the military aircraft as a Ka-50 Black Shark High-Performance Attack Helicopter, listing its weaponry and firepower. He observed three, probably on a search and destroy mission, now too fanned out to hit at once. He would choose one, hoping to draw in the others. But which one? As he drew closer, Colonel Gordon could see the flashes of weapon fire emitting from the center chopper. It was slowing to perform a 180°.

*   *   *

Focused only on the Black Shark's next maneuver, the fugitives gasped as the helicopter prepared to sweep the area from the opposite direction, executing an immediate high-speed coaxial-rotor flat turn. Frozen with fear, no one attempted to run. Where? Which direction? Only a matter of seconds before the unrelenting Shark would be on top of them. The violent, thunderous repetition of killing gunfire bursts began, again ripping and shredding anything in its path.

*   *   *

Sojourner dove for the Ka-50 as it initiated its final approach of terror, crossing the chopper's flight path above the gunfire at 525 mph, causing the helicopter to lose stability. Colonel Gordon broke into an Immelmann Turn, trading airspeed for altitude during a 180° change in direction, pulling the first half of a loop while rolling to an upright position when completely inverted. Now, Sojourner hovered at a much higher altitude than the Black Shark, providing Gordon an unseen vantage point for the hit, excellent for maintaining secrecy. After the Russian pilot deftly regained control, he frantically searched the sky for whatever had caused his helicopter to react as it had. Colonel Gordon activated G-BoF.

"Did you see what happened?" Alexei screamed in Russian to Nikolai. "The helicopter looked as if it would crash. Why?"

"I do not know!" Nikolai shouted.

As they watched the helicopter regain stability, then searching wildly, a brilliant flash occurred followed by a blue halo enveloping the Ka-50. Its twin engines failed instantly and the war machine plummeted into the forest. Everyone waited for an explosion but…nothing.

An eerie, momentary silence ensued until the "thumpa, thumpa, thumpa" of the two remaining Black Sharks grew increasingly louder as they approached in response to the strange sight they witnessed. Still in awe, the fugitives gathered near the stream concentrating on the helicopters hovering over the crash site a half mile away.

After several minutes above the site, one helicopter swung around to depart to the south only to be struck by a blinding flash and the enveloping blue halo, tragically dooming it to the forest floor. The final Shark spun madly in search for the source of the destruction of the advanced military machines.

Colonel Gordon maneuvered Sojourner in a tight figure 8 in order to maintain sufficient G-BoF charge. Constant firing from a stationary position would drain the 'capacitor', the holding cell for the electrical charge. Returning to a similar position above the Black Shark, well-aware he must put down the Shark, Colonel Gordon squeezed the grip locking the beam on the target and fired. The ball of lightning ripped across the beam at the speed of light sentencing the Shark to the same fate as the others.

* * *

Samantha gripped Nikolai's arm. "Did you see that? Why did they just fall out of the sky?"

Nikolai could only whisper, "I do not know. Is...I do not know. But...it...we are alive." Not removing his eyes from the scene, he questioned, "The American?"

Her heart raced at the thought. Could she be that close to escaping? Could this be the end?"

* * *

Glancing at Sojourner's readouts, he saw fuel usage still registered within safe parameters; he had kept unnecessary flight to a minimum to this point. He still had to find Samantha, although the Black Sharks proved she must be within a several mile radius of his current location. Reassured by the activated Chromatoskin, Jim felt certain he could perform low sweeping scans of the area without detection. Regardless, the quick dismissal of three top-of-the-line Black Sharks could not be easily ignored, although Sojourner did not detect any radio chatter during the encounter.

* * *

"Back under the trees. Take no chances!" the fugitive's leader commanded. "We must wait. We cannot afford to leave."

As the weary band left the vulnerability of the small clearing, Nikolai stepped upstream a bit. Samantha followed. He pulled his weapon from his pocket and removed the magazine, holding it in his open hand. "Oh, Lord, we are so close. Let this work," he prayed in Russian.

"What are you doing?" he heard Samantha ask.

He explained honestly, "This is signal to American. I shut down before so Helicopters not find us. I will…turn on again."

"Samantha looked in amazement. "Is that what I hid in my pocket the day they took your ammunition and gun?"

"Da…yes. You are brave, you help.

Samantha responded, "Nyet, ni nada"

Nikolai laughed. "Good, you learn Russian. But, there is need to say you are brave. Yes!" He handed the magazine to Samantha. "You turn on. You tell American you here."

She nervously gripped the magazine, turning it over, looking for how it was activated. Nik pointed to the side. "Need for transmitter. See button. Push."

In a symbolic gesture, Samantha held the magazine high, pressing the button while she spun slowly in place looking skyward. She stopped and handed the transmitter back to Nik. "Will it stay on or do I have to keep pressing the button?"

"Nyet," he smiled. "No…signal stay on. We wait…but in trees. We stay not seen."

As they made their way up the hill back to the tree canopy, Samantha mentioned, "Your English is getting very good. We can easily talk. You don't know how that has helped me through all this."

"I am sorry this…happen. You are nice. I hope God bless you with James. Maybe it to be. I pray for that."

Samantha halted her climb and turned to the young Russian. "Thank you, Nikolai. That probably won't be…after all these years. But, thank you."

Alexei nervously approached Nikolai. "Do you think the American will return? Where did he go? Where is he?"

Nikolai wanted nothing to do with Alexei at this stage. He could not forget that he and Samantha were to be killed at the dacha, but not him. What is his purpose in all this? He could not trust Alexei.

"He will! Why are you so concerned?' he barked. "If that was the American, he will. He did not come this distance to leave without her. Settle down, Alexei! You are making me nervous."

Samantha scrutinized the faces of the two men, previously friends. Alexei portrayed anger, fear, while Nikolai seized the dominant role of strength and control, silencing the man she suspected of, what? Nothing substantial…not yet. If her ordeal was near an end, let it end now, she prayed. The pressures of fatigue slowly unraveled the thin bond holding everyone together. Only by the grace of God had she been able to come as far as she had. She prayed God give her and Nikolai the several more hours of strength necessary.

As she sat on the steep hillside awaiting the arrival of her 'ride', she wondered how her American rescuer could get to her. What could someone possibly land here? Her location was ridiculous; a small clearing by a stream! How? But what that had seen earlier was miraculous. Twenty seconds more and they would have been dead. Where is he? He was so near, whoever he is.

Nikolai called the leader of the operation over to Samantha and him. "You put your lives in danger to save us." He hesitated, "What is your name?"

A weak smile crossed the face of the Russian. "Sasha, my name is Sasha."

Samantha extended her hand in friendship. "Thank you for getting us here. I will never forget you and your men. Thank you."

He shook her hand; his weak smile grew to a grin of appreciation. He asked Nikolai to tell her "all will be good; she is going home."

Nikolai relayed the message, after which he expressed his gratitude for their valor. The only reason Samantha made it as far as she had was due to what his men accomplished today.

Turning to his three remaining men, Sasha repeated Nikolai's words and finished with, "It is time…go home. Thank you! Now, go!" He and his men shook hands before the three disappeared into the woods, not looking back.

*   *   *

Concentrating solely on his instruments, Colonel Gordon ever so carefully began his scan of the area the center Black Shark had covered. Abruptly, Sojourner's screen sprang to life with the acquisition of the signal. He got an immediate lock and slowly advanced toward the origination point which proved to be less than a mile from his confrontations with the Black Sharks. His landing area appeared more than adequate, a clearing adjacent to a small stream, the terrain relatively flat at the bottom of a ridge. Hovering for only a moment, he eased the craft lower and lower, finally extending the landing gear. Needles, leaves, and dirt exploded in every direction from the force of the landing thrust as Sojourner touched down on the surface well within the necessary parameters for safe takeoff. Jim initiated shutdown and exhaled a long sigh of relief; he was on the ground…in Russia…to pick up Samantha Marissen. Was she all right? Had the Black Shark done its job? He had to find her.

Lowering his head, he thanked God for bringing him safely to this point and prayed for the strength and courage to complete the mission. The memory of a line from a letter she wrote to him after the float trip flashed into his mind, "You treat me like I'm the most valuable person on this earth." She was…and still is. This time he would live up to her description. Today he would be the man he should have been.

Surveying his surroundings, he surmised all safe and secure. After running over the entry code CLEAR— CLEAR—CLEAR, 4-2-7-9-5-6,* + twice, Colonel Gordon finalized shutdown. The Chromatoskin would remain active for twelve hours but that length of time would not be necessary. A couple of hours at most, he thought, would be all he required. The signal stopped. Were they close enough to see him land?

He released the canopy and disconnected the air supply. Bracing himself on the seat, he eased out of the cockpit onto the wing and down to the ground. Leaning forward, he unlatched and removed his helmet, immediately hearing the reassuring, soothing sound of the stream flowing not too far away.

* * *

Sasha, Alexei, Samantha, and Nikolai strained to see what could have caused such a disturbance as to have blown nature's debris in every direction, and yet remain unseen. Pointing in the direction of interest, Sasha whispered, "There, do you see? Something is down there! You cannot see it but it is there!"

As the three struggled to visualize what Sasha observed, the backside of a man mysteriously stepped to the ground from… nowhere? Baffled, they cautiously moved to a better vantage point and watched silently as the visitor bent over slightly and removed a helmet, exposing a head silver gray.

Nikolai chuckled quietly to Samantha, "I do not know how…your country send old man to rescue you."

She laughed under her breath amid tears she could no longer hold back. But, this was no time to cry. It didn't matter who they sent; she was going home. She anxiously moved to join the American.

"No, stop!" Nikolai whispered as he grabbed her wrist. "Wait…to see if pilot watched by soldiers. Be safe."

He was right, she knew. Once more, she crouched low until the pilot turned to place his helmet and gloves on a…a… something. She broke from Nikolai's grasp and weaving through the trees, ducking her head and blocking branches with her arms, she passionately fought her way to the clearing.

*   *   *

Placing his helmet and gloves on the oddly invisible wing of Sojourner, Colonel Gordon abruptly turned to confront a commotion hastily progressing toward him from the wooded hillside. As he realized he had neither the time nor the dexterity to defend himself, a figure slid the final few feet from the shadows into the confines of the clearing. She rose slowly, awestruck, not fifteen feet distant.

"James?" She remained motionless, unable to believe her eyes. Hands interlocked, she rubbed her lower lip with steepled fingers, tears rolled down her cheeks as she absorbed the beautiful sight of not only her rescuer but also her lost love.

As Jim stepped toward Samantha, Nikolai, Sasha, and Alexei cautiously entered the clearing, weapons drawn. Without removing her eyes from him, she extended her right arm back, hand open, "Stop, please! It's OK. I know this man!" Softly, she added, "I know him well."

"Samantha!" James clumped a step toward her as she rushed to him.

She stopped short, not wanting to do anything that might… oh, how confusing is this? She deeply wanted to hold him, begin again…but she knew nothing of his situation. Was he…

with someone; was he married? What was he doing here? Who could imagine James would be standing here, right here, right now! These questions stalled her in a moment of indecision. Should she just ask? That would sound so ridiculous, especially at this time.

Finally, she stammered, "I...I don't know what to say...or ask...or do. Are you...?"

Samantha's expression communicated her dilemma to Jim. If she was the woman he remembered, she would not make an assumption she might later regret. He wanted to hold her again but realized he was the unknown factor. Her life had been exposed for all too see during the highly publicized divorce. He clumped a few more steps to her and reached for her hands. She looked up and took his fingertips.

Jim smiled as he began, "I hope I'm answering what you're asking. No...I'm not."

With that brief confession, Samantha rushed into his arms, sobbing. He embraced her as best he could in his flight suit. She could not believe she was in his arms, arms of strength and protection. For the moment, nothing had changed; years melted away, exposing a love once smothered. As in the beginning, he held her as long as needed.

As she eventually pulled herself together, James' focus shifted to the three Russians, weapons now pointed to the ground. "Who are your friends?"

Not releasing her hold, Samantha explained, "They are responsible for my escape. They risked everything to free me. There are others but they are already gone."

"Thank you." Jim's brief smile to the three broke the tension of the morning. Oddly, this meeting brought some peace to the group; the skirmish at daybreak and the escape from the killer Black Sharks weighed heavy on everyone's shoulders.

Turning to the three, Samantha motioned to Nikolai who slung his weapon over his shoulder and made his way to them. Holding Jim's hand between hers, she went into a strange introduction, "Nik, this is James, the man I told you about from long ago.

"James, this is Nikolai. He has protected me from many things during this time." Attempting to continue, she faltered, "I don't believe…I don't believe I would be alive today…if not for him." Samantha leaned into Jim once again and broke down, reliving the fear and anguish of the past months in the safety of his arms.

As he held her close, Jim reached out to Nikolai, "Thank you for everything you've done. Really, thank you."

Shaking his hand, Nikolai added, "You save us. We would… have died. You stopped. Thank you!"

Nikolai paused before nodding to Samantha, "She is brave lady, very brave. Sam is why you hear signal. Ask her later. OK?"

Jim smiled at the odd request. "I will, I promise."

After Nikolai walked off to the side, Samantha raised her head from James' chest, eyes glistening. "I'm not brave; I'm so scared. I've never been so scared in my life. I can't believe what happened. I didn't do anything. They arrested me. They think I'm a spy. Isn't that just crazy? I—

He reassuringly rubbed her back as he continued to hold her. "Bravery is doing what needs to be done, even when you're scared. You are brave. Don't worry, we're gonna get out of here…safely…and soon. We'll lift off in about thirty minutes, no more."

Samantha freely allowed her long-lost pilot to comfort her as she pulled herself deeper into his arms. Her breaths quivered, but, with him she could endure this final segment of her long nightmare.

With calm determination, Jim announced, "We've got to move; time is not on our side."

"Yes...yes." She reluctantly backed away, turning her attention to the eerily transparent Sojourner. "What is this?" straining to make out the shape. "We're getting out of here...in this?"

"Yeah, something like that." He chuckled as he picked up his gloves. "This is your ride home."

From the direction of the three Russians soldiers came a single voice, "Not today."

SONORA COMPLEX, ARIZONA

HE TAPPED LIGHTLY on the slightly cracked door.

A muffled voice hoarsely responded, "What is it, Merrill?"

Merrill crept into the dark office, Ed silhouetted by the soft light of his desk lamp.'

"I just want you to know we haven't heard anything. We know Colonel Gordon fired on several targets but nothing more."

A heavy sigh emanated from the old man's shadow. "You're the only man I know who reports nothing new."

"Sorry, Ed, I only wanted to keep you up-to-date on the mission."

"No, no, I meant that as a compliment. I can depend on you for most anything."

He leaned forward in his chair holding the 8 x 10 picture of Rose and Samantha he had shown Jim during their first meeting. He breathed heavily as he struggled to speak.

"I've made a shambles of my family. Look at this picture, Merrill. Where am I? Where was I? Why was I not with them? Look at what I've done to Samantha, to Rose…to Jim. All because I thought I was doing the right thing for my sister. I felt I was taking care of Samantha, protecting her, watching over her. Instead, I smothered her; I choked life and love out of her. I've done the same to Rose. She's alone, having to go through this without me…if she would even want me there."

Merrill eased quietly into one of the chairs and edged closer to the desk. "Don't do this to yourself. You're under a great deal of pressure right now. You spoke to Jim; you told him everything. All you can do now is concentrate on getting Samantha and Jim home. And…you can see to it that Rose has someone to be with during this time. Isn't there someone?"

"There is, but I don't know if they will allow it, all the secrecy they want to maintain," Ed acknowledged in resignation.

Merrill quickly responded, "I believe they will; Rose deserves better and you can make it happen. Give me a couple of minutes, I'll speak with Director Jamieson."

Rubbing his eyes with heels of his hands, Ed agreed to Merrill's suggestion. "Good, thanks. If they need a name, its Reynolds. That young friend of theirs, Jim's friend, Larimore, knows about this. Tell Jamieson it's that group I want Rose to be with; she has spent time with them this summer. Jamieson already knows about them."

"Right, will do." Merrill stood to leave. "I'll be back as soon as I know."

Marissen leaned back in his chair. "Don't leave yet, I'd like to go over something with you."

"Sure." Pierce hesitantly returned to his seat. "What is it?"

Ed pushed back his chair, walked around and sat on the corner of the desk, and folded his arms. "Merrill, you have been the Director of Operations during the entire project and have performed beyond all expectations, handling everything thrown your way. I have relied heavily on your expertise, knowing you would take care of any problems or decisions effectively and efficiently."

Pierce, who normally anticipated Ed's requests, was at a loss as to where his boss headed with this discussion. He remained silent.

As Ed placed his hand on Merrill's shoulder, he inhaled deeply. "I'm retiring…finally, the moment the OV touches down. I want you to take over as President and CEO of Marissen AeroSpace. For now, I want us to work on getting my daughter and Jim and the OV crew home safely. After that, you'll be running the show. I've been hanging on much too long. I need to focus on rebuilding my family." He sighed, "I intend to spend my remaining years trying."

He extended his hand to the soon-to-be President and CEO. Stunned, Merrill rose and took his hand in a firm grip.

"Thank you, Ed. I don't know what to say, except…I'm honored you feel I can do the job. But, I agree, first we get everybody home, safely."

"Let me get on your request for Rose. I'll be back as soon as I know." Merrill left the office.

* * *

Thirty minutes later, Merrill knocked sharply at Ed's door and stepped in with Director Jamieson.

Jamieson immediately began the conversation, or report. "Mr. Marissen, we have information the financier of our saboteur, Cole Chambers. Zygman is calling your people together but I want you to know before the briefing."

"Come in, Director. Do you know who he is? Is there more to this that can possibly jeopardize the mission?"

Jamieson stepped to Ed's desk; Pierce stood next to Ed. "I want you to hear this before the rest; the other man is your son-in-law, or ex son-in-law, Robert Barrett IV."

Intense anger seized Ed as a searing hatred coursed through his blood. Rising from his chair, he paced about the office, breathing heavily, like a bull preparing to charge. The vilest thoughts about a man so evil electrified him until he cut short his hate. Barrett was unworthy of such effort. Ed did not allow himself to be dragged into the gutter of a man of so little character, knowing one day, Barrett would have to answer to his actions."

"One question," Marissen calmly asked, "Is there anything more to his involvement?"

Jamieson faced Ed. "We are certain he never knew anything about the mission. His was a personal vendetta against you; he wanted to bring down the project; he wanted to destroy you. He ended up destroying only himself."

Before Ed could respond, Merrill interjected, "What do you mean 'destroying himself?' How did you find it was Barrett?"

The director cleared his throat, "I have always said, 'evil is stupid.' Tracing financial transactions can be difficult but, generally, can be done. People think they're so smart with this off-shore banking, but they're not. These days, that's the first thing we check. It's a slow, tedious process, but once we get that nailed down, we just follow the money, building our case each step of the way. Timing is the important factor.

"Barrett was in Chicago leaving his hotel for the airport. He had booked a direct flight to Frankfurt, Germany. We wanted to pick him up before he reached the airport to avoid any resulting commotion. He got spooked on the way because he suddenly began speeding through the streets like a fool.

"Now for the stupid part: he turns into a parking garage. Where can you go after entering a parking garage? Our men follow. He speeds up to the fifth level, smashing several cars on the way, finally losing control before crashing through the wall at high speed, ending in the street below. He died at the scene. Thankfully, no one else was injured or killed."

"You say he's dead?" As horrible as it sounded, Ed knew Samantha would be relieved to know he was gone forever, a very sad chapter of her life had closed.

"To tell you the truth, I think he decided on suicide rather than face the justice system and prison. He was already in his own personal prison. When this story gets out, I believe most people will know your daughter did not do any of the things he testified to in the divorce proceedings."

"You know, Mr. Marissen," the Director added, "had Colonel Gordon not survived his ordeal, we may never have known what really happened."

In order to satisfy his own mind, Ed inquired again, So, you're saying no others are involved other than Chambers and Barrett? No other loose ends? This is the end of any espionage possibilities?"

"No others, Mr. Marissen. We are certain Barrett and Chambers acted alone. This was simply blind hatred for one man and money for the other. Just to clarify, the official story will be true; we cannot release the facts behind it. Barrett wanted to take down a new fighter Marissen AeroSpace was developing; an inside man, Cole Chambers did his dirty work – twice. But the effort failed the second time; the test pilot and plane survived the sabotage and the resulting information pointed directly at the two men.

"We can concentrate on the mission 100%. Latest reports inform us armed skirmishes are happening throughout Moscow, but appear confined to Moscow only…for now. The general consensus is—removal of the unstable government is entirely possible after Ms. Marissen is proven to be free; their 'ace in the hole' will be gone. The only unknown is, what will such an unstable force do to hang on?"

"Pierce had informed you there's no news on Colonel Gordon, but, a short time ago, Gordon activated the weapons system several times before landing. Sorry, Pierce would have told you. As we know, all systems must be shut down once he's on the ground to avoid tracking by the enemy. We can't have the international community reporting we have invaded a sovereign country—even if by only one man."

Zygman leaned into the doorway, "Sir, everyone is ready for the briefing."

"OK, Ray, be right there," Jamieson paused, "Mr. Marissen, are you good to go?"

"Actually, Jamieson," Ed responded, "I haven't felt this positive in quite a while." Holding up his index finger to stall the Director, he went on, "Did Merrill approach you about my wife…Rose, she's alone and I would appreciate if she could be with friends at this time. She worries so much about Samantha. I want her to know we're working on it."

Without wavering, Jamieson placed his hand on Ed's shoulder and affirmed his plea. "I discussed this with the President yesterday. He agrees, tell her what's happening today. She should know, and to be with friends would be the best."

He thought a moment, "From what Merrill told me, you're speaking of the Reynolds and Scott Larimore. I believe Larimore would be the guy to work through since he's aware of the mission. Contact Larimore first, then talk to your wife; let her know Larimore will make the arrangements with the Reynolds. I'll speak to my men about transporting Mrs. Marissen wherever she needs."

On a serious note, he reminded Ed, "Remember, no mention of Colonel Gordon. His name must remain unknown throughout the mission. I'll have Ray get you Larimore's number."

NORTH OF MOSCOW

"WHAT ARE YOU—

Two rapid shots struck their intended targets before the question could be completed. Sasha's body dropped to the cold, damp earth. Nikolai reeled backward, slamming against the considerable base of an evergreen and slid down to an almost reclining position, head slumpled, his chin to his chest. He did not move again.

Horrified, Samantha screamed, "Nikolai!"

As Jim grappled to grasp the tragic turn of events, Alexei, waving his weapon, commanded, "Everybody, shut up! Do not move! I will kill the next one to move!"

Frantic with fear, his hand trembled with the weight of the gun; he hadn't figured on killing either of his Russian comrades, at least not immediately. He had panicked and now his panic forced him into a position well past the point of no return. Any act from this moment would be to save his neck; he knew it best to stay with his original plan.

"Remove the flight suit; put it into the aircraft; and step over to the woman…now!" Alexei nervously pointed the gun first at Jim, then Samantha.

Without performing one of Alexei's commands, Jim calmly reached into Sojourner and pressed the release causing the canopy to slide into position, close, and lock.

"What did you do?" Alexei demanded.

With a slight grin, Jim confessed, "She's locked and loaded… so to speak."

Angrily, the Russian shouted, "What? What does that mean?"

"I mean…the aircraft is sealed tight and set to self-destruct in twenty-four hours…sooner if tampered with. Even I can no longer gain access." Jim did not disclose the remote entry he carried or the required code, fearing the mad Russian would threaten Samantha with harm if he believed a method of entry existed.

With his defensive motions handicapped by the flight suit, the infuriated, illogical Alexei slammed his weapon across Jim's forehead, opening a deep gash above his left eye, bringing him down on the wing of Sojourner unconscious.

"No!" she cried. "Stop!"

He swung around, taking aim at her head. "Silence! Be quiet or I will kill you.!"

Turning his attention to the limp body, he took aim at Jim's head, bragging, "You foolish American. Your valor cost you your life. We will find a way to overcome your nuisance defenses. I will be a hero, killing the two traitors and the prisoner's rescuer, while capturing the woman attempting to escape and seizing the American aircraft. I will be honored for saving the Russian Federation from American aggression."

Samantha, with tears of intense anger, cautiously, silently lowered her hand into the jumpsuit pocket without taking her eye from the enemy, palmed the small handgun and slipped the safety to the off position.

The Russian backed off a step for what he thought a cleaner shot. Samantha raised the gun with both hands, focused the sight between Alexei's shoulders, and slowly squeezed the trigger. Two shots rang out simultaneously, echoing through the narrow valley. Alexei's head jerked back, his body twisted downward, lifeless eyes staring blankly into hers as he collapsed.

4:05am
Sonora Complex

With communication silence of the utmost importance, the news of an incoming satellite report of the shutdown of Sojourner at 0400 hours Mountain Time brought about a collective sigh of relief among the exhausted group of scientists, Generals, and Government agency personnel knowing Colonel Gordon had safely landed on the opposite side of the world. The question of the moment—is Samantha Marissen at or near the site? The unthinkable—is she injured? Is she alive? The timetable, at this point, no longer relevant.

Ed paced the room; two more hours before 6:00am, St Louis time. He would wait until six to call Scott Larimore before contacting Rose. Perhaps, by then, he could tell her Samantha was safely on her way home. Regardless, he would let her know he wanted her to stay with the Reynolds until this was over; Scott was making the arrangements. He hoped the Reynolds didn't mind the imposition—of course they wouldn't, he hoped. Director Jamieson had notified his men to transport Mrs. Marissen to the Reynolds' home without media knowledge.

His desire, after the mission, the successful mission, was to return home to his family, to Rose, Samantha…and Jim. He would see Samantha reunited with the friends he had forced her to leave behind, those he hoped to grow to know. He prayed God grant him the time and the ability to accomplish these things. He prayed God return his daughter and Rose to him.

1:40pm
North of Moscow

"No, no, NO!"
Samantha dropped the gun and ran to James, taking his

hand into hers and held it to her face.

"James, James," she sobbed, as staggering grief overwhelmed her.

Abruptly, she ceased crying, wiped her eyes to look at his hand, his wrist. Did she imagine she felt a faint beat, a weak pulse? The harder she tried, the less success she had at finding a pulse. In frustration, she bent over him, listening for any sign of breath, anything. She swore she could feel a slight warmth on her cheek from very shallow breathing. She turned her face to his, staring directly at the bleeding gash above his eye.

His wound was bleeding; he was alive; he had to be. Samantha frantically searched his face, head, and upper torso for a bullet wound, but found none. Utter fatigue took control from the relief she experienced, knowing James still lived. Dropping to her knees, she prayed, "Oh, my dear Lord God! Thank you, thank you for sparing his life. Help us, Lord, help us to get out of here. I don't know how, but please help us." Her prayer trailed off to soft weeping as she nearly slumped to the ground.

Suddenly, she froze! What was that? Straightening up, she listened intently for several seconds. She heard it again…a grunt…then, a groan. Slowly, Samantha looked over her shoulder; Nikolai had repositioned his leg, his knee raised. He struggled to move.

Samantha bolted to his side and kneeling next to him, gasped, "Nik! You're alive! Praise God, you're both alive!"

She wanted to help, but how? She needed to get back to James, but Nikolai was conscious. She looked over her wounded guardian; the bullet had entered his left shoulder, a large bloodstain marked the area. When he painfully leaned forward, she told him of an opposite stain on the upper backside of his shoulder. Relieved, he explained with difficulty, the bullet must have passed through and did not lodge somewhere in the shoulder. If possible, this was the best scenario.

Grimacing, he leaned back against the tree and roughly whispered, "You are alive too."

"Yes…yes…but James is unconscious…still, and bleeding. I need to get to him."

"Sam, help me…up. Get me over…by him. We stay close… together. I will…protect."

"Nik, you have done plenty. Rest, if you can."

"No, you are to help."

"All right, let's go!"

Samantha offered support to his good side as he pulled himself, grunting and breathing heavily, to a standing position. She braced her shoulder under his arm, taking his weight on as he struggled across the clearing to James and his odd-looking aircraft.

Reaching a rock protruding from the hillside, Samantha assisted Nikolai to a sitting position. She immediately checked James, hearing the shallow breaths she felt before. "James," she uttered, "I will never leave you again. Stay with me, please. Somehow, with God's help, we'll get through this. I love you, James, with all my heart."

Although he hadn't heard her caring, reassuring words, she simply desired to tell him. Holding his hand next to her cheek, she prayed for his life; he had been unconscious so long.

Nikolai strained to express, "James is…a good…man, Sam."

Softly, she agreed, "He came for me; he risked his life for me."

The sudden sound of footsteps stumbling down hillside, followed by a hushed, "Nikolai!" startled the two. They turned to recognize one of the Russian men involved in her escape that morning.

He spoke in Russian, "I waited in the hills to see how the woman would escape. I was foolish, but I didn't see how the rescue could be done." He stared briefly in amazement at what he could make out of Sojourner. "Unbelievable! What is this?"

His astonishment caused him to speak faster. "I heard two gunshots, and then nothing. I came closer to see what happened and I saw only you and the American woman. Alexei is dead? Sasha? What happened? No! Do not tell me. I do not want to know anything. I know you Nikolai; you I trust."

He slipped his pack from his back. "Is the American pilot dead? I see you have been shot. Let me help. I am a doctor."

Extending his arm, halting his advance, Nikolai demanded, "No, the American pilot is alive. Help him first!"

After Samantha explained James' injury through Nikolai, she stepped aside to make room for James' medical attention. As the doctor reassured Nikolai of his education at the Volgograd State Medical University nine years earlier, he pulled a towel from his pack and motioned for Samantha to soak it in the stream for use as a cold compress. Bending over the unconscious pilot, he examined Jim's breathing and searched for unequal pupil size or unusual eye movement. Upon her return, the doctor attempted to bring his patient out of his unconscious state by gently pressing the cold towel along his neck and forehead, carefully avoiding the bleeding gash. Samantha held her breath and Jim's hand as "Doc" performed his duty. Finally, a long, low groan seemed to exhale from Jim's lips; his eyes fluttered before squinting into the eyes of his three observers.

Before Jim could sit up, Doc held him in place and instructed Nikolai to inform the patient he was not to move until cleared of any head or neck injury. Nikolai, in turn, relayed the message to Samantha.

"James," she whispered. "Don't move. This man is a doctor and he wants to be sure your head and neck are all right first. You do have an awful gash on your forehead. Please just lie still and let him do his job. I don't want anything more to happen to you."

He barely nodded as he strained to focus on her.

Doc went on with the checkup continuing the three-person rotation of asking Nikolai to have Samantha repeat a question to Jim. Did he feel any drowsiness, disorientation, headache, memory loss, nausea, or blurred vision? With some difficulty, Jim told of a severe headache, and that he had trouble focusing his vision.

Slowly, carefully, Doc had Jim sit on the edge of the oddly defined wing with Samantha's assistance to check further for muscle weakness. After determining there appeared to be no other injuries or weakness, Doc asked Nikolai to explain to Samantha that he needed to clean and stitch the head wound in order to stop the bleeding and for any hope of leaving relatively soon. She passed the information to James, to which he simply stated, "Do it." She remained at his side during the procedure, which had to be performed with little anesthesia since Doc's mobile supply ran fairly low. Thankfully, plenty of antibiotics were available for both men as he turned his attention to Nikolai.

While the Doctor observed Nikolai for symptoms of shock or injury to his lung, Samantha attempted to make Jim as comfortable as possible, if possible, in his flight suit. He would not allow anyone to remove any part or portion. His obstinate refusal convinced her he was in no way ready to throw in the towel. She knew at that moment whatever he needed her to do, she would do, no questions asked. They were going home, although she acknowledged an unsettled feeling about their mode of travel…but she would not question him.

KIRKWOOD, MISSOURI

"SCOTT! WHAT BRINGS you here so early? The get-together doesn't start till noon." Rich refused to classify it as a party…not this year. Besides that, he could see much more was on Scott's mind. "Come in, come in."

"I'm sorry…I had to tell you face-to-face."

"It's about Jim, isn't it? Have a seat. Let me get Gina. Samantha's here, she stayed overnight. Of course, you know that, you brought her here last night. Never mind, I'll get the girls."

Before Rich could turn, Gina and Samantha scurried into the living room, wrapped in their robes. "We heard you guys talking. What's going on?" Gina exclaimed.

Samantha interrupted, "Something about Jim? Did I hear you say something about Jim?'

Scott jumped from the chair. "Yeah! Yes, it is! The mission is on!"

"Now?"

"Right now! They're coming home today!"

Excitement immediately filled the room but ended just as quickly when Rich asked, "Wait a minute. How do you know this?"

"Ed Marissen called—

"Ed Marissen? The Ed Marissen called you…this morning?"

"Yep. Told me Jim was at his target and they were waiting

for liftoff. At this time, no one knew exactly when that would be. There's been no contact with Jim for several hours but that was to be expected; the schedule had to be changed, too many unknowns."

Someone had to ask, Samantha did, "But why did he call you? Does Mrs. Marissen know? She needs to know."

"She knows. That's why he called; he doesn't want her to be alone. He wants her to be with friends and we were the people he wanted. He asked if she could be with us today. Hope I didn't overstep my bounds, but I figured you wouldn't want it any other way, so I said it would be OK."

"Of course, it's OK." Gina hesitated, "Rose is coming here? What time will she be here?"

"Hon, relax. Everything is fine. I don't think we can be more ready. You've been preparing all week just to keep your mind off what's happening."

Rich turned to Scott. "So, how will she get here? What time?"

"Ed didn't say how, but she should get here about nine this morning."

"Nine! That's just a little more than an hour!" Gina declared. "I've got to get ready. I can't look like this when Rose arrives."

"You're always beautiful, Babe." You'll be fine," consoled her caring husband.

"Yeah, right!" as she hurried up the stairs with Rich casually following.

"Your dad certainly knows how to treat your mom...and you know she loves it," Scott commented quietly.

Samantha went to his arms. Scott, I'm worried...scared, I don't know...both. Just hold me till it's over."

He wrapped his arms around her. He was scared too...and worried, probably both.

7:50am
Sonora Complex, Arizona

"You'll be in good hands today, Rose. You'll be with people who love you…and I love you. I will be the man you thought you married; the man I should have been these many past years. I thank God you stayed with me. I pray we can be the family God meant us to be…and I mean all of us…you, me, Samantha, and Jim. I learned much too late what a fine man he is, something you knew all along…but I've learned.

Ed felt a tremendous weight removed from his shoulders as he recalled his confession of love and regret made to his wife during the early morning phone call. A poignant sadness swept over him when he heard her softly crying as he told of surrendering his life to Christ several weeks earlier. His priorities now reflected God's order: His Lord first, then Rose, and family.

KIRKWOOD, MISSOURI

FOUR SETS OF eyes peered out the front window as a small, red car eased up to the house, came to a full stop, then turned slowly into the driveway. The driver, a slightly balding man of about forty, stepped out dressed in a Cardinal baseball jersey, dark blue shorts, and tennis shoes and casually walked around to open the passenger door.

"And you thought they would pull up in a black limo surrounded by motorcycles," Scott laughed, as he ribbed Rich about his vision of Rose's arrival.

"A little more reserved than I thought," Rich had to admit. "But, if you want to be inconspicuous, this is definitely the way to do it!"

"Maybe we should let them come to the door instead of making a scene in your front yard, you know, maintain that inconspicuous look, if you know what I mean." The razzing continued.

"That is a very mature thought, Mr. Larimore, exactly what I was thinking," exaggerated Rich.

"Will you boys stop! I don't know if I can take much more." Gina feigned in her motherly way. "Scott, you seem to give Rich an excuse to think he's hilarious. You should see when Jim and Rich get together…it never ends."

"I look forward to that."

They watched through the living room window as Rose

made her way to the door, classically dressed in her backyard barbeque best, followed closely by her cardinal fan driver. Once in the safe confines of the Reynolds' home, all pretenses dropped exposing a most vulnerable woman.

"Gina, Rich, thank you for having me. I couldn't believe when Ed called this morning and explained what was happening. I still can't believe it! My baby might be home today!"

"She will be home, Rose, she will." Samantha didn't make the comment blindly. Although her fear persisted, she had the utmost faith in Jim.

"Odd though," Rose considered, "To everyone else, today is just another holiday. Little do they know of the potential danger. A bunch of juveniles pretending to play with the big boys is all they are…and they have made my Samantha a pawn in their game." She shook her head in disgust as she sat on the edge of the couch.

Suddenly, Rose stood again. "I'm so sorry. Where are my manners? This is David, Dave Riesen, isn't it?"

"Yes, ma'am."

"And he's so formal. He'll get over that by the end of the morning, won't he?"

"David, I think of these people as my family, Richard and Gina, and Scott and Samantha. Richard and Gina were…are… my daughter's best friends from some years back."

"Rose, Dave, would you like some breakfast or coffee?" Gina offered.

"Coffee, black please." Dave responded.

A cell phone rang a simple ring tone, Jim's tone. Scott answered. After a moment, he replied, "Yes, sir, she is here. All is well." A pause as he listened. "Yes. Sir, hold on, I'll give him the phone. Rich, here you go…Mr. Marissen."

Turning to Rose, Scott relayed, "Mr. Marissen asked me to

tell you he was sorry but he couldn't talk—too many things to take care of at the moment. But he said to tell you…he loves you. Wow! I've never been asked to do that before!"

Samantha laughed, "That's the first time I've heard you say that!"

Rich broke in, "I'm going to continue this at the computer. I'll tell you what's going on when I'm finished."

Perplexed, Gina asked, "What's that all about?"

"I don't know," Scott affirmed. "But, that's the second conversation I've had with him today. He has a certain authority about him, doesn't he?"

"Yes, he does," Rose agreed, "But, he was so kind and sweet this morning. He told me of his plans for after this is over. I cried as he told me. There are some things I want to share with you in a bit. You'll understand why I cried."

Samantha handed Dave a black coffee and Rose hers with cream and sugar. "Well, I do think you should tell us. Would you gentlemen mind moving to the kitchen for a while?

6:40pm
North of Moscow

Doc cleansed Nikolai's wounds of damaged and potentially infectious tissue, packing them with strips of sterile material while administering necessary antibiotics to prevent, or at least, delay the onset of sepsis, to which his exceptional good health and strength worked to his advantage. However, if he was not transferred to a hospital environment relatively soon, he could begin to experience chills and fever, rapid and shallow breathing, and an abnormal heart rate eventually leading to death.

Meanwhile Jim quietly informed Samantha his vision had returned to normal, although he experienced a great deal of pain about the stitched wound. Over a short time, a serious black eye had developed, one of multiple shades of purple and burgundy with some swelling. The swelling and bandage wrap could adversely affect his ability to maneuver Sojourner in strategic flight, a worthy concern. If alone, his personal ability would not be an issue, today he carried a precious passenger.

He cautioned Samantha not to divulge his visual improvement; he needed to understand, to be fully aware of the situation before trusting anyone. He especially did not want to provide access to the aircraft until certain of friend or foe. A sudden panic struck; the code—he couldn't recall the code!

Samantha could now appreciate his distrust; his earlier blind trust proved nearly fatal. Her recent taste of military conflict exposed its inescapable conclusion—trust no one. Her comfort lay in the knowledge that she could safely place her full trust in God and, in turn, James.

As Jim began to ease himself off the wing, Samantha hurriedly slid off to help, offering her hand to steady him during his first few heavy steps. With a deep sigh of relief, he felt he had regained his equilibrium, his steadiness, and squeezed her hand as a signal, so far, so good. Letting her hand slip from his, he stretched and walked several yards away and returned to her side.

"Ooh, James, your eye…it looks just awful, like the worst black eye ever. Are you sure you're OK?"

"I'm better than I was, but I've got one heckuva headache," he whispered, finding himself still comforted by her soft, southern manner. He kept the loss of the access code to himself, no sense dumping additional worry on her. Besides, he thought, something would trigger his memory. Perhaps visualization— try to picture the pad and its configuration.

"James?" Samantha spoke softly.

He stopped and quietly responded, "Sorry, I was going over

the departure plan. I don't want to be surprised again. Once is enough. I still can't believe I let my guard down like that. You know, never assume—

"James," she whispered louder.

Stepping before her while glancing to the left, he smiled, "Yeah, I still ramble, don't I?"

"I love your ramblings, I always did." She paused, searching his eyes, "I…I just want to thank you for coming for me. I see a wonderful man, the same man I knew long ago. I want you to know that no matter what happens, I will be forever grateful for you."

Although not the time, he needed to express his feelings before anything else could be accomplished. "Samantha," he held her by the shoulders, "I am so sorry that I didn't fight for you. I'm sorry that I let you go. I'm—

"James, you don't have to—

"Yes, I do. You were a wonderful woman…and I loved you." He inched closer. "I still love you. Will you forgive me for walking away? I will never leave you again."

She leaned forward into his chest, her hands grasping his flight suit. "James, I'm so ashamed for letting you go. Of course, I forgive you…but you must forgive me. I'm so sorry. I have had a lot of time to think…I was going to try to find you, to see if you had married. If you had, you would never know I tried. But now, I know, and I will not let you go, ever again. I love you, James."

Continuing to hold her shoulders, he confided, "I forgive you," and slowly, lightly kissed her.

As they parted, he returned to the matter at hand. "OK, back to business. We're leaving, it's time."

"Yes, sir!" she stated, saluting properly.

"It's good to see you haven't forgotten."

"There are many things I haven't forgotten." She laughed, as she used to laugh with him. "With your eye and the way I look a mess, we must love each other."

He smiled in agreement.

Before returning to the wing, he motioned Samantha over. "There is something I think we need to do but I need you to do it. My head is still throbbing."

"What's that?"

"The Russian guy that hit me with his gun…we need that gun, just in case. Can you get it?"

"Me?" Samantha remembered the promise to herself that she would do whatever was necessary. "Yes. I think I can, I think."

"You don't have to."

"No, I will, I think."

She stepped over to Alexei, the dead soldier, and bent down only to see the bullet hole at the base of his skull. Fighting the reflex to throw up, she searched visually for the weapon, realizing it must be under him. She grabbed his jacket and slowly rolled him over exposing the gun still in his hand.

Jim advised, "Ease the gun out of his grip, the direction his fingers point. If you notice any pressure at all, stop. Don't take any chances."

Samantha did as instructed; the weapon slipped from the dead man's hand. She carefully carried the gun to Jim, barrel pointing away from everyone. Setting the safety, he removed the magazine.

"Three rounds are missing, one still in the chamber, so, one for Nikolai and one for the other soldier. He never got a shot off at me."

"But I heard two shots. I know I did."

From several feet away, Nikolai tried to explain, "I shoot… but miss. I look. Small round hit."

Samantha went to James and rested her forehead on his shoulder. "I was all right until I saw what I did. I know I had to, but I think I'm going to be sick."

Still holding the gun, he wrapped one arm around her. "You saved my life, thank you."

She raised her head. "I don't ever want to be without you."

"You never will…you never will."

As Jim held Samantha, he tried to picture the keypad, hoping the image would help. He imagined just prior to locking Sojourner down going over the code in his mind. Part of the code struck like a bolt out of the blue. CLEAR, three times… yeah, three times! CLEAR ~ CLEAR ~ CLEAR…4? Yeah, 4! 4…2…umm…4…2…7…what? 4~2~7…9…5? Yes, 5! One more, just one more…6? Oh, yeah, 6! **4~2 ~7~9~5~6~+~***.

"Hold on! I have to do this right now." Jim released Samantha as he kept repeating the code while retrieving the remote from a hidden pocket on his right thigh.

She looked quizzically, "What is that?"

"This is the key to our limo. Stay here. I have to go the other side to gain entry. Jim stepped around to the left side of the cockpit and pressed the button, releasing the locks, allowing the canopy to lift. He laid the gun on the seat and looking down to the lower left sidewall, located the keypad. OK, two minutes, he had two minutes. Methodically, he punched the keys, CLEAR ~ CLEAR ~ CLEAR ~4 ~ 2 ~7 ~9 ~ 5 ~ 6 ~ + ~* and focused on the small screen. To his horror, the word ERROR flashed continuously. Had he made a mistake? He repeated the code to himself. No, he was certain he had it right.

Again, he punched in CLEAR ~ CLEAR ~ CLEAR ~4 ~ 2 ~7 ~9 ~ 5 ~ 6 ~ + ~* and again ERROR flashed. All right! What? He then realized he had been concentrating solely on the numbers. Time was running out!

He looked up and shouted, "If I yell RUN, get up and run. Get behind something 'cause this thing is going to blow!"

Carefully and deliberately, he punched each number a last time until reaching the final two entries. Taking a deep breath, he steadily pressed* followed by +. Immediately, the beautiful word DISARMED scrolled across the readout.

"Oh, my good Lord, thank you," was all he could utter. His head pounded and his knees were weak but he reported, "Everything is OK. Problem averted. Samantha, we're going home!"

That is, until he heard Nikolai. "Listen! Do you hear?"

Jim slowly picked up the gun from the cockpit seat and released the safety.

Three Russian armed military men scrambled down the hillside in the dim evening light and pointed their weapons in the direction of Nikolai, the doctor, and Samantha. "Drop your weapons!" one shouted in Russian. Another yelled, "You are under arrest!" in English.

Never removing his eyes from the three, Colonel Gordon quickly raised his weapon and fired five rounds. The sixth jammed.

9:02am
Sonora Complex, Arizona

"Alright, everybody, listen up!" Director Jamieson barked. "We just had confirmation that the self-destruct mechanism of Colonel Gordon's aircraft has been disarmed. Obviously, the timetable is out the window. Somehow, this operation is holding together. Based on what little we know they could lift off within the hour.

"On the political front, skirmishes are still flaring up around Moscow. We also can report that every country bordering

Russia is at full military alert. I can tell you, and this should please you, no one has any inclination we have a vehicle in orbit right now. You program appears to be a success." There would be no reaction until Colonel Gordon and Samantha Marissen stepped onto the tarmac of Sonora.

The Director scanned the room before announcing, "The next update will be when Sojourner lifts off...or if something unforeseen comes up."

The voice of Ray Zygman echoed through the hall as he ran to the large conference room, "Director, Director!"

Entering the room at a half-run, Zygman attempted to maintain some dignity as he stepped briskly to the front. He and the Director spoke in hushed tones before Jamieson faced the suddenly alert audience. "We have been informed that the President of the Federation told the Russian people Ms. Marissen has arrived in the city of Moscow and will be held in a secure area until her trial begins next Thursday."

Immediately, the room broke into murmurs of disbelief.

"Quiet...please!" Ray pleaded. "You have not heard everything! There is more to this claim."

Director Jamieson cleared his throat, glancing over the note before he spoke, "This is indeed a strange turn of events since there have been no satellite surveillance images to confirm such action. Our latest images show the destruction of the dacha and the remnants of Colonel Gordon's encounter with the Ka-50's.

"We suspect his landing site is near that vicinity, but the forest canopy and the Chromatoskin of Sojourner make a visual sighting extremely difficult, if not impossible. Let me state this as succinctly as possible—Samantha Marissen is not in Moscow! The story out of Russia is a total fabrication to buy time. Our main concern is, where will they go from here? When Ms. Marissen's arrival proves false, what happens next?

These Russian 'boys' bit off a bit more than they can chew when they devised the plan to swap Ed Marissen's daughter for their agents.

"We are going to let the media cover this as a 'true' news item. Nothing will interfere with the mission. We'll play their game…but keep in mind; we must stand ready to help the Russian people when their government implodes. We can do nothing until we know Ms. Marissen is safe."

The six scientists remained in the conference room, too numb to leave. Without mission details, all they knew was Jim Gordon and Sojourner kept plugging away, each step painfully attained. No one realized just how painful.

"Ed, how are you holding up?" Jamieson inquired, making their way back to Marissen's office.

"I'm as worn out as a five-year-old rubber band, but I'll make it." Ed stopped in the middle of the hallway and grasped the Director's arm. "Allen, tell me straight up; do you truly believe Samantha is not in Moscow, that she is close to coming home?"

"Honestly, Ed, there is no way she is in Moscow." He removed his glasses. "That dacha was totally destroyed and every Russian soldier killed. We have excellent surveillance of that. We know your daughter was taken from the dacha to a pickup point. That is where we are now. There is no way she was taken from that dacha to Moscow."

He laid his hand on Ed's shoulder. "I would bet my life on that."

Relieved, Ed confided, "I didn't think you would try to dazzle me with some song and dance routine."

"I wouldn't."

"I must let Rose know that what she hears on TV is not true. She must know the truth!"

Jamieson reassured Ed, "I believe that computer link with

your family is ready. It's CIA, so it will be secure. You can use that to maintain contact. It's a video link!"

Although rushed, Ed noted the reference to his 'family.' Back on task, he asked, "You got someone to show me how to use it?"

"C'mon, we'll get you set up. Ray will accompany you. Actually, there's nothing to it."

KIRKWOOD, MISSOURI

"RICH! COME HERE! There's news about Samantha on SNN (Satellite News Network). Maybe it's about her coming home. Maybe it's over!"

"I have it here…in the family room. The laptop is set up with Sonora. I can't believe this. I know this sounds crazy… the CIA did this for Ed…for Rose." Rich could barely contain his excitement.

The SNN breaking news logo flashed across the television the same moment Ray Zygman's image filled the laptop screen. Giving Sonora priority, Rich muted the SNN report.

"Mr. Reynolds, are you there?" Zygman repeated, Mr. Reynolds!"

Rich rushed to the laptop and planted himself in front, filling the Sonora screen with his face.

"Yes, we're here!"

"Great, but first you should move back from the camera."

"Gotcha!"

He quickly stepped to the center of the room. "How's that?"

"Good, good. OK, stand by for Mr. Marissen."

Ed moved into the picture, nudged closer to center by Ray. "I hope I reached you before you saw any news stories about Samantha this morning. I want to reassure you that any reports on TV are fabrication…a lie put out by Russian officials.

"They are reporting that Samantha arrived in Moscow a

short time ago for the trial later this week. That is not the case; we know differently. She is at the pickup site with Colonel Gordon…Jim, and should be preparing for departure. I couldn't tell you about Jim before. Ask that young man, Scott Larimore, he'll fill you in. The part about Jim's involvement cannot be released to the public. No one must ever know, but we will.

"Rose, Samantha is not in Moscow! That government could fail…probably will. It's good she's getting out of there. She's in good hands. You know that; you've known that all along.

"One last thing—thank you all for taking Rose in today. She needed to be with friends, and I know you are. I hope to meet you soon. Forgive me, please." He finished with, "I love you, Rose."

"I love you too," she responded before the screen went blank.

"He looks so tired," Rose worried. "I imagine he hasn't slept in days."

Rich aimed the remote at the flat screen; SNN blacked out. "We won't need that. We've got the real thing." He turned to Riesen, "Dave, have a seat, the waiting game has begun. Rose, everybody, make yourselves comfortable. At least, we're all together. I suppose everyone else will be showing up about noon, right Hon?"

Gina looked at the clock. "Oh, my! I haven't started a thing! Samantha, I'll need your help. It'll be good to have something to keep me busy. You guys make sure we don't miss anything! Figure out what we are going to tell our friends when they get here.

7:18pm

North of Moscow

As the third Russian soldier dropped, a burst of rounds fired off from his assault weapon in a reflex action. Jim panicked, but as he looked over the situation, he observed no movement.

Thankfully, they had been in a tight grouping with no wide gaps between shots. He ejected the jammed round, stepped off the wing, and cautiously moved around the nose of Sojourner to Samantha, the doctor, and Nikolai. Doc had already stepped to the three soldiers and motioned to Nikolai they were dead.

Nikolai remarked to Jim about his marksmanship when Jim looked to see Samantha on the ground clutching the right side of her neck, blood running over her hand.

"Samantha!" he shouted as he ran to her as best he could and knelt at her side. "You've been hit! Don't move!"

She laid on her side, still holding her neck. "I'm OK, I'm OK. It only nicked me."

"Doc, get over here! She's bleeding! Help her!" Nikolai relayed the plea in Russian.

Doc grabbed his pack on the run, reaching Samantha quickly, and began the examination of her wound. Jim held her bloodied hand as the doctor cleaned the area. She flinched occasionally, squeezing his hand as a release. "Don't worry, Hon. You're going to be fine. I'm going to take you home. We're going home." She squeezed his hand again as she grimaced.

"Did you make that face because you want to stop somewhere on the way?"

"No, because you can be such a smart aleck!" She made a painful attempt to laugh.

"We're going to have plenty of time to laugh."

"I like the sound of that." She inhaled sharply as Doc applied pressure to the wound to stop the bleeding.

"You're doing great. This'll make a good story at one of Rich and Gina's parties."

Doc finished for the moment, providing some relief for Samantha. "Do you still see them? How are they? How is Carol? Oh, my gosh, I have so many questions!"

Jim grinned, glad she still held a deep interest in their friends and that she seemed so strong, so ready to continue with the mission. Of course, she wanted to get home; he realized nothing would stop that from happening.

"After we're outa here, I'll fill you in on everyone. Just know, they are praying for you; they never forgot you."

"I never forgot them." She squeezed his hand again.

Nikolai spoke from his sitting position, "Doctor say he put medicine on, may hurt, be ready."

Samantha sighed, "Tell him I'm ready."

12:05pm
Rich & Gina's Home

Carol handed the platter to Rich as she and Ted entered the living room. She hugged Gina while repeating what they heard, "Did you hear about Samantha this morning? The news reported she's in Moscow; her trial starts this week. I can't believe it's gone this far."

"So, you saw that on the news? Come into the family room. I think we can put your mind at ease; everybody is here."

The usual group greeted Ted and Carol when they entered. Bob began, "Late as usual, I see."

Not ready for battle, Ted explained the obvious, "You know us better than that. We couldn't pull ourselves from the news. Everything is about Samantha being in Moscow. That's crazy! How far are they going to drag this?"

Suddenly, a voice from the past, "Hello, Ted, Carol. Nice to see you again."

They turned quickly to the somewhat familiar southern utterance. "Oh, my gosh, Mrs. Marissen! How are you?"

Surprised, they went to her immediately, but had no idea what to say or ask. Rose began to explain about the events unfolding in Russia; the true story of where Samantha is; and why she is at the Reynolds' home. Afterwards, Rich continued the explanation, filling everyone in on all that had transpired that morning, minus the name, Jim Gordon. Rose assumed the omission by design, since his name could not be involved.

By the time Rich finished, their friends sat transfixed, unable to speak. Finally, Bill asked, "Why the laptop? What's the story with that?"

"This," Rich bragged, "is how Mr. Marissen keeps in touch with us. We have a direct secure link with him. Think of it like a super video phone. We already had a conversation with Mr. Marissen earlier from Sonora, Arizona where he has an aerospace complex. Anyway, we'll hear from him when Samantha and… whoever the pilot is, depart from Russia."

Bob, with a look of concern, lamented, "Too bad, I'll bet Jim would give anything to be that pilot. I suppose where Jim is, there's no way he could know about Samantha this morning. Well, maybe he knows; everybody knows, except, he won't hear the truth."

Without dishonesty, Scott responded, "None of us have spoken with Jim since he left. Consider this, he's closer to the action than if he was here."

Well played, Rich laughed to himself. No one had talked with Jim since that Saturday, and if he was in Israel, he would be closer. Well done, Scott, well done.

Samantha entered the family room with the man who drove Rose to the Reynolds' home. "You weren't going to let this poor man sit in the kitchen all day, were you? This is Dave Riesen, the agent who managed to get Mrs. Marissen here with no one noticing.

"Mr. Riesen, these are my Mom and Dad's friends…and they are all friends of Samantha Marissen; knew her, what… twenty-five years ago?"

"Yeah, something like that, but who's counting?" Ted

answered jokingly.

Anticipating a movie script plan of numerous details and secrecy, Scott probed, "Dave, can you tell us of the intricate plan to get Mrs. Marissen here this morning? How did the media miss that? This has to be pretty good."

Chuckling mildly, Riesen ran his hand over the top of his head, scratched the bald spot, and openly admitted, "I suppose I can share this with you. Mrs. Marissen and I got into the car while it was in the garage. The plan was so simple: as two black limousines drove slowly to the Marissen residence, the media would concentrate solely on them. When the front gates opened, the limos would drive through while we drove out. The best we got was a passing glance from some young reporter. The tinted windows took care of the rest. They were so wrapped up in who was in the two limos. The phony news release from Russia will keep them busy the rest of the day."

"So, who were in the limos?" Out of curiosity, Bill wanted to know.

"The only people in the limos were several guys in suits bringing breakfast for the agents at the house." Riesen laughed, "Unfortunately, since I drove here, I missed out on whatever they brought."

"Well," Rich interjected, "we have plenty of food today. You want something now?"

Riesen waved off the offer, "Maybe in a while, thanks!"

Rich motioned for Gina to join him at the laptop while Scott took her place on the couch next to their daughter. Gina recalled the great relief the young Samantha experienced when Jim completed his tour during the Mideast Conflict. Today, she appeared to relive the stress of worry for her father's best friend, her 'uncle.'

9:22pm
North of Moscow

The travelers readied themselves in darkness, only dim light from the cockpit aided in the assembly of their suits. Hours of practice with Dr. Kerrick made his efforts preparing Samantha successful with only minor difficulties, mostly working around her injury.

"How are you feeling?"

"I'm doing fine. It hurt trying to get this flight…suit, right? flight suit on, but it's better now."

"You've been great with this. You wouldn't believe the plan we worked out to make it as easy as possible. The people in Arizona will be very pleased how well it went."

"Arizona? What people in Arizona?

Jim decided a moment of truth to be the best response. She deserved that. He faced her. "Marissen AeroSpace. Your father arranged this to get you out. I've been training in Arizona for a month."

Tears welled up as she spoke, "My father? My father did this?"

Jim touched her cheek. "Your father loves you; he loves you more than you know."

"And you've been working with him? How…how was—

Purposely looking straight into her eyes, he answered, "Good, very good. Your father and I did what we should have done twenty-five years ago. Your father is a good man who only wanted the best for you…he just didn't know how to go about it. Now, he wants you safely home where you all can begin again."

"I…I want you there for that," she confided.

"I'll be there."

Samantha caressed his face and kissed him, offering a silent prayer, "Oh, my Lord God, thank you for your many blessings. Thank you so very much."

"OK, let me stick this on the back of your neck." Jim stepped behind her, peeled off the protective backing and pressed it to her skin just beneath the bandage wrap and the neck ring of her suit as she raised her ponytail out of the way.

"Do you know how long it's been since I wore a ponytail. Many, many years! And now I've had it like this for months." A serious case of nerves had begun to set in but, as she decided earlier, she would trust James with whatever he needed.

"What are these patches we have to wear?"

"They are a precaution against space motion sickness," Jim explained. "Weightlessness can cause nausea. Have you ever experienced motion sickness?"

"No...wait, what do you mean *space*?" The look on her face expressed it all.

Taking a deep breath, he attempted to come up with the best explanation. "Here's the story in a nutshell. This is our only way out of here. I have a limited amount of fuel remaining and we can't land in another country. We're going to rendezvous with another ship in orbit and then land in Arizona."

Her eyes grew wider with each second as she thought about his explanation. "What?"

"That's as deep as time allows. I'll explain everything as it progresses. Right now, we have to get out of here. I will not allow anything to happen to you. Will you trust me?"

Samantha viewed the man she should have trusted all along. "Yes...yes I will, I do."

"Alright, we're ready. Just the helmets and gloves."

"Your neck is well-protected. The helmet will not affect the injury. Just try not to turn your head too much or too quickly, OK?"

"Yes, Captain…wait, what are you now? I'm sure it's not Captain anymore."

He smiled at her question. "I retired as a Colonel."

She returned the smile. "Look everybody, I'm going out with a pilot, a Colonel!"

"And you said I was the smart aleck!"

Before beginning the final stage, he removed a small item from her flight suit pack.

"What's this?" she asked, as Jim handed the miniature instrument to her.

"That is our communication device. Insert it into your ear, whichever one is your best, like which ear do you favor when talking on a phone?"

"My right, I guess."

"OK, gently insert it into your right ear, not too far but snug. All the radio equipment is located in the helmet. We'll be able to communicate with each other. We'll check it out before we lock down your helmet."

He assisted her in assembling the gloves to the sleeves of her suit, noting for himself the steps required. Before reaching for her helmet, he took her gloved hands in his and prayed, "Lord God, we are ready to go home. Bless us and protect us on our journey, take us safely home where we can continue to do your will together. We love You, Lord, and we thank You. We ask this in Jesus' name."

Together, they completed the prayer, "Amen."

As Jim raised her helmet, she asked, "Can we share one more kiss before we leave?'

Without answering, he moved closer, leaning forward until their lips met. When they parted several moments later, he simply declared, "I love you, Samantha."

"I love you, James."

"Sam…James!" Nikolai called out in the dark. Removing

an earplug, he reported weakly, "I hear on radio, sending MiGs to search…destroy. I do not know number. Wait for late night to attack from south."

Urgently, Jim demanded, "Nik, can you use your radio to contact someone to get you out of here?"

Everyone froze. Russian voices speaking in very broken English followed a sudden rustling of trees with beams of flashlights bouncing across the clearing, "He will not have to…we are here." Nikolai peered into the lights to finally make out the small band of men under Sasha who returned when Sasha did not show during the late afternoon. All but one flashlight were quickly turned off. The doctor and Nikolai detailed the events involving Alexei and Sasha and later, the three Russian soldiers. Two of the men prepared Sasha's body for the trek out of the forest.

"MiGs to come," an older rugged revolutionary reported as he nudged the bodies of Alexei and the Russian soldiers. "You…leave, now!"

Jim grabbed Samantha's helmet. Samantha shouted, "Nikolai, thank you for your protection! Thank you! God bless you!" just before Jim lowered it carefully over her head and locked the latches. He inserted his earpiece and slipped the helmet over his head, avoiding, as best he could, any contact with the stitches above his eye, and locked it in place. He could hear Samantha breathing. Good! Communication works! Get the temporary oxygen connections next. OK!

"Samantha, can you hear me?"

"Yes…I can."

"How's the oxygen, OK?"

"Yes, it's good…cool."

"Good. Let me get this stuff out of your seat."

"What is that?"

"I needed this weight to take your place on my way in, balance the aircraft."

"How much weight is it?"

"You don't really think I'm going to answer that, do you?"

Jim repositioned himself on the wing and extended his hand. "Come on up. Let's get you into your chariot."

She grabbed his gloved hand with hers and pulled herself onto the wing.

"This will be a little tight getting you in…" With minor maneuvering and shifting, Samantha lowered herself into the seat. Jim quickly made the necessary connections, switching the oxygen lines first. "Leave the temporary air tank attached to your leg; we'll switch back when we reach the Orbital Vehicle."

"Yeah, I don't get all that, but I leave it to you."

"You're doing great! How's your neck?"

"Not too bad. I think the doctor did a pretty good job. How are you? Your eye?"

"It's good," he lied.

Jim waved everyone back from the aircraft, way back. He settled into the cockpit and lowered the canopy.

11:57am
Sonora Complex

"Sir!"

"What is it, Ray?" Jamieson responded to his assistant's nervous call.

"You've got to get in here right away. The DS-20 satellite has detected motion toward the area we believe Colonel Gordon to be located." With confidence, he continued, "I believe it's imperative to transmit this data to the OV immediately to pass on to the Colonel."

Not wasting a moment, Jamieson agreed, "Make it happen, Ray. We're on our way."

With a slight curl of a smile, he confirmed the order, "Yes, sir, immediately."

Ed and Merrill matched Jamieson's pace step for step, as Ed worried, "What could it be? What's taking them so long to get out of there?"

Already standing in front of the flat screen in the command center were Gagnepaign, Townsend, and Forsythe. "Transmission to the OV complete," Ray informed his boss, "including orders to relay the data to Colonel Gordon."

"Excellent! Do we know what's moving out there?"

Leading Merrill, Ed, and Jamieson to the screen, Ray pointed out a gray dot gliding over a luminescent green ground, a night vision overview directly from the DS-20.

"Enlarge view," he ordered, and the dot broke into six separate objects. "MiGs, six of 'em, nothing larger, heading toward Colonel Gordon's coordinates."

"So, they're looking to take out that area to prevent escape." Gagnepaign surmised.

"Looks that way, sir."

Turning from the screen, Jamieson rubbed his face, thinking. Facing the screen again, "Is that where we think Colonel Gordon is?"

"Yes, sir," Zygman pointed to the area, north of Moscow, where the last contact originated, when suddenly, a small object sprang to life somewhat farther north than thought.

"Could that be them?" Ed questioned.

Within moments, a controller monitoring Sojourner blurted, "That's her! She's lifting off!"

10:05pm
North of Moscow

Rising slowly above the treetops, Colonel Gordon rotated Sojourner to the south when data began streaming across the screen, supplying Jim with the coordinates of the incoming MiGs.

"You alright back there?"

A shaky voice returned an answer, "I think I'm good. This thing stuck in my ear is weird; it's right out of some spy movie. But I can hear you fine. Are you OK?"

He lied again, "I'm OK." After a brief hesitation, he continued, "Hang with me here. We're going after those MiGs. We have to stop them." He deactivated the Chromatoskin.

Samantha tried to relax. Thankfully, the fresh oxygen reinvigorated her. She gave a short but direct response, "I'm OK. Just do what needs to be done."

"Yes, Ma'am."

"How can he," she wondered, "maintain such a low-key attitude during something like this?" Then, she remembered watching Jim depart St. Louis in his F-16 so many years before. "I suppose I will really see firsthand what he does."

Without warning, Sojourner jumped to life with tremendous acceleration forcing her deep into the seat. The firm confines of the seat and restraints reassured her, allowing very little body motion, although the helmet felt claustrophobic, if she thought about it. Imagine placing a fish bowl over your head with no way to scratch your nose, if need be. Frightened as she was, she remained silent as Sojourner climbed steeply into the night sky.

She began to speak, but stopped. She didn't want to distract her pilot, but then, "James?"

"Yeah," he responded.

"I just need to tell you before anything else happens…I love you."

Never words he heard from a control tower prior to take off, he chuckled, "I love you too, Samantha."

They bore down on the MiGs.

12:13pm
Sonora Complex

"What is he doing?" yelled Jamieson. "He's heading right for the oncoming MiGs without Chromatoskin! He needs to just get out of there!"

Forsythe attempted to calm everyone, "Colonel Gordon is experienced both in flying…and in war. We don't see what's behind the scene. All we can do is watch and wait."

Hamilton, Thurmond, Garcia, Kerrick, Rice, and Burchfield, along with IV Commander Parker and Captain Moore quietly entered and stood against the rear wall watching their pilot and aircraft on the real-time satellite display. What they viewed was no longer practice; stakes were high and lives real. Years of intense labor boiled down to this moment. Lisa Kerrick held Nate's arm with both hands as her eyes remained locked on the screen. Outwardly, Ed projected his calm, stoic demeanor, yet, internally, torn apart by what he saw. That small object on the screen signified his daughter and Jim fighting for their lives.

Those standing in the rear took a step forward as the objects grew closer. "Obviously," General Forsythe explained, "Colonel Gordon's airspeed matched the MiGs to conserve fuel. For whatever reason, he wants to draw the MiGs from the area they just left and wants the MiGs to see him." As Colonel Gordon flew above the MiG squadron, he lit up every radar screen.

"Once he passed over the MiGs," Forsythe informed everyone, "he went into a Wingover maneuver, which is a quarter loop into a vertical climb, letting the speed fall as altitude increases, followed by a flat-turn over the top, diving to complete a quarter loop at the original altitude, but going in the opposite direction." A basic description only an Air Force pilot would understand.

Forsythe broadcast, "A brilliant maneuver—manages energy by conserving both airspeed and altitude. He is now behind the MiGs…plus they have turned away from the area he seems to want to protect."

Aboard Sojourner

"You OK back there?"

"Actually…yes! I just closed my eyes when you started all the turns. What are you doing?"

"We've got to protect Nikolai and the others. They are going to annihilate the area; that's got to be their only mission. There's been enough killing today. I'm going to see if they will pursue us."

"What if they do? What then?"

"We can outrun anybody with this bird. You'll see."

Jim lowered his altitude, increased airspeed, and rose a mile ahead of the squadron. Without the Chromatoskin activated, the MiGs easily locked on to Sojourner. Colonel Gordon returned to the Immelmann maneuver, performing a half-loop and when completely inverted, rolled to the upright position. As the MiGs attempted to follow, he had to decrease airspeed to allow them to catch up. Meanwhile, Jim activated Sojourner's program to lay in the proper vector for orbital insertion.

"OK, hang on! I'm sure they're going to fire missiles. I want to show we can outrun them before we leave. They are so far from our Russian friends on the ground, they have no reason to go back."

Samantha swallowed hard. She left it all in God's hands.

Suddenly, a steady alarm sounded, as well as a flashing signal; the MiGs had fired their missiles. Simultaneously, the heads-up display alerted him orbital insertion could begin within the next fifteen seconds—his call. Nothing to call, he thought. Now! He raised the protective cover and flipped the switch. In a glorious burst of speed, Sojourner climbed faster and higher in the night sky, accelerating for orbital insertion.

Colonel Gordon inquired of his passenger, "How are you holding up?"

Pressed back in her seat, Samantha forced an, "I…I'm OK. Where are those missiles?"

"They're still following but losing the battle; they're going to drop off shortly. Get ready for the final push for orbital insertion."

"Orbital wha—

Suddenly, Sojourner shot upward with a final explosion of acceleration, forcing Samantha deeper into her seat, the pressure growing heavier in her chest and face, yet she remained focused on the expanse of stars beyond the canopy. Regardless of what happened next, the most remarkable adventure of her life surely unfolded with Captain, no, Colonel James Gordon. Although the cockpit seat blocked her view of him, she felt as safe and secure as in the past. How could she have ever thought a life with him would be less than what her father desired years earlier? Nothing would interfere with their love again.

She witnessed, first-hand, James' intense focus on what must be done and then, to follow through, requiring split-second decisions with no margin for error. An excellent example, she thought: his decision not to shoot down the Russian jets in pursuit. What would be gained by such an action? Not only could he fly with skill, his critical choices seemed flawless. Oh, if only this pressure of acceleration would back off, she hoped.

As Jim tried to ignore the throbbing pain above his left eye, the intense jump in acceleration forced his body further into the seat. He hoped the bleeding would not restart as a result. He worried about Samantha's neck wound. Good decision to have those NASA doctors waiting in the Orbital Vehicle. Be patient, the orbital insertion program would proceed on its own. Check the readouts: vital data streamed continuously across the screen, not interfering with the normal heads-up flight display. To him, the most important piece of information—the fuel level, looked good…so far.

As an amateur astronomer, Jim never tired of seeking his favorite stars, constellation, and planets, but not now. Instead, he closed his eyes in exhaustion, a hard-earned respite from an unbelievable experience. He thoughts drifted to Samantha's father and their newfound bond of…what? Jim had felt the beginning of a close, fatherly relationship, one he desired to see flourish. Perhaps, after all this time, Ed, Rose, Samantha, and he could experience a true family love. How great would that be! Oh, man, if only this thrust would stop, give my head a break!

As if on cue, the crushing acceleration shut down. Sojourner had reached orbit with an apogee, a high point, of 650 miles and a perigee, or low point, of 105 miles. Periodic corrections would eventually place Sojourner in a far less elliptical orbit, leaving the Orbital Vehicle the responsibility to 'catch up' for docking. The current orbit would not place them over the Russian country for some time.

"Samantha?"

"Yes?"

"You OK?"

"I think…Are we where I think we are?"

"If you think we're 120 miles above the Earth, then you're right."

"You're serious, aren't you?"

"I am."

"What happens now?"

"Our private spaceship will keep making corrections until

we're into a more consistent orbit. Right now, we're in an extremely elliptical orbit…one side is very high, 650 miles, and the other is lower, 105 miles. Another ship, the OV, will pull up and let us hitch a ride back with them in a couple of orbits." Jim hoped his explanation would help, her breathing seemed short and fast.

"How is your neck? Are you experiencing much pain?"

She laughed nervously, "I suppose that's the good thing. I'm so amazed by all this, I haven't paid much attention to my neck. It hurts, but nothing I can't live with. How are you?"

"OK. I'm just glad you're out of there."

"I'm just glad I'm with you." She took a deep breath and exhaled slowly, attempting to relax. "I must say, this is the oddest date we've had."

Her humor reassured him she would be OK. Samantha was glad to be with him, he thought. He was ecstatic to have her alive. The slightest difference in angle and the bullet that grazed her neck could have easily hit her carotid artery or…he didn't want to think of what might have been.

Sojourner initiated a long final burn to place them in a 200 mile by 250 mile slightly elliptical orbit, nothing to cause uncomfortable pressure, just an orbital correction. Once Jim checked to ensure that to be the last, he prepared to perform a minor maneuver of his own.

"I'm not sure this is necessary, but close your eyes…only to avoid any motion causing sickness. I'm going to roll this bird over. There's something I want you to see."

"You're going to turn us upside down?"

"Up here, you won't know the difference."

"OK…I think I'm ready."

Using the nitrogen thrusters, he slowly rotated Sojourner into position, allowing a view through the canopy of the Earth's nighttime surface revolving into one of the multiple sunrises they might observe today. "All right, check this out!"

All Jim heard, "Oh! Would you look at that? It's amazing… beautiful." The canopy grew darker with the sunrise, providing additional protection from ultraviolet rays, as the blue, white, and various shades of brown and green planet rotated into full view.

Samantha gasped at the beauty of her world. Both watched in silence, in absolute awe of the continents, mountains, valleys, oceans, and clouds, the many, many clouds, believing this moment to be a God-given reward for the years lost. Samantha whispered to herself, "Who can believe there is no God?"

After the day's events, the calm afforded them time to refocus, to relax, until Samantha inquired, "James? How much time will we have up here?"

"I suppose as long as it takes the OV to reach us…maybe a couple of hours." Was there a problem; was she doing OK? Jim hoped fear wasn't taking over.

"That's good," she reassuringly stated. "I am really beginning to enjoy this. Two hours? I'll just relax and look at this as something no one I know will ever do."

Remembering her ability to make the best of any situation, he laughed. "Believe me, Bob and Liz, Ted and Carol, Neil and Sue, Bill and Nancy, and Rich and Gina never will."

She had no response.

"Are you OK?"

"I just feel so bad for what I did to everyone…to you. I don't see how they would ever take me back." A true sadness spilled over with her statement.

Jim hoped to convince her of the group's feelings. "Believe me, they are still your friends, worrying and praying for you throughout this whole ordeal. None of them ever forgot you. You were their friend and they were yours."

"They remember me?"

"Like yesterday."

"Honestly, I…I can't wait to see them…again. I want to renew those friendships, soon. I have missed them so much."

"You will, I promise!" The idea of Samantha returning to his life brought a surge of joy.

"How is everyone? Are they all still married? There must be a lot of children and even grandchildren by now."

And so, it was. Jim, or James once again, spent a great deal of time bringing Samantha up to date while they viewed the Earth from a vantage point never to be experienced again. Their time alone provided ample, albeit strange, opportunity for renewal. Samantha asked, James answered; the pattern continued until the crackle of a distant voice popped into their ears.

"This is the Commander of the rendezvous ship, *Nemesis*, calling Flash of the bird *Sojourner*. Come in Flash."

Kirkwood, Missouri

"Did you hear that? Someone is making contact with the pilot of that space…what? Spaceplane? What did you call it, Scott?" Bob initiated the excitement at the Reynolds' home.

"That's probably as good a description as any!" Scott fell short of words earlier, when he attempted to explain the rescue mission to the close-knit group. In his excitement, he slipped up mentioning his knowledge of the operation, then covering the mistake by reminding everyone he spoke to Ed Marissen that morning, who had filled him in on what was to happen. He feared for his future remembering the threatened consequences if he divulged any information regarding the mission.

The response transmission came next, "*Nemesis*? Great name! Better than OV. *Nemesis*, this is *Sojourner*, reading you loud and clear," careful not to mention any names. "All readings nominal, we're just enjoying the view."

Now, Bob questioned the identity of the pilot, "Wait a

minute, I know we're hearing this guy over radio or something, but he sure sounds like Jim. Not only that, his call sign is 'Flash.' That was Jim's."

Rich attempted to throw Bob off the trail, "Maybe, but Jim's retired. This might be some new guy."

"Yeah, maybe so. I guess." He tried to let it go. "But he sure sounds like Jim."

The friends next heard the Commander inquire, "Ms. Marissen, how are you holding up?"

"I'm…fine," she announced.

The Commander added, "You're in good hands with the Colonel."

"Yes…yes I am," she readily agreed.

With the family room steeped in silence, no one wanted to miss anything Samantha might say. Her voice exuded an unexpected calmness.

"Oh, my!" Gina broke through the quiet. "She seems so relaxed." Her statement released the friends from their self-imposed restraint.

"OK," Bob argued, "that Commander guy just described the other pilot as a colonel. Jim's a colonel…with the call sign *Flash*."

"C'mon, Bob, what are the chances of that?" Ted asked, not thoroughly convinced himself.

Rose interjected a comment to steer the conversation away from the 'Jim' controversy. "At least, Samantha seems to be all right."

Gina took her hand the moment she noticed tears forming and whispered close to her ear, "She and Jim are together, where they belong. They'll be home soon." Rose squeezed her hand in an appreciative response.

The close-knit group kept an eye on the small laptop screen

displaying the Mission Control Center, anxiously awaiting another transmission. Statements of "I can't believe this!" or "I would be scared stiff!" or "I'm just glad it's almost over." continued until Bill voiced the obvious, "It's too bad Jim's not here."

A monotone instruction by the Commander grabbed everyone's attention, "Sojourner, we will rendezvous at the perigee of your orbit in approximately one hour. Your present orbit is as good as it gets within the allotted timeframe. I'll contact you as we make final approach from beneath. If you want, rotate Sojourner to watch for us. Our approach will be on the dark side."

"Roger that. We anticipate rendezvous in one hour."

Aboard Sojourner

With several short bursts of the nitrogen thrusters, Colonel Gordon repositioned Sojourner with nose pointed down 60°, providing a view of the Earth seemingly rolling away. The confines of the small ship along with Jim and Samantha being so well-restrained prevented any motion sickness symptoms. Sojourner settled into a hypnotic weightless drifting across the ever-changing face of their world.

"I will never forget this sight, especially the thin blue shell of the atmosphere you pointed out. Our world is simply amazing and…joyfully fulfilling to see what God created."

A deep gratification filled Jim that, despite everything, she had never sacrificed her childlike wonder and love of God for all He did and continues to do.

Apprehensively, Samantha shared a portion of her emotions, "I am so relieved to be out of there, James. It was absolutely horrid, awful. If not for God, I never would have survived… and I would have been lost without my Bible, which Nikolai made sure I had. I know God placed Nikolai there; he was my guardian. If not for him, they would have killed me. He is a lot like you."

Softly, she added, "I am very grateful you were able to keep those jets from killing Nikolai and his friends."

"I regret so many lives were lost; the bombings in Moscow; the dacha; the landing site, so pointless," he sadly recounted.

For a moment, he heard only her steady breathing, then softly—

"I understand, really. I…I killed a man today."

"You saved my life when you shot him. You did what had to be done. Thank you." Jim realized he would never be able to relate exactly what she had done for him. She had made a monumental decision and carried it out without hesitation.

Locked in the confines of Sojourner, he could take no physical action to comfort her, only a weak alternative, "Are you going to be all right?"

"I promised I would not react; I would not break. For the first time in my life, I want to be strong."

"You are strong. I look at all you've been through to reach this point, you had to be strong."

Almost inaudibly, she responded, "Thank you."

Several minutes passed in the utter quietness of space; no words, no sound, just an occasional exhaling of a lengthy breath before Samantha inquired, "How are you doing? How's your forehead?"

Again, he lessened the injury, "Much better. I think the stitches can be removed tonight."

Samantha laughed to herself. At least, she thought, he felt well enough to throw up a quick front. She slowly turned her head; her neck ached as she did, but not horribly.

With the North American land mass giving way to the

Atlantic Ocean, she poignantly raised the question, "So, James… where do we go from here?"

He began, "Where do we go from here? That's a very good question. But first, may I ask you a question?"

She wondered, what kind of question? Well, only one way to find out. "Yes, what's that?"

"Samantha, I love you. Will you marry me?"

What! Did I hear him correctly? Yes, I did. I know I did!

After only a moment, "Yes, yes, I will marry you! I love you, James! Oh, my goodness, I can't cry in this getup; what a mess that would make!"

They laughed in their joy…and at her predicament, although Jim's eyes displayed similar symptoms.

"Oh, no," she suddenly cried. "I must look simply hideous… my hair, no makeup, nothing. I'm so embarrassed."

"Don't be," he implored. "You are the most beautiful woman I have ever known."

As she laughed, she thanked him for his kind words.

"I wonder if there has ever been a proposal up here or, are we the first? Whatever! This is our story!"

The conversation of the newly-engaged couple continued as the Earth turned below. There would always be time to share what transpired during her captivity. As for now, the anxiety over her flight and spacesuit diminished, they kept an eye on the horizon for the OV, or Nemesis.

Kirkwood

After consulting with Dave Reisen, Rich and Scott managed to properly and securely connect the flat screen to the laptop computer. The screen snapped to life displaying a much broader and impressive picture of the panoramic curvature of the planet. Immediately, all eyes transferred to the much larger screen.

Bob uttered in awe, "Would you look at that! I mean, just

Look! Samantha is up there, somewhere ahead." The Nemesis Commander broke radio silence, "Sojourner, we have a lock on you and will be there in twelve minutes. Do you have a visual on us?"

Sonora and Kirkwood anxiously awaited a response.

Finally, "We have visual, Commander. We see your strobe."

"Excellent! Just kick back and relax; we'll be there shortly. Ms. Marissen, how are you holding up?"

With a strong response, Samantha informed the Commander, "I'm good! Thank you for asking."

A collective sigh of relief escaped the Reynolds' home, having waited a little more than an hour since the last contact. Both Sonora and Kirkwood strained for a visual of Sojourner, although an actual sighting would take time as the craft registered much too small for distant observation. Since the OV nor Sojourner currently operated with activated Chromatoskin, the rippling colors should display quite clearly.

"Colonel, there will be constant contact from here on; things will happen quickly."

"Roger that, Commander."

*   *   *

Gina, noticing her daughter exploring the screen for any sign of her uncle, whispered, "Are you a little more relaxed the closer they get to home?"

"A little. I know anything can happen. I'm glad we're all together."

Rose affirmed, "I'm thankful to be with all of you. I wouldn't want to experience this alone."

After a moment of hesitation, she blurted out, "You know, I can picture Jim as the pilot of that smaller one. I don't know why." She sighed, "Just wishful thinking. I mean, Jim suddenly had to leave a month ago. Ed had some important things going on in Arizona during August. I don't know. Just a silly feeling."

Bob immediately voiced, "Yeah, I know. All that 'Colonel' and 'Flash' stuff we heard. That's Jim's rank and call sign. Makes you wonder."

Scott and Rich looked up. Both realized what Rose had done. Imagine, managing to plant the idea of Jim as the pilot without suffering any consequences. They were now free to speculate without fear of reprisal.

"LOOK!" Ted excitedly pointed to the screen. "Is that them?"

Aboard Sojourner

"Oh, my," the only words Samantha could utter as she grasped the immensity of the approaching Orbital Vehicle.

"Imagine the aircraft that lifts it for orbital insertion!" Jim exclaimed. "The whole process is mind-boggling."

As Nemesis approached rising slowly above Sojourner, the visual effect of the rolling rainbow ripples assaulted the eye with mesmerizing beauty, as if alive. Soon, Samantha thought, they would leave the restricting confines of her rescue craft for the mammoth vehicle floating overhead and return to the safety and gravity of the Earth. Her journey home would forever remain a glorious memory.

"Sojourner," came the call from the Commander positioned in the control bubble above the bay. "Align your craft with Nemesis for rendezvous. Clearance is nominal for rotation."

Activating the heads-up display, a green rectangular outline representing the bay doors appeared, as did a horizontal outline of Sojourner, displaying the distance between the two craft. Jim gently maneuvered into position and notified the Commander, "Sojourner ready for entry."

"Acknowledged. Opening bay doors…now."

Jim and Samantha watched through the canopy for separation of the massive doors.

"What's happening?" Samantha hesitantly asked.

"Nothing," came an equally hesitant reply.

Kirkwood

With the camera trained on Sojourner as it hung just under the bay, the now supposed figure of Colonel Gordon appeared somewhat visible in the cockpit, while only Samantha's helmet stood out. The family had witnessed in awe the maneuver into position. Now, each member pulled and prayed for the final success of their safe return. Low conversation noted the skill and ability of the pilot as they awaited the opening of the bay doors.

A grim realization something may be awry stirred the group as they overheard the verbal concern of the Sojourner occupants hovering just beneath the massive OV. Rich's cell phone rang, startling the small gathering. He answered, listening as he stared at the screen.

"What's the problem, Rich?" Scott asked as an uneasy feeling settled in the pit of his gut.

Turning from the TV, he addressed his silent family and friends, "It's Ed. He said a small problem has come up…the bay doors aren't opening, but," he quickly added, "it can be rectified or another option can be used. They're working on it."

He hushed everyone as they spoke at once, "They want to cut our feed until the problem has been solved—

"No!" Rose insisted. Tell him we must see what's happening! She's our daughter, and we need to see!"

Rich, caught in the middle, raised his phone, "Mr. Marissen—

He stopped to listen, finally, he responded, "Yes, sir, I'll pass the word. Thank you, sir," and shut off the phone.

"OK, Rose, everybody…they are not going to cut the feed unless something goes wrong. He wants us to remain calm;

everything will be all right. And, I agree. Those are good people in Arizona and in that Orbital thing. What more is necessary? And with Samantha in the backseat…really…what more do they need?" Not an uproariously funny joke but it did take the edge off the tension.

Rose asked, "What made them change their mind about us watching?"

Rich grinned while chuckling, "Ed said he heard your insistence and strongly requested it be left on. Who here has the pull?"

Sojourner

Stress, tension, and the helmet added to the pain Jim experienced from his injury, but to Samantha, he appeared fine and, for her, remained so. Regardless of the current situation, they were going home. This day will be a success. He prayed "if it was God's will, grant them a long life together."

After forty minutes of communication between Sonora and Nemesis, during which he and Samantha conversed calmly about the future, the OV made contact, "Flash, Commander here." Formalities vanished, replaced with straightforward talk, still without names, "We have determined, and I know this sounds overly simplistic, the opening mechanism is hung up on something and will not budge. Power is there but, mechanically, gets hung up."

"So, what do you need me to do?"

All ears at the Reynolds' home perked up as sound suddenly returned in the middle of Jim's response to the Commander, halting the subdued conversation carrying on at the time.

"OK, here's the plan. We don't want to force the bay doors. Since we don't know the cause of the jam, we don't want to get them to open, only to have them not close."

Jim's response, "Makes sense."

"The Captain will maneuver the OV into position to give you access to the emergency hatch located just below the starboard cockpit viewing window. The Captain is very capable of handling this maneuver; we believe it better left to him.'"

"Roger, I agree. So, we're coming in through the emergency hatch?"

"Yes, that's the plan."

"What's my responsibility?"

"After the Captain backs away from you, we'll give the signal to turn your craft over 180°. Once you're there, you will receive step-by-step instructions. Believe me, Flash, I feel confident, working with you, we can pull this off without a hitch."

"Hey, thanks for the vote-of-confidence. How about a brief explanation of what we do after everything is in place?"

"You will have to exit your ship and work your way down to us in order to maintain a safe distance between both ships."

"Just asking…how will we come down to you? And why down?"

"Be easier to explain that as it happens. Trust me. This way we can maintain visual contact, otherwise, you would be under our wing and out-of-sight."

"Got it. We're going to leave our ship here, in orbit?"

"No, what little nitrogen fuel left for the thrusters will be used to reduce its altitude until it burns up in re-entry."

Jim's final reaction to the plan, "Wow! So, after we flip over, we will sit here as you maneuver around us, until we are above you on your starboard side, exit our ship, and work our way down to the OV using a system you'll explain as we go. That's it!"

"Pretty much!"

Samantha remained silent as Jim discussed the solution with the Commander of the OV. Without asking, she understood the dangers of the maneuver and the ramifications of any misstep that might occur. Well-aware no other solution existed, she braced herself for what was to come, thanking God for His presence.

Kirkwood

Not a sound emanated from the group as they remained glued to the flat screen, knowing no action film could possibly match the real-life drama unfolding before their eyes. The life of their friend hinged on the success or failure of this untried procedure.

All held their breath as Captain Dan Malone inched the OV, or Nemesis, back from Jim and Samantha's ship, coming to a stop fifty feet from the craft. At that point, Jim received the OK to turn Sojourner over. Leaning forward, everyone waited in anticipation until the craft rotated upside down to the OV. A sigh of relief escaped their lips.

Next, they heard, "Well done, you're in position. Now, reattach your oxygen lines to your tanks and prepare to depressurize your spacecraft. Check that. In your case, to help Ms. Marissen, depressurize the cabin first, with your oxygen lines still attached to the supply. Throw the red lever on the lower starboard side and watch the gauge right above."

"Now?"

"Yes, now."

"Done...the gauge is dropping; the air pressure is below nominal...she registers zero."

"OK, Flash, here's the fun part. Release the canopy latches as if you were exiting the craft."

"OK, but give me a few minutes to explain all this to Samantha, Ms. Marissen."

"You got it. Sorry...rushing things a little. Let me know when you're ready."

Rose strained forward, listening intently to hear Samantha, to know how she was doing. Scott and Samantha viewed the operation from their standing position across from the screen, squeezing each other's hands tightly. Rich and Gina, Bob and Liz, Ted and Carol, and Bill and Nancy simply stared at the TV, hardly able to believe the activity. The maneuvers required to survive seemed beyond comprehension. No one dared say anything; nothing made sense.

"Samantha," they heard in a calming tone, "I'm sure you heard all that. Are you OK?"

She inhaled deeply, "I am. Whatever you need me to do, just tell me. God has gotten us this far; He will get us the rest of the way."

"Yes, He will. With God's guidance, I will let nothing happen to you. I promise, believe me."

"James, you know I do."

"OK, Commander, we're ready!" Jim braced himself for what was to come.

Shocked, Carol exclaimed, "Did you hear that? She said James! I know she did!"

"Really? Are you sure?"

Rose raised her clasped hands to her chin. "Thank you, Lord, thank you for Samantha, Jim, and just everything You do for us. You are great; You are good!"

Sojourner

"Alright, here we go! Release the canopy latches as you would if you were exiting the craft."

"Roger."

"See the small compartment door directly to your left. I would say 'port' but, right now, left seemed easier."

"Roger."

"Push in on the upper lip."

"Roger. It opened to show a red button."

"Good. Press the button."

In the silence of space, the canopy disengaged from Sojourner, floating away into a slight tumble toward the Earth below.

"Done. I guess that gives us all the clearance we need to get out."

"Yes, but not yet. Sit tight, we'll maneuver into position now."

"Roger."

The lower camera gave precedence to another imbedded above the cockpit, Sojourner momentarily out of view. Malone lowered the OV, which appeared to observers as Sojourner rising, stopping with Jim's ship twenty feet above the OV, the planned clearance between ships. Malone nudged his ship forward until the emergency entrance registered directly below Sojourner.

Samantha raised her eyes to view the planet passing beneath, bravely fending off the anxiety of their predicament, the decisive moment. The thought of so many individuals struggling to bring them home briefly overwhelmed her.

Jim reached into a compartment under his seat and located a pouch containing an item of great importance to Samantha— her Bible. Nikolai made certain Jim had it in his possession before departing. Jim clipped it to his suit, not willing to risk leaving it behind. He reminded himself they were only twenty feet from the safety of the OV. Don't look at the big picture, only what needed to be done at that moment. Take care of the immediate business, then move on to the next.

Ed remained glued to the control room screen, while his friend, Merrill, worked feverishly with his crew to overcome the orbiting dilemma. Ed prayed as never before for a successful conclusion to the crisis and for the hopes and dreams of his family.

At the Reynolds' home, the only words perceived were the prayers of young Samantha as she stood back from the TV with Scott, hands clasped. Rose and the others repeated them silently in their hearts, awaiting the next step.

Suddenly, the sharp voice of the Commander, "We have depressurized the OV and are in the process of opening the safety hatch. Once the hatch is opened, five four-foot-long carbon poles will be assembled to reach you and Ms. Marissen. OK, the hatch is open. This twenty-foot pole is attached to the OV, which makes it stable and safe. Any questions, so far?"

"Nope. I can see the open hatch."

"OK, next step. We all must be tethered to something. Cap and I are tethered to the OV. Ms. Marissen?"

"Yes, me?"

"Yes. On the upper back of Flash's seat, you will see a zipper. Open that compartment. There will be a five-foot rolled up tether. Flash, I want you to carefully release your seat restraint and stand with your feet braced against the sides, facing Ms. Marissen."

Breathing, grunting, and the occasional groan from the pain of the stitched gash were heard as Jim performed the Commander's orders. "OK, I'm standing, facing Samantha."

Samantha added, "And I unzipped the compartment. I see the tether. Should I take it out?"

"Pass it to Flash. Flash, attach the end clip to your belt and the second clip to Ms. Marissen's belt. The other end has a large eyelet or hoop, right?"

Jim pulled the end of the tether to his visor. "Yes, it does."

"Slip the eyelet over the end of the pole which should be reaching you about…now."

"Hey, careful! You could put an eye out with that thing."

Samantha groaned, "Tell me you didn't really say that!"

The three separate locations felt some relief with the light-hearted banter. Jim noted Samantha's rapid breathing had slowed, her speech more relaxed. Perhaps, the last twenty feet will be OK.

Reaching out to the red and white pole, Jim slipped the three-inch diameter eyelet over the tip and slid it as far down as he could.

The Commander continued, "Now comes the time for the airline transfer. Remember, connect the tank lines before disconnecting the lines from your ship. Got it."

Back to all business, Jim replied, "Yes, sir. In process."

The oxygen tank still attached to her upper leg, Jim snapped Samantha's tank line into her suit and popped the other line out. He performed the identical operation to himself.

"Lines are transferred. Tether attached to the pole. What's next."

"Ms. Marissen, the best thing for you to do is let Flash lift you out of the seat."

Jim took her gloved hands and slowly raised her out of the seat, a much easier process without the canopy and no gravity. He smiled as she kept repeating "Oh, my; Oh, my; Oh, my…" as she slowly rose from the seat.

"I gotcha."

"I know you do. This is amazing. It's so hard to tell what's up and what's down!"

"Don't forget, we're tethered together and to this pole, which is attached to the OV. It is attached to the OV, isn't it?"

The Commander chuckled, "Yes, it is."

"Are you sure you're OK?" she asked. "Sometimes, you sound like you're in pain."

"I'm OK. We're almost there; twenty feet, that's all. How are you doing?"

"It hurts, probably more irritated than anything else. But,

I'll be OK."

"All right, let's go. Very slowly grasp the pole with both hands. I found out the hard way—sudden moves can make you look very foolish. Remind me to tell you that story! Anyway, you go first, I'll follow and move the tether as we go." Jim coaxed Samantha to try the distance alone, sort of.

She objected, "Aren't you going to hold on to me?"

"We are together." His words reassured her.

"Yes...we are." Beginning with two inch increments, Samantha, floating without gravity, worked her way down the pole, around the 90° bend at the bottom, and finally, the two feet to the hatch.

The Orbital Vehicle (OV)

Commander Webster, tethered to the exterior of the OV, waited at the hatch entrance to assist her. Inside, at the ready, was Captain Malone with the two NASA doctors. The Commander unhooked her tether clip once Samantha began entry into the hatch. Captain Malone took her by one arm, Dr. Benoit the other, easing her completely into the ship.

As Jim made certain of Samantha's safe entry, Commander Webster stated with great respect, "Colonel, it has been an honor to serve with you on this mission."

"As it has been for me. Thank you, Commander."

Jim reached for a handle near the hatch entrance and maneuvered through the three foot by three foot opening as Captain Malone and Dr. Brinker took hold of his arms and led him toward the center of the flight deck. Once Commander Webster disassembled and stored the emergency rescue pole, Captain Malone closed, locked, and sealed the hatch for return to the comforting confines of ground and gravity.

Commander Webster stated what needed to be done, still without names, before returning, "Captain, let's pressurize this cabin, get some air in here; Doctors, when we can, get those helmets off Ms. Marissen and the Colonel—see what those injuries they spoke of, are; the Captain and I will see about the disposition of the additional spacecraft."

Within minutes, Malone alerted Webster the cabin pressurization gauge read nominal; time to get the helmets off. After Malone and Webster removed their helmets, they assisted Samantha with the removal of hers at Jim's insistence as she reclined partially strapped into one of the crew seats directly behind the flight deck. Dr. Benoit stood ready to examine the injury before performing a complete checkup on Samantha in one of the available crew quarters. The magnetic boots proved a winning idea providing her the ability to move around while she worked.

As the helmet raised past Samantha's chin, the protective bandage wrap glared red with blood, causing a momentary panic. "We need to get the rest of the suit off before I can do any more."

Jim offered assistance immediately, "I can help with that. Where do you want to do this?"

Dr. Brinker had suggested that Jim remove his helmet, since he would know which motion caused pain and which didn't. He had the helmet to his nose when he responded to Dr. Benoit's need. Taking a deep breath, he continued until it cleared his head. A several-inch diameter area of blood-soaked bandage became visible along with the red, blue, and purple cheek and forehead.

"You look even worse. Are you sure?" Dr. Brinker questioned.

"Positive. Let's do it." Jim managed to get his magnetized boots on the floor and stood, ready to do whatever necessary. Extending his arms, he requested, "Could one of you get these gloves off?" Malone did.

"Take this earpiece too. Thanks"

"All right," Benoit allowed, "This should take just a few minutes then, you get your time!"

"Deal!" He stepped to Samantha, released the strap holding her in place and took her by the gloved hand. "Let's get you fixed up."

"Where are we going?" she wanted to know.

"Just around the corner."

Dr. Benoit and Jim guided Samantha into the small quarters and situated her in a chair/bed with loose straps. He prepared to separate the suit at the waist and remove it as two pieces but first had to remove her gloves.

He smiled, "You know how there is always one thing that gives you trouble. For me, it's these gloves! I can get them on and off somebody else but not me. See, yours are off already. I don't get it."

She touched his cheek. "From here on, I'll help you with your gloves."

He laughed, then grimaced, "Wow, I walked right into that one, didn't I?"

"Oh, yeah. Before I forget, hand me your earpiece. I don't think we'll need that anymore."

"Probably not, but it sure worked well." Samantha pulled it out by the small tab.

After some thought, Jim reported, "I think this would be better if Samantha was off the chair, just weightless. I could do this a lot easier. Don't move, I'm going to let you float in place while I remove the suit, OK?"

"OK, but…I was only joking about the gloves."

Even Benoit began to smile at their silly give and take.

Jim undid the straps and slowly moved Samantha to a horizontal position, then released the small latches that maintained the seal between the upper and lower half. Dr. Benoit stabilized Samantha's lower torso as Jim gently removed the upper portion of the suit, not allowing any contact between it and the injury to her neck.

Relieved, she sighed, "It feels so good to get that off."

Moving around to her legs, Jim asked Benoit to steady Samantha by the shoulders. "This should be a lot easier. Point your feet down." Using his magnetic boots for stability, he slowly slid the lower portion down and off. Dr. Benoit passed the suit paraphernalia to Captain Malone for stowage in a rear compartment.

"What a relief! This cooling getup is much more comfortable without the suit. I feel like I'm wearing a pair of long-underwear." Jim watched her with amazement. What a trooper, he thought. The hell she's been through: held captive, almost shot in the neck—she could have been killed, and this unbelievable attempt to get her home. He also figured this terrible experience would have to eventually take some kind of toll on her.

Dr. Benoit guided Samantha back to the chair and loosely refastened the restraints. She ordered Jim, "OK, Flash, let Dr. Brinker fix you up. I'll take care of Ms. Marissen."

"One moment, Doctor." James moved slowly to Samantha's side; she took his hand.

"James…"

"Let the Doctor do her stuff. I'm here for whatever you need. I'll always be here."

"I know you will. I love you."

"And I love you."

Thankful for her unwarranted trust in him, he leaned over and kissed her lightly. She squeezed his hand, then touched his cheek, just before he glided out of the small enclosure.

Kirkwood

Mesmerized, the family group remained standing, watching and listening to everything occurring 200 plus miles above, impatiently awaiting Samantha and Jim's safe return. Suddenly, Bill shouted, "Look! It really is Jim! Really! Where's Samantha?"

"I guess she's still in that room…wherever they took her with the doctor. I hope she's all right. Her neck looked horrible, all that blood. I wonder what happened?" Gina's worry grew more obvious when she realized the extent of Jim's injury. "Oooh, look at his eye, that looks so bad. How in the world did he make it this far?"

Rose returned to the couch, drained of strength, as she absorbed what all happened to free Samantha. "I will never be able to thank that man enough for what he has done. I am so happy they seem to be all right. They are hurt, but…they are together." Her voice trailed off, "They are together."

Scott and Samantha joined Rose just as Carol pointed out, "Did you see her going from that small ship with Jim to the pole…and then she went the rest of the way by herself after Jim explained what to do. And, like you said, Rose, both of them are hurt. Can you believe it?"

Rose leaned toward Samantha and Scott, "She is a different person when she's with him. It's as if she feeds off his confidence, building her own. That's what I mean when I say they are so good together. She brought out so many things in Jim that he had; he just didn't know how to use them. Like the time they performed the piano piece at church. I didn't even know Jim could play until then."

Samantha chimed in, "Yes! I asked Mom and Dad if they knew he played. They did but forgot. Maybe they'll do it again sometime!"

"Maybe…maybe they will," Rose imagined wistfully.

"OK, quiet everybody! I think they're talking to Jim!" Bob alerted everyone to the conversation.

The Orbital Vehicle (OV)

Free of his suit, Jim moved to one of the crew seats behind the flight deck. Commander Webster commented, "Funny how quick you get used to the magnetic boots, isn't it?'

"Really, I tried to put my feet on the floor but nothing happened."

Dr. Brinker took over, "Let's get you strapped down so I can check this out."

Slowly, carefully, gently, he removed the bandage from Jim's wound.

Before beginning to clean the injury, Dr. Brinker affirmed, "Overall, Colonel, I would say whoever did this did a good job, especially in the field. He must have been experienced. I'm pretty sure the reason you and Ms. Marissen had such bleeding was because of the G-forces you faced on your return. How bad is the pain on a scale of 1– 10, 10 being the worst?"

Jim looked toward Samantha's quarters. "She can't hear me, can she?"

"Show me the number of fingers then." Brinker responded.

He displayed nine fingers, then pulled back one.

From the crew quarters came a voice, "How many fingers did he hold up?"

"Two!" Dr. Brinker answered quickly.

Jim grinned weakly and nodded 'yes'.

"Wasn't there a stretch timaterial, you pull over your head, that goes with the suit?" Webster inquired.

"Yeah," Jim grunted. "I made a command decision not to use them. Too painful to get on and off for both of us."

"Good call. Obviously, you did OK without them."

Brinker continued his cleanup and examination, while

Malone and Webster continued to ready Sojourner for its flaming end.

* * *

"Uggh, that looks terrible! He really got hit hard! What a mess!" Ted set the record straight when he stated, "We can almost say with certainty that Jim was hit by something. Samantha's injury is another story. I can't figure that one out. We'll just have to wait."

Everyone seemed to relax a bit, knowing both Samantha and Jim were safely aboard the Orbital Vehicle, or Nemesis, neither designation easy. Bill had to laugh reminding them of Samantha trying to find out how many fingers Jim had raised, and the Doctor covering for him.

Samantha Reynolds took Scott's hand in hers, finally giving in to her emotions. Burying her face in his chest, she broke into sobbing. Her uncle was safe but hurt, soon to come home with his Samantha, also injured. He is a hero in the eyes of everyone at the Reynolds' home, yet, the same quiet, good man. She felt so relieved and so very proud. Gina and Rich happily accepted their daughter in the arms of another quiet, good man, a man hand-picked by Rich's best friend.

* * *

After some time, Dr. Benoit contacted Sonora. Facing the camera, she disclosed, "We have completed our examinations of the patients and conclude both are in relatively good health and able to withstand the pressures of re-entry despite their injuries. We decided against the use of a painkiller and are going to numb the areas of injury until landing. Then we will re-evaluate the situations. We don't foresee any problems; we want to avoid the use of medications prior to and during the landing. I have also taken pictures of Ms. Marissen's injury… just in case…if you know what I mean. For your information, she was grazed deeply by a fairly large caliber bullet, narrowly missing her carotid artery. Another fraction of an inch would have been fatal. Her injury did not require stitches, although I have packed the wound and she has received an antibiotic injection. A fresh protective wrap will be applied once the area has been numbed. She will be fine…a little sore, but fine."

"Doctor, would you like to take over with your report?"

"Thank you. Flash was struck across the eye by a military handgun wielded by a Russian soldier in a blindside attack shortly after landing. He is not certain how long he was unconscious but recalls Ms. Marissen and a Russian doctor at his side when he came to. The Russian doctor appears to have done a good job stitching his wound, which was necessary. Good enough, that I decided to leave the stitches for now. Just like Ms. Marissen, his wound has been cleaned and he has been given an antibiotic injection. Once I numb the area, he'll get a new bandage. He's going to look pretty bad for a while but he's going to be fine. So, that's it for now. I'll turn it over to the Commander.

"Ok, Freedom Base, we have prepped XM2 for re-entry over the Pacific. She's about seven miles ahead and ready to enter the atmosphere. She did a great job; did everything she was built for. We salute you, Sojourner. Sorry we couldn't take you home.

"The camera is trained on her location. You may be able to witness her ending. Just keep an eye on your screen in about thirty minutes. Just got the word, our patients will both be up front in about ten minutes. We're set for re-entry once everyone is buckled in. For the first time today, we are back on a schedule."

Dr. Benoit led Samantha by the arm to the flight deck crew area and placed her in the seat next to Jim. He held her in place as Malone ensured she was restrained properly.

"How are you feeling? Are you good and numb?"

"Oh, yeah," Samantha replied. "My neck hasn't felt this good for hours. Thank goodness I didn't have to get any stitches. How are you?"

"This feels very strange…I mean, no feeling. I can't even tell if I'm blinking. But, it sure feels better." Finally, since the injury, Jim spoke truthfully of his pain, or the lack of pain.

"I would lean on your shoulder, except I can't bend my neck. So, I'll just hold your arm, if that's OK with you."

"Definitely. We're almost home. Maybe we could still make the party at Rich and Gina's." Jim simply smiled. So many years, and now they could be with friends, together again.

Samantha did laugh at his line, aware she truly desired to see those people again; renew the long-lost friendships; and explain how sorry she was for her decisions so long ago.

"I feel so bad for you; your eye looks absolutely dreadful." Her compassion soon turned to a comedic attempt, "You look like you just tried out for a part in a mummy movie."

"Oh, thanks. That will build up my confidence." He chuckled as he noted, "We even look like a team. Pretty klutzy, but a team."

Samantha tightened her grip on James' arm. "I'm not supposed to turn my head, so would you lean over; I need to tell you something?"

He did, as best he could, considering the restraints. She stretched as close to his ear as comfortably possible. "I have missed you so much; I can't even tell you. Thank you…again, for what you did. I promise, I truly promise I will love you for the rest of my life."

James' heart melted at her words. She said nothing she hadn't said earlier; as always with Samantha, the manner she spoke moved him. He turned to her and whispered, "I promise you, Miss Samantha, I will love you as long as I live…and I hope that to be a long, long time."

Sonora Complex, Arizona

"All right, people!" Merrill bellowed. They'll be braking for re-entry in twelve minutes. Are we ready? All systems go for re-entry? I don't want any oversights at this late stage. Talk to me!"

Reports from every facet filtered through efficiently, each within satisfactory parameters. Merrill thanked all controllers upon receiving their report.

"All is good, all is ready." He advised Ed. "The remainder of the mission rests on Webster and Malone's shoulders."

Al Jamieson remained in constant contact with President Burton. His affirmative nodding implied a presidential request. "Yes, sir, I'll see that it is done…but, I do ask for time for those involved to reunite, to be together, to experience the relief that it's over."

"Definitely, definitely!" the President replied. "If possible, I would like to speak with Colonel Gordon and Samantha Marissen on a secure phone later."

"Yes, sir! That should not be a problem; I'll see to it." The call ended.

Jamieson approached Ed. "The only exposure the President requests of your daughter is a brief clip showing she is here in the United States and definitely not in Moscow as the Russians keep reporting. He also wants to make sure people notice her injury—not to make an issue of it, but that the average Joe notices it. How does that sit with you?"

Placing his hand on Jamieson's shoulder, Ed's only reply, "You'll have to talk to Samantha about that," and readied himself for the landing.

Kirkwood

Gina rushed into the family room, bursting with enthusiasm, "I have just had the greatest idea! No party today—no way! Too many things happening. What if we have the party after Jim and Samantha get home? We all heard Samantha can't wait to get together again. I'm sure we'll see her before then, but let's surprise her soon with a party…for her!"

Carol jumped out of her seat, excited by the possibility. "That is a wonderful opportunity to do something for her. I agree, this is something we should do!" The family room vibrated with cross conversations of when and how they could surprise her and what should be served. Young Samantha rose quietly, led Scott to the kitchen and out the back door onto the patio.

"Are you OK?" Scott asked as she stood with her back to him, arms folded.

"I had to get away from all the silly planning! There are no guarantees right now. Jim and Samantha are facing the most dangerous part of coming home. They have to pass through the re-entry part…and from everything I've seen and read, that's the most dangerous. I know other ships have burned up doing that. I'm sorry, I just had to get away from it."

As he attempted to step in front of her, she kept turning away, not wanting eye contact. Finally, Scoot took her by both shoulders and hugged her from behind. "It's all right, I understand. But maybe that's the way they handle the same stress and worry you're feeling. I know they are just as concerned; they get relief looking past that and talk like Samantha and Jim are already here."

Samantha took one hand from her shoulder and faced Scott, searching for a place of refuge. He held her close as she released her fears and concerns of the last month. The back door opened; Rose leaned out looking toward the two. Scott raised a few fingers to show all was OK. She gently closed the door and returned to the family room.

Looking up to the man consoling her, Samantha forced a weak smile, stating, "You're right. They're aware of the dangers; I know they are. I'm being overly sensitive. They know God has His hand on all this. I should know that."

Folding her hands into his, Scott asked, "Why don't we pray for Samantha and Jim and the crew?"

With foreheads touching, Scott led the prayer,

"Dear Lord God, we humbly ask you to protect Samantha, Jim, the doctors, and the crew during re-entry, and bring them home safely to families who love them. Let the process go as planned with no problems or issues of any sort. We ask that we may shortly be celebrating their successful return with thanksgiving and praise. In Jesus' name…Amen."

Samantha raised her head. "Thank you. I think you just reminded me of my Uncle Jim and what he would have done. You are a kind, sensitive, manly kind of guy." Without hesitation, she kissed him.

Samantha and Scott returned to the family room. "You didn't miss a thing. We couldn't see Jim's ship enter the atmosphere. We think it was too far ahead. We're just waiting for—

"Freedom Base…Nemesis here." Malone's voice startled the watchful family. "We are coming up on the Indian Ocean and prepared to fire engines for re-entry. Force-field in full function."

Orbital Vehicle

Jim, Samantha, and the two doctors observed the procedure through the cockpit windows as the nose of the spacecraft dipped slowly downward until orbiting upside down, rear thrusters facing eastward. Nemesis' re-entry procedure mirrored a typical NASA shuttle re-entry. Soon, the main engines would fire, lowering the orbital perigee into the upper atmosphere. After the main engine burn, Nemesis would resume full revolution to its nose-first trajectory.

Samantha fully appreciated her final view of the earth passing beneath, noticing James every bit as enthralled. In passing, she confessed again, "I'm anxious to get back to St. Louis to renew the friendships I so foolishly let go."

Laying his hand on hers, he comfortingly responded, "They'll be waiting for you. I only wish they knew you were on your way home now."

Waiting for an opportune moment, Dr. Brinker broke in, "You're both from St. Louis? I grew up in the county—Fenton. Do you know Fenton? I guess I should ask what high school you went to, eh?"

A groaning laugh resulted from the age-old St. Louis question. A non-resident would have no idea of the importance of that information but, in St. Louis, that significant portion of life registered as ones' coat-of-arms.

The engines fired for up to three minutes, slowing the craft to re-entry speed. An ever-so-slight shudder passed through Nemesis, similar to a commercial airliner slowing for final approach.

*   *   *

The Kirkwood crowd watched in awed silence as the onboard camera focused on a side view of the Nemesis flight deck, Webster and Malone at the controls, the doctors and Samantha and Jim strapped in their seats. The view would not last. Interference from the ionization of molecules would soon black out all communication. To see their friends so close to end of their ordeal, left them in a state of near-exhaustion, drained of all strength. Rose did not remove her eyes from Samantha the entire time she was on-camera.

The burn complete, Nemesis returned to normal flying position with a 42° nose elevation at the brink of descent. Over the mid-Pacific at 400,000 feet, the aircraft encountered increased air density as it rode the compressed molecules to a reduced speed. Samantha first noted the rougher ride and increasing G-forces as re-entry speed decreased, igniting an intense orange glow of the electromagnetic force field colliding with thicker air molecules.

* * *

As the private band of family and friends observed the flight deck, crew, and passengers, the pixels composing the image began to freeze, then break up—and, finally, blackout, the period of unknowns. Samantha Reynolds gripped Scott's hand the moment the screen went dark. Three minutes or more would pass before communication resumed, an eternity for those watching.

Not a breath dare escape for fear of an unnecessary sound at Sonora or Kirkwood, as no one uttered a word during the blackout period. One minute passed—then two—three, nothing. At this point, some began looking at one another, hoping, praying all was well. Almost four minutes—flight control radioed, "Nemesis, Freedom Base here..."

Rose, Gina, Rich, the entire group at the Reynolds' simply stared at the screen, praying for the return of their precious cargo falling from space. Rich muttered, "C'mon, you guys can do it; c'mon home."

Jim and Samantha did not realize the extent of the rough ride involved with re-entry. She squeezed Jim's hand tightly as they bounced their way through the atmosphere, all the while experiencing increasing G-forces as flight speed drastically slowed, although not as strong as James' earlier maneuvers and eventual rocketing into orbit. Jim compared the white-hot glow of re-entry to sitting inside a neon tube of burning gas. From his one-time experience, he determined the end of re-entry should be near.

* * *

"Nemesis, Freedom Base…

"Nemesis, Freedom Base…

Merrill muttered under his breath, pacing the floor, "C'mon…we need a response…c'mon."

* * *

"Freedom Base, this is Nemesis! We are on our way! All systems intact; re-entry a success!"

Absolute pandemonium spilled out at both locations with the knowledge the spacecraft survived the ride through hell, protecting everyone inside, although many understood the true protection came from the God of the universe.

Almost immediately, the image of the flight deck returned to the screen. The voice of Ed Marissen came through, "Welcome home, Nemesis! Welcome home, Samantha!"

"Dad…is that you?"

"Yes, baby, you're home."

"Is Mom there?"

"No, but she's with your friends, watching."

"She can see us?"

"She can…and she can hear you, but you can't hear her."

"Mom? Oh, Mom, Dad! I love you! I can't wait to see you!

565

I thank all of you, each and every one of you for what you've done. Thank you! Thank you!"

Jim closed his eyes, remaining silent during the brief interchange between daughter and mother and father, a beautiful time of healing, the beginning of renewal. He thought he heard Ed explain Rose watched with their friends. How? Doesn't matter, they know she's safe; she's coming home.

*   *   *

Rose slowly eased herself onto the couch, buried her face in her hands, and wept. Surrounded by friends, she confessed, "Samantha never called us Mom and Dad, ever. Oh, my Lord, this is so wonderful, so beautiful." She laughed while she cried.

*   *   *

"Freedom Base, the engines are fired up for powered flight. ETA, about forty-seven minutes. I think the Colonel would appreciate a hot cup of coffee when we pull in." Malone seemed almost giddy with the success of the mission. "We'll come in overhead, sweep out and around, making our approach from the east."

Commander Webster added as a precaution, "Double-check the air traffic in the area. There never is; we're so remote. But, let's not overlook anything now."

"Copy that."

"And," Webster continued, "We'll exit through the emergency hatch, since the problem with the bay doors. Have a platform truck out there."

"You got it!"

*   *   *

Scott and Samantha slipped into the kitchen where she could quietly breathe a sigh of relief. Everything should be fine from here on, their return not due for another fifteen minutes. Scott grinned when Samantha suggested she should tell her uncle "no more crazy trips." Rose almost stepped into the kitchen as Scott approached Samantha near the counter, placed his finger under her chin, and whispered, "I love you, Samantha Reynolds, and there's nothing you can do about that." He kissed her.

As he stepped back, Samantha responded softly, "I don't want to do anything about it. I love you too." And she returned the kiss.

Rose could not contain herself, as she hurried to the young couple, threw her arms around them, and declared, "That was just so beautiful. I'm so happy for you!"

Embarrassed, Scott and Samantha could only smile and hug Rose back.

"Don't worry, I won't say a word," she bubbled. "This is your news. I'm just so happy. Jim and Samantha will be so happy. You know Jim hoped this would happen. Oops, maybe I shouldn't have told you that! Oh, well, this is wonderful!"

"OK, everybody! They expect to see them any minute! Get in here! There's a camera focused on the western sky." Neil didn't want anyone to miss anything. The family room refilled in a hurry. Even Dave Reisen found a good seat.

Suddenly, everyone snapped to a heightened peak of attention. A very distant object appeared on the screen, so small, it appeared to bounce as the camera attempted to focus. The cameraman locked onto the object and switched to a high-powered lens, sharply displaying Nemesis diving toward the landing area.

"Wow! Would you look at that!" Bob reported in a mesmerized state. "That definitely looks science fiction." Heads nodded in agreement.

While conversation increased, Rose's phone rang. "Rose, are you watching? She's almost here! I don't have long but I'm sorry you're not with me. I'll make sure you get to talk with her. Then I want to get you out here. I call you again after she lands. I love you, Babe."

"I love you," Rose managed before her extremely excited and busy husband had to hang up. That was fine; he called. She thoroughly enjoyed the attention Ed blessed her with the last month.

"Gina!" Rose happily called out. "That was Ed. He said I would be able to talk with Samantha when she lands. I want you to talk with her too! All of you!"

What more could happen to highlight the day? Nancy presented a great thought, "After Rose and Gina talk with her, we all, at one time, welcome her back and let her know we can't wait to see her again! What do you think?"

"That's a great idea!" Carol excitedly agreed. "Then, she'll know we still love her and miss her!" So, that was the plan.

* * *

Several states west, Ed Marissen stoically observed his people working feverishly to bring Nemesis through the final leg of its journey; Merrill Pierce requesting orders and answers to last minute questions and concerns. Ed reminded himself of his wise decision to step down for Merrill to take the lead.

Project scientists, engineers, and technicians, being who they are, fretted over the smallest of details, not resting until the ship touched down with the crew, doctors, and Jim and Samantha. Although a failure of the bay doors occurred, this group took on a childlike giddiness that a successful solution had taken place and that all other facets had functioned as planned. Occasionally, a hint of nervous laughter rippled across the room.

Finally, nothing more was required; all was ready—everyone in position at Sonora and in Kirkwood. Onboard Nemesis, Captain Moore turned to his passengers, "You are home, Ms. Marissen, you are home. Glancing at Jim, he gave a quick smile and nod, as if to say, "Well done, Colonel."

* * *

Nemesis decreased the angle of its steep descent and leveled off as it flew just north of the Complex, banking hard to starboard as it swung around to line up for final approach.

"Nemesis, this is Flight Control. You are cleared to land on runway 001A."

The final view for Sonora and Kirkwood caught Nemesis in the final majestic moments of the starboard bank, easing into the landing approach, lowering the landing gear, and nosing up for rear wheel touchdown. Samantha squeezed James' hand in anxious preparation.

"This may sound odd, but I'm enjoyin' these tight turns and maneuvers," she whispered. "I'm so happy to be home!"

"Me too. I think I need a vacation." Exhaustion began to overtake Jim, but rest would have to wait. A great deal of activity remained to be handled today, most of it probably political. More importantly, time with Samantha minus outside concerns ranked number one!

* * *

Ed stood for a better view the control center screen. So close, so very close, he thought. You're almost here, Samantha, almost here. Lord, I ask that we can begin anew. Give me the opportunity to be the father I should have been, the husband I should have been. I thank you for bringing her home, for Rose, for Jim. Everything came together your way. Thank you.

* * *

Samantha Reynolds moved closer to the screen in awe of the aircraft as it came into view. Scott stood behind her, hand on her shoulder. "Amazing, isn't it? We can only look at it; Samantha is in there, having the experience of a lifetime."

She turned to him. "You would fly in that?"

"In a heartbeat!"

Everyone stood to better see the moment the craft touched the runway. All eyes focused on Nemesis growing larger, closer until the multiple rear wheels touched the airstrip in a cloud of smoke, followed by the front landing gear beneath the nose of the aircraft lowering slowly to the concrete surface.

"Freedom Base, we have wheels down!" Commander Webster proclaimed.

Sheer joy exploded at Sonora with shouting, whistling, and laughter, much laughter, as the extreme pressure of the mission gave way to ultimate relief over the safe return of all. A similar reaction of a smaller nature took place at the Reynolds' home. Tears flowed at both locations. Sonora employees mobbed Ed and Merrill; overjoyed that years of intense labor came to fruition with the successful rescue of Samantha Marissen from a treacherous situation half way around the globe.

While the noise of celebration filled the Kirkwood house, Samantha Reynolds thought rather to throw her arms around Scott's neck and kiss him. As the kiss ended, he declared loud enough for her to hear over the din, "Miss Reynolds, I believe I love you!" To which she resoundingly replied, "Why Mr. Larimore, I believe I love you too!"

The couple froze with embarrassment upon realizing the room had grown strangely silent with the booming report of their love for one another.

Rich stepped before the two with Gina. "Well now, this is good news, although not altogether unforeseen." He slapped Scott on the back. "I guess Jim got his wish. Which one of you is going to tell him?"

Scott shrugged, "I knew Jim set up our meeting; I never knew he planned that far ahead! We'll both tell him…later. He seems to have his own story going on right now."

Always looking to add a good line, Rich threw out, "All I can say is—it's a good thing Samantha has her own apartment or I'd be saving up for a ladder right about now!" Scott and the celebrating friends broke into laughter and more applause.

Gina jokingly rolled her eyes at his comment before Samantha half-seriously stated, "What I don't get is, why Scott thinks Dad is so funny."

"Don't forget," Gina explained, "Jim hand-picked this young man. They're like two peas in a pod. Remember when you would say, you hoped to meet someone like Jim…" She knowingly pointed to Scott.

Rose joined Gina in celebrating, grinning to Scott and Samantha, "Thank goodness, I didn't have to keep that a secret for too long!"

By the time their attention returned to the screen, Nemesis rolled to a stop and shut down.

Inside Nemesis, Malone worked through his checklist while Dr. Benoit freed Samantha from the restraints and led her to the crew quarters for a quick reexamination of her injury. Dr. Brinker began the same but Jim asked if he could check it later. Dr. Brinker saw no problem with that.

Webster approached to give Jim a hand with the restraints

and, smiling, mentioned, "So, you and Ms. Marissen, you knew each other before?"

Jim figured, why worry about this now? Just be honest. "Yeah, some time ago."

Webster surprised Jim with his next statement. "I'm glad for you. It's not right for a good guy to be alone; I hope all goes well for you and her. Whatever you have, it worked well for the mission. I'm not sure anyone else could have pulled this off. Let me know what happens."

"I will," Jim promised. "Thanks for your friendship."

Webster offered his hand to help Jim out of the seat. Jim took hold and slowly stood. His knees would take some time to adjust to the weight of gravity.

Samantha returned to the flight deck directly to Jim. "My legs feel like I've been on a boat or something. I'm doing better, but it was pretty strange at first."

"Me too. I need to stretch, walk around a little."

She laughed. "The Doctor asked me about us. I guess some of the things we said up there might have led people to think certain things. I just told her the truth. I will never deny what we have."

"Neither will I." Jim looked around, saw the crew and doctors busy with one thing or another, and stole a quick kiss.

Samantha grinned, "You are such a bad boy, kissing me in my father's spaceship!"

He simply smiled.

Webster stepped to the center of the flight deck. "Since the bay doors are not operating properly, Dan is opening the emergency hatch again for us to exit. Thurmond will be in here soon to take a look at the doors. My guess is they will open now; the lack of gravity caused something to jam that the lack of weight couldn't handle. Just an amateur guess. A platform truck will lower us and we'll get a ride to the hangar. No cameras here, so Ms. Marissen, no pressure. You are back in the United States."

'Back in the United States', how often did she take that for granted in the past. Everyday life—just so simple. For nearly five months she lived a life of fear, not knowing from day-to-day what would happen next. Then, to return to a life of complete freedom, to have the ability to come and go as she pleased once again. She vowed to appreciate every day, as if the last.

Samantha thought of Nikolai; did he make it? What of Anechka? What kind of life did she and Nikolai have to look forward? She understood she must know his fate; she couldn't let him fade into obscurity.

Captain Malone swung the emergency hatch inward, allowing a blast of desert air into the flight deck, not unbearable but hot.

"Man, it's good to be back," Jim spoke in an undertone. "I never thought I would miss the desert, but…it's good to be back."

"This is where you trained…here?"

"Yep, right here."

Dan approached from the exit, informing the small group, "The platform is ready. We'll just go out the way you guys came in, except you'll have to back out on your hands and knees instead of floating. The platform will take us down to a van for the ride to the hangar. Piece of cake, right?"

Pointing to Samantha and Jim, he relayed special instructions, "Drs. Benoit and Brinker are to get you guys to the Med Center for a thorough examination and evaluation." Giving them both the 'once over', he finished with, "You look like you need it."

Extending his hand to Samantha, he warmly expressed,

"Welcome home, Ms. Marissen."

Taking his hand into both of hers, she responded, Thank you so very much."

Turning to Kyle, she reached for his hand. "And thank you, thank you both for your courage and…well, everything. I feared for my life. I just know I would not have survived another day.

Tears gathered in her eyes.

Malone stepped up to Jim. "Colonel, congratulations on the mission. You really know your stuff. I have to tell you—I would not have been able to do what you did. I owe you my deepest apology."

Jim led Malone to the side. "Our duty is to perform our responsibilities to the best of our ability. And you did. None of this would have been possible without your cool head to get us in here after the bay doors failed. That could have been chaos. Nice job!"

"OK," Webster instructed, "Here's how we'll exit. Dr. Benoit will go first, followed by you, Ms. Marissen. Then, Dr. Brinker and Colonel Gordon, with Dan and me last."

Samantha spoke up, "I would like Colonel Gordon with me."

* * *

"Well, what are they waiting for? C'mon out!" Bob shouted at the screen. "We know you're in there!"

Laughter popped up continuously as the 'family' waited impatiently for the couple to make an appearance on the balcony, as they referred to the platform. Thankfully, the wavy rainbow-like appearance of the OV managed to keep the group occupied, similar to a cat hypnotized by a tiny red laser dot on the floor.

"There at the door," Liz announced, "You can see motion inside. I think they're ready to come out!"

As instructed, Dr. Benoit exited first, followed by Dr. Brinker. All eyes riveted on the small opening, waiting to see Samantha show herself. The general consensus seemed to be, this is not real until we see her! Another body worked its way out of the exit backwards. What a disappointment, it was only Jim, one-third of his head bandaged. The room broke out in celebration for the return of their hero, a title he would not accept. He squatted before the opening, as the next person worked feet-first to get out. He took her by the hands and helped to raise her to a standing position.

The sight of Samantha standing on the platform, truly home, brought forth every emotion. Rose wept in the knowledge she was hurt but home with the man who truly loved her. Gina stood before the screen with her hand over her mouth, seeing her best friend finally safe with Jim. And so it went, clapping, whistling, laughing, or crying.

Shielding her eyes from the Arizona sun with one hand, Samantha stood in plain view on the platform, holding Jim's arm with the other. A windowless, oversized yellow van backed up to the descending platform. The rear doors opened. Jim stepped off the platform and assisted Samantha to the runway. Taking her arm, he led her to the rear doors of the van. Standing near the back to greet her was Ed.

She did not notice at first, stepping into shadow from intense sunlight, but when she did, "Dad? Are you really here?"

"I should be asking you that," he replied as he held his arms open wide.

She fell into his arms. "Oh, Dad, I love you, I love you."

When Jim entered the van, Ed relinquished his paternal protection and released Samantha to his arms. "James, we're home, we're home." Out of sight, she broke down, giving in to her emotions and sheer exhaustion, sobbing in joy and relief. The remainder of the crew waited understandingly at the doors until the proper moment.

Shortly after, Jim motioned the Doctors and crew to climb in for the short ride to the hangar, as a small celebration of their own took place with good words, grins, and congratulations.

The massive doors to the hangar parted enough to allow the van entry, the same hangar Jim returned to at the end of his life-threatening test flight. Merrill designated this gathering as private—just between the crew of Nemesis, the core group of scientists and technicians, and Samantha and Jim…no cameras.

Hamilton, Thurmond, Rice, Garcia, Kerrick, Burchfield, and Pierce were hastily ushered to the front of the crowd. As the van doors opened, the occupants stepped down to applause and cheers, which increased dramatically with Samantha and Jim's appearance. In an instant, the couple and crew found themselves surrounded by well-wishers, giving and accepting thanks and credit for a job well-done.

* * *

Later that day, Samantha spoke with her mother, then Gina, in a tearful, loving reunion using the same link as before. Both she and Jim reunited with their friends in a lengthy, sometimes humorous, sometimes heartfelt conversation of what had been and what was to come. Samantha happily discovered her fear of losing her extended family profoundly pointless. The conversation drew to a close with Samantha softly confessing, "I want to thank y'all for your forgiveness, your kindness. I love you! I love you, Mom! I love you, Gina!" The roomful of friends joined together to express, "We love you!" before signing off.

The most difficult portion of the evening belonged to

her father as he told of her ex's part in nearly destroying the attempt at rescue and how he perished trying to escape the authorities. Samantha listened with little emotion as she heard of his death earlier that day. Strangely, she felt no remorse, and oddly enough, some relief. Thankfully, Ed had insisted Jim be present during the breaking of the news.

Much later that evening, after Samantha agreed to a short video interview by Ray Zygman for the CIA to prove she had never been in Moscow while casually displaying her near-fatal neck injury, Samantha and Jim met in a quiet recreation room to enjoy privately the quiet company of each other. In her lap lay the Bible James had brought back from Nikolai, opened to Psalm 139. She read it aloud just before they fell asleep on the couch; James sitting with his head back and Samantha resting her head on his chest. Next to her lay the poem she carried for years, no longer just words.

Lisa Kerrick and Nate Garcia slipped into the room to visit but seeing them fast asleep, Lisa whispered, "Let them rest. We can tell them tomorrow."

The following five days consisted of the debriefing of all personnel in the details of the mission, Samantha and Jim included. Drs. Benoit and Brinker subjected them to x-rays, scans, and tests of every sort to determine any hidden injuries that might have resulted from Jim's blow to the head or Samantha's beatings at the hands of Igor and, thankfully, found none.

Rich would later report at every gathering that they x-rayed Jim's head and found nothing.

Dr. Brinker thought it best to reopen, clean, and stitch again Jim's head wound in the sterile conditions of the Med Center. Exhaustion appeared to be the main source of concern for both Samantha and Jim. Several days of rest and relaxation proved to be the best medicine, during which Jim provided a tour of the operations and early morning hikes in the desert.

A tearful, yet joyous reunion between Rose and Ed, and Samantha and Jim culminated with the announcement over dinner of Samantha's engagement to Colonel James Paul Gordon, Retired. Rose nearly danced with happiness at the news, while Ed simply hugged Samantha lovingly and in a fatherly gesture, heartily shook Jim's hand, expressing, "Welcome to the family…son."

Their debriefing stretched over two days, Samantha revealing all details of her four and one half month confinement and mistreatment under her original captors until the arrival of Nikolai, her guard. She spoke most highly of his protection and determination to ensure her escape, breaking down at the thought he may have lost his life defending hers.

CIA Director Jamieson interrupted her testimony clarify to the committee that Nikolai, a young man whose descendants lived under the oppression of communism, volunteered to serve as a plant to observe and protect Ms. Marissen and to assist with her escape. He also reminded the committee of the intent of the raid—to prevent the elimination of Ms. Marissen, which was to take place the day of the rescue. "Elimination" he explained, meant execution.

Samantha shuddered, recalling Nikolai's shooting of the Captain determined to kill her as she lay defenseless on the floor of the dacha. She remembered his distorted, disfigured face the moment of his death. She relayed her experience of killing Alexei, the soldier who figured to make good by her capture; killing James Gordon; and holding the strange craft for Moscow. Samantha's testimony did not falter, did not waver as she spoke of the events calmly and succinctly. Jim listened in silent awe of the ordeal his 'fragile southern belle' endured and how she rose to conquer her fears.

The Russian military, because of Samantha's escape, seized power two days later, followed by the guarantee of the election of a legitimate government body. Officially, no mention of the rescue surfaced, probably due to the ease of entry and escape of the American pilot with Ms. Marissen. To the world, Samantha Marissen simply returned to the United States, which set well with President Burton and the involved government agencies. If the Russian Federation did not wish to pursue the matter, so be it. The prosecution of the Russian spies and their American counterparts would, however, continue as planned.

Jim's debriefing began with the rainy Saturday visit of the Big Brass and ended with the landing of Nemesis, covering every step between, taking the committee through every point three separate times. As grueling as the debriefing was, Jim proved a capable testifier, relying heavily on his memory of the debriefing procedure following his disabled jet incident during the Mideast conflict. Samantha listened intently as she learned of the strength and courage of the man next to her.

After two weeks, the committee closed the investigation, satisfied the incident would not raise its ugly head in the future. The Russian Federation would not risk embarrassment with the revelation of any portion of the rescue to international ears. Eventually, as happens all too often, unspoken events never seem to have occurred.

Remaining true to his word, Ed retired, turning control of Marissen AeroSpace over to Merrill Pierce, occasionally lending his expertise on a consulting basis; otherwise, Merrill captained the ship most effectively. The Orbital Vehicle, Merrill dreamed, could deliver living quarters for future colonies on the moon, and from there…

September 19, Saturday

Prior to their late-night departure, Director Jamieson boarded Ed's private jet to inform Samantha he received word

Nikolai had survived; he would make a full recovery. He also told of their quiet attempt, if Nikolai wanted, to assist him in coming to the United States. Samantha explained to Jamieson about Anechka and she must be included in the arrangement. He only nodded and said he would look into it.

The mid-September return to St Louis proved quite uneventful; once a story loses its heat, coverage soon disappears. With the secrecy of James' role; the lack of Russian Federation furor; and deprived of public interest; the two-week period since Samantha's rescue provided ample time for the media to sniff out another so-called lead to some obscure, yet to be identified, tragedy.

October 3, Saturday Afternoon
Kirkwood, Missouri

"It feels good to get out! I can't believe we haven't gone anywhere since we got back." Samantha stretched her arms in the front seat of James' jeep as they turned the corner toward Rich and Gina's house. "I am so nervous about this. It's been so long—I won't know what to say."

James consoled her, "Rich and Gina are still the same, and they still love you. We're just going to have a nice, quiet reunion with a couple of good friends. You'll be fine! Look on the bright side! We're healing up pretty well; we won't scare them off! Besides, isn't it nice with all the media coverage gone. We can get around like normal people again."

"There's nothing normal about you!" Samantha grinned.

"Nor you!" he laughed.

The jeep bounced into the driveway, coming to a stop at the garage door.

"We survived in space, but I'm not sure about this car!"

"Jeep!"

"OK, jeep!" She looked around the front of the Reynolds'

home, "Oh, my, the same house, same street; I feel like I've never been gone."

James twisted in the seat to face Samantha, gently pulled her toward him and kissed her. She closed her eyes and touched his face as their lips met. She sighed when parting, "I like when you kiss me for no reason."

"We have a lot of years to catch up."

She smiled the smile he remembered.

"Well, are you ready?"

"As I'll ever be."

James stepped around the jeep and took her hand as she worked her way out. She laughed, "This car—jeep, is kind of fun. Don't get rid of it. You want something different? OK, but keep this."

Hand-in-hand, the couple proceeded down the side of the house to the gate and entered Rich and Gina's back yard, Samantha first.

"Surprise!!" came the loudest, most shocking greeting Samantha would never have anticipated. Covering her mouth, she couldn't decide whether to laugh or cry. She simply stood still, taking in everyone: Rich and Gina, Ted and Carol, Bob and Liz, Bill and Nancy, Neil and Sue, Ed and Rose, and a young couple she didn't recognize.

James stood behind her, hands on her shoulders. "What do you think, Hon? Surprised?"

She couldn't speak, the surprise overwhelming. Suddenly, Samantha ran to Gina, threw her arms around her and broke into tears of joy. At that, the group crowded around, welcoming her back to the 'family' with hugs, kisses, and many, many kind, loving words. Scott and Samantha Reynolds remained in the background.

Jim made his way to the young couple, allowing his

Samantha the time to fully understand the depth of love these people had for her.

"I'm so glad you're home!" the young Samantha cried, as she hugged her uncle. "You sure had me worried!"

Jim held her as he reported, "I understand a certain young guy spilled the beans of my whereabouts not two hours after I left. Is that right?"

"I did." Scott confessed sheepishly.

Samantha looked up. "Yes, he did, and I'm glad he did. If there isn't something crazy going on with you, no one would ever pray for you!" She smiled and touched his forehead. "At least your eye looks much better. I'm so relieved you're all right."

He grinned broadly. "You know, little lady, you remind me of that woman over there. Give her a few more minutes. I want to introduce you to her…and you too, Scott. Man, it's good to see you!"

"Good to see you too!" Jim actually hugged Scott, which the young man quickly returned.

Feigning a need to know, Jim inquired "I hear there may be something happening between you two; is that true?"

"There is, but we'll tell you about it later. This is your moment." Scott barely got the words out before the family descended upon Jim, clamoring to welcome him home after Samantha had been properly reunited with her friends.

With Samantha at his side, he shared how good it is to be back with friends and how much he appreciated the homecoming. As some years ago, she stood with her arm around his waist, his around her shoulders as conversation continued from every direction. After several minutes, Jim hushed the group and motioned for Scott and Samantha to join him.

"Samantha…this Samantha…you, I want you to meet

someone you haven't seen in a long, long time." Without rambling, he took Miss Reynolds by her arm, "This is Rich and Gina's daughter, Samantha, the little girl named after you. Samantha, this is Samantha."

Jim's Samantha looked at the young lady with a sudden awareness. "I've been wondering who you are. I should have guessed." She held her arms open. "My gosh! Come here!" The young Samantha quickly went to her, expressing, "I had always hoped to see you some day. This is a wish come true." They embraced, like family.

Continuing the introductions, Jim motioned Scott closer. "This young guy is Scott Larimore who seems to like Samantha. For some reason, everybody says they remind them of us. I don't see it, but sometimes you have to let people have their fun."

Samantha immediately responded, "I think I can see it. Scott's a young, handsome man…like you used to be…and don't you dare say anything about me! You know I'm just kidding, my handsome Air Force Colonel pilot."

"Oooooh," the group echoed in unison. The remainder of the afternoon rolled on with laughter and quips and banter and barbs as before, with Samantha experiencing full restoration of the friendships she sacrificed years earlier, especially with Carol, whom she spoke with for almost an hour. However, there would be no talk of her ordeal today. Today meant renewal and a return to what was and should have been.

To add to Samantha's enjoyment, Ed and Rose easily partook of the day's festivities, finally sitting around before dinner talking and snacking on chips, veggies, and dip. Ed prayed before the meal, thanking everyone for their forgiveness and acceptance, having expressed sadness for the distress his selfishness had caused his daughter and Jim. Rose never loved him more for his courage to openly confess his mistakes in judgment.

Rich responded for everyone as he reassured Ed that was then, this is now. Today is a new beginning and nothing could change that. God has blessed all of them with this day. He wrapped it up with, "Let's eat!"

As the group passed through the food line, Jim explained Gina's Labor Day menu to Samantha, Rose, and Ed, how it never changes…but is always good. He pointed out the bar-b-que pork steaks, potato salad, baked beans, corn-on-the-cob with lots o' butter, rolls, homemade chocolate chip gooey butter cake, lemonade and sweet tea. One unfamiliar item sat on the table, until Samantha exclaimed, "This is Mom's chocolate sweet cake! Oh, my gosh, you brought your cake. That is so sweet…and so is your cake!"

Ed asked, "Are you always like this with Jim?"

Before she could respond, Jim replied, "Always!"

* * *

The day passed much too quickly. As the guests began their ritual for leaving, Jim called for Samantha, the young one. She wandered over. "What can I do for you, sir?"

"Wait, before you begin, I see you drove that jeep thing today. How did Samantha like it?"

Glad she asked, Jim was more than happy to reply. "She likes it! Said it's fun! She wants me to keep it! What do you think of that?" A positive reply was not expected.

She hugged him, "That's good! Scott and I enjoyed riding around in it. Since you were gone, I grew attached to the darned thing 'cause it reminded me of you. Kind of brought you closer to home."

Jim scratched his head, "I never know what to expect from you. You always keep me guessing. I love you, Sweetie."

What? He never called her that. Is this part of the new Jim, the guy who has his love back. Excellent! "I love you too, James."

He snickered at her attempt to keep it up.

"So…Jim, what do you want?"

Shaking his head, he asked her to keep it low. "Would you be able to go to a bank with me tomorrow?"

"Why? You want to give me a chunk of money?"

"Not now. Seriously, I want to show you something, something no one ever knew about. But you can't tell anyone… except Scott. Can he make it?"

"No, he has a flight. He'll be gone a few days."

"Oh, I wish he could." Jim looked over his shoulder. "How about Monday afternoon. I'll pick you up at work…in my jeep."

"Woo-hoo, I can't wait! No, that will be fine. You make this so mysterious."

"Great! I'll be there at three. Don't forget…you cannot mention this to anyone."

October 5, the Bank—3:20pm

What a strange situation, waiting for Jim and a bank employee to unlock a safe deposit box on a Monday afternoon. Samantha had no idea Jim even had one, or why he had one. All she knew, Jim came to close this one out. He would take whatever was in it home. Why? She had so many questions, especially, why did he want her with him?

At last, the box opened; the employee left the room. Jim looked into the box, almost as if something sacred lay inside. Finally, he reached in and removed a small black velvet box. Inspecting the case, he held it up for Samantha to see. She said nothing, leaving anything spoken to Jim. Slowly, he opened the small velvet package, exposing an oval cut, one-carat diamond engagement ring in a silver setting and band.

For only a moment, she noticed a very sad expression soon replaced by a smile. A beautiful ring for sure. When did he buy it? Why was it in this bank box? "It's beautiful, Jim. When did you get it? Does Samantha know?"

"She liked this ring twenty-five years ago. She never knew I bought this right before we broke up. I've had it ever since. I couldn't get rid of it, I just couldn't. And now, I can give it to her."

Very excited, Samantha raised the question, "You're going to ask her to marry you?"

"I already did, right after we left Russia."

"No, really? While you were in space? There?"

"Shhh. Yeah, right there. She said yes."

"You guys keeping it secret?"

"Well...with everything going on, we haven't had much time to talk about it. I want to take her to dinner and ask again...make it official." If possible, Jim appeared to blush.

"This is wonderful! I'm so happy for you!" She paused, "Wait a minute, now you expect me to keep this secret?"

"I do. We're going to dinner Thursday evening at the restaurant on the top floor of the building where your mom and dad's reception was held."

"Where you and Samantha spent your first evening together?"

"Yeah, I thought that might be nice."

"That is very nice! You are such a romantic. This is so exciting!"

"Remember...no telling. Maybe Scott, but no one else, OK?"

"OK!"

Looking into the deposit box, she asked, "What else do you have there?"

"Just a few things. Here is the Bible she gave me that first evening; and some candleholders from the wedding reception, and a pearl necklace my mother wore on special occasions." He held up the necklace. "When Samantha and I get married,

I'd like you to wear it."

"It's beautiful."

"It's yours…if you want."

"Oh, Jim, I would be so honored. Thank you."

"Why don't you put it on…one less thing to carry."

October 8, Thursday

"This place is still beautiful. Thank you for bringing me here." Remembering how much James liked the outfit she wore to Rich and Gina's reception, Samantha found a deep blue evening dress that covered one shoulder with a matching wrap. The ensemble did not go unnoticed. The elevator door opened. After entering, James pushed the button for the top floor restaurant.

"I thought this might be enjoyable. I haven't been here since that evening."

"Neither have I."

As always, their hands came together. "One thing I'm not sure of…and you'll know as soon as we get to our table."

"What's that?"

James paused a moment, "I reserved a table next to the windows. Afterwards, I remembered you felt pretty uneasy that close to the edge."

Samantha smiled. "Don't worry about it. I think I'll be fine. After being 200 miles up, floating around, looking down at the Earth…I think I'll be all right. If not, I'll let you know."

The doors opened to an elaborate lobby, the restaurant to the right. The maître d' led them to the table, next to the floor to ceiling windows, and pulled the chairs out, first for Samantha, then for James.

"Are you OK with the window?"

"Actually, yes. I like this." She gazed toward the Arch

and Mississippi River. "Yes, this is very good!" She hesitated a moment. "Isn't this near where we stood that night?"

"It is. I asked for this spot."

The sparkling water and appetizer complimented their intimate conversation as they enjoyed one another's company, although James grew increasingly nervous with anticipation. Focusing on her beautiful expressions and listening intently to her pleasant, soft southern articulation only served to emphasize Samantha's inner beauty, the beauty of a woman who truly desired to follow God's will in all her thoughts, words, and actions. Carefully, slowly, he withdrew the black velvet box from his pocket. Reaching across the small table, he took her hand in his, came to her side, and knelt on one knee.

Samantha covered her mouth with her free hand as James held the open box for her to see, and in a hushed voice expressed, "Miss Samantha, I love you with all my heart and promise I will for the rest of my life. Will you marry me?"

"Oh, my precious James, I love you so very much, and I will forever, I promise. Yes, I will marry you…I will." Her eyes sparkled with emotion.

The small number of couples in the restaurant applauded her acceptance. James slipped the ring snuggly onto her finger. Gracefully, she rose and they kissed. Holding her hand as she sat, he then pulled his chair around to be closer.

Without removing her eyes from the ring, Samantha wondered aloud, "Where in the world did you find a ring like the one I thought was so beautiful?"

He lovingly held her hand as he replied, "This is that ring."

Caressing his hand to her cheek, she whispered, "I don't believe this. The very ring I slipped on my finger so long ago at that little jewelry store. And here it is…the very ring…on my finger…again. It's so beautiful."

Gently touching his face, she smiled and confessed, "I am so happy we are together, and will be for the rest of our lives. I love you so much."

Looking intently into Samantha's misty eyes, James simply and sincerely responded, "I love you Samantha." After a moment, he added, "God does work all things for good for those who love Him and are called according to His purpose."

Softly, she agreed, "Amen."

www.ingramcontent.com/pod-product-compliance
Lightning Source LLC
Chambersburg PA
CBHW022249310726
48973CB00001B/19